Y0-BDB-912

MONTEREY SHORTS

Stories by
Fiction Writers of the Monterey Peninsula

Monterey Shorts is published by:
Thunderbird Press in association with
Fiction Writers of the Monterey Peninsula
22597 Black Mountain Rd.
Salinas, CA 93908
Visit us on the Web: www.fwomp.com

Edited by Walter E. Gourlay, Chris Kemp and Frances J. Rossi

Library of Congress Cataloguing-in-Publication Data
Monterey Shorts / FWOMP—1st Ed.

ISBN 0-9676848-4-6
Printed in the United States of America

For all the writers who dared to dream
and continue to dream.
Let the dream spill onto the page.

Lead the way.

— Byron Merritt

Monterey Shorts

Foreword
by Brian Herbert

This collection of short stories set in the Monterey area will appeal to a wide audience, as the tales cover a range of intriguing subjects. One of the contributors to this collection—Byron Merritt—is the grandson of Frank Herbert, the legendary author of *Dune*, universally considered the greatest science fiction novel ever written. Byron is my nephew, so from a young age he was immersed in the life and culture of a great writer, just as I was. This did not, however, mean that the writing craft would come easily to either one of us.

The writing profession is a difficult one, and only an infinitesimal percentage of its practitioners ever make a living doing it. The old adage holds especially true for us: "Keep your day job." After working in the insurance business for a decade, I did not begin to write until I was almost 30 years old. Then, for years afterward, I followed a career as an insurance agent while producing science fiction stories during every spare moment. Byron, while working in the medical profession, began to write at around the same age as I did.

When Byron came to me a few years ago to ask for writing advice, I was pleased to help. I could see that he had a great deal of natural talent, but I knew that he could not compose stories in a vacuum. He needed to network with other writers so that he could exchange ideas and get feedback from them. For years I had been in a writing group, a closely-knit unit of half a dozen members. This had been an important support group for me, with people I could trust not to steal my story ideas or hurt my delicate psyche . . . writers who genuinely wanted me to succeed, just as I wanted them to do the same. Based upon this nurturing experience, I recommended that Byron join a writing group himself.

When he looked around the Monterey area, however, he could not find anything suitable. So, intending to organize a group himself, Byron ran advertisements in the Monterey Herald and looked on the Internet, where he found local writers, whom he e-mailed. The response was strong, and for his first meeting in January 2000, 38 people showed up! He realized that this was far too many, so he quickly reorganized into ten members—six men and four women. With tongues planted firmly in their cheeks, they named themselves Fiction Writers of the Monterey Peninsula. It seems that the acronym for this, FWOMP, represents the sound a manuscript makes when it hits the slush pile, that inglorious place in every publishing house where unwanted stories end up.

In this anthology, ***Monterey Shorts***, none of the stories belong in the slush pile. It is a marvelous collection of fiction, all set in the beautiful Monterey Bay area. Byron Merritt composed a science fiction detective story, while his fellow "FWOMPers" produced yarns that fall into a variety of genres and sub-genres, including literary, historical, fantasy, crime, diving, and life styles, with delightful touches of John Steinbeck, Sam Spade, and Frank Herbert.

— Brian Herbert
Seattle, Washington
September 2002

BRIAN HERBERT, son of Dune *author Frank Herbert, is the New York Times Best-selling author of the* Dune *Prequels:* Dune: House Atreides*;* Dune: House Harkonnen*; and* Dune: House Corrino.

The Undiscovered Monterey Peninsula
by Chris Kemp

Welcome to the Monterey Peninsula you thought you knew, or imagined you did.

Where skin divers, burned out businessmen, Carmel Valley farm kids and middle class families rub shoulders with ghosts, Russian fugitives, homicidal maniacs and doppelgangers.

Where Dinosaur Town is just a midnight ride away.

Where the hot tubs talk to each other.

Where aliens threaten to overrun the human populace—in the future, at least.

Yeah. *That* Monterey Peninsula.

Ten local authors—writing stories set in or around this magical area—have scoured their imaginations, pooled their talents and scrupulously critiqued each other's work to come up with the book you now hold in your hands. Known collectively as the Fiction Writers of the Monterey Peninsula (FWOMP), their approach is as staggeringly diverse as it is unique, making ***Monterey Shorts*** a volume with something for everyone.

Don't take our word for it, though. Taste and see for yourself. Like peanuts or chocolate drops, if you sample one story, you won't be able to stop. These are the Monterey area's newest voices, with a vision that is compelling, entertaining and profound. Whether you are lucky enough to live on the Peninsula, or are one of the thousands who come to soak up its beauty, serenity, and history, ***Monterey Shorts*** is for you.

Just understand that you may never view the Peninsula the same way again.

— Chris Kemp
Pacific Grove, California
September 2002

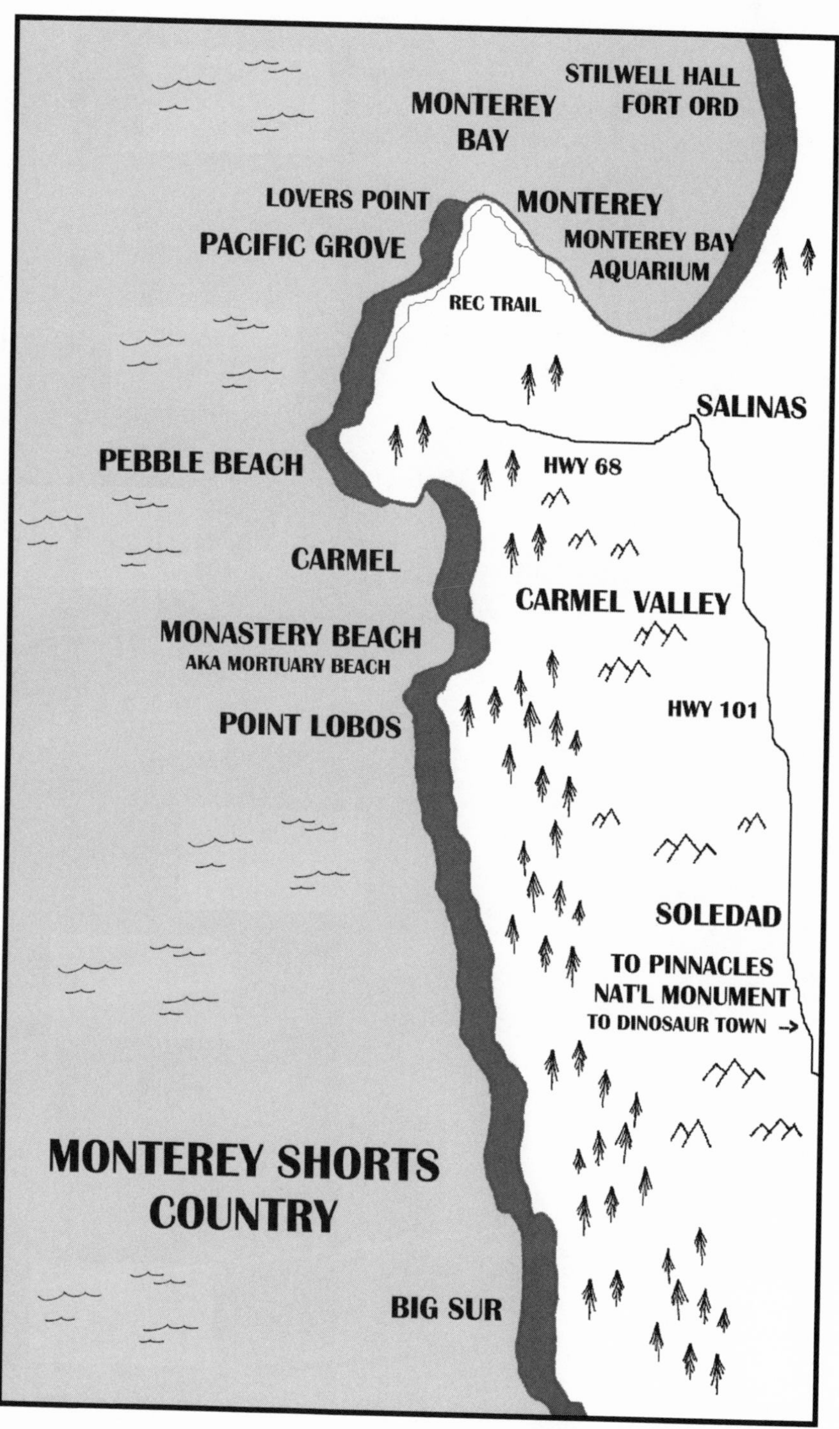
STILWELL HALL
FORT ORD
MONTEREY
BAY
LOVERS POINT
MONTEREY
PACIFIC GROVE
MONTEREY BAY
AQUARIUM
REC TRAIL
SALINAS
PEBBLE BEACH
HWY 68
CARMEL
CARMEL VALLEY
MONASTERY BEACH
AKA MORTUARY BEACH
HWY 101
POINT LOBOS
SOLEDAD
TO PINNACLES
NAT'L MONUMENT
TO DINOSAUR TOWN →
MONTEREY SHORTS
COUNTRY
BIG SUR

Reunion

by Walter E. Gourlay

Life is but a fleeting dream
And man the dream's mistake
So let him tread with dreadful care
Lest he the Dreamer wake.

— *Adele J. Gourlay 1926-2002*

On a crisp, beautiful fall day, Dr. John J. Ackerman, Emeritus Professor of Anthropology at Michigan State, got into his new Lexus, intending to stop at the Faculty Club and have a couple of drinks with the dean before going home. Instead, he went to California.

He didn't know he was going to California. He was thinking of the empty house awaiting him. And the barren years he'd spent driving the same route, back and forth, literally and figuratively. So on a sudden impulse he went directly home and packed a light suitcase. He drove to the interstate with no conscious destination in mind. Goodbye, he thought. Goodbye to his books, his house, his routine, his scholarly pretensions. Goodbye to all that. Goodbye, Professor Ackerman, Ph.D. Goodbye to the man he'd become, the man he'd once thought he wanted to be. He'd leave it all. Tear it up and throw it in the wastebasket. God, it felt good! The most impulsive, irresponsible thing he'd done in years. In how many years? Since before he'd married Harriet.

Good, sweet devoted Harriet. As uncomplicated as a glass of tap-water. True blue Harriet. A cheerleader in high school. The girl next door. Industrious, tireless, sincere, tidy Harriet. As wholesome as sliced Wonder Bread and just as dull. A Stepford wife. Those empty years with her until her death a few months ago had eroded his being away. They'd eaten at his spirit, his manhood, the Johnny Ackerman he once had been.

It wasn't entirely Harriet's fault, he had to admit. If anything, it was more his fault for having married her.

He remembered being just plain Johnny, before becoming Dr. Ackerman, Ph.D. Eager for adventure. He'd gone mountain climbing in the Adirondacks and the White Mountains, a glory of orange, red and yellow in the fall, with the crackle of oak leaves underfoot. He'd inhaled their heady fragrance as Laurel, the blonde swimming instructor, enthusiastically introduced him to sex in a tiny pup tent while the leaves drifted and whispered around them. And the hot humid summer he'd sweated as a longshoreman, heaving those bales of raw cotton on the asphalt docks of New York, before saying the hell with that. He'd hitchhiked and hoboed westward across the great American tableland. A year driving cattle in Wyoming and another ranching in Big Sur near Cambria, then hitchhiking back to Manhattan. There his freedom ended. His draft board zonked him. Greetings. Classified 1-A. Fit for combat. The price he paid for good clean living. A ticket to hell in the Pacific.

He didn't want to remember the war. It was sealed up somewhere in a dark corner of his memory, not to be looked at again. After his discharge, complete with a Purple Heart, he'd tried to put himself together again. Pick up the pieces. Start a new life. He'd gone to sea on a tramp steamer for a couple of years, then gone on a long fishing trip in the Maine woods. When he decided he was ready for civilian life he rented a cold-water flat on Bedford Street in the heart of the Village, and entered Columbia on the GI Bill.

He'd entered Harriet at about the same time. They'd met on the double-decked open top Madison Avenue bus. It had started to rain and she was ever so sweetly grateful for the loan of his jacket. Harriet was pretty, blonde, brown-eyed and direct. The only daughter of a wealthy Republican father, she'd been very properly brought up and properly educated at Bryn Mawr. She was in New York, she said, "sort of studying ballet."

"Please do it to me," she'd said at his pad on their first date. They'd been drinking Lambrusco by candlelight; Pachelbel's *Canon* on his hi-fi. "Take me, John!" She'd decided to lose her virginity, she told him, in her direct, no-nonsense way, and was bestowing the honor on him. It was probably the most daring thing she'd ever done in her life, he thought, her one token of resistance to dear Daddy. Naturally, he'd done what was expected of him. It was pleasant, not as memorable as some encounters he'd had, but pleasant. Harriet was duly grateful. She'd been wearing a black lace bra and panties. Buying them was probably the second most daring thing she'd ever done.

Why had he married her? Because she helped to wash away memories of the war, helped him to settle down and lead a normal life. He'd been seduced into marriage. Not by Harriet's maidenly charms, as she probably believed, but by the appeal of the comfortable slot she offered—not so much the pretty one between her legs, but the soft niche that would await him as the loving husband of the only child, the darling sweet little girl, of her multimillionaire Daddy.

As a condition of marriage, Daddy had demanded he shave off his beard, that intolerable symbol of nonconformity. He'd complied without a struggle, to Harriet's giggling approval.

Dear Daddy thought his chosen field of anthropology was suspiciously liberal, if not downright Communistic. "Pinko professors," he grumbled. "Free Love. Communal property. Sex among the Hottentots." But grudgingly he'd supported John as he went through graduate school and during his early years of teaching. Harriet had cheerfully given up ballet lessons and in due time produced three children, two boys and a girl, all now grown and each of them respectable, Republican, and as predictable as Harriet herself.

After earning his doctorate he got a job as an Instructor at Michigan State, quickly rising to Full Professor. When Harriet inherited her father's wealth they became a popular couple socially, bought a huge house overlooking the Red Cedar River in Lansing, and hired a gardener, a maid and a part-time cook "so you can entertain your colleagues," she explained. As a rich man's daughter, Harriet had inherited a first class ticket and a first class attitude to life. As was expected of him, he joined the faculty club and the exclusive country club and hobnobbed with General Motors executives in the state capital. As expected of her, she became a volunteer at several local charities, and made sure that everyone knew her husband was a university professor and that she was a graduate of Bryn Mawr.

She became chairwoman of the Women's Republican Club and its major fundraiser. One year she was offered the Republican nomination for Congress in their liberal (university-infected) Democratic district. She turned it down. "I'm just a simple housewife. My first duty is to my family." They turned to him, but backed away when he pretended to be a closet socialist.

Too late he realized how much of her father had been imprinted on Harriet. Over his objections, she insisted in introducing him to acquaintances as "Doctor Ackerman." And she scolded him in private for encouraging his graduate students to address him by his first name. By the time he admitted to himself how little they had in common, the first child came, and then the others, and he resigned himself to being a token husband and father, bought and paid for. He buried himself in his research, and became a workaholic.

He'd been highly successful professionally. His doctoral dissertation had been seminal, was widely cited, and led to his appointment at Michigan State. He'd published several textbooks and numerous monographs, had held a prestigious Guggenheim Fellowship, had become chairman of his department, and before his retirement had been elected president of the American Anthropological Association.

Of course, Harriet thought all this was wonderful. She made sure to go to every black tie reception, and saw to it that their acquaintances and the local press were duly informed of his various successes. But to his amazement, she'd never once looked at any of his books or articles, attended any of his lectures, or even asked him about his work. "I'm just a simple housewife."

When he'd gone abroad on field trips or attended conferences elsewhere in the States, invariably she decided to stay behind. "You go," she'd say, "while I take care of our beautiful home." By then he didn't miss her. They had little to say to each other except for feeble make-talk, and he was glad when he could be free of the obligation to undertake even that.

He'd been an effective teacher, he knew. He'd tried to bring to his lectures his sense of irony that challenged the tribal taboos and sacred cows of American society, a skepticism about its norms and mores that impressed and amused his students and made his courses popular.

His classes were always full, mostly with adoring young female undergraduates who in the early Seventies would sit in the front rows, braless, wearing miniskirts and see-through blouses.

It was sheer loneliness and boredom with his marriage, he thought, that had led him to an abortive, unsatisfactory affair with Claudia, a scrawny, neurotic, worshipful student in Anthropology 101. When he discovered how easy it was to seduce them (praise their intelligence, recount stories about the sex life of aborigines, ply them with wine and play Ravel's *Bolero* on the hi-fi in his comfortable third-floor office) he bedded several in quick succession, not all of them scrawny, but all neurotic, and after the initial excitement none of them satisfying and all of them ultimately boring. Except for one he became really fond of, even began to fall in love with—bright, dark-eyed Susan, braless, beaded, and slit-skirted, an aspiring artist with an outrageous wit and a rollicking sense of humor—but she left him for a callow youth her own age who wrote purplish poetry, and bade him a tearful, affectionate, but determined goodbye.

When the university adopted strict rules forbidding hanky-panky between faculty and students, he'd chosen the safer and more socially acceptable path of seducing (or being seduced by) the wives of his colleagues. They proved to be almost as boring as the students. They gossiped about the other wives, talked about their kids, or complained that their husbands ignored them, usually all of the above. Why did he bother? Because they were there, he thought. Minor adventures. Ignoble substitutes for climbing the Alps or exploring the Amazon jungle. If you couldn't be an intrepid explorer, there was always your colleague's wife to conquer. Less challenging, but much less dangerous.

And so his best years had gone dribbling away.

And Harriet, poor dear self-circumscribed Harriet, had she ever been unfaithful to him? He doubted it. He'd never even considered it until now. But she *was* pretty, and sexy in her straight-arrow way, and someone among his colleagues or his neighbors (*or his students?*) could conceivably have found in her a small Alp or a patch of unmapped jungle. He hoped so, for her sake. Somehow the thought that probably she had never even briefly tasted forbidden fruit filled him with pity for her, and a profound sadness.

Impelled by some inner directive that he couldn't name he took U.S. 69 south, then 94 to Chicago, and U.S. 80 due west, intoxicating himself as he had done in his youth with the immensity and infinite variety of the continent, staying in Ramada Inns, Great Western Motels, Motel 6's, Quality Inns, and dingy mom-and-pop places smelling of mildew and insecticide that you'd never find in a Triple-A guide book. In search of . . . in search of what?

Maybe he'd know when he got to wherever he was going. Or was the trip itself the answer? He was renewing his acquaintance with America in all its spectacular beauty and all its man-made ugliness. The sprawl of filling stations, mini-malls and carpet outlets, used car lots and new car lots, housing developments endlessly reproducing like the marching morons who'd built them.

He took back roads through the cornfields, flat pastures and rolling hills of the Midwest, then bustling noisy interstates across the sluggish Mississippi, through the lonely prairies, the burnt brick, orange and purple mesas smelling of creosote, with their arroyos of cottonwood, the magnificent Rockies muscling themselves up from the bedrock of the Americas, then through the tumbleweed deserts of Utah and Nevada, searching, yearning, for something the sense of which eluded him. Through the Sierras into California, down across the flat, green San Joaquin Valley and then over the green hump of the Coastal Range to Big Sur, to Cambria where he had worked on a ranch in those days before the army grabbed him. The muted roar and the refreshing salty scent of the sea recalled where he'd been born and raised, in Patchogue, Long Island. When he saw the Pacific ahead, its gentle blue sparkling under a milky sky, he sensed he was getting close to wherever he was going. Up from Cambria through Big Sur on the narrow ledge of Highway 1, sculpted between the mountains and the terraced waves of the sea, and then on the freeway through Monterey without stopping.

On his left, through the dunes, he caught glimpses of Monterey Bay. Squawking sea gulls spiraling and soaring, pelicans gliding effortlessly above the wind-drift, the surf barely audible. The waves in wave language telling tales of the distances they'd come, led by the wind like him, to California on the edge of the great continent.

He passed Seaside on his right, a dismal congery of strip malls with a K-Mart just off the freeway, presided over but not improved by a ten-story box pretentiously called the Embassy Suites Hotel, lonely and badly out of place. He hadn't been to the Peninsula since the war. 1943, to be exact. There hadn't been any freeway or Seaside then, only a tiny no-name huddle of rickety shacks inhabited by whores and vagrants. Monterey had been a town of decaying adobes, booming with raucous soldiers, honky-tonk bars and hookers. The Embassy Suites reminded him that he'd have to find a place to stay for the night, and it was already getting dark. Still he kept driving.

Suddenly, ahead of him, a sign. *Fort Ord.*

He'd been stationed at Ord, in the fall of 1943. "Planet Ord" the soldiers had called it, or sometimes just "The Planet". Out in the middle of nowhere, usually surrounded by fog so thick that it seemed an alien world floating in space and time, disconnected and unrelated to the rest of the Peninsula and to the rest of the earth. "Go to the end of the world and turn left," they used to say.

A couple of years ago he'd been surfing the Internet for an article on Native Americans of California. He'd found a reference to the Ohlone who'd left middens of abalone shells and primitive tools in the Fort Ord area. Mildly curious, he'd opened a link mentioning that Ord had been closed down and that Stilwell Hall—which he'd known as the Soldiers' Club—was on the brink of demolition because the bluffs on which it stood were being eroded away. "The Club". He hadn't thought of it for years. Now, strangely, here he was. "Fort Ord".

The Club had been the inspiration and gift of General "Vinegar Joe" Stilwell, who'd wanted the lowly GIs to have a place of their own, and had beaten back persistent attempts by the chickenshit brass to build an officers' club instead. Later it had been renamed Stilwell Hall in his honor. And his memory. Beautifully constructed and furnished as one of the last

Federal Arts Projects of the depression-era WPA, the Soldiers' Club had sat among the dunes overlooking Monterey Bay. *Was it still standing?* he wondered.

Without stopping to think, he turned off Highway 1 at Marina and took the Eighth Street exit to the bridge leading toward the Club. The fog had lifted as it sometimes did, especially in the early fall. Yes, there it was.

Silhouetted against the sky, dark and abandoned, not yet fallen into the bay, the Soldiers' Club hugged the dunes. On a night like this, he remembered, near the end of September 1943, the Club had officially opened. At that time it stood the length of a baseball field from the dunes that buffered it from Monterey Bay, the dunes that were eroding away.

Like us all, he thought. Give us time and we all erode away.

Two stories high, California Spanish in architecture with a terra cotta roof, the Soldier's Club had been an enlisted men's palace. It had a vast ballroom with parqueted teak floor, crystal chandeliers, frescos and murals by local artists, a library, meeting rooms, and a 40-foot bar said to be the longest in California. Big dance bands—the most noted in America—performed on the ornately furnished mezzanine high above the ballroom floor. On opening night more than a thousand women, carefully selected by the Red Cross and the local USO, had been bused in from San Francisco and elsewhere to dance with the soldiers. General Stilwell was absent; he'd been put in command of the China-Burma Theater, so his wife dedicated the Club and stood in for him on the long reception line.

Other dances, other parties, followed. And one memorable night in late October, just before his battalion shipped out for the Pacific, he'd met Terry. Memories opened up. *Terry.* Tall, redheaded Terry with the blue-indigo eyes. That party . . . the dance. Was it almost sixty years ago? Eons in a man's life.

God, but he was really bushed, suddenly exhausted from his long drive.

Very carefully, he pulled over to the shoulder to rest a bit.

He awoke to the sound of his radio. Funny, he didn't remember having turned it on. Tommy Dorsey's orchestra, playing *Boogie Woogie.* He hadn't heard that tune in years!

Directly in front of him, he saw the Club strangely ablaze with yellow lights, music and the sound of voices loud, the wind fresh and sea-scented with a slight hint of kelp, the sky clear with its stars winking at him, as on the night he'd met Terry.

This is a crazy dream.

He found himself walking toward the entrance, toward the music and the voices, the laughter. In uniform, young, vigorous, virile, the warm, familiar but long-forgotten touch of dog tags on his chest. He stroked his left hand, searching for the shrapnel wound that had earned him his Purple Heart on Okinawa, but his fingers were supple, his skin smooth.

If this is a dream, I don't want it to end.

He pinched himself to make sure he was awake. *Not a dream.*

If not a dream, then what was going on here? *Einstein*. Einstein said that past, present and future exist side by side, like bends in a river. That was it. He must have stepped right over a time loop, like in a science fiction novel, back to 1943. October 1943, to be exact. He was sure of the date. He really was walking toward the Club, in October 1943, toward the lights and Big Band music. What were they playing? *Tuxedo Junction*. He was young again, new corporal's stripes on his sleeve, dog tags jingling, his carriage erect.

"Stop slouching," Harriet had always told him.

Dear Harriet. If she could only see me now.

Tonight was one of those rare starry nights in October, Indian summer on the Peninsula, just before the rainy season, when the skies are clear for weeks on end and the days are warm and sunny. The caressing whisper of the surf, the green scent of the dunes plants instantly familiar. Tonight a slight haze, a gentle breeze, unusually warm, as he remembered it had been that other time. Everything seemed more beautiful, more vibrant than before.

Was this what it was like to be young? Did young eyes see everything with this crystalline brilliance?

Feeling unreal, he showed his dog tags to the bored MP at the entrance and pushed his way into the lobby. The Club, aromatic with cigarettes and beer, was cheerfully noisy and jammed with soldiers and assorted women—wives, girlfriends, Red Cross girls and even a few enlisted WACs in uniform. A pair of broad stairways on either side of the lobby led to the mezzanine, where a band was playing *The Last Time I Saw Paris*. He thought he recognized several men from his platoon, but ignored them as he pushed into the ballroom. Terry. Was she here?

Yes. Terry, a vision in a long red taffeta dress, was there as he remembered her, standing at a table across the room, talking to a couple of overly attentive soldiers who looked vaguely familiar. Yes. That same red dress. Terry. And she seemed to have expected him.

"Johnny!" she called. "You're here!" She pulled a red rose from a vase on the table and put it in her hair just as she'd done that time so long ago. She ran over, her face radiant, and hugged and kissed him. There were those indigo eyes—such a deep blue that in the world he'd just come from he would naturally have assumed they were contact lenses. But in 1943 contacts weren't even imagined and her wonderful eyes were colored as if by magic.

He took her hand. Warm, perfectly manicured fingers, nails neat, not long, a reasonable shade of pink, not crazy colored claws like some women back in the time he'd come from. She wore those same beautiful jade earrings.

Why had I ever let her go?

It struck him that the band in the mezzanine was playing a rumba.

"Do you remember, Johnny? Do you remember what I said when I walked over to you that night?"

Oh yes, he remembered.

"Yes," he said. "You asked me if I could rumba."

"And you answered 'I can do anything you ask me to.' And that's when I began to fall in love with you. And then you said that my eyes were indigo. And I thought that you were probably the only soldier in the Club who knew what indigo was. But Johnny," she grinned, "you couldn't really rumba, you know. We won that dance contest because of my dress."

He looked down at the long crimson dress almost covering her red pumps and remembered how later he'd pulled that dress up to her waist and they'd made love under the stars.

"It was this long skirt," she said. "It covers my feet. You kept missing the beat and you couldn't lead and I had to keep shifting my feet. Nobody could see it because my dress was so long. And so we looked like the perfect couple. And of course we were. And are. What a woman will do for a man," she said, rolling her eyes. "Tell me, Johnny, can you rumba?"

"I can do whatever you ask me to do."

They began to rumba. Johnny was a bit awkward at first, but helped by Terry he got into the beat of it, and remembered to keep his hips and knees loose. "I wish I could do this forever," he said. "Be with you forever."

"You can, Johnny, you can." She kissed him. "Do you remember what we did that night?" She gripped his hand, looked into his eyes and grinned mischievously.

Oh yes, he remembered. Remembered telling her that they would be shipping out the next morning, remembered their mutual hungriness, remembered taking her out there where the dunes began. Remembered the two of them returning to the Club, hand in hand, sand on their clothes and in her hair as his buddies hooted, hollered and applauded, Terry looking embarrassed but somehow triumphant at the same time. He remembered. Oh yes, he remembered.

They walked back to the table where she'd been sitting. "Johnny, You remember Bryan Wilson and Joe Biondo." They didn't get up, but made space for him.

"Hello, Joe. Hello, Bryan."

"Hello, Johnny."

"What's new, guys?"

"Nothing much. The latest scoop is we ship out tomorrow. Five a.m. Eat, drink and be merry, as the man says. Especially drink." Bryan hiccupped. *Big, blond Bryan had lost his leg to a land mine in Okinawa, back in what was now the future. Back in the future? I'm not going to rack my brain trying to figure that out.* Could he go back to his own time? Did he want to? Suppose he stayed here with Terry now? He'd survived the war, he knew. Survived, and married Harriet and became a professor. That was a million years from now. But maybe he had a second chance, a chance to start over, Terry and he. He pulled Terry to the dance floor. High above, the chandeliers twinkled and cast fleeting shadows. "Tonight is beautiful," he said. "You're so beautiful."

They danced. *Chattanooga Choo-Choo. "Pardon me, boy, is that the Chattanooga choo-choo? On track twenty-nine."* God, that brought back memories.

What had happened between him and Terry? After he'd gone overseas there'd been letters back and forth. Passionate, erotically explicit at first, pledging eternal devotion, then his gradually becoming fewer and more distant until she'd stopped writing. Distance fatigue, he'd called it. A "red shift" of emotions and memories as the distance increased. A casualty of war. She'd sent a snapshot of herself in a two-piece bathing suit that he'd posted by his bunk in the barracks, to the whistling admiration of his buddies. Somehow between invasions he'd lost it, and then lost her address. He'd filed away the memory of her as a wartime souvenir, "a really great stateside piece of ass." He thought he'd turned over the page she was written on. But the page was still there, he realized.

"If only we could live over again," he said.

"Sorry, Johnny, it doesn't work that way." She rested her head on his shoulder.

The White Cliffs of Dover. Promising love, laughter and peace ever after when the world is free. *God we were naive in those days.*

"What is this, some kind of a time warp?"

She raised her head and studied him. "You could think of it like that."

"How should I think of it?"

"It's reunion time. Your class reunion. Your going-away party. Our anniversary. Come on, Johnny, loosen up. Live a bit, if you'll pardon the expression."

"I wish we could be this way forever," he said.

"We have now. Now is forever. We can be together now." She pulled his head forward and kissed him. "Please Johnny," she whispered, "please make love to me again."

He took her out to the dunes as he had on that night so many years ago and pulled her dress up to her chin as she whispered his name and clutched his back and it was all as beautiful as it had been so many years ago.

Then they walked back, hand in warm hand, under the powder-soft stars, the whispering ocean breeze on their skin, surrounded by the susurrus of the surf, the scent of the sandy grass, and feeling not exhausted but exhilarated. "They're all gone now," he said, waving his hand at the shadowy dunes they'd just left.

"Now? When is 'now'?" she said. "Now is now. Even when the Club is gone, we'll be here and we'll be now." He looked at her in puzzlement. "Oh Johnny," she said. "You'll see."

This time there was no sand on them, no cheers or whistles, as they walked into the ballroom alive to the beat of *The Jersey Bounce*. "If this is some kind of mixed-up dream," he said, "I don't want to ever wake up."

"It's no dream, Johnny. It's the way it was meant to be." She gripped his hand, hard. "Johnny, I've missed you. I've come back every year looking for you."

"Every year? You do this every year?"

"On the anniversary. The anniversary of the battalion's going away party. It's our anniversary too, Johnny," she said, pulling him closer.

He had to excuse himself to go to the men's room, as he always had to after sex. *This can't be a dream,* he thought at the urinal. *You piss in a dream and it wakes you up. Piss is damn real. About as real as you can get.*

I wonder where she's been all these years. Maybe she's married now, has kids. But not in this crazy dream or time travel or warp or whatever we're in. The orchestra. What was it playing? "We'll meet again, don't know where, don't know when." His eyes were moist as he walked back to her. *Must be the cigarette smoke.*

"I'll get us a pitcher of beer," he said.

He turned brusquely and shouldered his way through the crowd to the Tap Room. Behind the bar were those amusing, corny paintings he remembered. Cartoons, really, of black-bearded whalers and fishermen in floppy nineteenth century oilskins, obviously inspired by *Moby Dick*. Shit. The beer, damn it, was that awful insipid 3.2 percent alcohol. America's mommies had made Congress decree that no military installation could serve anything stronger to their dear boys being sent out to kill and perhaps to die. But the hell with it, it was better than nothing, especially at only two-bits a foaming pitcher and when it was drawn from kegs by smiling, bouncy-breasted young barmaids with upswept hairdos, their every flounce and bounce studied avidly by the lonely soldiers lined up at the double brass rails. *If you wanted stronger stuff, buddy, either female or liquid, take your hard-earned bucks to lower Alvarado Street in Monterey, the center of sinful life on the Peninsula. And watch out for muggers.*

On his way back, carrying a pitcher and two glasses, he bumped into Tommy Goodson, beaming, full of life and spirits. It opened a wound, seeing Tommy. *Tommy. Screaming when his guts were blown open on Okinawa.* "Johnny boy! Good t'see ya!"

Johnny forced a smile. "How ya doin' Tommy?"

"Great! How're you, Johnny?"

"Never better!"

"You can say that again! Ain't this a great party? You with somebody, Johnny?"

"Terry. The tall redhead."

Tommy whistled. "That ball-breaker? The ice woman? Let me tell you, Johnny, you're wasting your time. She don't let nobody but nobody get near her ass. Well, best of luck, Johnny."

When he reached her, Billy Larsen was towering over her. Big, brawny Billy. The poor fucker had lost it at Ie Shima. Panicked under fire, abandoned his squad, was court-martialed and dishonorably discharged. Here the poor bastard was, showing off his new sergeant's stripes.

Male buddy talk:

"Hi, Johnny."

"Hi, Billy." *You miserable bastard.*

"How's it goin'?"

"Can't complain."

"Great party." Billy drifted away. *Good riddance.*

Terry was looking at him curiously. "What's the matter, Johnny?"

He shook his head. "Nothing."

He told her what Goodson had said. She threw back her head and laughed. "Me? The ice woman? I've been saving myself for you, Johnny. My Johnny. I knew you'd come back some day."

God. Where had life gone wrong? Don't let this end.

Terry reached out to him. "C'mon, Johnny, let's dance." She led him out on the crowded floor. The chandeliers were winking. The band was playing *Stardust*. "This is my favorite," she said. She rested her head on his shoulder. Her fragrance smelled like lilac, her breasts pressing against him. They held each other very close. *This is where I belong. I'll settle in here and stay forever.*

He looked about the room. All of them were here, he supposed, the 500 men, more or less, of his battalion. He recognized many of them, but could recall the names of only a few. Even some of the officers were here dancing with army nurses and WACs. Funny. They don't usually mix socially with the enlisted men. Of course this was a special night. A reunion, no less. Their last night at Ord. There's arrogant chickenshit Captain Leary and that beetle-browed bastard, Lieutenant Vogel, and 90-day wonder Lieutenant

Franco who always looked confused and ill at ease in his uniform. Should have stayed a civilian. Fat-assed Major Callahan, pudgy, sweaty, and self-important as always. *Third Platoon almost all wiped out because of his fucking stupidity. Ordered them right into an enemy ambush. Naturally they promoted him to Lieutenant Colonel. It figures.*

What a miserable bunch they are. Were. *We* were. The "Greatest Generation". *Where did that stupid name come from?* He shook his head. The connection eluded him.

Sneering, loudmouthed Sergeant Truax, whom he instinctively disliked and always avoided. And poor sneaky little Gorzinsky, who'd be caught cheating at poker and have his life made miserable. And Sonny Quinlan, that illiterate retarded hillbilly. How the hell did he ever get in the Army? He'd raped a teenaged girl in Japan after the war ended and wound up in Leavenworth. One by one they came over and shook his hand. It was a shock to recognize Sergeant Lacey, whose head would be ripped off, spattering Johnny with blood just as he himself was hit by shrapnel and earned his Purple Heart. Here was Hummins, who'd die of pneumonia, and Hennessey, who'd be killed by a land mine. Fat, crazy Sam Goldman, who'd bitched and griped all through basic training but would single-handedly hold off a Japanese platoon on Leyte and earn a battlefield commission.

"You're a good man, Sam," he said. Goldman looked puzzled, but grinned back at him.

"You're doing okay yourself, Johnny," he answered, looking at Terry.

Didn't any of them know? Was he the only one who could see ahead? He gazed at Terry. *What did* she *know?*

He looked for his best drinking buddies, Joe Vaccaro, who'd been seasick and puked his way all across the Pacific, and Benny Segal, who got the clap in Guam and swore off women forever. And kept his vow until that uproarious night in Kobe after the war was over. And got the clap again.

Terry took his hand. "What's the matter, Johnny?"

"I'm missing a couple of buddies. Not everybody's here."

She looked at him and smiled. "Of course not. But they'll come when they're invited. Maybe you'll see them next time. Or the time after. Sometime soon, anyway."

"You mean we'll do this again?"

"We'll always be here, Johnny. You'll see."

"How come I wasn't here before?"

"You have to be invited."

"And tonight I was invited?"

"Oh yes, Johnny," she said, taking his arm and cuddling close to him. He smelled the lilac. "You were invited."

They danced for hours, joking and laughing, bodies moving in wondrous unison. Jitterbugging. *Cow-Cow Boogie. Pistol Packin' Mama. Praise the Lord and Pass the Ammunition.* They held each other close for more sentimental tunes. *White Christmas. You'd Be So Nice To Come Home To. Sleepy Lagoon.* Johnny hummed as they danced, surprising himself that he remembered the words to all of them. *When the Lights Go on Again. As Time Goes By. I'll Be Home for Christmas.* Terry seemed tireless and so was he. Then, all too soon the band was playing *Three O'Clock In The Morning* as a sign that the festivities were over, and Terry led him out to waltz.

"Terry, can we stay together tonight?"

She gazed at him in surprise and then with tears in her eyes. "Oh Johnny, dear Johnny, you still don't understand, do you?" She stopped dancing. "You can't change the past. This is all we had, Johnny. It's all we'll ever have."

The evening was winding down. One by one, the others had disappeared. Even the band was gone. A cold wind was blowing from somewhere.

"The last one to arrive is the last to leave," said Terry. "That's you, Johnny. That's the rule. That's the way it is."

"Terry, I'd give ten years of my life to stay with you tonight."

"Oh Johnny, please try to understand. You don't have ten years." Then she suddenly vanished.

The vast ruined hall was a silent, dark and empty vault. Damp chilly fog and the odor of kelp drifted through broken windows. Seagulls flapped their wings flying through the panes. Gone were the chandeliers, the murals on the walls. The floor was buckled, encrusted with animal dung and stinking of human excrement. And the sea roared closer, much closer, beyond the dunes, sounding angry. There was a louder roaring in his ears, and now, finally, he understood it all.

From the *Monterey County Herald*:

PROFESSOR FOUND DEAD BY STILWELL HALL

The victim of an apparent heart attack, Dr. John Ackerman, a retired Professor of Anthropology at Michigan State University, was found dead in his car at 7:30 a.m. yesterday near Stilwell Hall on the site of the former Fort Ord. He was discovered by workers who had come to partially demolish the building, which is in danger of falling into Monterey Bay. When contacted by telephone, a university spokesman in East Lansing, Michigan, said they were unaware that Ackerman had gone to California, and suggested that he may have been doing anthropological research on the Ohlone Indians, who used to inhabit the area. After a medical investigation into the cause of death, his body will be sent back to Michigan. Professor Ackerman is survived by two sons and a daughter, none of whom was available for comment.

Johnny walked up the path to the Soldiers' Club, lively again with light, laughter and music. A band was playing *Boogie Woogie.* He was in uniform, young and vigorous. And happy. He knew he'd see Terry again. And again. And again. Even if the Club slid into the sea. She'd always be there in October 1943.

Author's Note:

The Soldiers' Club, renamed Stilwell Hall in 1966, in honor of General Joseph ("Vinegar Joe") Stilwell, served as the on-base recreation center for some two million soldiers who passed through Fort Ord, California during World War II, the Korean War, and the Vietnam War. Of these, about 100,000 were wounded and 30,000 killed in action.

During its fifty years of service, most of the Big Bands of the era entertained the men and women in the Army. Such noted figures as Duke Ellington, Count Basie, Bing Crosby, Bob Hope, Jack Benny, Edgar Bergen, Lou Costello and the Dorsey Brothers appeared at the Club.

A prime example of Spanish-Californian architecture, the building serves as a memorial to General Joseph Stilwell, who led the Allied Forces in Burma during World War II, and to the soldiers who served there (my own son among them).

Since the closing of Fort Ord in 1994 the future of Stilwell Hall is highly uncertain. Where generations of soldiers laughed and danced, the rooms are now dark, the floors are buckling, and the windows broken.

The Army has given the land on which the building stands to the California Department of Parks and Recreation, to be part of the new Fort Ord Dunes State Park. But erosion has worn away the dunes protecting the building from the sea, and the Army is preparing to demolish it. State Parks would like to save Stilwell Hall by moving it away from the cliff where it now stands, and restore it as an information center, a museum and community center. The effort has lagged for lack of funds.

A group of community leaders is actively trying to raise the necessary money to save this memorial to California's past, and keep it from being used as landfill. You can help by writing a check to "The Stilwell Hall Preservation Society" and mailing it to:

P.O. Box 5688
Presidio of Monterey, CA, 93944

To exchange memories of Fort Ord and Stilwell Hall, you can e-mail: foaa@monterey.edu or write to:

Fort Ord Alumni Association,
100 Campus Center,
Seaside, CA 93933-8001

I am indebted to Ken Gray, Staff Park and Resource Specialist of the California Department of Parks and Recreation, Monterey District, for taking me on a guided tour of Stilwell Hall, and for sharing with me his enthusiasm and extensive documentation. Thank you, Ken!

— WG

About the Author

A native of New York City, WALTER E. GOURLAY moved to the Monterey Peninsula after retiring from teaching at Michigan State University. He has a doctorate in Chinese History from Harvard and has done considerable academic writing. Before his teaching career, he was a freelance writer for men's adventure magazines. For some time he worked in public relations, and managed a concert hall in New York. He has now returned to writing fiction. A founding member of FWOMP, *he belongs to the local chapter of the National Writers Union. The* Pebbles *writing group in Carmel, of which he is also a member, has recently published two of his short stories in a collection. He's now writing his wartime memoirs and researching a historical novel set in New York City, Java, and Japan during the Napoleonic Wars. Walter lives in Carmel, California.*

Mortuary Beach

by Mark C. Angel

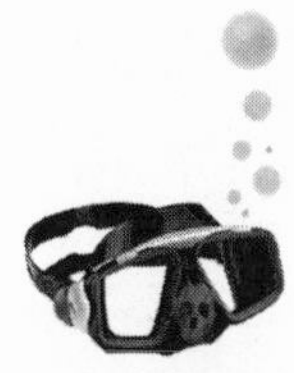

According to California State Park statistics, the scenic bay off Monastery Beach, just south of Carmel, has claimed the lives of at least sixteen divers and sightseers during the past ten years. Local emergency response agencies regularly perform rescues in these beautiful but treacherous seas. The gallant efforts of these teams have helped keep the above statistic to a minimum.

One of the most extraordinary places to be stuck in traffic is a little stretch of Highway 1 between Point Lobos State Reserve and the city of Carmel-by-the-Sea. When you are in your car squeezed between opposing bumpers, a fresh salt-sea breeze or a stray wisp of fog will often waft in through your open window.

Northbound from the pine forest of Point Lobos, the highway passes the grassy expanse of the Riley Ranch horse pastures. A little further down the hill, you cross over the San Jose Creek Bridge. To the right you'll catch a glimpse of a Carmelite monastery and to the left is the Pacific Ocean, so close you can practically skip a stone on it.

There the waves of Monastery Beach suck and slobber rhythmically on the steeply sloped sand in a dance of subtle ocean power. This beach is the entry point for some of the most spectacular kelp-forest diving in the world. But it can also be a death trap.

Jerry Wilcox and Spike Johnson had little in common save their love for the water. Both were starters on the varsity water polo team as freshmen at California State University Bakersfield, where they rapidly became friends.

Jerry grew up in Iowa, born into an idyllic nuclear family and reared in Oskaloosa, southeast of Des Moines. He had a square jaw, well-kept brown hair, and the build of a farmer, though his hands were soft. He spent most of his early summers living in a houseboat that he had helped his father and uncle build on the south arm of Lake Red Rock, a popular Midwest summer habitat for athletic youths. Swimming, fishing and water-skiing were among his favorite pastimes. He had been valedictorian of his high school class and captain of the swim team. Accustomed to success and wanting more than life in Iowa could offer him, he planned his escape from the harsh Midwestern winters and applied to CSU Bakersfield.

Matthew "Spike" Johnson was a teenage refugee from a bitter divorce. He earned his nickname from his wiry red hair and abrasive attitude. At fifteen he moved from his father's cattle ranch near Palestine, Texas, to his doting mother's townhouse in Fresno, where he ached to free himself from the clutches of her evangelical husband.

As a young cowboy, Spike wore his Stetson high and his jeans low. Though he never quite lived up to his parents' academic expectations, he excelled at roping calves and aquatic sports. His idea of a good time was chasing soft girls with ponytails and hard whisky with beer. He earned a high school letter in water polo but just barely graduated. Then Spike found himself headed to CSU Bakersfield on a swimming scholarship.

The summer before their senior year, Jerry invited Spike to join him on the family houseboat in Iowa. Spike took Jerry up on the offer. He fit right in at Lake Red Rock, given that the most popular of the activities there involved water sports and chasing the opposite sex.

"How'd ya like to try breathing underwater?" Jerry asked Spike one morning at breakfast on the houseboat deck as they watched small waves in the lake lap up against the rocky red shore. They were recovering from a long night of overindulgence.

"Yeah . . . right," Spike laughed, and sucked in another spoonful of cereal, milk dripping from his lower lip.

"For real, dude," Jerry replied. "I'm talking SCUBA diving. I've got an extra set of gear down below. All we gotta to do is get the tanks filled."

"That could rock!" Spike said. "Breathing under water's got to be at least as cool as tipping cows." He demonstrated by pushing over the cereal box, as if it were a cow standing asleep in a pasture. They both laughed as they watched the contents scatter onto the table and floor.

"It'll be fun, Spike. I'll explain the rules."

"Aw, now you have to go and spoil all the fun!" Spike protested. He wiped the dry cereal off the table into his bowl and added more milk.

"Dude, this is serious," Jerry insisted. "You usually need a diver certification card to rent gear or go out on a boat or anything like that. But here on the lake it's pretty laid back, so I figure we can just go out a little. It'll be easy to get to the surface if anything goes wrong."

"What could go wrong?" Spike asked.

"Just about anything," Jerry explained. "I mean, think about it, bro'. Humans weren't meant to breathe underwater. So if something goes wrong with the gear, or you freak out or something, that could be it. You come up dead, or darn near."

Spike glanced up with an uncharacteristic expression of doubt, but then smiled at the thought of the risk.

"We won't go too deep," Jerry continued. "Then, if you like it, you can get certified somewhere and someday we can really go for it."

Jerry gave Spike his first dive lesson on the swim deck of the houseboat. He explained how all the SCUBA equipment worked and how to use it properly. After he finished, he helped Spike get into his gear and then donned his own. "Don't worry about how the gadgets work," Jerry said. "I'll adjust them for you as we go. The one thing you always gotta remember is never hold your breath, especially when you're going up. You could pop a lung."

"That could be a major bummer," Spike said, grimacing at Jerry's description.

Jerry finished his instruction and the two jumped off the swim-step splashing into the tranquil water. Once they regrouped on the surface, Jerry took hold of the dump valve on Spike's buoyancy compensation device (BCD), an air bladder vest that functions like a life jacket and holds the tank and gear.

"You ready?" Jerry asked.

"Ready as I'll ever be," Spike acknowledged, floating comfortably in the water near the houseboat.

"Then put your mask on, stick the regulator in your mouth, put your face in the water and breathe like we practiced on the boat. And remember, if you have a problem once we're under, just move your hand like this." Jerry held his hand out flat, twisting it back and forth.

Spike did as Jerry instructed, submerging only his mask. The water was clear enough so he could easily make out individual blades of lake grass growing on the bottom.

"Good," Jerry said. "Now I'll let the air out of our vests and we can drop down. Remember to hold your nose and blow out to equalize the air pressure in your inner ears early and often. And stay close to me!"

Spike nodded, his face still in the water. Jerry put his regulator into his mouth and proceeded to bleed the air out of both their BCDs. The two young men then dropped beneath the surface and soon settled on the lake bottom, their depth gauges registering fifteen feet. The flat bottom of the houseboat was visible overhead and the faint buzz of an outboard motor penetrated the silence between their breaths.

Jerry checked to see if Spike was okay by holding one hand up with his thumb and forefinger forming an "O", his three other fingers extended. Spike returned the sign indicating he was fine. Jerry adjusted the air in Spike's BCD to make him neutrally buoyant. Then, with a gentle kick of their fins, they glided away, stirring up a cloud of silt on the bottom. The zero gravity experience gave Spike the sensation of floating in outer space. He thought it probably resembled what astronauts felt during a space walk, only divers could propel themselves forward by kicking their fins.

As the underwater world came into view, they saw a few grassy plants, a bit of litter and the occasional freshwater fish. It was unremarkable, but for a first dive experience that's a good thing. After twenty minutes they made their way back to the houseboat.

"How'd ya like it?" Jerry asked after he had inflated each BCD vest at the surface to keep them comfortably afloat.

Spike spit the regulator out of his mouth. "It was great!" he replied excitedly. "I felt like I was flying through the water. But it was a little cold once we got down below the surface." He crossed his arms around himself and rubbed his naked shoulders.

Jerry climbed back onto the boat and removed his gear. Then he took Spike's fins and helped him aboard. "It's pretty boring in the lake, but my dad once took me to Monterey and we dove in the kelp forests. The best dive we did was at a place called Monastery Beach, near Point Lobos State Reserve. The visibility was at least 50 feet, but talk about cold . . ." He paused for a moment as he hugged himself. "You think this lake was cold? In the Pacific Ocean," he waved west in the direction of the afternoon sun, "it's close to 50 degrees and you need a thick wetsuit to prevent hypothermia."

They began to disassemble the dive gear and hang it out to dry.

"The part I liked most about diving in Monterey," Jerry continued, "was looking up through the seaweed jungle. I could've burned a whole tank of air just lying there on the seabed, looking at the giant kelp reaching for the sun and swaying in the ocean surge." It got quiet as he drifted off into a momentary remembrance.

"Hey, I got an idea," Spike said, interrupting Jerry's reverie. "Why don't we go diving there next year after graduation?"

"Great idea, but if we go, you're gonna have to get certified. I'm not diving with you in those waters unless you get some proper training."

"I'll find a way. I've got a year to work it out."

The next year Spike took SCUBA training while on winter vacation in Baja, earning his SCUBA certification or C-card, which indicated he was a certified open-water diver. By the time summer rolled around again, he could hardly wait to dive the Monterey area. Any site on the Peninsula would have sufficed, but he especially looked forward to diving at Monastery Beach.

The young men planned their dive trip carefully, reserving accommodations at the Monterey Youth Hostel near Cannery Row. They loaded their stuff into Spike's 1978 Dodge Colt wagon, which he fondly referred to as the "Old Nag", and began their journey from Bakersfield to the Central Coast.

The hostel proved a perfect base. It had a comfortable and friendly atmosphere and was within walking distance of town. It wasn't long before they stumbled upon Monterey Dive Center, one of the several dive stores in the Cannery Row area.

"Hey, dude," Spike waved at the attendant as he entered the store. "What are some of the best dives in the area you can do without a boat?"

The attendant pulled out a laminated map of local dive sites. "What level of diving are you looking for?" he asked.

"I suppose we can dive just about anywhere," Spike assured him, proudly presenting his new C-card. The attendant took a close look at it then scrutinized the young men. He smiled at their enthusiasm, but shook his head at their overconfidence.

"I dove Monastery Beach a few years back," Jerry offered. "Isn't it one of the best dives in the area?"

"It's great when the conditions are right," the attendant replied. "But the west swell has been nasty the past few weeks. You might want to stick with the north shores like the Breakwater or Lovers Point."

The attendant returned Spike's C-card as he continued his report. "Even when conditions are perfect, Monastery is pretty advanced." He pointed to a spot on the map. "Whaler's Cove, inside Point Lobos State Reserve might be okay, but if you're going to dive there, you have to get a reservation."

He circled the sites he'd mentioned, along with a couple of others, sold them a guidebook and wrote down the number for the dive reservation line at Point Lobos. "One more thing," he added from behind the counter. "If you're determined to dive any of the more exposed sites, get there as early in the morning as you can, before the wind picks up. And plan your dive so you exit while the tide is still going out. That's when it'll be at its best. But even so, I'd stay away from Monastery Beach if I were you."

The attendant rented them the appropriate wetsuits, tanks, and weight belts to supplement the gear that they'd brought along.

"Thanks a lot, guy," Jerry said as the pair left the store with guidebook in hand and gear in tow. Spike struggled a bit with the lock on the hatchback of the Nag, but with a little finesse, got it to give in. They loaded her up with 60 pounds of lead weights and four 40-pound air tanks, not to mention a couple of 200-pound men. The Nag's suspension nearly burst and she choked and bucked a little, but with a belch of hot gas and an expletive of encouragement from Spike she rumbled down Cannery Row, groaning at every bump and crack in the pavement.

For their first dive, Jerry and Spike chose MacAbee Beach near El Torito Mexican Restaurant. It was relatively easy to access, parking for the Nag was nearby and there was a freshwater shower for rinsing their gear after the dive.

"The guidebook says there's an old sea anchor at a depth of 40 feet, straight off the point," Jerry said as they both struggled into their wetsuits.

"That'd be cool!" Spike replied enthusiastically.

"Seems like a good place to get used to the conditions around the Peninsula," Jerry continued, not letting on that he was feeling a little apprehensive. He hadn't been on a cold, open-water dive since he visited Monterey with his father more than five years before. It made him especially nervous to be diving with a newly certified buddy who had never dove in such frigid water.

"We can kick out a few hundred yards before we drop down, then head that way," Jerry said, swinging his hand from right to left. "We'll explore the rocky bottom shown on the map, then find the anchor and come back in over the sand."

"Sounds like a plan," Spike agreed, wiggling the zipper of his booties up over his neoprene wetsuit.

"Help me shoulder my tank, would ya?" Jerry asked, turning his back to Spike to receive the 60-pound bundle. The regulators and gauges hanging off the tank's top looked like a four-legged octopus dangling its tentacles around his neck. After Jerry was set, he helped Spike with his gear. Not long after he started, Jerry snapped his fingers with a look of consternation.

"What?" Spike asked.

"I forgot to put on my weight belt."

Spike looked into the back of the Nag and saw the belt, threaded with 30 pounds of lead, partially hidden by a towel. He reached into the car and passed the belt over, snickering at his friend, then held the tank up out of the way while Jerry put on the belt.

When they finished adjusting their gear, they waded into the gently rolling waves like awkward sea monsters. Waist deep, they stopped and spit into their facemasks, wiping the saliva around to keep the glass from fogging up. Then they rinsed the masks out with ocean water and slipped the straps over their heads, positioning them securely on their faces, careful to get all of their hair out of the seals. Next, they put their snorkels between their teeth and pulled on their fins. It was not a graceful process, but it worked. Now, ready to start their dive, they dipped into the water and began their surface swim, expelling distorted expletives through their snorkels as the cold water penetrated their wetsuits, reaching every warm patch of skin on their bodies. After a few minutes the inner layer of water warmed to body temperature and the divers adjusted to the 50-degree sea.

Since both were competitive swimmers, kicking out proved little trouble. Once they got past the shoreline kelp beds, they signaled one another to drop down.

On the bottom, Jerry soon realized that Spike was nowhere in sight. Visibility was at least twenty feet, but Jerry had still managed to lose track of him. He looked around for about a minute; then, as he was trained to do during his certification course, he surfaced. After safely ascending 25 feet, Jerry popped his head above the water, filled his BCD with air and searched for his friend. He saw Spike a couple yards away, struggling to keep his head above water.

"What the hell happened to you?" Jerry shouted as he swam toward Spike. He was a little out of breath, both from the general anxiety of getting separated from his friend and from SCUBA diving in the cold ocean for the first time in years. When he got close enough, he could tell Spike was gasping for every breath.

"Get the air for me . . . would you?" Spike heaved.

Jerry quickly opened the valve on Spike's tank and added some air to his friend's BCD, lifting Spike's face out of the water. "Ya okay now?"

"Yeah," Spike choked. "Just lost my breath for a minute. These weights are pretty heavy . . . when you don't have air in the vest . . . to help float."

Spike sputtered some more as he caught his breath. "I forgot . . . to turn on . . . my tank," he said, acknowledging a mistake common among novice divers. "I started to go down . . . then couldn't get air out of my regulator or inflate my BCD. I kicked like mad to get back to the surface. Good thing

I don't have too much extra weight on my belt."

"I sure am glad you didn't have to drop your weight belt," Jerry added, trying to make light of the situation. "I was right under you."

"I'll be all right in a minute." Spike ignored Jerry's attempt at humor. "I just gotta catch my breath."

Jerry watched his friend struggle to regain his composure and realized then that they had forgotten to check each other out thoroughly before getting into the water. Feeling guilty because he was the more experienced diver, Jerry made a mental note never to skip a full safety check again.

Despite Spike's near mishap, the young men decided almost immediately to descend again. This time they faced each other and stayed close, neither being in a mood to prove anything. They held each other by the vest and slowly let air out of their BCDs. Visibility at the surface was poor, but as they dropped below the thermocline, the water cleared up.

On the bottom they adjusted their buoyancy by adding spurts of air into their vests until they could control their vertical position by breathing in and out. Taking a deep breath, Jerry slowly rose in the water. When he exhaled, he descended.

Spike found his balance point, too, and quickly achieved neutral buoyancy. He was still breathing heavily. Each gave the "OK" sign to the other, then began finning along a few feet above the ocean floor, eager to explore the splendors of inner space.

Kelp swayed to and fro in the gentle push of the water. Greenlings, gobies and groupers went about their business, avoiding the clumsy aliens who passed them by. Only a small, orphaned sea otter, which had been rescued as a pup by Monterey Bay Aquarium research divers, seemed to pay any attention at all to the strangely attired invaders. Once the otter realized neither was his surrogate mother, he also paid them no mind.

The explorers soon found the old rusted-out cannery pipe that the site map had depicted. They knew it would point them toward their objective. They peeked inside the pipe and saw a well-camouflaged decorator crab searching for bits of food, then followed the pipe until it ended. There they found a few links of a massive, rusty anchor chain. They signaled their mutual excitement by extending their thumb and pinkie fingers and clenching the three others.

They navigated along the anchor chain, which disappeared into the sand then emerged again. At a depth of 40 feet, they found what they were looking for: an imposing iron sea anchor, rust-encrusted and covered with strawberry anemones and a myriad of other sessile creatures. The concave iron disk, designed to stabilize a ship while at sea during a storm, was eight feet in diameter. From its center, a six by eight-inch rectangular iron shaft projected at a 45-degree angle toward the seabed. The chain was linked through its huge iron eye.

On the base of the shaft, near the chain's eye, the ganglionic mesh of a kelp holdfast secured a single, thick stalk of kelp that reached up into the hazy waters above, disappearing into the glare of the sun. The stringy tentacles of purple, orange and white tubeworms reached up from the sandy bottom and into the currents, continually waving through the waters, searching for tiny plankton. Several sienna senorita fish sallied serenely by, nibbling on edible flecks of stuff stirred up by the cumbersome divers bumbling about their undersea world. A well-camouflaged flounder resting beside the anchor skittered away, undulating off the bottom to avoid a random fin kick unnoticed by the underwater tourists.

Jerry checked his air gauge and noted that he had half a tank. He signaled for Spike to do the same and was disappointed when Spike held up five fingers, indicating he had only 500 pounds of air left—plenty to make it to the surface, but not enough to make the underwater swim back to shore.

So they began a controlled ascent, careful not to rise faster than their bubbles, in order to avoid dangerous decompression injuries. They watched as their exhaled bubbles rose and expanded due to the diminishing water pressure closer to the surface. That expansion, which would continue until the bubbles burst into the air above, graphically reminded them of what could happen to excess nitrogen dissolved in their blood during a dive—nitrogen built up from breathing compressed air—if they didn't surface slowly. Ascending too quickly could cause residual nitrogen dissolved in their blood to form bubbles. These bubbles could expand and lodge in the capillary beds of their joints, muscles and organs causing the bends, embolisms . . . or worse. By surfacing slowly, however, the divers ensured that the nitrogen had time to return to their lungs on its circulatory journey to be safely expelled through normal respiration, allowing them to avoid such problems.

They arrived on the surface safely, inflating their BCDs so they could float comfortably.

"That was so cool!" Spike exclaimed. "Totally amazing! Did you see those orange fish? They were nearly chewing on our ears!"

"Senorita fish," Jerry affirmed, curtly.

"That was the best! The lake was nothing compared to this!"

"Yeah, but your tank is almost empty. We're going to have to kick back to the beach on the surface." He pointed to the line of shore several hundred yards away.

"Hey, look at the kayakers," Spike said, his mind still unable to focus after the excitement of the dive.

"It would be nice if we had one right now," Jerry said. "You could paddle back and get another tank."

"It's not that far," Spike said. "How much air do you have left?"

Jerry checked his gauge. "Nearly half a tank, you pig. You gotta learn to take long slow breaths so you don't burn your air so fast."

"Maybe I should get a bigger tank."

"Just take long, full breaths. If you take short, choppy breaths, a lot of air gets wasted in the dead space of the tubing, regulator and hoses."

"Easy for you to say, you've been diving since you were a kid."

"You'll be fine," Jerry said, easing up a bit. "But we have to be more careful, like making sure our tanks are turned on and stuff."

"And our weight belts are on," Spike added before rolling onto his back and kicking toward the beach.

"And our weight belts are on," Jerry said, conceding Spike's point. He put his regulator back in his mouth and followed beside his friend, face down, trying in vain to see more of the dive site through the murky water.

Once they made it back to the beach, they clambered up to the washdown area. "Where do you want to go next?" Jerry asked, as Spike finished rinsing the sand off his wetsuit.

"A beer would be nice."

Jerry had no argument against that. He collected his gear. "Got the keys?" he asked, extending his finger to receive them, his arms full of equipment. Spike hung the car keys on it and went back to washing his gear.

When Spike got up to the Old Nag, Jerry was leaning on her hood. All his gear was behind the car. "The Old Nag wouldn't let me back in," he said and handed the keys back to Spike.

"She just doesn't love you like she does me," he replied, slipping the key into the back lock. He pushed down hard at the hasp area with his free hand, twisting and wiggling the key until the lock released and the hatchback opened with the melodious creak of rusty hinges.

"See, no sweat," Spike smiled while taking a stick out and jamming it between the bumper and the hatch so it wouldn't slam down onto their heads.

After loading the heavy, wet gear and changing into some dry clothes, the two college buddies went to do what college buddies do best. They found a good seat at El Torito and ordered cold brews.

"Where do you want to do our second dive?" Spike asked.

"I don't know. Why not take a break and do another one here? We can switch out the tanks and then go that way." He waved his hand toward a dive site on the other side of MacAbee Beach.

"Nah, I want to try another area," Spike insisted, raising his mug to his lips. "Some place new. Maybe Lovers Point or something."

"How about we drive along the coast and see what looks good?"

"Sounds like a plan."

After a more than sufficient surface interval between dives, they reluctantly abandoned their comfortable chairs, turning away from the striking view of the Monterey Bay, to sally forth on their next dive adventure beneath it. They got into the car, paid the parking attendant and pulled out into the street. The Old Nag grudgingly chugged along Cannery Row, past the Monterey Bay Aquarium and down Ocean View Boulevard toward Lovers Point in Pacific Grove.

They ended up choosing Otter's Cove beach past Lovers Point, for their next dive. It wasn't as visually interesting as the dive at MacAbee, and the sea grass was a mess to swim through on the way out. But once they got to the rock outcropping where the environment turned more interesting, they enjoyed themselves, and the dive unfolded without any major mishaps. By the time they'd exited the cold water, both were ready for a hot shower, a good feed, and a peaceful nap in the warm afternoon sun.

By their fourth day of diving, Spike and Jerry were feeling more comfortable with their gear and more confident with their diving skills. They had completed several of the best beach dives the Peninsula had to offer, including the spectacular but exhausting Butterfly dive off Scenic Avenue near Carmel Beach. However, they remained unable to get reservations to dive Point Lobos. And Monastery Beach continued to manifest heavy surf and a strong surge.

"I can't believe we came all this way to dive Monastery Beach just to get closed out by a little bad weather," Spike said, sipping a cool micro-brew at Sly McFly's, a bar near the aquarium.

"That's just the way it goes in this sport," Jerry said, shrugging his shoulders.

"I bet once you get under the surface it isn't so bad," Spike said, wiping beer foam off his lip with his sleeve. "I say we give it a shot tomorrow. It *is* our last day here."

Jerry chewed on Spike's suggestion while Spike chewed on a spicy chicken wing. "I mean, whatta we got to lose?" Spike continued after swallowing. "If we have to ditch the dive, we just come back over the hill and dive somewhere on the Monterey side." He finished his beer and ordered another.

After a slight pause, Jerry responded. "If we're gonna do it," he said, "we'd better get up early and go there at near sunrise. That's when the tide will be best, according to the local chart." He grabbed his guidebook from the seat next to him, opened it and began to study it, mindlessly wiping a fresh drop of red cocktail sauce off the map of Monastery Beach with his thumb. "Maybe it'll be easier to get out then," he added. "The tide should be going out, so the waves might be less of a problem."

Jerry paused again, and pointed to the entry site. Spike looked on with interest as his friend shared his thoughts. "If we dive the north end first, we can do our deep dive on that wall and around Boulder Gardens." Jerry's finger traced the route on the page. "Then we can do a second dive on the south end in the kelp forest if conditions don't get too bad."

"That looks like a good place for a second dive," Spike agreed. "Not much deeper than 40 or 50 feet."

"How deep do you want to go on the first dive?" Jerry asked.

"As deep as we can," Spike said, wryly. He slid the book back over to Jerry and pointed at the depth lines. The map showed where the Submarine Canyon merged with the Carmel River Canyon, precipitously dropping to the ocean floor, nearly a mile below the surface where it met the Monterey Canyon.

"I don't think I want to go quite that deep just yet." Jerry smiled and took another chug of beer, watching a waitress in a tight miniskirt and see-through blouse pass by. Spike caught his friend's stare and followed it enthusiastically.

Jerry tapped a spot on the dive map to bring their attention back to the book. "Just past this wash rock here," he said. "I remember diving around some really cool boulders. It drops off in a fairly steep angle into the canyon after that."

Then he pointed at another spot where the depth was 100 feet. "If we drop down here," he continued, "and work our way back up the wall into the boulders, I think we could get the best out of the dive. How many have we done so far, nine?"

"Ten, if you include the one where that regulator you lent me blew out and I lost most of my air before I got back to the surface."

"Sorry about that. I never had any problems with the gear before."

"First time for everything." Spike smiled.

"We better head back to the hostel and get some rest," Jerry suggested.

They paid the bill, tipped their waitress generously and walked back to the hostel.

An early fog blanketed the Monterey Peninsula when Spike and Jerry went out to fire up the Old Nag the next morning. Large water droplets fell off the pine trees, splattering on the pavement, and the air was thick enough to chew. The divers were still a little groggy, but sufficiently excited about the dive to make the effort.

The Old Nag seemed even groggier than they were, at first resisting all efforts to start. But she finally coughed up a belch of black smoke and roared into action. The old car huffed and puffed up Prescott Avenue, chugging over the hill behind the hostel to Highway 68, where it eventually intersected with Highway 1. It seemed as though the vehicle might come to pieces right then and there, but Spike coaxed her on successfully.

They continued south until Monastery Beach came into sight, then found convenient parking at its north end past the Little Red Schoolhouse on their right. The fog was so dense they could hardly make out the monastery across the highway, and the fishy smell of low tide filled their nostrils.

Spike killed the engine. The sound of waves crashing roughly over the coarse sand was muted by a nearby grove of soggy eucalyptus. Menthol from the fragrant leaves saturated the cool, misty air, completing this somewhat mystical scene.

"This doesn't look much worse than the water conditions in the bay," Spike noted.

"Don't let the surface activity fool you, dude," Jerry cautioned. "It can be deceiving. Don't forget that the shop guy said it can be a lot more challenging than it looks."

"C'mon, let's do it," Spike said, wrestling with the handle of the door. He gave it a gentle nudge with his shoulder and it surrendered without further struggle. He stepped out and stood facing the beach. Jerry joined him.

Leaning against the Old Nag, they pondered the vision before them. Soon the fog began to recede, allowing the sun to shine through the trees on the hill behind the monastery. Glimpses of blue sky were peaking through the white glow and foamy gray waves became visible, crashing over Point Lobos in the hazy distance.

"I guess the swell is breaking from the other direction this morning," Jerry said. "The waves are only a couple feet high. The north side looks doable."

"Shall we?" Spike asked, moving toward the back of the wagon.

"We shall," Jerry said. "And the sooner the better."

By the time they'd got their gear together, the fog had drifted back behind the breakers and the tide was almost fully out, making the floating kelp especially thick. The shore waves had picked up a bit, but not alarmingly so. The divers donned most of their gear at the car, carrying their masks, fins and snorkels as they trudged across the beach and down to the surf.

"Ready for a final check?" Jerry asked.

"Ready," Spike replied, and began calling off the various check items. Jerry lifted his arms and turned around. Spike looked for any loose or incorrectly assembled gear and checked his tank valve. "Looks good," Spike said, and went through a similar routine under Jerry's scrutiny.

"Wait," Jerry said. "You put your weight belt on backwards." He lifted Spike's tank while his buddy dropped his heavy belt and placed it back on in the proper position with the quick release hasp lying securely to the left, so his right hand could pull it loose if need be. "One more reason to do a safety check," Jerry commented.

"That's for sure," Spike agreed as they finished the drill and put on the rest of their dive gear.

Fins on feet, the divers waddled down to the water. They stood face to face, as the waves broke against their sides. They rinsed and fitted their masks and regulators; then, slowly, each with one hand supporting his buddy and the other holding his mask and regulator on his face, entered the sea. The relatively small waves buffeted them with surprising force, their powerful wash nearly ripping the divers' feet out from under them. The two stumbled awkwardly into the water, deep enough to float, then kicked out past the tenacious waves.

Spike and Jerry soon switched from their regulators to their snorkels to conserve air as they made their way out to the drop point.

"You okay, Spike?" Jerry called.

"Yeah, just got some seaweed caught on my tank," Spike replied, his voice muffled by the sounds of the water as he struggled to remove the long, thick strands of leafy brown rope. "How about you?"

"I'm okay," Jerry replied. "Kick out around the kelp, over here." He pointed south toward Point Lobos, which lay across the small bay.

"I'm trying," Spike said. He managed to get his tank free but found his regulator, entangled, blowing off air. He quickly rectified that situation and continued swimming.

Jerry swam out past the wash rock (indicated on the map as a key landmark for the dive site), and watched as Spike made his way through the mat of thick kelp, fighting relentlessly with the weeds that seemed deliberate in their attempt to restrain him. Finally they met at the designated spot and reestablished contact.

"How're ya feeling, Spike?"

"Fine, now that I'm outta that mess," Spike said, floating close to him.

"It didn't look nearly this bad from the beach," Jerry said, as they bobbed up and down in the surface chop.

"I thought we saw a channel through the kelp before we entered," Spike recalled.

"We did, but it closed in on us. Why don't we go ahead and drop down here to 70 feet? According to the dive tables, if that's our maximum depth we can do a 30-minute dive."

"I thought we were gonna go to 100 feet and then work our way back up?" Spike said, spitting out some splash from a white cap.

"That would cut our non-decompression limit to twenty minutes. Besides, I don't think there's much to see past 70 or 80 feet with the water this stirred up."

"I guess you're right," Spike conceded. He had looked forward to making his deepest dive yet, but he saw the logic in Jerry's reasoning. "Let's get under. I'm getting a little seasick slopping around on the surface like this."

"Okay. How much air do you have?"

"Twenty-seven hundred pounds," Spike replied.

"I still have 3,000. Go easy on your air." Jerry stuffed his regulator between his teeth.

"Yes, dear," Spike said and mouthed his own regulator before signaling he was ready.

Jerry pointed downward with his thumb. They bled the air out of their BCDs, allowing their lead weights to drag them down. As they got deeper, they added air into their vests to slow their rate of descent.

Jerry checked his depth gauge. It read "65 feet". His wetsuit was more compressed than it was at the surface, and the chill of the colder, deeper water began to get through the diminished insulation. When they got below the debris and particulate matter sloshing around in the surface layer, the visibility increased to nearly twenty feet. Jerry kept an eye on Spike, who seemed to be coping pretty well with his buoyancy.

When Jerry's gauge read 80 feet, he leveled off and saw that Spike had dropped well below the planned depth limit. Jerry went deeper to stop him. Once he had his buddy's attention, he waved his flattened hand back and forth in a horizontal motion, signaling Spike to level off. Next, he put his thumb and forefinger together to see if he was okay. Spike signaled back that he was and they leveled off at 95 feet.

There was nothing to see in the middle of the cold, dark water so they had no reference point except for their gauges. Already they found that the turbulent sea was toying with them.

Jerry grabbed Spike's vest, bringing them face to face. He clenched his fist and pointed his thumb toward the surface, signing his partner to go up.

Spike squeezed his nose between his thumb and forefinger, attempting to equalize pressure in his ears, giving Jerry another "OK" sign with his free hand.

Jerry checked his compass and signed again to go up. Then he extended his fingers, pointing to show that they should head toward the shore.

Spike signed "OK" and began to kick in that direction.

In a few minutes, they had risen to their planned depth of 70 feet and saw a gray, rocky slope rushing toward them. By the popping of their ears, they knew they were changing depth rapidly. The pressure between their outer and inner ears equalized uncomfortably, as the surge moved them back and forth, and up and down. The wall zoomed in and out. Jerry grabbed Spike again and signed to go further up, and in.

Spike readily agreed. He was breathing hard and using air fast, but being a strong swimmer, he fought the currents and followed Jerry. They didn't see much of anything until they got up to 60 feet, and even then the surge was stirring up the bottom so badly that visibility had deteriorated to ten feet. For a few minutes, the turbidity seemed to ease, making underwater navigation and maneuvering a bit easier. The last set of heavy swells that had tossed the divers around appeared to have passed, allowing them to get their bearings.

But no sooner had they regained their sense of direction than another set of swells pummeled them. While heading back toward the shore, Spike was in front of Jerry. He had gotten too far ahead and was barely in sight when the new siege of turbulence hit. The last image Jerry had of Spike was of his fighting to hold onto the wall and signing that he was low on air. Jerry signed back instructing him to go up to the surface, but he couldn't tell if his friend had seen him. As the giant swell receded, it swept Jerry around a precipice and dragged him back down into the canyon.

Jerry lost sight of the wall and became totally disoriented. He was aware only of the painful sensation in his ears, a clear indication that he was going down further and further. The chill penetrated his bones as his wetsuit compressed more tightly against him with each foot of added depth. He tried to kick toward the surface but soon realized that, after being whipped around so much in the currents, he didn't know which way was up. By the time he was able to grab his depth gauge, it read 135 feet. He could no longer mask his panic.

To make matters worse, the nitrogen dissolved in his blood was playing havoc with his mind. It was as if he were on laughing gas, yet he struggled to keep his wits. He knew that if he didn't do the right thing now, it would likely be the last thing he ever did.

He looked at his air gauge and found that he only had 900 pounds of air left. Adding some air to his BCD, he looked again at his depth gauge, assessing the speed and direction of his movement by noting the exhaled bubbles coming out of his regulator.

Before long he arrested his descent and knew that he was, indeed, finally rising toward the surface, but much faster than his bubbles were. The violent water was playing havoc with his attempts to control his depth. Painfully aware that he was in serious danger—that the nitrogen in his blood might soon bubble and create a bloody foam in his veins—he spread his legs and extended his fins to slow down. In a final attempt to avoid decompression sickness, he dumped the precious air out of his BCD, allowing the 30 or so pounds of lead around his waist to again counter his ascent.

At 50 feet and sinking again, Jerry kicked his fins frantically in an effort to achieve a greater measure of control, going up at the safe rate of one foot per second. Breathing through the regulator was now becoming difficult, indicating that the air in the tank was getting very low. Flipping his gauge over, he saw that he had less than 100 pounds left.

It became harder and harder for him to contain his panic. With 40 feet left to go to the surface, he took one last, slow, deep breath, sucking his tank dry, then released his weight belt and let it drop into the depths. Like a helium balloon freed from the grip of a child's hand, he floated steadily upwards, not caring where he was going to end up or how he was going to get back to the beach.

Jerry exhaled slowly as he rose toward the surface, releasing the pressure of the expanding air to avoid rupturing his lungs. He retained a good enough sensibility to know that this didn't help rid his blood of the tiny, potentially lethal bubbles. So he spread his feet and turned his fins up to reduce the speed of his ascent. Unfortunately, with no weight belt, the buoyancy of his wetsuit and empty tank still propelled him upward faster than the bubbles he'd exhaled.

On the surface, he gasped for air, but got a mouthful of water. Coughing and sputtering, he managed to clear his mouth and breathe deeply. He manually inflated his BCD by putting his lips over the dump valve and blowing air back into the vest. Once he had a vest full of air to help keep his face out of the water, he tried to relax and lay motionless on the surface, bobbing up and down like a black and blue cork. He was thankful he had survived. He prayed that he could get back to the beach without further problems. But Jerry didn't feel very well. He felt nauseous from the saltwater he'd swallowed, and suddenly puked. He felt a little better after that but he was getting cold and stiff and feeling a bit dizzy. In the distance, he could see the beach being pounded by the waves as the tide vengefully reclaimed the land it had abandoned earlier that morning.

Jerry was exhausted, sick, cold, and feeling pain all over, but it wasn't long before his despair faded into euphoria and he experienced a sense of peaceful acquiescence. He eventually stopped struggling and resolved to kick gently toward the shore while lying on his back, slowly succumbing to his ailments as they became progressively worse.

Forty feet deep, Spike clung to a rocky outcropping in the wall. The brutal water ripped mercilessly at his gear and body. Seeing Jerry carried away in the grasp of the sea, Spike tried to signal that he was getting low on air, but didn't know if his friend had seen him. The best Spike could hope for was to meet his partner on the surface. He fully accepted that the dive was over.

As soon as the turbulence slackened, Spike released his hold on the rocks and began to ascend through the boulders and kelp. His basic SCUBA training had taught him that if you lose your dive buddy or get low on air, you should go to the surface and regroup. But he had miscalculated his exit and was coming up in the middle of thick kelp, and much too close to the shallow rocks. So he fought against the brutal breakers, attempting to return to the relative safety of deeper water, well away from the pounding surf.

To his dismay, Spike found his efforts to clear the kelp had the opposite effect. He was so tangled he couldn't even find his gauges. He suspected that there were only a few more breaths of air in his tank, so he pulled the quick-release on his weight belt, thankful that Jerry had helped him get it on correctly. At once he lurched toward the surface, but only moved a few feet upward before his tangled gear held him fast. Before he knew it, the kelp had him yet again, ripping his mask off and exposing his eyes to stinging salt water and shocking cold.

Squeezing his eyes shut against the painful blur, he gripped his regulator tightly in his teeth and climbed out of his BCD, extricating himself from the snares of the brown, rope-like plants. Once free, he sucked in one last breath of air then spit the regulator out. Letting go of the dive gear, he fled for the surface, squirming frantically through the dense, slimy jungle of giant algae.

When he reached the surface, he found himself battered by one heavy wave after another. Despite the onslaught, Spike managed to crawl onto some rocks. He saw a fisherman on the shore.

"Help!" Spike cried. "Help me! Get some help! I lost my buddy out there!"

The man seemed to hear him and began to make his way toward the distressed swimmer, but then another wave attacked Spike and the sea devoured him, sucking him back into its gullet. He again struggled for the surface, hoping that his call had been heeded. When he popped up just outside Boulder Gardens, he was able to climb through the kelp into deeper, safer water. The fisherman was running up the beach and Spike prayed he was going for help.

"Highlands Fire!" The words crackled out of the stale speaker like dry rice paper. "Respond to a report of divers in trouble at Monastery Beach."

The crew on duty snapped into action.

"Heads up everyone," Engineer Goodman said, dropping the footrest on the Lazy-Boy with a clunk. "It's ours."

"Goodman, take Layton in Rescue 7361 and get the boat in the water at Whaler's Cove," Captain Mortlan ordered. "I'll take a volunteer and then head for the south end of the beach to set up command." She then answered dispatch to acknowledge the alarm.

"Hey, Layton," Goodman called downstairs to the workout room. "We've got a live one off Mortuary! Let's shake it!"

Firefighter Layton came running up the stairs in his shorts and socks, carrying his duty boots, slipping slightly on the smooth wood steps. The rookie had recently finished water rescue training and was bursting with anticipation about going out for a real rescue. He passed the engineer, ducking under his arm as the older man held the door.

"Get a wetsuit on and put the portable radio in the waterproof bag," Goodman barked, while following the firefighter out. Goodman put on a bright orange exposure suit, climbed into the rescue vehicle beside Layton, fired up the diesel and flicked on the lights and siren. The engineer grabbed the mike and said, "Dispatch, show 7361 responding to Whaler's Cove," indicating that the rescue vehicle was staffed and heading out to help the divers.

Goodman navigated his rig through the entrance to Point Lobos State Reserve. He waved at the part-timer in the kiosk before winding around visitor traffic and into the oncoming lane toward where the rescue boat was stored. When he got to the cove, he staged his rig next to the boat shed at the near end of the crowded parking lot.

The men got the inflatable rescue boat (IRB) ready for deployment and with the help of some bystanders, put it into the water. They climbed in and fired up the Yamaha 35. In less than six minutes since they'd received the call, they were on their way to the rescue.

In the meantime, Captain Mortlan established command at the south end of Monastery Beach. She was advised by dispatch that the Coast Guard helicopter was 35 minutes away.

Spike watched as the red shapes and flashing lights of the fire engines and other emergency vehicles arrived. He saw a rescuer in an orange life jacket come toward the surf line. He swam toward her with the little strength he had left, but the roaring surf wouldn't let him out of its clutches and he couldn't move one leg.

Captain Mortlan spotted Spike. "Go out!" she called, waving him back toward deeper water. "Wait for the rescue boat!"

Too exhausted to think for himself, he complied gladly and remained floating just beyond the waves. Mortlan keyed her radio and relayed the location of the victim to the rescue boat. She could see her rescue crew exiting Whaler's Cove as she spoke.

Spike waved weakly at the small rescue boat. It bobbed in the swells coming toward him. The rescuer in the bow of the rubber craft waved back. Spike relaxed a little and closed his eyes, the buoyancy of his wetsuit keeping him afloat.

"Layton!" Goodman hollered over the sound of the boat's motor. "Jump in 'n grab him. Hold onto this line!" He thrust one end of the bowline into Layton's hand. "I'll pull you both out a safe distance past the breakers, then we can stabilize the diver and get him aboard!"

Layton leaped into the water and swam the few remaining strokes to Spike. When Layton made contact with him, Spike was barely conscious.

"I got you. What's your name?"

"Spike Johnson . . ."

Layton grabbed Spike's extended hand and pulled him around so the victim's back was to the rescuer's breast. Then Layton threw his arm over Spike's shoulder, grabbing him across the chest. Once Spike felt secure in the rescue hold, he went limp. Goodman reversed the IRB's motor and slowly pulled the pair away from the breaking waves to the relative safety of deeper water. Then he put the motor into neutral.

Goodman pulled Layton and Spike along the side of the rescue boat. "He's breathing and has a pulse! His name is Spike Johnson!" The firefighter reported.

Layton took the neck brace from Goodman and placed it around Spike's neck as a precaution, in case Spike had suffered a traumatic injury during the dive. Goodman then lowered an orange, floating backboard into the water and Layton slipped the rigid device under Spike. Using five nylon straps, they secured him to it. Finally, they affixed Spike's head to the backboard and were ready to bring him in. Layton climbed into the boat and together they pulled him aboard.

"We have the victim," Goodman reported to the captain.

"We'll have the ambulance meet you at Whaler's Cove," her voice crackled back over the portable radio.

Goodman acknowledged, and navigated the boat back through the high swells. Spike came to again.

"Where's Jerry?" he muttered.

"Who?" Layton asked.

"My dive buddy," Spike repeated and tried to get up.

"Don't try to move. You're strapped to a backboard. Another team of rescuers is looking for your friend," Layton lied, trying to be reassuring. There were no other rescuers in the water. "Can you tell us his name?"

"Jerry. Jerry Wilcox."

"Okay, Spike. Do you remember what color his gear was?"

"Black . . . with some blue, I think."

Layton patted Spike on the shoulder. "Just relax, we'll find him." Over the sound of the boat motor, the rookie reported the information to Goodman who radioed back to command.

At Whaler's Cove the rescue team got Spike back to the boat ramp and into the ambulance. Then they headed back out to look for Jerry.

Flickering red, amber and blue lights littered the perimeter of the beach and the parking strip along Highway 1. Eight emergency agencies had responded, including fifteen vehicles and more than 30 rescue personnel. The local press swarmed around the area like yellow jackets at a picnic. And curious gawkers looked on from a number of vantage points.

The Coast Guard helicopter had arrived as planned and began searching immediately. The pilot contacted Mortlan at the command post. "We've spotted something in the water," he said. "We're going down to check it out."

The pilot lowered his craft closer to the water. "Looks like dive gear, but there's no diver in sight. We're going to continue our search." They watched as Goodman headed the IRB toward their position at full speed. Before the IRB got near, they pulled up and continued their search. The crew watched from the air as Layton grabbed the gear. He immediately checked the gauges and reported back over the radio. "The depth gauge reads 145 feet and the tank is completely dry," he said to Mortlan.

"Copy," Mortlan sighed hopelessly over the radio.

"Sounds like a body recovery to me," the chopper pilot said to Joe Tapin, the rescue diver in the bird.

"Let's give him a chance," Tapin said, imagining how he would feel if he were the one in trouble. "Maybe he made it to the top and ditched his gear. After all, the vest was inflated and intact."

After another fifteen minutes of searching in ever-widening concentric arches, Tapin spotted Jerry. The pilot immediately went on the radio. "We've spotted the victim floating off Point Lobos. He's on his back. Seems to be . . . kicking out to sea. We're going to drop our rescue diver in and hoist him up."

"Copy," Mortlan acknowledged. "The second ambulance will be waiting near the landing site."

Tapin leaped from twenty feet above the ocean swells, splashing down near Jerry. The victim seemed oblivious to the commotion. When Tapin got to him, he had a slight smile on his lips and was finning gently. Tapin looped a rescue harness under Jerry's arms and secured it firmly. The chopper crew hoisted Jerry aboard. Tapin waited for the IRB to pick him up while watching the helicopter whisk Jerry back to the landing site on shore.

The waiting ambulance transported him directly to the barometric chamber at the Pacific Grove Fire Station where Dr. Torison and the volunteer medical treatment crew were standing by to receive him.

Epilogue

Spike sat alone, nursing a mug of Carmel Wheat in the lounge of El Torito. He lifted his glass symbolically to his friend Jerry who now lay comatose in a bed at Community Hospital of the Monterey Peninsula. Resting his broken leg on an extra chair, Spike looked at the wrinkled pages of last week's paper lying on his table. A blurry color photo on the front page showed Jerry being hoisted out of the water by the Coast Guard helicopter.

Spike read the caption to himself:

Divers rescued from treacherous waters off infamous Mortuary Beach.

He reflected morbidly on the alternate name the locals assigned the wretched place, and took another swallow of beer. Then he read from somewhere in the middle of the article:

> *. . . most of these accidents could be avoided if people participating in ocean sports were more knowledgeable about the dangers. For more information on ocean safety, contact the California State Parks, the Monterey County Office of Emergency Services or any coastal fire department.*

"Blah, blah, blah . . ." Spike mused, silently scanning through to the end of the story again. He folded the paper and put it in his bag.

He looked out the window at the sun shining on the lovely Monterey Bay. It looked as calm now as Jerry's unconscious face did a couple miles away in the hospital. Spike wondered if *this* might not have been a better day for a dive.

Author's Note:
Several of the actions portrayed in this story are contrary to safe diving practices and should not be emulated.

About the Author

After nearly twenty years as an emergency services professional, MARK C. ANGEL has worked in ambulance services, firefighting, ocean rescue, disaster response and community emergency preparedness. A volunteer with the American Red Cross since high school, he most recently spent three weeks in New York City assisting with disaster relief efforts. In his spare time, he practices Tai Chi and volunteers as a scientific diver with the Monterey Bay Aquarium. He has a bachelor's degree in psychobiology and music from the University of California at Santa Cruz, and has traveled and dived extensively on four continents. Mark is currently in the process of publishing his first novel, Rexriders.

The Lizard Catcher

by Lele Dahle

Wherever this life may lead you
Whatever your fate shall be
Remember the summer wildflowers
And think of me, think of me.

It is summer in Carmel Valley. A balmy day like so many were then, with cotton candy clouds trapped inside a hopelessly blue sky. I am ten years old, and my name is Rose Ann Stuckley. I'm positioned upon my belly near the river, with Alex crouching beside me. The river has dwindled to a lazy meandering stream, and the exposed rocks are green with slimy moss. Cottonwood trees make a jungle wall that accompanies the watercourse some six or seven miles downstream from where we are to its mouth at Carmel lagoon. Fragrant clusters of purple lupine flowers are in full bloom along the sandy banks, permeating the air with a heady scent.

The air is still. Expectant. A big alligator lizard is crouched motionless in the sand ahead, poised to flee but for one swift motion of my hand. My pony Apollo is tethered to a nearby tree. Juanita is in the scene too, she is clumsily scrambling up the riverbank to gather bits of grass to feed him; I don't really see this because I'm focusing on the lizard, but it's what she always does. I can hear her grunt as she toils to reach the top where the lush grass grows.

The Lizard Catcher

Whenever my mind seeks out memories of the sunny days of my childhood, the spotlight eventually falls upon this business of lizard catching. I swim happily backward in time, to find myself kneeling in soft river sand, the sun's warmth radiating, and leaves lightly rustling overhead. I dig hungrily, and colors, scents, sounds, spill into my consciousness.

Suddenly, I reach a precipice, and the eidetic images unravel as I totter over the brink. Nightmarish scenes assault me. Blood rushes hotly to my face. Just before I manage to clamp the heavy doors shut, I catch a fleeting glimpse of a girl; she is wild with terror and grief, running, her heart furiously pumping. I can hear her screaming something over and over.

I remind myself that this bad thing happened a very long time ago. Then, if I'm able to securely lock away these mangled recollections, I will bask for awhile in the crippled happiness that preceded an undoing of childhood innocence, to recall the days when I was the best lizard catcher Carmel Valley had ever known.

My dad was in his mid-thirties when he inherited a good piece of farmland in the lower Carmel Valley. This was just before he married Mom. Perched on the edge of our fields, about halfway between the Valley road and the river, was the farmhouse that my great grandpa built. It had a river-rock foundation, and the remainder was of redwood log and plaster, with high open beam ceilings. The Stuckley name wasn't one of those Carmel Valley land baron names like the Hattons, or Jacks. We were modest landowners by those standards.

Dad was known for being a pretty good horse breaker. He'd grown up in the Salinas Valley, where his parents had a small ranch, but moved to Carmel Valley in his mid-twenties to help my great grandpa, who was in poor health. When Grandpa passed on, he left the place to Dad. In his youth, Dad had been a rodeo competition rider and reputed hell-raiser, but he injured his back after being trampled by his stallion, Midnight, and that put an end to his rodeo days. It ended for Midnight, too, because Dad shot him afterwards.

Mom was eighteen years younger than Dad. She had long black hair that she wore braided down her back or twisted around her head, and almost always wore shorts, so her slim legs were tan, even in winter. She was only eighteen when they got married, and nineteen when my sister Kristin was born. Mom had Bohemian leanings, and spent a good deal of time hanging out in Carmel, or down the coast with her artist friends. She also loved to garden. We always had fresh vegetables that she'd grown, and bright bunches of flowers at the table.

Even back in my childhood days, being a true farm family in Carmel

Valley was becoming uncommon. All around us, clusters of suburban housing developments were sprouting, as ranchers sold off parcel after parcel of land. But Dad doggedly subscribed to the principle of traditional farm life, and Mom, who'd been raised in Wyoming, embraced it just as fervently.

Sometimes it felt like Kristin and I were little more than indentured servants, catering to a dying cause. Our mandated chores were ceaseless. Not only did we have to daily feed and water the horses, goats and a couple of steers that Dad kept for meat, but we also had a big Holstein cow named Mumu, who we milked every morning and night. Kristin was three years older, and managed to bully me into doing the lion's share of the work. I got stuck being the one to do the milking most mornings, which caused me to smell of cow at school, and throughout the winter months my hands stayed red and chapped from exposure to the cold.

If my sister and I were somewhat neglected by modern standards, the upside was that we were left to do pretty much what we wanted, as long as the chores got done. Our parents would tell us two things: be home by dark, and don't get hurt. If I did get hurt, I didn't ever dare to mention it unless it was something really bad that I couldn't hide, like the time I fell off Apollo while racing Kristin with her horse down Wolter's Road, and ended up with a deep head wound that needed to be stitched at the hospital.

Our big redwood barn would fill up as hay was harvested, until the stacked bales almost kissed the high beams. Kristin and I were allowed to sleep out there during the summer months. We'd climb to the top of the stacks, and with groaning effort arrange hay bales so we'd have cubbyholes to put our sleeping bags in. Bats stuck themselves up in the rafters, and at twilight they came alive and swooped outside to find bugs. Mice living in the hay made furtive little noises all night long, attracting stealthy-winged and marauding owls.

There was only one downside to hanging out in the barn and his name was Raymond. He was the meanest kid at Carmelo school. His dad oversaw the task of baling and putting up our hay, and he kept Raymond pretty busy all summer, which was a relief for us. He was Kristin's age, but had flunked two grades, so was only one year ahead of me in school. We all secretly called him "The Gorilla", because he was big and heavy, and walked around with his shoulders slouched forward. He was prone to dark fits of rage that could erupt suddenly. I once saw him have a screaming fit in the barn. His dad went to him, knocked him flat and started kicking him viciously in the stomach with pointed cowboy boots, until Raymond was wailing and begging him to stop.

Raymond's cruelty was boundless. If we happened to encounter him in the barn, he'd grab a hay hook, search until he found a mouse, impale it on the hook, and wave it around in our faces. After that, if the mouse showed any sign of still being alive he'd yank it off the hook and stomp on it, grinding it into the hard packed dirt of the barn floor with his mud-caked Wellingtons.

The end of third grade marked a turning point in my young life, and is actually where this story begins. Sissy, who'd been my best friend since kindergarten, moved away the day after school got out for summer. Her dad was a military officer, and they got sent someplace overseas. It happened suddenly. I only had two days notice of it and then she was gone forever.

Sissy possessed this magical ability to spin reality into an alluring moonglow, and had managed to entrap me in her silken web, where I felt cherished. I could barely remember my life before. I'd become completely habituated to her presence; sitting on the bus with her, hanging out at Martin's Fruit Stand or Wolter's Market sharing penny candy; sleeping high up on the haystacks together; giggling endlessly on the telephone when we were apart. Having her gone felt like death. Not so much of her, but of me, strange as that sounds. Outside her sphere of perception I felt unremarkable and dull. To this day, I can still occasionally catch fleeting sounds of her Orphean laughter echoing hauntingly through the hollows of my heart. After Sissy left, there was only one thing for me to do. I angrily extracted her from my mind. At least I tried to.

About a week into my gloomy summer, Mom took me up the Valley with her to the egg farm, owned by the Sanchez family, who sold or bartered eggs, mostly with the locals. You couldn't exactly call it a working farm; it wasn't much more than a jumble of chicken cages behind their house. Mom traded milk for eggs.

When we got there, she told me to go play while she went inside and talked with Mrs. Sanchez. I meandered over to the chicken coops and was surprised to find a girl there I'd never seen before. She was a skinny brown-skinned girl with coarse hair and a sad expression in her big eyes, about my age. I found out later that her parents were migrant farm workers who'd left her while they followed the summer crops. Only as it turned out, they never got around to coming back for her. Her name was Juanita.

She'd been ravaged by polio, and one of her legs was as thin as a beanpole and shorter than the other. She stood with her back against a chicken coop, her head turned away from me, looking pathetic . . . which aroused my curiosity. I went over next to where she stood and pretended to look at the chickens, giving her side-glances to see if she would look back at me.

She stayed frozen.

I finally couldn't take it anymore, so I inquired, "Do you live here?" She turned her head to give me a brief stare and then resumed her stony stance. "I have a pony. His name is Apollo, and he's a pinto." There was still no response. Then I remembered that I'd stuffed some Jacks and a ball into my jeans pockets earlier. I held the Jacks out.

"You wanna play?" Still no answer. "Okay, then I'll play by myself!" I was starting to get peeved at being ignored.

I sat down and carefully smoothed out a circle in the dirt. Then I proceeded to go through onesies and twosies, giving her side-glances. By the time I was on threesies, she was watching, so I said, "C'mon, sit down." I motioned with my hand and she came hesitantly over and sat. "Don't you like Jacks? Why can't you talk to me?"

"Chocks?"

"Yes, Jacks!" I noted her Hispanic accent. It suddenly dawned on me that she probably couldn't speak English. I wasn't being snubbed, just not understood. I took on an air of authority. I had a project now. Summer was beginning to look up!

The next day, I rode upriver to the egg farm. The egg farm road was a bramble-infested, dusty dirt road, ending in a footpath that wound down to the river. When I arrived, I asked Mrs. Sanchez if I could take Juanita for a ride on Apollo. She seemed surprised, but said that it would be okay as long as I was careful. She cautioned me that Juanita couldn't speak a word of English, and that I had to look out for her weak leg. I said that I'd teach Juanita some words, and that seemed to make her happy, because she gave me a big smile and a hug. When Juanita saw Apollo her eyes widened to full moons. Then she gazed over to me, and the envy I saw caused my heart to quicken with pride.

That summer I introduced Juanita to my world, and she followed after me breathlessly. We rode up and down the river, seeking out deep swimming holes guarded by huge trout. And explored the trails on Saddle Mountain, where smells of horehound and sage blended with a faint odor of seaweed, carried in by the inevitable afternoon fog. I took her out to long dirt roads that traversed the artichoke fields, and kicked Apollo into a frenzied gallop so that she could experience the exhilarating rush of unbridled power and speed. In those dusky evenings, I hauled her up to the top of the hay, where we made tents with bed sheets slung between hay bales to sleep in.

I painted my world with bold, bright strokes of primary color in an effort to block out the delicate sunset pinks and mauves that were Sissy's hallmark. Sometimes at night with Juanita sleeping soundly next to me, I'd allow thoughts of Sissy, and my chest would ache from stifled sobs. I imagined her inside glossy picture books that showed faraway places, smiling and waving while riding a gondola down a narrow canal in Venice, or dancing through fields of tulips in wooden shoes.

The sun slowly graduated southward, and the inevitable day came when Mom told me we were going to Holman's in Pacific Grove to buy new clothes. It was a week before school was to begin for the fall.

Fourth grade began gloriously for me. At first recess, pretty, perfect Mary Reid, one of the most popular girls in my class, asked me to play jump rope with her and one of her friends. Then the two of them invited me to have lunch with them. Over the summer I'd fantasized about something like this happening. I'd waltz in on the first day of school in my new clothes, maybe a party dress, accessorized with ballet-style shoes and socks trimmed with lace. All the girls would surround me and want me to play with them. They knew, of course, that they *couldn't have* played with me before this, because I hadn't ever needed any friends besides Sissy. Even shabby Rose could have dreams.

Instead of party attire, I wore one of my new dresses from Holman's, an ugly blue and white checked thing that Mom had picked out despite my protests, saying that it was practical and would hold up for washing. I'd slopped milk down the front of it before school, while carrying a full bucket in after milking, and it had dried into a stiff, conspicuous stain that I tried to conceal with my hands.

While I was doing my best to be pleasant and charming toward Mary at lunch, in the back of my mind I was wondering where Juanita could be. She hadn't been on the bus that morning. By the time school was out and I was sitting beside Mary on the bus, I'd forgotten completely about her. Then, after everyone was seated and we were starting to roll, I saw Mrs. Larson, waving for us to stop. Walking crookedly alongside her was Juanita, looking ragged and miserable. Everyone stared as she limped toward the bus. Then, when she got on, not one kid moved to let her sit. The driver had to walk back and bark at someone to move over, and this caused snickers all around. It would not be my best moment. When Mary giggled and twittered, so did I.

For the rest of the afternoon I tried not to think about Juanita, but the image of her hobbling out to the bus swam around and around in my head and wouldn't quit. Sometimes her face would change into Sissy's, and I would fight back tears. I knew it wasn't going to be possible to be friends with both her and Mary Reid. Juanita was no different from all the other farm labor kids who came through the Valley and to Carmelo school. They never stayed long, and when they were gone, nobody missed them. To most of us living in Carmel Valley, these migrants who followed the crops were barely acknowledged, except as ghostly shadows that were sure to fade away by the next setting sun. I wanted to be friends with Mary Reid pretty bad; I *had* to be friends with her now that I didn't have Sissy anymore. So I made my decision. Juanita would have to go.

I racked my brain for a solution about what to do with Juanita, short of abandonment, and then came up with a brilliant idea. Maybe she could become friends with Maria Elena and Esperanza, two Mexican girls from the third grade who kept pretty much to themselves the way Sissy and I had. Thinking this made me feel better. Tomorrow I'd help.

The next morning, the bus drove right past the egg farm road. At school I asked my teacher where Juanita was, because I hadn't seen her at the bus stop. I was sure she should've been in my class. What he told me was almost unbelievable. He said that Juanita had never been to school before and couldn't read or do arithmetic, so she'd been placed with Mrs. Larson in the first and second grade classroom. He assured me that she was in school; he'd seen Mr. Sanchez drop her off himself.

Imagining Juanita sitting with those little kids was a lot to bear. I shivered remembering how her scrawny little arms had felt wrapped tightly around me as we rode together on Apollo, those dark eyes brimming with worship.

Too many images of Juanita were invading me. I'd have to take immediate action. During lunchtime I looked for her on the playground, but she wasn't there. So I went to Mrs. Larson's classroom and found her sitting alone at her desk eating lunch. I called from the doorway and when she saw me her eyes lit up. "C'mon, Juanita. Let's go play." I motioned with my hand.

When I got her outside, I scanned the playground. I needed to find Maria Elena and Esperanza. I spotted them at the far side of the blacktop; they looked to be playing hopscotch. This wasn't so good. My plan had been to somehow get Juanita to join in on whatever they might be doing, but I didn't think she would impress them much with hopscotch.

But I had to go through with it. I took her hand, pulling, to try and hurry her over, all the while scanning for signs of Mary Reid or any of her cohorts. I was lucky, they were nowhere in sight. Juanita was beaming. She held her mouth tightly shut, as if she were afraid to breathe, but her eyes sparkled like two dark jewels, and she did her best to walk without a limp. Finally we were there. I paused for a moment; I really hadn't planned ahead what I would say.

Esperanza stood, watching Maria Elena hop. My voice came out strained with niceness. "Hi Esperanza!" Juanita at this point was hanging behind me and she'd gone rigid. I backed up a few steps then pushed her toward them, trying to ignore the expression of horror on her face. "Juanita wants to play." Maria Elena stopped dead in her tracks, one knee still bent up. Both girls stared at us.

Then Maria Elena broke the silence. She said something to Esperanza in Spanish, and they both started laughing. I didn't understand what they'd said, but whatever it was caused Juanita to bolt. Which was a good thing, because she didn't see what happened next. Esperanza began to imitate Juanita's limp. She made a grotesque face and hobbled about, chanting something over and over in Spanish. For a few seconds I became lost in a mental fog. Then I turned to see where Juanita had gone. She was making a beeline for the classroom.

For the next several days, I snuck into Juanita's classroom during lunch hour. That first day, she kept her head lowered and ignored me. But I worked on her and soon had her giggling once again at my dumb jokes that she couldn't begin to understand. Guilt wasn't the only driving force, although I'll admit that was part of it. I'd become dependent on the adoration she'd gifted upon me those past months, and now that it was going to be lost, an irrational sense of panic had seized me. I was frightened at the prospect of not having her close at hand, no matter that she was lowest ranking girl at school.

Near the end of the first school week, Mary was beginning to act strangely when I was present. She didn't at first discourage me from hanging around with her and her friends, but she'd periodically whisper things to them, and then they'd sneak looks at me with mysterious little smiles on their faces. Soon I stopped being invited into any of their activities, but like a fool I hung around, wondering what I'd done to her to deserve this treatment. The more I wondered, the more desperately anxious I became. It felt like sinking into quicksand. By the following week it all didn't matter anymore. Mary was looking through me like I was a clear glass of water.

Finally I faced the misery of my fate. I was high priestess of the outcasts now, so how could it hurt if I were to be seen publicly with Juanita? I took her hand and bravely led her into the luminous autumn sunshine.

Raymond had been too busy with his dad during summer to be much of a problem where Juanita was concerned. But on that first day I brought Juanita out of the classroom to play, I saw him staring maliciously from the far end of the blacktop. Not long after, the assaults began. And continued.

Raymond also began to occasionally follow Juanita and me after school, usually when we rode Apollo down to the river. He tried to be secretive by hanging back, crouching, and hiding behind trees, but was so ridiculously awkward and loud that it didn't take much for me to figure out what he was up to.

At school, Raymond would parody Juanita's limp and make derogatory comments. If we were out in the fields where a teacher couldn't see, he'd knock her down and raise his foot over her, like he was going to deal a kick. If I screamed at him to stop, he just laughed. I kept a constant wary eye on him, trying my best to minimize any trauma or pain to Juanita. But it wasn't only Raymond. Taunts of all kinds became a daily ordeal at school. I became Juanita's armor. I had no choice.

By early October, the days were bright and warm, yet there was a crispness to the air that foretold of winter. Amber and crimson leaves were torn from tree limbs by sudden gusts of wind, and tossed high into the sky, where they skated and swirled, before finally settling to the ground. Kristin's best friend, Joyce, spent a Friday night at our house. The next morning her mother called to see if she could leave Joyce's brother Alex with us for the day. My Mom said yes, and when Alex was dropped off, he had his buddy Shawn with him. The first thing the two of them did was head out for the eucalyptus grove that bordered the river, about a half-mile from our house.

Shawn and Alex were in my grade at school and were as inseparable as Sissy and I had been. Alex and I had something in common. His big sister Joyce was the same age as Kristin, and just as big a bully. I went outside to watch as they made their way toward the grove, and began to get angry. This was my turf! I was also mad because Joyce and Kristin hadn't let me play with them, and now here were Alex and Shawn without so much as a grunt in my direction, running off to have fun by themselves. I went out to the pasture and got Apollo.

I dismounted just outside the grove and tied Apollo to a tree. Then I Indian walked slowly into the forested interior. Eucalyptus are notoriously messy with their constant shedding of leaves and bark, so I couldn't help some crackling underfoot. After spotting the boys in a clearing by the river, I hid behind a tree trunk, to see what they were up to. They were both on their hands and knees staring ahead, backs to me. Then I saw Shawn make a lunge forward, his hands making a grabbing motion into the sand ahead of him.

"Shit! He got away!" Shawn's exclamation startled me and I took a crunching step backward. They both turned in my direction. Shawn spoke. "What are you doing here, Stuckley? You just ruined it for me. I could'a caught that alligator!"

Then Alex chanted, sounding exactly like his sister Joyce had earlier that morning. "Get outta here Rose, we don't want you here!"

"Yeah, get outta here! Go back to your moo-cow, Rose!" Shawn stuck out his tongue and made a face.

That ignited me. I stormed up to them and shouted, "You're STUPID, Shawn, you're a stupid poison oak eater!" The comment was inspired by the fact that in the first grade Shawn had eaten a fistful of poison oak to show he didn't get it, and was swollen for weeks after. A momentary glint of pain crossed his face. I couldn't think of anything bad to say to Alex. "I'm a better lizard catcher than either of you. I'm the best lizard catcher . . . and you'll be sorry!" Then I stomped away and jumped on Apollo, kicking him cruelly all the way home.

Things should've ended there, but didn't. Later that day the boys approached me. Alex spoke first. "Rose, you can come hunt lizards with us if you want."

"Yeah," Shawn chirped.

After I'd recovered somewhat from the shock, a realization hit me that this was probably some kind of trick, a ruse to get me somewhere, where a cruel encounter would surely be waiting. I glared into their faces, trying to cook up my best nasty retort. Shawn was wearing a slight scowl, probably remembering that I'd earlier called him stupid. But Alex stared curiously at me through robins-egg-blue eyes, displaying a demeanor that begged an amicable response. My cynicism melted under his gaze, and I became further disarmed by a sudden attack of shyness. But my imagination started racing ahead of itself, assessing the possibilities . . . me, a lizard catcher! On the tip of my tongue were words, nearly blurted with gratitude, saying yes, yes, I'd go! But then remembered, I'd lied to them earlier. I'd never before had any interest in catching lizards and couldn't dare let them know this. I responded poorly, "I can't go right now, I promised Juanita a ride on Apollo." With a desperately driven smirk, I swaggered off.

As I walked away, a light feeling arose inside and expanded till I felt as buoyant as a helium balloon. *I was wanted!* Even sought after! I knew that I would rise to the cause. I was going to become a lizard catcher, and I'd be so good that Shawn and Alex would beg me to catch lizards with them. All the boys would. Then I'd show them, I'd show everybody how great I could be.

But by the time I was up on Apollo's back and not halfway down the driveway, the swelling of pride had deflated, giving way to an aching inside, a craving to belong. I was growing weary from deflecting all the taunts thrown at Juanita, and it was just the start of the school year. This couldn't be articulated clearly then; I only knew that something had begun to color me black and blue inside.

After that day, nothing was the same in my life. Chores went on, afternoons with Juanita trekking down to the river or to Wolter's market continued. But I had a new awareness, a mission. At school, every time I went out to the playground, I was looking for lizards. While riding Apollo my eyes never stopped scanning. I became Pocahontas in the wilderness, and developed a gliding walk so as not to scare my prey. Bluebellies and alligators were the most prevalent, but there were others; horned toads, skinks, and tiny salamanders, they all fascinated me now. I fashioned snares and nooses out of sticks and grass. I became possessed.

One blustery Friday afternoon in early November, Juanita took the bus home with me because she was staying the weekend. I wanted to get some lizard practice in, so we took Apollo and went off to the eucalyptus grove.

The grove is about a quarter mile in length bordering the river, and almost as much in breadth. At the west end is a barbed wire fence where the trees abruptly end, separating it from a neighboring hay field. A horse trail winds crookedly through, end to end.

I'm at the west end now. I decide to push through a heavy thicket of blackberry bushes that are growing against the fence, leading toward the river. Earlier I'd glimpsed what looked like a nice patch of clearing in there from the river side, but had been unable to get through because the eroded bank was too steep. I crawl on my hands and knees into the bushes. Juanita is with Apollo some ways back, because I don't want his heavy step to disturb the lizards.

I come into the sandy clearing; it's a lot smaller than I've imagined. I still my body as I've practiced to do, and my eyes scan the ground for lizards. Then I look to the fence posts. For a moment I'm not sure what I'm seeing, because my mind registers only shock. I get up from my knees and step over to the fence. There are dead field mice stuck to the barbed prongs of the wire, at least a dozen of them. I'm momentarily confounded; how could mice have gotten stuck on the barbed wire? But I look closer, and see that one of them has its belly slashed neatly open, with miniature entrails hanging out. With another, two sticks are jammed into sockets where once were eyes. A few of them look like they'd been literally ripped apart, right on the barbed wire. I see hanging chunks of fur and flesh. Legs are neatly snipped off here and there; some don't have heads. I'm struck with horror, yet somehow mesmerized. I can't unglue my eyes from the gallery of tiny mutilated corpses.

A sudden gust of wind rattles the trees, and dappled afternoon shadows dance at my feet. My heart pounds in my chest. I crouch down. Then I hear footsteps coming in my direction from down at the river. I crawl back the way I came as quickly and quietly as I'm able. Uneasiness pervades me. I don't want to catch lizards now. Juanita asks to take Apollo to the river, but I say no. I mentally seek refuge from what I've just witnessed, but the images won't go away.

The Lizard Catcher

Thanksgiving week arrived and I would have four days free to go lizard catching. There weren't too many lizards out due to the advancing cold, and the ones that were around were sluggish and too easy to catch. That was my excuse for not going to the eucalyptus grove to hunt. But the real reason was Raymond. I'd only been back to the grove once since witnessing the mutilated mice. On that day, I rode Apollo to the end of the path and halted cautiously at the fence. I let the reins out so that he could graze, and that's when I heard sounds coming from beyond the brush where the clearing was. I strained to hear, and as I did, an electrifying shock coursed through me. The voice belonged to Raymond. He seemed to be talking to no one but himself, in angry, accusing tones. I didn't stay to listen, but kicked Apollo into a hard gallop, not daring to breathe until I was safely home.

After Thanksgiving there would be no more outings, as winter settled in with a vengeance. The sky stayed fitful and dark. One storm after another battered the coastline and forged inland, to be spent across the Santa Lucia and Gabilan Mountains. Water ran off everything, and soon the ground was soggy, then great puddles formed, as the earth could hold no more. Old-timers talked excitedly about how this might well end up a flood year, maybe even a great flood, the hundred-year kind.

Raymond began to stalk us around school. Everywhere we went he'd be skulking nearby. As if in accompaniment to the foul turn of the season, he'd acquired a new persona. The taunts and show-off bravado previously exhibited had passed out of existence. In its place was a brooding intensity to his expression, an almost desperate look. He was now "silent Raymond", who never uttered a word. I didn't know how to react to him. It was so creepy that I almost wished he'd go back to his old ways. At least before, I had known what to expect, what to prepare for. How could I then have had any idea what lay inside that head of his?

The river swelled bank to bank, its dark water carting down uprooted trees and debris that accumulated in high heaps at the lagoon, looking like makeshift hobo huts. Rising water threatened to spill over onto the flatlands, and people living nearby began nervously filling sandbags. Mercifully, the rain let up some before the banks overflowed, but continued to fall sporadically through April.

Inside those cabin fever days, I spent long hours alone in my room, engaged in fantasies. One of them was that Sissy had come back. At first there was a problem with Juanita being in the picture alongside Sissy, but I was beyond the point of letting her go, so I had Sissy like her. I even made Juanita's leg better, and had her speaking perfect English, instead of the self-conscious stuttering that she barely managed to murmur.

The three of us—Sissy, myself and Juanita—are sitting next to the faucet on the side of my house, the one that never stops dripping. We're fashioning flower dolls from all the delicate flowers in Mom's garden. Bright anemone-like dahlias, or ruffled hollyhock blossoms turned upside down become their skirts, and then we stick barely opened daisy buds on top for the heads. Under the faucet we arrange stones and mud, making a swimming pool for the flower dolls to float in. We gently set them down into the water and watch as they gracefully glide. Juanita gets up, she is laughing . . . so happy! She runs over to pick more blossoms, because our dolls need a change of clothes after swimming, so they can have something to wear to the princess ball.

My high reverie was followed by melancholy lows, as reality seeped through like winter wet, causing the crystalline images to bleed away into mud.

Another winter musing involved Alex, and the lizard catching. Alex and Shawn would be out in the field at school during lunchtime, seeking out the first frisky lizards of spring. I'd saunter up with one of my special lizard catching "devices", perhaps the one with a delicate grass noose attached to a slim willow switch. I'd see a lizard nearby, then pull the noose out and ease to my knees. This would cause them to turn and watch. Slowly, I'd lower the noose down in front of the lizard's nose . . . then snatch my prize and hold it up triumphantly for all to see. Finally Alex and Shawn would ask me to go with them to hunt lizards. They'd beg me to show them what is the best grass to make a noose, how to walk like Pocahontas, and praise me for my amazing skill.

This is pretty much how it happened one windblown March day, give or take a few details, such as the begging, praising, or most of that other stuff. At first they pretended not to watch, but by the time I'd carefully snuck my noose out in front of the lizard's nose, I had their full attention. They tagged along as I made a second catch, this time with my bare hands. Afterwards, the three of us looked around, surprised to realize that lunch hour was long spent. Mr. Powell, our principal, was halfway across the field with a scowl on his face. But the best part was something I hadn't even fantasized about. As we were being scuttled back to class I exchanged a brief eyeball-to-eyeball gaze with Alex, and he smiled at me. Not a smirk, but a genuine, sweet smile.

I held my breath for the remainder of the school week, waiting to be invited to catch lizards, but Alex and Shawn totally ignored me. On Saturday I was moping around the house feeling angry and tense. I'd prepared insults to unleash on them that I was rehearsing over and over in my head, when Mom came and told me that the boys were at the door. It was a full ten minutes before I had the courage to go out and meet them. Alex gave me a cheery smile. "Hi, Rose!"

I waited in the doorway for an insult. When it wasn't forthcoming, I invited one. "What do you stupid-heads want?"

Shawn, who I knew didn't like me the way Alex did, offered, "If you're gonna be mean, then maybe we won't tell you. We won't tell her, will we Alex!"

Alex ignored him and continued, "Hey Rose, wait'll you see the noose we fixed up! We're gonna go and try it out. Wanna come?"

I was ready to respond with, "I'll go and get Apollo," but stopped myself. I thought with wonder, *I'm one of them now.* They had bikes. I floated out to the garage to get mine.

The light feeling continued throughout the weekend. It had been a day I could've only dreamed of. Shawn, Alex and I down at the river, a camaraderie of like minds dreaming up new ways to catch lizards. We discussed nooses, traps, and the merits of hunting alligators versus bluebellies. They accepted me as one of them, or at least Alex did. Shawn treated me with a polite coolness, as one would treat an uninvited guest who'd be leaving soon.

Come Monday, Alex and Shawn ignored me at school. Monday passed, then Tuesday. Then, during lunch hour on Wednesday, the two of them rambled over and invited me to go lizard catching with them after school. I'd been holding a rage back for two days. I didn't know if I wanted to challenge, get even, or if I'd just explode. In a moment of self-preservation, I managed to choose what I thought was the least destructive course of action. I responded, in a mocking voice, "Only if Jua-nita can come too."

Shawn's words blistered me. "I don't even want YOU along, Stuckley!" Then he turned to Alex. "I told'ya I didn't want Stinky Rose to go catch lizards with us, and now LOOK!" His eyes were blazing, while mine stared back defiantly. Alex grabbed Shawn by the arm and dragged him away. I watched as they huddled nearby, out of my earshot, Alex talking, and Shawn gesticulating wildly.

They came back to me. I heard a complete lack of conviction when Shawn spoke. "Juanita can come, but just this once." Alex was standing behind him with a roguish smile on his face that he beamed at me. I returned his smile, privately amazed that I'd prevailed in this battle of wills.

I sensed a chasm beginning to separate those two, with myself being the fulcrum. If I hadn't been so pinched by hunger, I might've been concerned for Shawn. But I wasn't. He was clumsy, and even aside from the poison oak episode, I thought he was pretty dumb, too. I couldn't understand what Alex saw in him that was so great. It never occurred to me that Shawn and I might have anything at all in common.

Juanita was now a member of the gang, whether Shawn liked it or not. He didn't like it, but settled into a sort of resignation, marked by long sighs and occasional glaring stares. I stopped taking the bike, and instead rode Apollo with Juanita riding behind, meeting them at predetermined places. Juanita never participated, and we didn't ask her to, either. She seemed content to stay by Apollo's side and entertain herself by braiding wildflowers into his mane and tail, or she'd wander to collect grass and wild oats for him to munch on. As we moved along paths, or down the river, she trailed behind, leaving a respectable distance so as to not disturb the lizards.

We spent the spring trampling through high fields of yellow mustard, and down to the river that was still swelled bank to bank, the rushing water murky with silt and dirt carried all the way from Chew's Ridge and the mountains beyond. My world was washed clean and filled with promise. The only darkness was the lurking shadow of Raymond.

A mountain lion came down from the hills and started killing. There were sightings of it in the fields, and roaming through people's backyards in the early hours before daylight. A neighbor's dog came up missing. Then one morning after milking, I went out to the small pen that housed our goats. A few days before, one of the goats had birthed triplets. The kids weren't quite walking normally yet; they wobbled around knob-legged, making brave leaps, already trying to play. I loved watching them. I noticed that one kid was missing, so I felt around inside the deep straw of the lean-to, but it wasn't there.

That night before bed, Dad left his shotgun resting by the front door. I woke up in darkness to the shrieking cries of an animal in distress, and then there was gun blast. I ran outside, but Dad yelled at me to go back, so I stayed inside the doorway and watched. He was cursing, the barrel of his gun pointed into the black fields. Then he went to the goat pen and I heard another shot fired. The puma, Dad called them pumas, had gone after the mother goat and torn a huge chunk out of her back end. The first shots were fired at the retreating cat, and the last one was to put the mama out of her misery. We didn't see the cat anymore after that night.

By the end of May, Carmel Valley was still leafy and green. All over the foothills, bright orange poppies opened their petals to the promise of summer. The hay was maturing early due to the massive amounts of rain that had fallen steadily since November, the fields were thick, the grain top-heavy. Raymond and his dad started showing up to ready the barn and baling equipment for harvest.

I guess it was because I knew Raymond would be tied up working most of the summer, that I gained new courage. If there would be fallout, it wouldn't last long, as school was almost over. Or maybe it was because he didn't seem as menacing anymore, only annoying, with those ogre stares and that blundering gait. So I confronted him at school one day. I left Juanita in the library during lunch with a stack of books and a teacher looking on. I didn't have far to go. He was right outside the library door, sitting on a bench. I walked straight to him and spoke in a tone that sounded more self-assured than I actually felt. My hands went defiantly to my hips. "You have to stop following me and Juanita!"

His glare silenced me. Staring back, I observed that he had a deep furrowed line between his eyebrows, and wondered why I hadn't ever noticed before. My eyes continued to survey his face, as if for the first time, maybe it was for the first time. His eyes were the color of mahogany, glossy, like the polished flank of a bay horse, and he had a sprinkling of soft black hairs growing on his upper lip and chin. Covering his forehead was a minefield of tiny pimples. His jaw tightened and I backed up, remembering the rages and tantrums, *the mice*. He shifted his eyes from me to the paper bag at his side, then took out an apple and started to eat it, staring ahead with an abstract expression, as though he was far away into his own head. Unreachably, spookily far. I stood for a few moments, unnerved, and then realized I was shaking all over. As I stumbled away, it sounded like I was yelling down a well. "You'd better stop! I mean it . . . I mean it . . ."

Summer vacation was only a day away. Alex came up to me at lunchtime, nervous and fidgety. "Are you going anywhere for summer?"

"Nope. Where's Shawn?"

Alex looked down at his shoes. "We're not friends anymore." I thought back on the last time I'd seen the two of them together. They'd fought. I caught only the loudest part of their conversation, when Shawn declared to Alex that he'd rather be playing with Jimmy Lindstrom than being stuck with him and the two retards. Then he'd gestured to Juanita and me. Alex had responded angrily, "Go ahead! Play with Jimmy, see if I care!" I could plainly see that this had come about because of me. Heat blazed up in my cheeks and spread painfully to my ears. I scanned the blacktop and saw

Shawn and Jimmy Lindstrom playing tetherball. Alex followed my eyes, then mumbled, "I gotta go do something . . ."

As he turned and walked away, kicking imaginary rocks from his path, I disintegrated inside. This was the end of it. Alex hated me now. He'd have to. Because it was true, I *was* only a retard, after all. How could anyone want to be with a misfit like me? After school, while walking to the bus, I glanced over my shoulder and saw Juanita trying to catch up, then hurried my step. I couldn't carry the burden anymore.

I'd once brought a polliwog back from the river in a peanut butter jar, and put it on top of my dresser. It had been a bullfrog tadpole, with the beginning of legs sprouting. It went around and around in exhausted circles inside its tiny fishbowl prison, swelling with agitation, trying in vain to return to the prismatic river world that had defined its existence even before time. Only when it was near death and gasping did I have the mercy to take it, maybe too late, back to the river.

The smoldering pain that had germinated inside since Sissy's departure one year before had finally erupted into something organic and living, and assumed possession of my senses. I'd become the embodiment of that anguished polliwog. I reeled through that following day, the last day of school, witnessing the outside world through trapped, polliwog eyes. I could see Juanita's distorted face peering through the glass at me, eyes weeping for joy at her august acquisition.

It was two weeks into summer vacation and I hadn't seen Juanita. Her English had improved to the point where she could speak in halting, careful sentences. She telephoned me three times the first week, and each time I lied and said my mom wouldn't let me play. After that the phone calls stopped. I'd lost interest in Apollo, in the lizards, in everything.

Then one morning, Alex showed up at my door all by himself and asked me to go lizard catching. I couldn't conceal my surprise and just stared dumbly at him. After I'd recovered somewhat, my first impulse was to slam the door shut. But while scanning his face, I read something there, anxiousness, or maybe a sadness that seemed to mirror my own misery. I knew that I had to go, to try and make things up to him.

It was different without Shawn around. We were shy and polite with each other, and I glumly wondered if he was really having as good a time with me as he would've had with Shawn, or some other boy. But when we parted, he said he'd be back tomorrow. It was as if my world had suddenly exploded into fireworks of dazzling sunshine. I ran straight to the phone and called Juanita. From then on, the three of us were together almost daily.

The Lizard Catcher

One lovely midsummer morning, I bridled Apollo, and then set out to pick up Juanita. Alex said he'd meet us at Rockface, a picturesque stretch of river that wound a tight course against the mountain, so named for the craggy cliffs that rose nakedly from its narrow sandy banks. The place wasn't far upriver from the egg farm, and had one of the best swimming holes in the Valley. Because of its proximity to the mountain, not a lot of sun reached the area and it possessed a dank, earthy smell. Giant ferns and big-leafed vines grew lavishly on the cliff side, giving it a wild, unkempt look. Alex told me that the previous summer he and Shawn had found a tiny lizard there, with a long, rainbow-hued tail. He wanted to go back and see if he could find one again.

I'd always felt a shiver upon arriving at Rockface. I fantasized about spirits of dead Indians dwelling there, so I never stayed beyond early afternoon if I was alone. The last time I'd ridden through, Apollo suddenly spooked and dumped me in the river. He would've run all the way home if he hadn't snagged a rein on a nearby tree branch. Remembering that incident added to my uneasiness.

When we arrived, Alex was nowhere in sight. But Raymond was. I'd spotted him in the bushes near the egg farm road when I picked Juanita up on Apollo. It irritated me that he was lurking about, but what could I do? I mentally pictured his dad getting mad for him sneaking off when there was work to be done for the harvest, maybe angry enough to knock him down and kick him hard, which gave me a small degree of satisfaction. A few minutes later, Alex showed up holding a glass jar, presumably to carry the lizard home in. I figured that Raymond would see Alex and slink away.

We decided to cross the river and start our search on the cliff side because that was where they'd found the rainbow lizard. We had to either hike upstream to find a shallow enough place to cross, or else get wet crossing where we were, so we decided to go upstream. I instructed Juanita to stay with Apollo. I'm sure she felt the spookiness of Rockface, and that's why she protested, saying that she wanted to go with us. But I told her that we had to hike way, way far upstream to find a shallow place to cross, and there were too many big rocks in that part of the river for Apollo's hooves to handle. What I didn't say was that there were too many rocks for a crippled girl to pass through, too. I ordered her, not in a nice way either, to stay put, that we'd be coming back down on the cliff side and would see her soon. I glanced back just before we disappeared around the bend. She looked like a statue, staring.

We hiked a good ways upstream before we found a place shallow enough to cross without getting soaked. There wasn't much bank between the river and the cliffs here, but it was wider than where we started out. Alex and I began scouting around the moist rocks for places where the lizard might dwell, working our way slowly back downstream. We came across a garter snake, two turtles, several ordinary lizards, and numerous frogs; but there would be no rainbow-tailed lizard for Alex to transport home in the jar.

By the time we got back to where we'd left Juanita, she wasn't there and neither was Apollo. I made a mental note that she'd probably taken Apollo away from the river to find grass to feed him, then gave it no more thought as we methodically worked our way back upstream. After about a half-hour or so we abandoned the search, waded across the river, and walked back to our original location.

When I didn't see Juanita or Apollo, my first reaction was anger. How dare she take him off so far and for so long! Alex had left his bike at the egg farm, so we headed in that direction. I was still feeling resentful by the time we got there, even after Mrs. Sanchez told us she hadn't seen Juanita since I'd picked her up earlier.

Then the phone rang. It was my mom, wondering why Apollo had shown up at home riderless. Inside of an instant, my indignation vaporized, leaving behind a spasm of shivers.

Alex and I went back to the river and started calling her. It was mid-afternoon by this time, but within the shadow of the mountain it seemed much later. A new anger had ignited, fueled by my conscience, and was furiously burning inside. I tortured myself with visions: I saw her waiting there, wondering why we hadn't returned; becoming increasingly frightened; panicking, trying to lead Apollo down the stony riverbed toward home, limping, stumbling, and Apollo, sensing her inexperience, stubbornly resisting, and then pulling away. Coiled pangs of guilt vibrated, in concert with the rhythm of my heartbeat.

By the time we'd retraced Apollo's wayward path back to my house without finding Juanita, the grownups were worried. Dad telephoned Mr. Sanchez and he came over, then the two of them went down to the river and scoured the same area Alex and I had just searched. They returned after dark, empty-handed. Dad called the sheriff, who said he'd give her till morning to show up, and then organize a search party if she was still missing.

That night in bed, my mind is racing. I think of a dozen scenarios that could've befallen Juanita, each one more gruesome. I finally lose all sense of rationality, and a jumbled assortment of dismembered images are being deposited at the doorsill of my consciousness in much the same way a cat would drop his catch, torn and bloody at his owner's feet. I'm as unable to block these perceptions as face the fact that Juanita is missing.

An image comes to me, a memory of when Apollo, while still a colt, is castrated. Dad ties Apollo's legs, the two back ones together, and the two front ones together. Then he pushes him toward the fence and leans over his back to pin him against it. The vet goes to Apollo's rear, and Dad holds the tail up while the vet takes a sharp knife and slices Apollo open under his tail. Apollo begins to bray, and blood spurts everywhere. Then the vet reaches his hand inside the incision and yanks out two bloody wads that he throws to the dogs. My six-year-old eyes recoil at the sight of blood coursing down poor Apollo's legs, staining his white tail red, and the dirt beneath his dainty colt hooves crimson-black.

My mind flips to another scene, and I watch helplessly as a calf of Mumu's tries to squeeze through the barbed wire fence and instead gets hopelessly tangled in it. The more she struggles, the deeper the wire cuts into her . . . Dad at first tries to free her, but we can see that the wire has imbedded so deeply into her belly that intestines are protruding. He places his hunting knife close to her neck and slices; her eyes slowly roll back into her head so that only the whites are showing, then a whooshing sound comes out of her throat, and her body collapses limply into the wire.

Pictures of Dad's prized stallion, Midnight, are hanging in the hallway like they always are, but now there is one photograph I've never seen before, framed in gold, hanging separate from all the others. In it the beautiful Midnight is lying on the ground, with a neat round hole right in the middle of his forehead.

In the eucalyptus grove, I see mangled mouse corpses impaled on barbed wire that is crisscrossing the high branches over the sandy clearing. Raymond is inside the marquee; he has the hay hook raised, poised and ready to rip down on Juanita, lying helplessly there beneath him, her terrified eyes as big as saucers.

I sit up with a gasp. I know where Juanita is. I clearly see her frail body lying on the small patch of sand in Raymond's secret place. The revelation feels like a jagged shard ripping into my flesh. I jump out of bed and start for my parents' room. I have to save her. I have to tell.

I get to the door, but freeze as a new thought comes to me. How can I possibly tell them about my discovery; that I know where to find Juanita? If I talk about the mutilated mice on the barbed wire, I'll have to say that I've been to that place before, and tell about all the unspeakable things Raymond is capable of. If I reveal any of this, they'll lay the blame squarely on me for not going to any grownup before the terrible tragedy happened. Once I begin, I'll need to confess that I'd been mean to her on that last day, and sometimes on other days, too. Then everybody will know what kind of girl I really am.

My heart was tangled in such big knots, that were they to come undone, would be the undoing of me. I thought of Alex. I needed him now. *He will help me,* I assured myself. *I'll call him in the morning, and we'll go together to rescue Juanita.* I spent the remainder of the night staring at the ceiling, anxiously awaiting the light of dawn.

Sheriff Westover was sitting at the kitchen table talking to Mom and Dad when I got up. Mr. Sanchez was there too. I guessed I must've dozed off at some point, because I hadn't heard them arrive. The sheriff asked me a lot of questions about Juanita, and asked some to Mr. Sanchez. I answered a bunch of useless questions, like did I see any strange men down at the river, or did Juanita ever talk about running off to find her parents. I squirmed in my chair. All I wanted to do was call Alex. Finally, the sheriff, Dad, and Mr. Sanchez left to search some more, and I went to the phone. I told him to come. I told him it was urgent.

While I was waiting for Alex, I headed for the fields to see if Raymond was there. His dad's truck was parked near the barn on the dirt frontage road just beyond our horse pasture. I could see two people. Raymond's dad was leaning into the back of the truck, and there was someone on the other side of it whose face I couldn't see. I sauntered across the pasture, pretending like I was going to catch one of the horses, so that I could identify the other person. Then Raymond came around to his dad's side of the truck. He saw me and halted. Our eyes momentarily locked, then he broke his stare and casually reached into the truck bed for some equipment.

I went back to the vicinity of the house as fast as I could walk. To run was unthinkable, because then he'd know I was on to him. My heart was beating like hummingbird wings. I stayed where I could see the truck and watch the goings on until Alex came. When I saw Alex riding down the driveway, I ran to him, nearly knocking him off his bike. I could feel my body vibrating, and my face was on fire. He looked at me funny. "Are you okay?"

I wanted to choose my words carefully, but they came tumbling out topsy-turvy and crazed. "Raymond did it! He kills mice with hay hooks . . . he was at Rockface yesterday. Didn't you see him? He was at Rockface, and he took her! C'mon, we have to go to the grove, we have to rescue Juanita!" I was pacing, ready to bolt.

Alex was momentarily quiet. When he spoke, his words came out measured. "Rose, what are you talking about? Raymond took Juanita?" He squinted suspiciously at me as if trying to penetrate my brain; to decipher what the hell might be going on in there. Upon seeing this reaction, I made an effort to calm myself before speaking again.

"I know where Juanita is."

As we walked down the road toward the grove, I unburdened myself. I told him all about seeing the mice strung up on the barbed wire that previous fall; about Raymond's hay hook antics; the way he terrorized Juanita, only to have it stop suddenly; how the stalking started, and continued. I reminded him that everybody, including him, knew how mean Raymond could be. I could see that Raymond had gone careening into madness and I needed Alex to know and believe it, too.

When we were at the entrance to the grove, Alex suddenly stopped. "What if Raymond is in there?" I detected fear in his voice and was somehow reassured by this.

"Don't worry, Raymond is with his dad at the barn. I saw him there just before you came."

So we continued. Once inside the grove I slowed down and began to walk in a careful, catlike manner, which calmed me immensely. I fell easily into my lizard catching mode. I led Alex to the fence, and we got down on hands and knees and began to crawl into the brush. By this time, I felt composed enough to handle any kind of grisly scenario we might encounter. But as I broke through the brush, my eyes weren't prepared for what was before me. I saw nothing. Nothing at all, except a pathetic little circle of sand with leaves scattered about. Alex and I both stood up.

"All right Stuckley, where is she?" His voice held a mixture of relief and annoyance.

I pointed to the barbed wire. "That's where Raymond stuck the mice! Juanita is here, I know she is!" I circled around and around, growing increasingly flustered, silently pleading for any sign that might tell me she was here. Not a remnant of the mice on the wire remained. Not even a footprint in the sand. It was a radiant day, bright and warm, with a soft breeze carrying the scent of eucalyptus and grass. I raised my face upward and looked through the canopy of trees. I could see cathedral glass patches of sky, framed by leaves and branches. The boundless blue made me feel infinitesimal and powerless. Nothing in these surroundings spoke of disaster. The day wasn't supposed to be beautiful. The sky needed storm clouds and lightning bolts, and this tiny patch of sand begged for Juanita.

"I'm going home." Alex had already gotten down on all fours and was disappearing into the bushes.

"You can't leave!" My voice was a high-pitched wail. I sank down into the sand, with tears starting. "You can't leave me . . ." I whispered. Then I was sobbing.

I'm not sure how long it was I'd been crying, when I felt a hand on my shoulder. Alex knelt beside me and put his cheek against mine. "Rose . . . stop crying . . ." Feeling the warmth of him only made me sob harder. "It's okay . . . Rose . . . it's okay . . ."

It was two weeks before I had the courage to get up on Apollo's back and ride down to the river. I felt like I was finally awakening from a dream. Juanita still hadn't been found, and yet life went on. It seemed as if I was the only one in the world still thinking about her, and I cursed the whole world for this. I hadn't seen Alex since the day we'd gone to the grove, but he'd called a couple of times to see if I was okay.

Harvest was in full swing. The high golden hay was being slashed down, and packaged into bales that sat neatly atop the scalped land. I caught glimpses of Raymond occasionally, out in the fields with his dad. Unlike before, when I couldn't get him to leave Juanita and me alone, he was now conspicuously avoiding me. I was beginning to doubt my earlier conviction that he was responsible for Juanita's disappearance. That left only myself to blame, and the guilt was a boulder, crushing me.

I wanted to try and find her. Just one more time, then I'd put it behind me, that's what I told myself. I rode upstream and dismounted when I got to Rockface. I was standing on the exact spot where I'd last seen Juanita's eyes forlornly staring, when Apollo suddenly snorted and bolted away from me. Several buzzards had taken flight ahead of us. My hands burned where I'd been holding the reins. I stared at the brush from where they'd flown. My mind raced. Nobody had thought to look upriver for Juanita.

I held my gaze on the bushes ahead and advanced slowly, growing more frightened with each step. As I moved closer, I could smell death in the air. I'd run across the rotting carcasses of animals plenty of times while riding; the putrid, sickly smell meant something was long dead. And buzzards always accompanied dead things. My legs felt weak and my body grew clammy. But I willed myself on. Then I saw through the foliage the delicate legs of a deer sticking out from its distended body, covered with flies. I retched and turned away.

Apollo had deserted me and gone home. By the time I'd walked back, my parents had already telephoned the sheriff, who was getting ready to form a search party. I wanted to tell them about the deer, and how we hadn't looked upstream for Juanita; wanted to talk about Raymond and my suspicions, tell them that I was lonely and scared and aching so bad inside that I wanted to die. But it suddenly all seemed hopeless and futile. I just said I was tired and went to my room.

The familiar sight of Raymond and his father toiling over our land would be no more. After harvest, they stayed only long enough to see that every bale was stored securely in the barn. I don't know what happened to Raymond's dad, he disappeared to somewhere, and Raymond joined his mother, who'd earlier in the summer packed up and moved to Los Banos, because his parents were getting a divorce. I imagine I should've expected to feel relief at Raymond's leaving, but I didn't. I thought about how he'd be released from it all now, to begin anew. He'd be able to forget. I had no such choice, no way to escape from my memories of her, my grieving, my guilt. From some untended place deep inside me, hatred smoldered.

It is the day after Thanksgiving. There's a big flatbed truck sitting outside the barn. Two men have been loading hay bales onto the truck for most of the afternoon, and now one of them is running across the pasture toward our house, I can see him coming from my bedroom window. He knocks, Kristin answers the door, and then calls Dad. I can't hear exactly what the man is saying, but I hear Dad exclaim, "Oh my God!" and he yells to Mom. I open my bedroom door. He tells her, "They might've found Juanita!"

I rush out.

The man is talking, while trying to catch his breath. "Uh . . . we got to the bottom of the stack, that's where we found the body. The bales had been arranged in such a way, uh . . . on the floor of the barn; we uncovered the top of it, a passageway leading to a hidden room, right there in the middle of the hay. It's a girl . . ."

I'm running ahead of everybody and Dad is calling at me to wait, but I don't. I run into the barn. I scream when I see her, because her body is half eaten by mice, and the mice, scores of them, are all spilling out from inside of her and scattering into the surrounding hay. Dad rushes to me and I'm yelling at him to get the mice off of her, and I try to get the mice off of her myself, but Dad grabs me and drags me away. "Raymond! Raymond!" I'm shouting his name over and over. "Raymond did it!" Whatever restraints I'd managed to hold myself together with crumble and fall away as Dad carries me into the house.

I can't now recall exactly what I said. I was hysterical. Somehow I was able to get the story out about Raymond, to the point where they at least believed me enough to investigate. I heard that when the sheriff over at Los Banos took him in, he became completely unhinged and had to be taken to a mental hospital. He did finally confess to killing Juanita.

One of the rumors going around the Valley was that Raymond tied her to a tree in the hills first, and tortured her with a hay hook for a few days before he entombed her in the hay. Dad told me not to listen to any stories. He said that Raymond chased her down the river, she fell and hit her head on a rock, and died instantly, right there. And Raymond hid the body in the hay because he was scared. I took some comfort in Dad's version of what happened, but deep down inside I knew that those other stories were most likely closer to the truth. For I knew Raymond. Mom and Dad told me I didn't have to go to school the following week; they didn't even make me do homework.

I would be returning to school in a couple of days, and the thought filled me with unspeakable dread. I was leading Mumu back to pasture after the morning milking, when Dad's truck and horse trailer pulled into the driveway. I watched Dad unload a pretty chestnut colored filly. Then he called for me to come over. When I got there, he made a sweeping gesture toward the filly with his free hand. At that she reared, straining against the rope. Dad moved nimbly aside and let out some slack.

"A yearling. She's got mustang in her, Rose. And you're gonna break her."

I stared into his face, puzzled. "I'm getting too old to be doing this on my own. It's high time you learned the horse-breaking business."

I took a few moments to study her. She was holding her head high, snorting, ears pinned back, furiously pawing the ground with her front hooves. The whites of her eyes were showing.

"Oh, she's pretty skittish. Been running wild too long." Dad gave the rope a little tug and she reared up again. "But we'll turn her into a nice show horse, Rose. This filly has jumpers in her blood. Maybe we can make a jumper out of her."

"What's her name?"

"Anastasia. Anna for short. What do you think? She's pretty nice, eh? Here. Put her away for now. Let her calm down." He handed me the rope and headed for the house without turning his head once to see how I was making out.

I stood there holding her, too afraid to move. If she wanted to run, she would. Dad maybe could restrain her, but I certainly couldn't. I looked to the paddock gate; it seemed far away. I briefly wondered if I should call Dad, but knew I wouldn't. So I turned to the filly and took charge. I began talking to her in a calm, soothing voice, and held my hand out to let her sniff it, then touched her nose and stroked her neck. She lowered her head for me and I scratched behind her ears. Then, very slowly I led her into the pasture, taking care not to make any abrupt movements. The moment I unleashed the halter, she took off like a flash. It was like watching raw beauty in motion. She raced around and around the pasture until she was foamy with sweat, then abruptly stopped, and daintily pranced over to the water trough to drink. *And you're gonna break her . . .*

I stayed for a while watching, temporarily exiled from reality. Then my thoughts fell back to Juanita, and sorrow descended, once again, like a shroud. I would've given almost anything at that moment to have her back. I would've told her all about the chestnut filly, and watched as those big eyes lit up, sparkling with wonder, momentarily masking the tortured countenance that mutely told her tale. I continued to observe Anastasia through a blurry window of tears; feeling like it was never going to be possible to escape this tangled web of despair.

It's been a week since high school graduation. Today is my eighteenth birthday. I'm at the Trail and Saddle Club, up the Valley, for the first horse show of summer. Today we took blue ribbons in pole bending and barrel racing. In the gymkhana contests, nobody can match Anastasia and me; we're like one body out there. Dad tells me that my times are good enough for the rodeo circuit; he wants me to go for tryouts, just like he'd done all those years ago. But I'll be going to college in the fall.

Twilight is upon the sky. I'm near the horse trailers on the far side of the big arena. I'm brushing down Anna. A band is setting up on the back of a flatbed truck over in the grassy barbecue area. The smell of charring meat is wafting to me. Everyone has pretty much settled in over there, for drinking, eating, and dancing under a canopy of sycamores and stars.

I hear footsteps. I turn and stare into the almost dark. I only see the silhouette of someone coming toward me, but recognize the springy gait. I'm smiling now, with anticipation.

Alex and I took a day recently and went to Rockface. Most of the fields and access roads leading to the river have long been blocked off by golf courses and nice homes, so we had to hike upstream for quite a while to get there. It stood unchanged by time. The same high cliff rose from a base of overgrown vines, with a tiny strip of moist sandy bank. As we stood on the spot where we last saw Juanita, Alex took my hand. Then he pulled me close. We stayed like that for a while, not talking, both of us lost in another time.

Up ahead I can see Juanita, standing crookedly on the riverbank, Apollo at her side. Woven into his mane and tail are colorful wildflowers. She has a matching wildflower garland in her hair and looks just like an angel. I watch as she gently leads Apollo up the river. Just before they round a bend, she pauses, turns her head and gazes back at me. Tears are running down my cheeks. I raise my hand in farewell. She gives me her sweet smile and waves back. Then she turns away, and the two of them slowly continue upriver, eventually disappearing from sight.

Alex leaned over and put his cheek up against mine. He whispered, "Let's go home now."

About the Author

LELE DAHLE *grew up on the Monterey Peninsula. An early love for reading led to her interest in writing. She has written many short stories and is currently working on a first novel.*

Monte-Ray Gunn

by Byron Merritt

Of all the Alien Enterprise Zones in all the galaxies, I had to pick Monterey, California. Of course there are other AEZs on Earth: one each in New Turkey, Shanghai, Rio de Janeiro, and two more in the good ol' Independent States of America, one in the Florida Keys and another in Fargo, North Dakota. I'll never understand why Fargo was picked. Somebody told me once it was because of linguistic variables or some such thing.

Who knows?

But, hey, that's none of my business. As a detective for MAH—Monterey Alien Homicide—my job keeps me fairly isolated in this incredibly diverse community.

Captain Terry Bryce, my C.O., woke me up today before the crack of noon, startin' me off in a foul mood. I'd been up late last night drinkin' Procyon micro-beer and eatin' live Purcovian Tschk! I'm not exactly sure what Tschk! is and I don't care. They taste good and don't run away particularly fast when you try to eat them, that's all that matters to me.

I also learned not to say Tschk! in front of others last night when a large opaque Tlinolian sat next to me and I ordered a third round for myself. Saliva left my mouth—involuntarily of course—and set off one helluva brawl . . . which started a terrific headache that's still with me this mornin'.

After leavin' the 400-tier apartment in Seaside where I bunk my tired hide, I travel downtown aboard a floater that wings itself to the top of the MAH Strata-Building on the Washington Flyway. Cloud cover is below the 200th tier so I'm greeted with sunshine as I step out of the floater's oval passenger belly and duck underneath its bat-like wings, their capacitor cells hummin' with the charges they receive from the wind currents of the Monterey Peninsula. The overly brilliant reflection of sun off the glass of the floater feels like splinters in my head, as I inadvertently glance back after exitin' the craft.

I don't like the sun. Never have. Especially after a night of drinkin' and Tschk! eatin'. Unfortunately my apartment lies well above the fog and cumulus, but it's the only thing a lowly detective like myself can afford. Although two million world-credits ain't too bad considerin' housin' costs around here.

I grab a newsdisk from a hover-dispenser, shove it into my shaded eyeglass monitor and watch the news as I descend in a digivator to the 95th level. These news people need to get a life. They're still talkin' about this millennium quant-computer bug. For Corsicans sake! Get over it! The year 3000 rolled over three weeks ago!

"One-hundred, forty-fifth tier, Mr. Gunn," a sexy voice announces. I grunt for the digivator to continue. It was nice of Digi to tell me. She knows I like to stop for Roolusian coffee on that level, but not today. I drank two pots before leavin' my place and besides, I've got to get into work and find out what's so damn important that I start early.

The digivator shimmers and I step off onto the main tier of MAH. "Have a great day," Digi says as I step off.

"Thanks doll," I reply and watch her doors vaporize as she heads off to pick up the next transport.

Captain Bryce's office is on the other side of this expansive level and, unfortunately, all the personnel levs are in use so I have to use my feet to get there. Oh well, it'll give me time to finish my newsdisk.

As I walk, the scenes and text from the newsdisk whip by my glasses. Oh for the love of Sirius! I can't believe these politicians are still bickerin' about buildin' a second floater zone into Carmel Valley. Last week it took me two minutes to get from Monterey to the mouth of the Valley. I remember when it used to take thirty seconds. "Build the damn thing," I mutter to myself.

I finally enter the cramped, cluttered office of Captain Bryce and find her sittin' at her desk talkin' to a cup of coffee. I think she's been at this job too long.

"Detective!" she squeals in that high-pitched voice of hers and embraces me with a powerful hug. Her orange and olive-spiked hair jabs me in the nose and mouth and I spit it out. Last week it was purple and gold. I can't keep up with her changes or her husbands; she's got sixteen of 'em and an equal number of hair spikes. She adopted the polyandry and free-lovin' theorem from the duck-billed Troskonians in the Ofarum galaxy, as did a few million other humans. I ain't one of 'em.

"What's the big idea?" I ask, gruffly. "Why you wakin' me up so early? It ain't even eleven o'clock yet."

I darken my glasses and crunch down into a nearby levchair. I feel the caress of air around my butt as I continue to spit out colorful strands of hair that taste like the kitchen floor in my apartment.

Don't ask how I know that.

I look up at the captain and she's got her bottom lip stuck out and her red scaneyes lookin' at the floor. I'm a sucker for women who pout.

"Knock it off already!" I say. "You know I hate it when you do that."

She smiles, sits in my lap and gives me another hug, fillin' my nose and mouth with her damn pelt again. I rasp tryin' to get rid of the stuff and push her to her feet. She doesn't seem to notice the displeasure her jabbing hair causes me.

Dames.

"I'm so glad you're here, Ray," she says while bouncin' around her office watering the multitude of plants surroundin' us. Some look pretty mean so I keep my distance. "I have an assignment for you."

She winks at me and smiles as she watches me tuck my crumpled shirt into the a-little-too-tight pants I threw on. She sighs wistfully.

"What this time?" I ask sarcastically. "Another lost Andronian fish?"

I ain't had a real case since I got here. There's not much crime around Monterey with the camsats and genetic restructurin' done to weed out unwanted tendencies. Personality changes are available to any who request it through the reformation centers that dot this sector of the Milky Way. I don't let anyone mess around with my head, although Captain has reportedly had several *enhancements* that make her more *pleasant* to work with.

Yeah, right.

"No, silly," she says puttin' down her water jug. A nearby plant picks it up and eats it. I pretend not to notice. I look at her red eyes and watch them light up, burnin' into mine. I look away, my head still achin'.

Then she says somethin' that catches my limited attention: "A murder!"

"What?" I ask, sittin' up in the cushy chair. "Where?"

"Monterey Intergalactic Aquarium," she says, eyes still beamin'. I know that she's lookin' at me to check my interest. No doubt she can detect my excitement as I feel my face flush. Those eyes of hers don't miss much.

"Show me!"

She slips behind her desk and activates a hologram. The room sparkles a silver-gray color all around me and suddenly I'm standin' in the middle of the main viewin' room at the aquarium. I can see the crime scene, sealed off with yellow forcefields sayin' "Homicide Scene! No Access!" I'll bet the lowly cops enjoyed puttin' that out. Probably the first time they'd ever done it.

I walk through the holo and scan the area. Next to the otter tank I see an odd-lookin' body layin' on the gold-tiled floor. As I approach I can see that it's a Sextan: pink skin, twelve eyes, four upper arms and six legs. These creepies remind me of a spider with too many eyes.

And Sextans have no hair. None. I never understood that, but I don't really care. Aliens aren't my type. When Homicide rolled over and joined Alien Homicide, yours truly got shoved into this ridiculous department. I objected, they didn't listen. Big surprise. But I've got a job to do so I'll do it.

I see somethin' white splattered on the otter tank forcefield and swirlin' around the floor near the alien's head. It's blood leakin' from the Sextan. I approach the tank to get a better look but the holo winks out and I'm back in the captain's office.

"What the . . .! Why'd you turn it off?" I object.

"You know the rules. No holo-investigations. You've got to get down there yourself and check it out," Captain beams.

I cringe. "You mean do an actual crime scene investigation? *From* the crime scene?"

She shrugs then grins at me. "I don't make the laws, Ray. I just follow them." She frowns a little. "Like you should."

"But that's ancient! Crime scene investigation? Come on," I say holdin' my hands out. She bolts toward me and gives me another hug as well as another mouthful of color. I spit. Again!

"Oh thank you Ray," she says, not waitin' for my response. She begins rompin' around the room lookin' for her water jug. I'm hopin' one of those plants will grab hold of some of her hair and remove it. I want to object some more, but I can tell she knows I'm excited about workin' a *real* case. I haven't done somethin' like this since the trainin' academy on Lunar Base Seven. But I had to make a show of it for her. Captain expects it of me.

"All right," I say with a hard stare, "I'll do it!"

"Great!" she cries, claspin' her hands together in front of her chest. "I'd like you to meet your live-in partner." She points to the coffee mug on her desk.

"What? I don't have a partner," I correct her. "Especially a live-in!"

"This time you do. Ray Gunn, I'd like you to meet Gelatos." She shoves the coffee mug at me. I take it and peer inside. A black layer of goo fills half the cup.

"This is my partner? A Gelatonian? You've gotta be kiddin'?"

She shakes her head quickly causin' her hair to blur and form an interestin' abstract design.

"Watch it, pal," I hear a deep voice come from the cup. "I'll melt that look right off your face. I'm none too happy about working with you either."

"Great," I say. "A Jello square with an attitude. Bryce, you know I don't work with aliens."

"You do now," Captain says and puts a new micro-battery in her right eye implant. "You'll do just fine!" She pushes me out her door with my new partner in hand.

I begin movin' through the maze of police desks and paraphernalia within the main office, holophones screamin', cops laughin' and eatin', and creepies filing complaints against other creepies.

"Don't like partners, eh?" the blob in the mug asks me.

"What was your first clue?" I respond, moving to a holophone that's ringin'. I yank out the silver connector to silence it.

"Did you used to work with your captain? She seems quite fond of you."

I laugh a short burst. "Women."

"You wouldn't mind if I asked the captain out for a drink or something, would you?"

"Why would I? And I didn't know that Gelatonians drank or . . . did other things."

A drawn-out sputter comes from the mug. "She's very pretty you know. Maybe she likes me and we can—"

"Hey! If you're interested fine, but I don't need to hear about your plans with her, all right?" We come up to the red anti-way to the digivator and step onto the soft carpet. "So you're a . . . male, I assume?"

"I am," he says proudly. At least we might have one thing in common.

"Thank Sirius for that," I say and take in a deep breath.

"You been a cop long?" he sputters in an irritating tone.

I look down with a sharp expression. "Long enough. Why?"

"Just wondering how long you've had that unfortunate name. Did you get it after you joined the force or did your mother really dislike you?" His breath stinks. At least I hope it's his breath.

"Look who's talkin', Jello-head," I say and step through the digivator doors as they materialize.

My gelatinous partner and I don't talk on the floater trip over to the aquarium, which is fine by me. We land on the roof of the towerin' white and gray structure, then take a digivator to the fifteenth level. I can't remember the last time I was this low in the strata-colonies. I'm usually stuck above 40 all the time. But the fog is layered overhead obstructin' the sun, a slight reprieve for my headache.

As I enter the crime scene, I'm stopped by a young officer wearin' shorts and a green, high-quality, Chircovian-weave shirt with the word "Lieutenant" imprinted on the lapel. "Where do you think you're going?" he asks, latchin' onto my arm. Before I know what I'm doin', I grab ahold of his right arm and twist it behind his back. He yelps in pain.

"Excuse me," I say. "Do I know you, kid?" He squirms and squeals somethin' about his mommy, so I let him go.

"You'll pay for that!" he shrieks and runs to a tall man standin' with his back to me. When the man turns to look at me, a grin crosses his face. It's Sergeant Boomer, a thickset Folorian-Asian with a steady smile and a set of biceps that could crush a small Irosian family. He walks over and slaps me on the shoulder with one of his large, powerful hands.

"Well, well, well," Boomer says, showin' all his teeth, "if it isn't Ray Gunn! They finally let you out, Ray?"

"Just for the juicy stuff, Boomer," I reply with a grimace, lookin' at the dead Sextan layin' face down in a pool of white blood. "I guess this qualifies."

I start to head over to the body but Boomer stops me, puttin' his right hand on the center of my chest.

"Hold it Ray!" he blurts. "This is our call. Lieutenant Quarterchef over there is in charge of the scene." He points at the kid whose arm got in my way.

I look up with a start. "Quarterchef? He's not Judy Quarterchef's kid is he?"

"The same."

Great, now I've irritated the son of a strata-district supervisor. Another blotch on my record, no doubt.

"Your call, huh?" I say holdin' out my cipher armpad with the captain's orders on it. Boomer looks up with astonishment.

"They really did let you out!" he laughs. I watch him walk over to Quarterchef and break the bad news. The kid storms out of the building threatenin' everyone and cursin' my name.

"Making new friends?" the black goo sputters from the coffee cup in my right hand.

"I don't have friends, Sludge-boy," I say, sharply.

"Can't imagine why," Gelatos gurgles. I guess that's his laugh.

"What do you need, Ray?" Boomer asks me when most of the activity caused by my entrance has settled down. I tell him "a little peace and quiet" so I can examine the crime scene. Boomer obliges and scoots everyone out of the room. Some of the aquarium employees thunder their objections but it doesn't bother me. Mostly aliens work here anyway with a few humans and some intergalactic mixes thrown in.

The Sextan is layin' face down on the gold tiles, not three meters away from the high-density forcefield of the otter tank. A few of the hairy rodents are still splashin', playin' and rollin' on top of each other, clearly havin' a better time than me. There's a white splotch on the shimmerin' shield. I move over to the body and lift up its head. Three of its eyes are smashed and white blood still oozes out of them. There's an imprint on the Sextan's face. A burn of sorts where it came into contact with somethin' hot.

"Hey, Boomer!" I call toward the doorway where he's standin'. "What's this burn here?" I hold up the dented, seeping face with all its lifeless eyes gazing blankly at me.

Boomer comes over. "Looks like a forcefield burn to me," he replies, then looks at the otter tank.

"You mean someone smacked this guy headfirst into the forcefield hard enough to kill him?"

Boomer shrugs. "Kinda looks that way, doesn't it?"

"That had to hurt," my gooey partner's voice echoes. Boomer looks at the coffee cup in my hand and his eyes go wide.

"Bad coffee," I say, then get back to the point. "Camsat footage?"

Boomer shakes his head. "Nothing seen. He stayed late working last night but no one entered after lock-up. There's no cameras in the viewing area here, either."

I raise my head and my eyebrows. Almost all places have some sort of digital feed for security and such.

"Privacy reasons for some of the species," Boomer says, seeing my surprise. He points toward a small tank with three green globs in it looking like odd-shaped, thistled leaves.

I sigh and shake my head. "DNA traces?"

"Just employees and they all have rock-solid alibis. Except for . . ."

"Except for who?" I ask, lettin' the Sextan's head smack back down onto the floor with a disgustin' *splat*.

"The aquarium director, Mr. Yuri Vladosky. We haven't been able to reach him yet, but it's only a matter of time. He's a very busy man. His terminal's locked down, too." Boomer glances toward a large doorway that says "Director's Office".

I enter the office and find it swirlin' with tubes imbedded in the walls, clear tubes with multi-hued fish dashin' here and there. On the far side of the room I see his Personal Access Terminal and head over to it. I put my face up to the gray screen.

"Enter security clearance, please," a droning, artificial voice says.

"What if I don't know the security code?" I ask.

"Then you can't access this system. Please enter security clearance," the voice says again.

"Otter tank," I say. It remains silent. I hit the desk with my fist after several more attempts.

"Let me try," my gooey partner sighs from the mug.

I laugh. "You think you can do better?"

"It's a quantum PAT, right?" the goo asks.

"Hell I don't know! I just use quants, I don't build 'em."

"Set me down," Gelatos says. I shrug and comply. I watch him trickle out of the mug, makin' some hideous slurpin' and squishin' sounds, then disappear into the terminal like a sheet of thin blackness.

"This guy doesn't even have a quadratic-tetrox compression protection filter!" his voice echoes from within the confines of the gray screen. "What a moron! Try it now."

"Access files," I say into the screen.

"Access granted," the droning voice says.

"Access latest entries by Yuri Vladosky." The quant slushes for a moment and then starts sprawlin' data across the screen. I'm taken aback by what I see. It appears that Mr. Vladosky is a big fan of aliens, so much so that he has them workin' at his home to pay off debts for their transport to Earth. Then I remember somethin' I'd read in the newsdisk on my way to Bryce's office earlier. Today is the arrival of the new alien colonists at the DoubleTree Hotel. I don't understand why they call it that. I've never seen or heard of a single tree bein' there, let alone two.

"Hey, Jello-boy!" I call toward the quant. "Let's get goin'. I've got an idea where we might find Mr. Vladosky."

The black putrescence slowly oozes out of the PAT and back into his cup. "The name is *Gelatos*, Gunn," he gurgles, irritably.

"Whatever." I carry him back out to the viewin' area where Boomer is standin', lookin' over the crime scene vigilantly.

"Anything?" Boomer asks me, while nudgin' the Sextan's head with his boot.

"Maybe. Anything else goin' on out here?"

"No. Just watching this guy coagulate," he blanches. I look down and notice the Sextan is startin' to change colors. I forgot about that. These Sextan's decompose quickly in our atmosphere.

"Get a stasis-field around him," I order. Boomer complies and sets up four small vertical rods around the body, then activates the field. The Sextan stops decomposing almost immediately.

Aliens. Always making my job harder.

"What was his name?" I ask.

Boomer looks down at his cipher armpad. "Gr . . . Greg . . . Gr . . . here!" He thrusts his blue-screen in my face. No wonder he's agitated! I look at the name: Grghk Pbgrwkskl. I download the information from Boomer's link and head out.

On my way to the door I see a crowd gatherin' near the entrance to the crime scene. The media is there, gobblin' up this stuff, along with a few rubber-neckers lookin' past me. Then I spot *her*: A Draconian woman, almost human-looking if you don't count the two left arms—one over the other—and her purple eyes. I could swear that I've seen this three-armed dame someplace before, but my Tschk!-befuddled mind can't place where.

It's her eyes that catch my attention. You see, Draconians are known in the colonies as "weepers", a derogatory term that I must admit I've used before. When Draconians are happy, they weep tremendously. Even when they're curious, they still weep. But when they're sad, they don't weep at all. This Draconian hasn't got a single tear in her eyes.

She sees me headin' toward her and as I reach the crowd, she disappears into it. I try to look above all the heads, some of them sharing the same body, but I can't see her.

I'm not the type to get all gushy over a woman, but she was a stunner. But Ray Gunn's gotta job to do and he's gonna do it! So I head up to the top of the aquarium and catch a floater.

"Where to, sir?" the flier asks me as he expands the wings.

"The DoubleTree. And soar, will ya!" I slump back into the comfortable mesh seat and close my eyes. The floater abruptly pitches upward causing last night's Tschk! to rise in my throat. Ugh!

For a guy like me, who's not fond of aliens, this definitely ain't the place to be today. The DoubleTree is crawlin' with 'em. Acronians, Epsilonians, Netorians, they're all here. There's a big welcome extravaganza goin' on as I use a lev to glide me across the room.

"Do we have an I.D. on this guy?" I ask my jiggly partner.

"Finally talking to me?" he replies, a note of sarcasm in that smelly voice of his.

"Don't be a wise-Gelatonian. Just give me the I.D.," I grumble. My headache is subsidin' but my patience ain't that great in a place where I'm rubbin' elbows with the slime of the universe.

"Yeah, yeah," he sputters. "He's two-and-a-half meters tall, retained his family's True-Russian heritage before the Great Intermix, Caucasian, green eyes and . . . he's bald."

"Bald?" I say with a start. No one needs to be bald. In fact, I can't remember the last time I saw a bald human. Oh sure, other species are bald accordin' to their genetic makeup, includin' the Sextans. Humans, however, have had that genetic heritage ripped out of their DNA chain. Or at least I thought we did.

"Yes, I know. Weird isn't it?" my partner spews.

"Weird? It's downright uncivilized. Why would you *want* to be bald?"

We continue through the gauntlet of infestations before I finally spot him sittin' behind a long, gleamin' black table with high-arching, Lorosian goldstone chairs around it. An assortment of aliens surrounds him.

"Mr. Vladosky?" I say, flashin' my cipher I.D. at him.

"Da. Und who might you be interrupting dis fine day of mine?" he asks in a thick Russian-Deltonian accent.

"I'm Detective Gunn, Monterey Alien Homicide."

He laughs. "So you verk for MAH." All the gathered aliens laugh in their unique way: triple tongues wigglin' wildly with shrill sounds; grotesque intestinal soundin' spurts that seem to emanate from the wrong orifice; howlin' laughs like those heard from hyenas on the ancient Serengeti. Some are so loud that my ears throb and the poundin' in my skull starts again. I didn't understand at the time that "MAH" in the Hetoria system and beyond, is the term used for a certain sexual position outlawed by the Alien Council of Ethical Conduct on Earth. When I read about it later, I nearly lost my lunch.

"Yes, that's right," I say impatiently. "We need to talk. Now!"

Mr. Vladosky's thick eyebrows rise up toward his gleamin' head. "Do not order me, Detective!" he sputters. "I know yur Captain and she vood not appreciate my being spoken to in dis manner. Now vy don't you finish your coffee and leave. Set up an appointment vith my office later. I'll be glad to speak to you ven I get de chance."

"Do you want me to melt his face off?" Gelatos offers.

Mr. Vladosky throws a puzzled look at the coffee mug in my hand then starts to laugh.

This is gettin' tiresome. I lean over the table and grab him by the lapel of his dark-blue, wrinkle-free coat, pullin' him toward me.

"Look, it's been a long day and I'm runnin' outta patience. Perhaps I should go back to my captain's office and tell her about this little alien colony you have here." I pull him closer so that I can whisper. "Especially the ones at your home. Workin' like slaves."

His eyebrows lower and worried creases form on the corners of his mouth. He stands up from behind the table and we lev over to a quiet corner near a beverage vendor. He orders Mooroscian wine and I ask for my Procyon micro-beer. The vendor laughs at me. I guess it's not a fit drink for such a fancy place.

"Give me what he's drinkin'," I say, and the vendor pours me a glass of silver wine. I take a swig of the incredibly sweet liquid and wince as it goes down. What I wouldn't give for some Tschk! right now.

"You seem to haf opened up a nano-can of Vloborian vurms, Detective," Baldy says through his wineglass, a glint of anger in his eyes.

"You seem to have a dead employee in your aquarium," I say flatly.

His eyes bulge and he scans the carpet as if searchin' for who it might be. "Who?" he finally asks.

I show him my armpad with the Sextan's name. I can't pronounce it either.

He drops into a hoverchair and sets his drink in his lap. "Grghk," he says somberly. "Ven did it happen?"

"Last night. After hours. Time of death: 0319."

"How did he die?" he asks, gulpin' down his wine now.

"Looks like someone smacked him into the otter tank shield hard enough to smash his head in. Not a pretty way to go," I say, slurpin' my wine.

"No vitnesses I take it. Dat's vy you're here now."

I nod.

"Well I'm afraid dat I vas at home vith my vife and family all night. Zey can confirm dat if you'd like, az vell az confirming it vith my floater recorder."

I look at him with surprise. "You have your own floater?"

He smiles. "Uf course. You don't tink dat de owners of de Monterey Intergalactic Aquarium vood let me use public transportation, do you?"

I forgot how rich those quantum PAT designers had become. The Loadard family owns the aquarium and it's the Loadard family name that's emblazoned upon almost all the PATs in this sector of the galaxy. I heard a rumor that they were so rich they still used water to take showers, rather than the sonics required by law.

"What can you tell me about Grghk? Was he mated?"

Mr. Vladosky nods. "To a beautiful female named Yprsdk Thrwsk Pbgrwskl," he says as if there were a load of Tschk! in his mouth.

"Is she local?" I ask, knowin' that Sextans sometimes travel long distances to work.

"She lives in Marina near de floater maintenance center and vasher. She's a lovely . . . lady." His eyes twinkle, but I can't tell if he's sad about poor ol' Grghk or if somethin' else put that twinkle there. I find it hard to believe anyone would find a Sextan lovely, other than another Sextan. All those spidery legs and eyes. Hideous!

I know this pile of Jolosian crap is bein' cooperative because of what I said to him about his alien collection at home, but I don't much care. I need information and there are two ways to get it: the right way and my way. Today, like all days, I choose my way. I know the information we scammed from his quant is inadmissible since we had no warrant but I don't give a Ligovian load! It's gettin' the job done that matters to me. That and gettin' outta here as soon as possible.

"What kind of worker was Grghk?" I ask.

"Very goot. Excellent in fact. He'd been putting in zum long hours lately so dat vee could expand de tanks ven de new shipment from Netus Seven arrives. A great crop of helium breathers from de depths of dat planet. They are—"

"Look! I ain't interested in floppy fish, just what happened to your employee in your aquarium."

He looks at me with disgust, as if I weren't worthy of the information about the Netus arrival. "Vill dat be all?" he asks sharply, puttin' down his wine glass.

"No. I have one more question." I take a slurp of silver wine again. "How long have you been bald?"

A startled look comes over him and his face reddens. "You voodn't understand if I told you," he says, dismissin' me with a wave of his hand.

"Try me anyway."

He sighs. "Some species find body hair repulsive. I kept my genetic disposition zo not to offend zem. Many of zem vork for me und de better vee can get along, de more vork vee can get done."

"I see."

He starts walkin' back over to his collection of aliens at the table where I'd found him.

"But hey!" I yell after him. He turns back to look at me, stiffly. "What if you offend me?" I say, and happily leave the hotel.

Old Baldy was apparently tellin' the truth. I confirmed his story with his wife and kid through the holonet and checked out his floater, which had been docked at his home all night. Figures. I never get a break. Nothin' comes easy to Ray Gunn, not work, not play, not . . . well . . . not even love. My last girlfriend ran out of the apartment yellin' and screamin' somethin' about "having had enough." Of what, I'm still not sure.

With Baldy's alibi revealed, this crime scene trail seemed as cold as outer space and I wasn't sure when or how I'd advance the case. I knew I had to meet up with the corpse's mate. I hate doin' that part of the job. Interviewin' the dead's family is never fun, whether they're human or not.

I glide into Marina a few seconds later on a low floater lane and the flier lands on a pad near the bright yellow maintenance station. The Sextan's home is behind the station in a set of oversize villas. I find the right place on the 65th tier and buzz the scanner. The green door slides open and a Sextan woman appears at my feet. She screams at me and scuttles away from the open door.

I hate this.

"Mrs. . . . Mrs. . . . whatever your name is, wait!" I say, and start to step inside. I bang into a forcefield and my headache starts up again. Perfect.

"Don't come. No. no. No hair. Don't come," she squeals. I forgot about the problem these Sextans have with hair. I've got a full, black mop so she's probably petrified of me.

"I'm sorry about the hair, ma'am, but I've gotta ask you a few questions . . . about your mate's death."

She reappears around a corner holdin' some flimsy clear piece of material. She shuts down the security system and hands it to me.

"What's this?"

"Filament cap. Must put on before coming in. Yes. Must wear," she says.

I roll my eyes and slip it over my head, feelin' it tighten around my skull. This isn't helpin' my headache.

"How sexy you look," Gelatos snickers from inside the coffee cup.

"Watchit or I'll toss you down the laser dump," I whisper and step into the villa. It's a nice place with fancy colored stone decorations on the walls and a Sextan resting pit lined with green Ulookisian silk in the far corner of the main room.

She allows me to sit down on somethin' resembling a couch only after coverin' everything I might touch with Clear Foam: a substance that dissolves with time.

"So sorry. So, so sorry. I must protect house. So sorry. What do for you now?" she asks quickly, bumblingly.

"Have there been any problems around work or the house lately?" I like to get right to the point when I question people . . . or aliens.

She rubs her . . . whatever it is . . . with one of her legs, as if ponderin' a thought. "No. No problems," she says but then begins to weep.

"What's wrong now?" I ask impatiently just wantin' to get on with this torturous task.

"He work so hard. All the time. Work, work, work. Hardly ever home."

"You mean you didn't see him very often?"

"Not lately. No, not lately."

I think of what old Baldy said to me earlier about this "beautiful" Sextan. I don't see it, personally. "It must get lonely around here with him gone all the time," I continue. "Have you two been gettin' along?"

She rubs that thing again with her leg and an injured look comes across her . . . whatever, before fading to a sternness. "We fine. No more. No more question. You leave hairy human." She opens the door.

"But I—"

"No! You leave now!" she says, pointin' two spidery legs at the doorway.

"I think we better go," Gelatos says.

I get up, head out and hear the door whisk closed behind me as the forcefield hums to life.

"Why should we go?" I ask my stinky partner.

"Because she had a level eight security system on us the entire time we were there."

"What? How do you know that?"

"It's a gift," he says. "As a Gelatonian I know when and where other non-carbon based life or intelligence is around and I can tell you with absolute certainty that she had an active, high-level, vaporization security system in there. It spoke to me."

"Oh? And what did it say?"

"It said that we'd better get outta there before she got mad. Which she was."

"Dames," I grumble, and head up to the floater.

When things aren't lookin' good for me, there's only one place to go. The pub. Tonight I go to Monterey Jose's. The place is crawlin' with creepies and humans I usually don't associate with, but I'm thirsty for some Grosolian whiskey so I let it slide. I haven't been in here for quite some time and the clientele has obviously slipped.

I'm chuggin' my drink down when I see her; the Draconian woman. So this is where I'd seen her before! My mind's a little clearer now that the sun's gone down and I've got a drink in my hand. Remarkably beautiful in all her movements, she has skin that's a light olive color, full red lips with high cheekbones, and a long but perfectly symmetrical neck with deep black hair hanging down past it onto thin shoulders. Her chest is narrow but sticks out nicely in front and her slender hips sway just enough for my taste. She's waitin' tables and wearin' some airy outfit showin' all that creation gave her. I'm not one to fall for dames you see, but this gal had it all, includin' a third arm—which I was willin' to overlook for the moment. Why hadn't I taken more notice of her before? I ask my waiter to send her over. He looks at me and rolls all ten of his eyes.

She comes over and when she spots my uniform I watch her eyes dry up. She's obviously upset about somethin'.

"What's wrong?" I ask.

"What do you's want?" she asks stiffly. She looks down at the coffee cup where Jello-boy is. "Would you's like some fresh coffee?"

I stare down at the coffee mug. "Is it hot?"

"Very," she says and begins moving a steamin' dispenser closer to the mug. I wave her off at the last second.

"Temptin', but no thanks," I say, grinnin' into the cup. I hear a slow fizzle come out of it that I interpret as a sigh of relief. "I saw you at the aquarium earlier and you seemed upset there, too. Somethin' troublin' you?"

"Only you's," she says and starts to walk away.

"You knew Grghk, didn't you?"

She stops, comes back to my booth and sits down next to me, her eyes as dry as the sun. Her scented skin, smellin' of crushed Yukulian rose pedals, wafts into my nose. I move away.

"Yes, I knew him's," she says.

I'm kinda stunned. I didn't expect her to know the deceased. It was a shot in the dark for me to have even mentioned it. The things you learn through police work.

"How'd you know him?" I ask and slam down the rest of my whiskey.

She smiles softly at me and I feel a lump form in my throat. "We's were lovers," she says flickin' her hair back. "He's was a very hot lover. Very hot."

I nearly topple outta my chair. "What? How's that possible? Sextans hate hair," I say pointin' to her long, dark locks.

"Grghk's was different. He's liked my's hair for some reason. He's actually enjoyed touching it, too's. He's told me's never to tell anyone's, though. He's kept it secret from everyone's." She trembles suddenly for some reason, then stands to leave.

"Just a moment Mrs. . . . Mrs. . . ."

"Ms. Olossc," she says.

"Well, Ms. Olossc, you need to speak with me some more. When do you get off work?" I stand up.

"Midnight."

"I'll be back to pick you up," I say and walk out. Midnight. I wonder if I can wait that long. What the hell am I sayin'? Snap out of it Gunn. Geez, I'm turnin' into a mush pile here.

And she's an alien!

I catch the next floater to Seaside and head to my apartment for a sonic shave and shower. I put on my best uniform and some fresh cologne. It's still nearly five hours 'til she gets off work, so I watch an ancient vid detective story to take my mind off of her. But I forgot about the spluttering glob in the coffee mug who'd listened to everything I'd said to her.

"Soft-hearted Ray Gunn," he needles me from my table.

I should've accepted the hot coffee.

She comes out of Monterey Jose's in a sparklin' silver outfit she must have changed into after clocking out. It sets off her purple eyes and dark hair, attractin' me to her like a magnet. She hops into the floater that I have waitin' and we wing off toward the beach.

I brush my relatively clean uniform with my hands, straightenin' any wrinkles I find and feel my squishy partner in my left breast pocket.

"Watch what you're touching, Gunn," he murmurs quietly.

"Shhh," I whisper into the pocket. "Keep quiet . . . and don't stain anything."

"Where are we's going?" Ms. Olossc asks.

"*We's* are goin' to the beach so that I can talk to you in private," I say as the floater changes altitude and drops below the scattered clouds.

The flier looks over my cipher payment for going so low and obviously realizes this is government business because he shakes his head but continues on. He won't get paid his usual outlandish fees for this excursion to ground level. Swallow that, fly-boy!

We descend to the beach near the defunct ruins of the Monterey Cineplex. I watch as the moon makes a rare appearance, coming out from behind a cloud, and giving us a moonlit silver view of the surf swellin' back and forth. We exit the floater.

She walks away, toward the beach. I catch up to her and notice that her eyes have dried up again.

"He's used to love the beach," she says watchin' a few cloned harbor seals barkin' at each other out in the kelp beds.

"Grghk did?"

"Yes. It's where we's met. Not far from here."

I cringe, not wantin' to picture them together.

"Grghk's was a great lover. He's was soft, caring and so hot." She looks out over the bay with her beautiful eyes. "He's would never have been accepted by another Sextan's. He's loved my's hair."

"He was mated, too."

"Yes, he's was," she says with obvious irritation. "But because he's was forced into it. He's left the Sextan system because of language."

"Language?"

"He's made the mistake of using bad language on his's home planet. They's kicked him's off. His's only attachment to home was being mated to another Sextan's."

"I see," I say, rubbin' my chin. "Seems to me that Grghk had quite a few problems accordin' to Sextan society. First language and now this hair thing."

"He's would have found someone other than me's if he's could. I's was too tall for him's. He's liked small women with hair. But none would have him's. So I's was his's choice. He's made me's very happy." Her eyes begin to stream.

I put my arm around her to comfort her, then realize that she's happy. I still get confused with these watery eyes. But she doesn't seem to mind and puts her head on my shoulder. The smell of her hair is intoxicatin'. I pull away.

"You's not like me's?" she asks coyly.

"No, that's-not-it-at-all," I say quickly. "It's just . . . well . . . you're an alien. I'm not too fond of aliens."

She moves closer to me. "Maybe you's just haven't met the right alien's." She moves her soft, red lips up to my ear and whispers, "You's have nice skin." She touches my right arm. "And firm arms."

"Psst," I hear come from my coat pocket.

"What was that?" she asks, snapping her steamy mouth away from my face.

"Nothin'. Would you excuse me for a moment?" I separate from her.

"What is it?" I ask impatiently into my pocket as I walk toward a retaining wall.

"Hey, lover boy, I just got an idea about the murder."

"Oh really?"

"We need to head back to the aquarium and check the crime scene again."

"What? Now?"

"We all have to make sacrifices, Gunn. Look at me. I'm sucking up lint in this cheap suit's pocket but I'm still willing to work with you and get this crime solved."

I sigh. "Okay. But give me a minute will ya?" I walk back over to the beauty facin' the tide.

"I've got to go. A . . . call," I say and cipher-summon another floater to take her home. She thanks me and kisses me on the cheek. I smile and help her into the floater.

"What's your first name?" I ask.

"That is rather personal of you's."

"It's for my report," I lie.

She smiles and says, "Plop." The door to the floater swings shut and I watch it soar upward into the clouds and disappear.

"Come on Romeo," Jello-boy bubbles.

"Romeo? Who's that?"

Gelatos and I arrive at the aquarium minutes after leaving Plop's company. I head over to the dead Sextan's body and look down at it through the stasis-field.

"So?" I ask my partner, lookin' into the cup that he'd oozed back into on our way over to the scene.

"We need to access Baldy's quant again."

"And why is that?" I ask, headin' toward the director's office door.

"I need to check the heat signatures of the room and the otter tank shielding. I think it might surprise us. Something that your girlfriend said made me think about it."

"She's *not* my girlfriend. And how can Baldy's PAT tell us anything about the murder?"

"Quants are very sensitive to heat. I'll access the time of death of the Sextan and we'll look at the wall nearest the tank in Baldy's office and see what we can see from the PAT's standpoint. The security system only shows visual pictures in the offices. But with the help of the quant, we can link the security system and the PAT together at the time of death and see what happened in the main viewing room. Maybe."

"Maybe? You pulled me away from my *girlfriend* for a maybe?"

Gelatos laughs, or whatever that sound is.

We enter the director's office and I set the coffee cup down on the large desk. Gelatos slides out of the mug then into the terminal. I hear the slushin' sounds again.

"Accessing data," the sterile voice says, then I see a red haze and gray pixels appear on the PAT screen. The red haze, I can tell, is the Sextan. He's standin' about twelve meters away from the tank lookin' at a pair of frolickin' otters that appear as another set of red images. Then I watch the haze around the Sextan expand.

"His body temperature rose sharply," I hear my gooey partner say as he watches from inside the quant.

"So I see."

The red haze around the Sextan peaks in intensity and he runs with incredible speed on his six legs toward the tank. He runs full-bore into the otter tank forcefield and falls back onto the floor, motionless.

I stand up from the table, a momentary sense of awe, anger, and pity fillin' my thoughts. "I can't believe this," I say to the ooze as he seeps back into his cup.

"I think Grhgk's hair fetish finally caught up with him, wouldn't you? He must have wanted a short, hairy female pretty bad," Gelatos says. "Definitely a *hot* lover," he jokes and gurgles.

"Well, Captain Bryce will be pleased that I solved the case at least."

"*We*, lover boy. *We* solved it."

"Oh yeah," I say. "*We*."

The followin' day the news hits the vids and the whole world knows about this Sextan and his little sexual problem. Thankfully, I was able to keep Plop's name out of my report since her part in this whole damn mess was simply incidental. I've tried holocalling her but she hasn't been home. Probably workin'. Maybe tomorrow I'll stop by Monterey Jose's and see if I can spot her.

Until then I'm at an old hangout suckin' down Procyon micro-beer and eatin' fresh Tschk! again. I stagger back home when they close the joint and pass out on my sofa-bed while watchin' old detective story lazdisks of my youth and thinkin' about *her*. When I wake up my holophone is screamin' in the corner and my head is gratin' against the inside of my skull. I slam down the green activation button on the phone and Captain Bryce's shinin' face appears.

"What time is it?" I ask quietly, my head throbbin'.

"It's almost ten a.m.!" she says cheerfully. "Time for you to start work. I've got another assignment for you, Ray! And for Gelatos. Hi Gelatos!" she squeals. "Next Friday night at Hilltop Bar and Swill would be fine!" Her eyes try to look behind me.

"Please," I plead, "not so loud. And it's too early." I slap the red disengage switch and disconnect it from the holo outlet.

I try to go back to sleep, but it's useless. Damn women. One tryin' to get me into work before the crack of noon and the other nettlin' my emotions. I get back up and pour myself a strong brew of Roolusian coffee. My headache eases enough so that I can turn on the vid-news without screamin' in agony. A pretty, young newscaster comes on and announces another "tragedy" at the Monterey Intergalactic Aquarium. I sink onto the sofa and listen intently as she continues with this "breaking story":

". . . it appears that two otters were found brutally slain today at the aquarium. Their bodies were mutilated and shaved clean of all hair."

I flip off the news and lean back, holdin' my head against the cool material of the sofa.

"No rest, even though we're weary," I hear Gelatos gurgle from his mug on my coffee table.

"Weary my ass," I say rubbin' my temples. "My head is killin' me."

I head into work two pots of coffee later and find the place bustlin' with activity: reporters and detectives all runnin' around. I ask one of the new detecs what's going on.

"Haven't you heard?" he says with a shocked look on his face. "Those poor otters were killed at the aquarium!"

I place my left hand over the overzealous detective's mouth before he blurts out anything else that'll cause my brain to explode. "Yeah, I know," I lean in toward him and whisper. "I think I've got a few leads on this one." I remove my hand from his face.

"*We*, Gunn," the coffee mug in my right hand sputters. "*We* have a few leads."

The young detective looks down at the coffee mug and grimaces as he sniffs the air above the cup.

"Yeah. *We*," I say.

I hate aliens.

About the Author

BYRON MERRITT lives in Pacific Grove, California, and works as a full time emergency room nurse and part time writer. He's taken first and third places in local writing competitions and has posted numerous science fiction stories/articles on the Internet at various webzines. He says that he derives much of his writing abilities via his genes; his grandfather was the internationally best-selling author Frank Herbert of Dune *fame. Byron is currently working on multiple science fiction and fantasy short stories, novels, and novelettes.*

Borscht in the Bay

by Ken Jones

Woody couldn't sleep. He stared at the ceiling and listened to the regular rhythm of his wife Helen's "sleep-breathing". Even if from time to time it reminded him of a semi-truck's compression brake, he'd learned *never* to call it snoring.

Quietly rolling his lanky frame out of bed, he collected his sweatshirt and faded khakis from the floor and closed the bedroom door behind him. Shuffling down the dim hallway toward the bathroom, he perused the gallery of photographs of a much younger Clarence "Woody" Woodall, each showing him smiling amid gatherings of his long ago Army buddies. He washed his face and dressed in the bathroom, wishing that just once he could wake up in the morning instead of the middle of the night. On his way to the kitchen, he paused in the tiny living room, quiet except for the familiar ticking of the antique clock on the mantel. There he regarded his wife's overweight orange ball-of-a-cat, Ralph, sprawled on the sofa sound asleep. "I ought to try 'Mixed Grill Feast' for dinner myself," he muttered.

He lit the burner under the kettle and rummaged in the cupboard for the ancient jar of instant coffee. It wasn't his favorite, but easy to make on only two hours sleep. The kettle began to rumble, rousing Ralph who had joined the household as an appreciative stray five or six years earlier. The cat voiced his disapproval and rolled over, turning his back to the kitchen.

When the water finally boiled, Woody poured it slowly over the aged crystals and stirred the mix into something that marginally passed for coffee at one-thirty in the morning. He slipped into his jacket, tucked his wispy gray hair under his favorite faded red 49ers cap, and took his cup out onto the front porch.

Taking a deep breath of the clear, salty-sweet air, he stretched and looked up, marveling yet again at the star show that played on those treasured but all too infrequent non-foggy nights like this one. He locked the front door out of habit and, coffee mug in hand, strolled the two short blocks to the bay listening to the waves washing on the rocks below Lovers Point and the sea lions yowling from the Monterey Harbor. After crossing Ocean View Boulevard, he walked a few hundred feet up the meandering recreation trail that hugs the bay. He smiled as he sat down on his favorite bench, almost glad he wasn't able to sleep. Closing his eyes, he absorbed the sounds and aromas of the night.

The Woodalls had lived in Pacific Grove, California for almost 25 years. They had bought the little Victorian house on Fountain Avenue when he'd retired after 30 years in the Army. He'd been stationed at the Presidio for a few years and had spent time at nearby Fort Ord. When it became unlikely that his name would appear on the full Colonel's list, he'd reluctantly decided to retire early and try civilian life. The size and feel of the little town of Pacific Grove suited them perfectly and so their ultimate return to the Peninsula had always been the plan.

Woody's weathered outdoorsy look gave no hint that he'd spent his Army years behind a series of unsatisfying desks. His tall thin figure could often be seen walking along the edge of the bay from Cannery Row around Point Pinos to the Inn at Spanish Bay. At 70, aside from a little arthritis, some occasional forgetfulness and now this sleep thing, he was in pretty good shape.

Convinced that vigilance was the defining responsibility of every good citizen—such as himself—Woody kept his eyes open and was quick to report suspicious activities or unusual occurrences, as well as loud radios, a neighbor's unkempt yard, or unfamiliar cars on the block; he was a one-man neighborhood watch. His alarms often turned out to be false, but he thought it better to be proven wrong than to be caught off guard. Over the years, he'd built a reputation within the Pacific Grove Police Department as a lovable busybody among those who knew him and as a certifiable head-case by those who'd only heard the stories.

For the most part, the police put up with Woody in deference to his one true ally in the department, Detective Sergeant Anthony Scaperelli. Sergeant Tony, as Woody called him, had 24 years with the Department and the two men had been friends from the days Tony had worked Fountain Avenue as a rookie.

On this night, though, nothing bothered Woody. The stars were bright and the bay was tranquil. The sounds and smells of the night wafted past him as he sipped his almost-coffee and stared out at the gently rolling water.

His peaceful reverie was interrupted when a small dark form on the water out past the end of Lovers Point caught his attention. At first he thought it was a line of kelp, but it seemed to be moving toward shore.

When he leaned forward to try to make out more detail he felt a bulge in his jacket pocket and reached in to see what it was. *My Binoculars! That's where they went*! He put his cup down and sighted through the small field glasses. After some trial and error, he located the object again and saw that it was an inflatable boat. As he watched, the craft came to within a few hundred yards of shore and three men slid over the side. The little boat soon flattened and sank.

The men swam toward shore only yards from where Woody sat. He got up and moved behind a nearby tree. Very strange, he thought. Why would anybody be out there this time of night . . . and why waste a perfectly good blow-up boat?

The men changed out of their wetsuits, retrieving dry clothes from their bags. They talked quietly but Woody could hear parts of their conversations. "My God!" Woody whispered to himself, "That sounds like Russian!"

After a few minutes, the three climbed up the bluff and walked away from the lights of Pacific Grove toward the darker streets in the direction of the Monterey Bay Aquarium.

Woody didn't know what, but something was not right. He hurried back to the house, picked up the phone and pushed the PGPD speed dial button.

"Pacific Grove Police Department."

"Oh, it's you, Fowler," Woody grunted. "Is Sergeant Tony on tonight?"

"Hello Mr. Woodall," Officer Fowler said with forced politeness. "Sorry. Sergeant Scaperelli doesn't come on until seven in the morning. What is it now . . . er, is there anything I can help you with?"

Woody thought about it. He'd dealt with Fowler before and found him a little slow on the uptake . . . too hard to get through to. "No, I guess not," he said, "I'll call back in the morning." He hung up and looked at his watch. A quarter past two. "I'd better make a pot of real coffee now," he told Ralph, who blinked at him from the couch. "Now what did I do with my cup?"

Just after sunset earlier that same evening, Petty Officer Aleksei Ivanov and Radioman First Class Ivan Smokitavitch bobbed in a small inflatable boat next to the dark hull of the Soviet submarine, *Boetz*. They floated five miles off the Central California coast slightly north of the mouth of Monterey Bay at the spot where the sub's batteries had finally given out.

Aleksei, a tall and muscular 23-year-old, had an unruly mop of blond hair, a quick wit and a natural bearing of authority that was supported in no small measure by his six-foot-two frame.

The young radioman, Aleksei's polar opposite, had celebrated his nineteenth birthday somewhere in the north Pacific. Ivan's face was round and boyish and at five-three, his shipmates often kidded him for having lied about his age *and* his height in order to be accepted by the Navy. He looked up to Aleksei more than just physically. The petty officer had become his role model and defender during their service together. Ivan had tried to add years to his appearance by growing a beard like Aleksei's, but the pathetically scraggly stubble had had the opposite effect.

The third member of their group, Engine Mechanic Vladimir Kraninskakov, carried out the last official operation aboard the sub.

The moonless sky was alive with stars, the air fresh and the surface of the sea calm. The men looked toward the outline of the shore, dark except for clusters of lights sprinkled intermittently along the edge of the land.

"Looks like a peaceful place, don't you think, Ivan?"

"I don't know," the nineteen-year-old grumbled, slumping forlornly against the side of the inflatable.

A great swell of bubbles rushed up around the bow of the sub and the small inflatable tilted as the foam boiled and hissed across the surface. Vladimir's stout, wrestler's body, squeezed like a sausage into his ill-fitting wetsuit, was briefly silhouetted against the horizon as he climbed down from the tower and stepped into the inflatable.

Vladimir was the oldest member of the trio at 43. He had been at sea longer than any of the others and was not shy about expressing his disdain for the general state of mechanical mayhem he had been forced to work with during his 26 years of service. He'd been in the engine room when *Boetz* made her maiden voyage in 1967 and over the years he'd watched in disgust as she'd deteriorated for lack of maintenance and replacement parts. It was Vladimir who had given the boat the unofficial nickname *Borscht* after she had to return to port on the third day of her first patrol when her periscope seals failed and flooded the control room. By the end of her second tour, *Boetz*, which translates ironically as "Champion," became forever *Borscht*, "Beet Soup," to her crew.

"It won't be long," he said, sitting heavily, "that damn boat's been trying to sink for years."

The men paddled silently toward shore, the only sounds being the rhythmic slap of their paddles and the rush of water under their boat. After they'd gone some 50 yards, a wrenching, metallic sigh from the *Borscht* halted their paddling and they turned to see the sub nosing down, her aft section rising out of the water to stand nearly straight up against the sky.

The dark form began to slip slowly down amid roiling mounds of foam and the screech of escaping air until its descent slowed and finally stopped with twenty feet of the tapered aft section still exposed above the gentle swells. The outline slowly oscillated in the starlight, its single large screw pointing straight up, as if trying to pull itself out of the deep. Aleksei looked anxiously at Vladimir, whose job it had been to scuttle the boat that now seemed reluctant to be scuttled.

"Ah . . . Vladimir?" he said softly.

"Damn boat can't do anything right!" Vladimir said, shaking his head.

"Ah . . . Vladimir!" Aleksei repeated. Vladimir never took his eyes off the *Borscht's* tail end. He simply held up his hand as if to say, "Be patient . . ."

They watched the slowly swinging form for several painful minutes. Suddenly a burst of air and a cloud of misty foam billowed up around it. The *Borscht* shuddered, then slipped smoothly beneath the waves, leaving only a swirl of phosphorescence on the surface. It was the end of October 1991 and the *Borscht,* nee *Boetz,* had ended her lackluster career with a terminal dive into the cold depths of Monterey Canyon. Only after the swirling iridescence had disappeared did the crew of the *Borscht* resume their rowing.

"I can't believe I let you talk me into this, Aleksei," Ivan said over his shoulder as he rowed.

"You were eager enough to come along, as I recall," Vladimir said with a chuckle.

"That was the drink talking," Ivan shot back. "If Aleksei hadn't suggested that we have a vodka in the torpedo room, we'd be with the rest of the crew now on the supply ship on our way home. Things were getting bad, sure, but I never really wanted to leave." He paused, then continued in a lowered voice. "I know about America. Americans drive their big cars too fast. Everybody in America has a gun . . . we're all going to be shot. I know it."

"And how is it you know so much?" Aleksei asked skeptically.

"I just know!" Ivan shouted. "I've seen many American moving pictures. Gun fights, automobile chases, one big party, all the time. They're all crazy. I know." Ivan paddled silently for a moment and then said quietly, "I just want to go home."

"Do you miss your mother?" Vladimir said, jokingly, as if to a child.

"No. Well, yes, but . . ."

"Ah," Vladimir said, knowingly, "then it must be the beautiful girlfriend Svetlana we've heard stories about, eh?"

Ivan didn't answer.

After they had paddled for several minutes, Aleksei said, "I could not have known the captain would order the crew to board the supply ship while we were sleeping."

"That's what makes me most angry," Ivan said, turning to face the other men. "How could they leave us like that?" He wiped his nose with the back of his shaking hand.

"They didn't 'leave' us," Vladimir replied, his voice full of contempt. "They just didn't bother to look for us. If we'd had all our torpedoes instead of just one . . ."

He shook his head and laughed. "One torpedo! What kind of Navy is this anymore? Anyway, if the aft room had been loaded, it would have been part of the watch. As it was, it was just good place to go drink vodka."

"But they tried to sink the boat," Ivan said with a forlorn sigh. "We could have died."

"We could have," Vladimir conceded. "It is a good thing most of the valves were rusted shut. To think . . . we owe our lives to sloppy maintenance. I'm glad we could close the rest before we took in too much of the sea."

"You moved pretty fast for an old man, Vladimir!" Ivan said, his mood lightening temporarily.

The mechanic feigned a backhand at the young radioman. "Outrun you any day!"

Ivan's smile didn't last long, however, and when Vladimir saw young Ivan's mood again revert to despair, he spoke up. "Without fuel or supplies *Borscht* was a dead boat," he said calmly. "Listen to us, Ivan. America is our best hope. Things will work out, you'll see." He gave his friend a gentle poke on the arm. "Besides," he went on, "I've seen a couple of American movies myself. American women are very pretty, like Svetlana . . . maybe prettier."

After a few minutes, Aleksei moved next to Ivan and put a fatherly arm on the young man's shoulder. In gentle tones, he said, "You worry too much, Ivan. Nobody's going to shoot us. Surely you remember how bad things are at home. You read the communications. There is so much confusion, nothing is working anymore."

Moving closer to keep the conversation private, he went on. "We are all a little scared, but are you not just a little bit excited, too? We will take a day or two to look around. We'll make sure nobody's shooting at us, and see if Vladimir is right about how pretty the American girls are. Then, if we like what we see, we will go to the authorities as we agreed. This is our best opportunity to start a new life. A free life."

When they'd rowed to within 200 yards of shore, the three slipped over the side and treaded water, using their sea-proof bags full of their shore clothes as flotation. Vladimir pulled the plug on the little boat and the inflatable sunk under the weight of four heavy wrenches tied to the rigging to guarantee it found the bottom.

"That makes two naval vessels I sink tonight," he said. "I should get a medal."

Ivan laughed, "You would, too, if they hadn't both been *ours.*"

"Swim!" Aleksei urged.

Exhausted, they swam through the rocky crags into the low surf and onto a little beach. When they'd reached the shelter of the bluff, Aleksei scanned the area and saw no one. "So far, so good," he said.

"That water is cold like Siberia!" Vladimir shuddered, peeling off his wetsuit and hurrying into his pants and woolen turtleneck.

Ivan hunkered down behind a rock, shivering, and peered cautiously over the top.

"Get changed, Ivan," Aleksei said, "there's no one there." Reluctantly, Ivan emerged and began to shrug out of his wetsuit, all the while looking as if the shooting was about to start.

After changing into dry clothes, they stowed their wetsuits in their bags and carefully climbed up the embankment to stand on a pathway that wove its way lazily in both directions along the edge of the bluff.

"Where do we go now?" Ivan asked. He was still poised to run.

"Fewer lights," Vladimir suggested, pointing in the general direction of Monterey.

"The less going on, the better," Aleksei agreed and the three headed up the pathway toward Monterey.

At the stroke of seven that morning, a light flashed on the PGPD switchboard.

"Pacific Grove Police Department, how may I help you?" Linda, the day shift telephone operator said into the tiny microphone of her headset.

"Sergeant Tony, please, Linda."

She recognized Woody's voice immediately. "Oh, good morning, Woody," she chirped, "how's everything this morning?"

"'Bout the same, Linda. Listen, I'd love to chat with you, but is Sergeant Tony in yet? It's important!"

"He sure is. Hold on a moment, I'll connect you."

Linda saw Tony as he rounded the corner from the coffee room and called to him. She held up her hand in the standard "call for you" gesture and mouthed the word "Woody."

Tony waved and headed for the blinking phone on his desk. He had come in an hour early to try to catch up on the paperwork he hated. Lately, the routine things he used to take in stride were beginning to sap the fun out his job. A call from Woody always signaled a break in the routine.

Pushing some papers out of the way, he put his coffee down and picked up the phone.

"Hey, Woody, what's up?"

"I can't tell you on the phone, Tony," he heard Woody whisper, "you'd better come over."

Scaperelli smiled. He tossed his glasses onto his cluttered desk and squeezed the bridge of his nose.

"What's on your mind, Woody, we've got a busy day going here already."

"I don't want to talk about it on the phone!" Woody said again. He sounded nervous to Tony. "They might be listening!"

"Who might be listening, Woody?" Tony asked, concerned for his friend.

"I'll tell you when I see you. How soon can you get here?"

Tony checked his day planner, an almost solid field of scribbles. It was Friday morning and the week was coming to an end like a train wreck. "How about I come over around eleven-thirty? I'll pick you up and we'll grab some lunch."

"No sooner?" Woody asked, sounding dejected.

"That's the best I can do today."

"Okay. But just you, Tony! Don't bring anybody with you, okay?"

"Sure, sure, Woody. I'll come alone." Tony chuckled to himself and hung up the phone. *Woody's read one too many detective stories*, he thought.

Woody hung up the phone and sighed. Ralph sat in the middle of the table, on top of the *Monterey Herald*, staring at him. He stared back. Woody always won these stare-downs with Ralph. He liked to think it was because he had the stronger will, but he suspected that Ralph was only humoring him.

Helen had come into the kitchen just as Woody hung up the phone. "Who'd you call at this hour?" she asked.

"Tony," Woody answered.

"Is everything all right?"

"I couldn't sleep again last night," he began, "so I got up and took a walk down to the bay. While I was sitting there, I saw three guys in a rubber boat come close in, then sink the thing, and swim the rest of the way. They were *Russians*. Tony's going to pick me up for lunch and I'll tell him all about it."

"Were they all right?" Helen asked, tightening the sash of her robe.

"They weren't hurt, if that's what you mean."

She opened the cupboard, reached for her favorite cup, and looked back at Woody.

"Why are you using *my* cup?" she asked.

He looked down at the cup in his hand. "I don't know what I did with mine."

Helen took down one of the good ones. As she stirred in a lump of sugar, she lifted a slat on the blinds over the sink and checked the thermometer mounted outside the window. "Already almost 60," she said absently. "Going to be a nice day."

She brought her coffee over to the table. "Wish you wouldn't let your cat up on the table," she said, pulling the paper out from under Ralph and swatting him onto the floor.

"He's *your* cat!" Woody barked in reply.

He'd never really trusted that cat; it was something in his eyes.

Helen breathed a sigh of relief when Tony pulled up outside a little past eleven-thirty. Woody had been driving her nuts pacing around the house all morning. Tony had become part of the family and Helen was comforted knowing that Woody wouldn't get into too much trouble while he was with him.

"Remember your right to remain silent," Helen said, looking out at Tony's cruiser.

"Very funny."

Sliding into the passenger seat, Woody wiped the perspiration from his brow and looked over at his friend. "Thanks for comin' Tony," he said.

"Not a problem," Tony replied. "You and Helen okay?"

"We're fine."

"What's this all about?"

"Saw something in the bay last night."

"And . . .?"

"You're going to think I've dropped my last marble, Tony."

"C'mon Woody, you know me better than that," Tony laughed. "Is The Grill okay with you for lunch?"

Woody flashed Tony a knowing glance. "You still seeing that short-order cook?"

Tony sighed. "We're taking a little break. Things got going too fast there."

"How long has it been, Tony, since your divorce?"

Tony grimaced at the thought of his ex. Nearly two years ago she'd left town with a window washer after eighteen years of what Tony thought had been a happy marriage. The terse note she'd left behind said her new love didn't work nights or get shot at. She said the only thing he brought home from the office was clean hands.

Tony didn't answer and the rest of the short drive was quiet.

They pulled into the little parking lot above The Grill at Lovers Point and walked down to the order window. The fog that had rolled in earlier that morning had burned away and the bay was a Color-by-Deluxe poster. The sky was a deep blue, clear but for the contrails washing across it in lazy wind-bent arcs. A crisp breeze ruffled the umbrellas at the weathered tables and gulls waited watchfully on the low stone wall that separated The Grill's eating area from the Lovers Point beach below.

Woody sat down at a table while Tony ordered the burgers.

"Anybody workin' here today?" Tony shouted into the empty little kitchen.

"Hold your horses!" came the reply. A woman in blue jeans, a faded sweatshirt and a well-seasoned apron emerged from the storeroom with her arms full of bags of buns. She blew a few unruly strands of salt-and-pepper hair out of her eyes as she dumped the buns into a bin and turned toward the counter. In her flat sandals, she stood eye-to-eye with Tony.

She smiled broadly when she saw who the rowdy customer was. "Well, hi, stranger!" she said. "Thought you must've transferred to the North Pole."

"Hi, Sara," Tony replied. "I guess I *have* been ignoring you lately."

"You're forgiven."

"Couple of cheeseburgers and two medium cokes, I guess," Tony said.

"Woody have another emergency?" she asked, spotting him over at the table.

"Yeah. He had a late night last night; saw something out in the bay."

"Not another sea monster!" Sara said with a laugh.

"Not this time," Tony said as he collected his change. "Probably only dolphin, or divers."

"Oh well," Sara said, "good to know somebody's looking out for us."

Tony rejoined his friend and the two men sat and waited for their order to be called.

"Okay, what's the deal?"

Woody looked around and then hunched over the table. "I think we were *invaded* last night."

Tony had heard it all—a few times—in his years with the department. He didn't surprise easily.

"That so?" he said calmly. "By whom?"

"Russians," he whispered.

Tony tried hard not to laugh. He gazed out over the peaceful water, not daring to look at Woody's worried face. "Don't see any boats. How'd they get here?" he asked.

"They came in a little inflatable and they sunk it right out there." Woody pointed out into the bay. "Three of 'em came up right over there, I could hear 'em talkin' Russian."

Woody folded his arms and looked at the sergeant, who was recovering from a sudden coughing spell.

"Tony, your order's up!" Sara called from the window.

Glad for the diversion, Tony got up quickly and walked over to the window.

"Don't be such a stranger, okay?" Sara said, sliding the bag forward on the counter with a wink.

"I'll be around," Tony said. "Call ya?"

"Hope so."

Tony handed Woody his cheeseburger and coke and sat down with his own. The two men were quiet as they enjoyed their lunch, stopping only to lick sauce off their fingers.

"We have a lot of folks in town from other countries," Tony said, finally. "You're sure they were Russians?"

"They were Russians! I could hear 'em. I was over behind that tree, there beyond the bench," Woody said, pointing up the coast. "I could hear 'em pretty good. They were talkin' Russian. I'm sure of it."

"Okay, so they were Russians," Tony said. "What makes you think they were invading?"

"Why else would they sink their boat? And in the middle of the night ta boot?" Woody said, as if it were obvious. "You're starting to sound like Fowler!"

"Okay, okay . . . so what happened next?"

"They took off. I wanted to follow 'em, but I thought better of it."

"What time did all this happen?"

"Around two this morning."

"For Pete's sake, Woody, don't you sleep anymore?"

"Not too much lately."

"Okay, tell you what I'll do. I'll make some inquiries. If I run across anything, I'll give you a call."

"Thanks," Woody said, with obvious relief. Then, while suppressing a small burp added, "Are these great burgers, or what?"

"Sara makes a great burger, all right," Tony said, wiping his mouth and ignoring Woody's mischievous look. He checked his watch. "Look, Woody, I gotta get back to work. Take you home, or are you okay here?"

"I'm okay here. I want to take another look around anyway."

"Remember," Tony said in his policeman's voice. "I don't want you doing my job. You just let me handle this." Tony couldn't help but love the guy. He could be a pain in the ass sometimes, but Woody's heart was in the right place.

Sergeant Scaperelli's occasional partner, Officer Paul DeBurke, was on his way out for a smoke when Tony returned to the office. "So what's shakin' in weird Woody's world today?" he asked.

"Go easy, Paul," Tony said, "Woody's okay. He saw some men come on shore early this morning after their rubber boat sunk. Says they were Russians."

"Sea monsters, alien spacecraft and now Russians," DeBurke scoffed. "You going to do anything with it?"

"I've got to meet with the Chief on something else this afternoon, why don't you check with the harbor people and see if they had any problems last night that didn't make our sheets. Ask 'em to check the area off Lovers Point for . . . whatever."

"Aw, c'mon, Tony. Why don't we just issue a 'be on the lookout' for three Russian spies?" DeBurke crumpled his coffee cup and slam-dunked it into his trashcan.

"Just find out if Harbor has anything interesting."

DeBurke made a sour face, but acquiesced with a shrug.

The three new arrivals had spent the night hidden under heavy branches in a clump of cypress trees near the recreation trail, able to fall asleep only after determining that the barking they heard was from sea lions in the harbor and not police dogs on their trail. The sound of joggers passing nearby awakened them into an early morning shrouded in fog. After the runners passed, the men emerged onto the trail.

"I'm hungry," said Ivan, pulling his wool coat tightly around him.

"Of course, you are still growing," Vladimir said, mussing Ivan's hair roughly.

"So are you," Ivan replied, poking Vladimir's ample midsection.

"Come on, you two," Aleksei said finally. "We have to eat. Let's keep going."

They proceeded along the trail through the fog, stepping to the side to let the occasional oblivious jogger or bicyclist pass them. Before long they noticed the smell of food in the air and their steps quickened. A building gradually came into view and it soon became obvious that it was indeed the source of the enticing aromas causing their stomachs to growl.

Aleksei smiled as he slowly read the sign on the building's blue awning: "Archie's American Diner". Their hunger overtook their natural caution. They put their sea bags down in the bushes beside the stairs next to the front door and eagerly entered the building.

The large room was filled with tables, only a few of which were occupied. The heavy scent of pancakes and bacon hung in the air. At the opposite end of the room they saw a counter and behind it the bustle of a busy kitchen.

"Morning," a cheerful young waitress said as she passed them with her arms full of overflowing plates. Aleksei took the lead and pushed the others toward an empty table along the wall.

In a moment a couple entered and walked to the counter. Aleksei had the most English, so he followed them and listened as they ordered their breakfast. Returning to the table, he leaned toward his shipmates.

"They asked for food at the counter," he told them. "Then they paid for it and sat down. I think I can do this." Aleksei rose and walked up to the counter, taken with the fact he didn't have to stand in line.

"Help you?" the boy working behind the counter asked.

"Three breakfasts and three cups of coffee, please," Aleksei said in his best English.

"Which breakfast?" the boy asked, pointing to the menu board hanging overhead. This hadn't happened to the others he'd watched and Aleksei was momentarily confused.

Just then the waitress who had spoken to them earlier came by with another armload of plates. He saw bacon, eggs and toast and pointed to it as it passed.

"*That* breakfast," he said. "Three of *that* breakfast and three cups of coffee, please."

"Okay," the boy said. "Three number 4's, scrambled and three coffees. That it?"

Aleksei looked at the boy, wondering if things were going well, or not well at all.

"Guess so," said the boy after a moment's hesitation and he rang up the sale. "That's $24.18, with tax."

Aleksei looked down at the bundle of strange green paper in his hand, his share of the American currency they had found among the Captain's abandoned effects. He held the bundle toward the boy.

"Ah, new in town, huh?" the boy said. He carefully picked a twenty and a five out of the bundle and smiled warily at Aleksei. He dropped the change into Aleksei's hand and put three empty coffee cups on the counter. "You're number fourteen," he said and handed Aleksei a little plastic sign with the number printed in red.

"Thank you, very much," Aleksei said, studying the little piece of plastic he'd been handed. He pointed to the empty coffee cups. "Coffee?" he said. The boy leaned over and pointed to the pump-top pots lined up at the end of the counter. "Caw-fee," he said, shaking his head.

Aleksei just stood there.

"We'll bring the food to you," the boy said, after a few moments. He pushed the three cups closer to Aleksei and pointed away from the counter.

"Thank you, very much," he said again to the boy. He slipped the plastic card in his coat pocket and picked up the three cups.

"No problem, comrade," the boy said, shaking his head. Aleksei stopped and glanced back at him. Over six feet tall, bearded and wearing his heavy woolen coat, Aleksei was an imposing figure. The boy held up both hands, palms forward and took a step back.

"Hey," he said, "just kidding."

The Russian hadn't caught the joke.

Aleksei figured out how to get coffee out of the pots by watching another customer. He carefully carried the three full cups back to their table.

Soon the waitress brought an armload of plates. "You guys are number fourteen, right? All the same, so it don't matter where they go," she said and put the plates down.

The men were overtaken by the hot, tantalizing smells rising upward towards them. They hadn't tasted a real egg in over five months and the sight nearly brought tears to Ivan's eyes.

"Look at this," Vladimir said, holding up a little package of strawberry jam. He zipped it open theatrically, scooped out a succulent dollop with his finger and rolled his eyes as he placed the sweet blob on his tongue, closing his mouth around it.

Ivan laughed and tried the same thing, but the package slipped out of his fingers, landing upside down in his lap. Undaunted, he picked up the jam and spread it on his toast. Vladimir grabbed the remaining packets and slipped them into his coat pocket. Aleksei savored his food. "This is good," he mumbled. The others mumbled their agreement.

"This is coffee?" Vladimir asked, making a face into his cup.

It was a quarter past nine when the three finished their first breakfast and an almost identical reorder. Their reorder had exhausted their funds—Ivan didn't get a second helping of bacon—but Aleksei had carried the purchase off much more smoothly.

"What do we do now?" Ivan asked, stifling a burp.

"That's a good question," Aleksei said. "What do you think, Vladimir?"

Vladimir sat back in his chair smiling and rubbing his stomach. "Don't know," he answered. "We can't stay here. Best to keep moving, I think."

They collected their bags and stood for a moment on the corner. The fog was giving way quickly to a brightening sun and there were more cars and people on the streets than before. Ivan suddenly grabbed Aleksei's arm and nodded to the opposite corner. A Monterey police car had stopped at the corner and a uniformed officer was out talking to a bicyclist on the curb. Ivan couldn't take his eyes off the officer's .45, securely strapped into its holster.

"Don't worry, Ivan," Aleksei said, but he, too, felt nervous. Without a word, Vladimir began walking up hill, away from the corner. The others followed.

The three new sightseers spent the morning wandering leisurely through Cannery Row then back along the recreation trail into Pacific Grove. They stopped along the way to watch brightly colored bicycle-driven surreys filled with laughing families tool along the trail, and later spent the better part of an hour sitting on a bench by the bay watching a drum-accompanied dancer perform for her unseen audience. When the dancer finally stopped and sat on the ground beside her drummer, the men continued their walk through the quiet neighborhoods.

They stopped short as they rounded a corner and saw a nearly life-size sculptured whale lying next to a wide stairway in front of a building directly across the street.

"Long way from the ocean," Vladimir said.

"He should have stayed at sea, too," Ivan said, remembering the policeman's gun.

"It's a statue," Aleksei said. "It isn't real." He nodded toward a small park across the street, opposite the whale sculpture. "Let's go try to figure out what to do," he said. They crossed to the park and sat on a bench away from the street.

"Are you sure we're better off here than we were on the *Borscht*?" Ivan asked.

"I'm sure," Aleksei answered, but without the assurance that had filled his voice in the empty torpedo room. The men sat watching as young people with musical instruments began to assemble on the small gazebo near the opposite corner of the park.

The gazebo soon bustled with boys and girls busily sorting through sheet music and tuning their instruments. The little park slowly filled with people and although Ivan was somewhat uncomfortable, Aleksei and Vladimir were enjoying the sounds and the warm sun that washed through the trees.

"I used to play the trumpet, did you know that?" Vladimir said to Aleksei.

"I didn't know," Aleksei said. "Did you play well?"

"No. We lived in such a small place, the neighbors complained. My father sold it."

As they watched, a man stepped onto the gazebo and tapped his wand on the music stand. The tuning stopped immediately. He raised the wand and, with his downbeat, the park filled with Glen Miller's *In the Mood.*

After his lunch with Tony, Woody walked home from The Grill past the spot where he'd seen the men come ashore. He searched for some evidence of their having been there but, finding nothing except his coffee mug sitting on the bench where he'd left it, he continued home feeling a little on the grumpy side. He knew what he'd seen and it could be serious.

His wife greeted him upon his return. "Aw, they didn't lock you up," she said, with mock disappointment.

"Ha, ha," he said, sarcastically. He hung his cap back on the peg by the door.

"What did Tony say?"

"He said he'd check around, but I don't know."

"If he said he'd check, he will. Tony's one of the good guys."

"Wish I knew what those guys were doing here," Woody said, brushing Ralph off the couch and sitting in his place.

"I think they're just lost, or runaways," Helen said.

"You're the one always reading those mysteries and spy novels. Is that the best scenario you can come up with?"

"I could be wrong, but there was another article in the *Herald* today about how bad things are in Russia. I couldn't blame them for trying to get away from that." She got up and went into the kitchen.

Woody pondered this, but he wasn't convinced that the men he saw weren't up to no good.

"Your cat is out of food," Helen said. "I'm not going to the store for a few days, could you go get some?"

"Sure," Woody said, then added under his breath, "Why is it *my* cat whenever it's in trouble or needs something?"

"What?" Helen called cheerfully from the kitchen.

"Nothing."

Woody looked at the clock on the mantel; it was almost one o'clock. "I'm going to take a little nap first," he said. "I'll go later."

"That's fine," said Helen.

After half an hour he awoke feeling refreshed and found Helen on the living room sofa, curled up with a book. Ralph was lying on his back next to her. She was absently scratching the cat's large white stomach.

"How many cans should I get?" he asked her.

"Oh, a dozen, I guess. Have enough money?"

He checked his wallet. "Yeah. Be back in a minute," he said, pulling his cap from its peg.

The pet shop was only a couple of blocks away, up the hill on Fountain. When he reached the intersection above his house, he could hear the Pacific Grove Breaker's High School jazz orchestra practicing for their Sunday concert in the park. Woody marveled at how accomplished the kids were. He'd tried to master, or at least tame, the clarinet as a youngster, but the attempt had totally frustrated him.

He turned and walked past the library and into Jewell Park. The park was full of townsfolk and tourists enjoying the big band sounds. He leaned up against a tree near the corner as the band finished with an energetic *Pennsylvania 6-5000,* which the audience enthusiastically joined providing vocal accompaniment. The band stood, acknowledging the crowd only briefly—mostly waving to their parents—and began to pack up their instruments as the crowd slowly dispersed.

The music helped Woody forget what he'd seen in the bay early that morning. Until, that is, he came face to face with three men wearing dark wool coats and carrying duffel bags. Even though he hadn't seen their faces in the dark, the clothes were the same, bags and all. There was no mistaking it: these were his Russians.

"Excuse me," the tallest of the three said. The man looked directly at Woody and smiled as he and the others stepped off the sidewalk to pass.

English! Woody thought. He was speechless. His mind raced, but it was a muddle. What should he do? Should he try to capture them? Should he call for help? Too many options competed for his attention and he could only stand and watch the three men turn the corner and disappear toward Lighthouse Avenue, Pacific Grove's main street.

After a few moments, when he'd regained his speech and mobility, Woody hurried home and again pushed the PGPD speed dial button.

"Oh, I'm sorry," Linda said, "Sergeant Scaperelli is in a meeting. Would you like to talk with someone else, or do you want his voice mail?"

"Nobody else, thanks, Linda," Woody said. "Voice mail, I guess." After a short wait, Tony's recorded voice told him to leave a message and he'd get back to him. *Harder and harder to talk to a person,* Woody thought.

"Tony," Woody began, "I saw 'em again, up close this time. There's three of 'em and they're wearing those long black coats, just like in the movies. I saw 'em goin' toward Lighthouse on Forest, up from the park. One tall one, one short one and one shaped like a redwood stump. They're in town, Tony, I saw 'em . . ."

Woody's message was interrupted by the annoying beep that meant his time was up. He hung up the phone and ran his fingers through his hair.

"Don't worry so, dear," Helen said in soothing tones from the couch.

Woody stood up and rolled his shoulders.

"Why don't you make us a cup of tea and relax a while," Helen said, patting the couch beside her. Woody turned on the burner under the kettle and got two cups ready for tea, then walked into the living room to sit beside his wife.

After a few minutes, the pot began to whistle. Woody fixed the tea and brought the cups back into the living room, putting Helen's on one of the catalogues lying on the coffee table.

"I saw them again at Jewell Park," he said finally. "Funny, but if they hadn't been wearing those big coats, I might have taken them for locals. Anyway, I called Tony just now to tell him, but he was in a meeting." He took a careful sip. "Left a message."

"I still think they're just running away," Helen said.

Woody put his cup on the coffee table, sat back with a sigh and folded his arms. "Well, even so, they shouldn't be running around loose," he said, frowning. "Tony's got to pick 'em up and find out what they're up to."

Helen smiled as she reached for her tea. Ralph sauntered in from the kitchen and stared at Woody. "Ralph looks hungry," she said. "Why don't you open a can for him?"

"Damn!" Woody said. He got up, pulled his cap from the peg and headed back to the pet shop.

Aleksei and the others crossed Lighthouse Avenue and stopped in front of a store window. Ivan was watchful; Vladimir was having another packet of jam, grape this time. Aleksei looked at their reflection in the glass.

"You know," Ivan said to his reflection, "we should get different clothes. Vladimir is starting to smell like bilge."

"You're no rose yourself, Ivan," Vladimir smacked, casually licking his fingers and glaring at his young shipmate.

"Ivan may have a point," Aleksei allowed, picking up a whiff of his own bouquet.

As it happened, the window they were standing in front of belonged to a small thrift shop. They could see various items of clothing hanging on racks just inside the door.

"Do we have any green money left?" Ivan asked. The three dug in their pockets but could only muster a few coins among them after their extravagant breakfast.

"Now what do we do?" Ivan asked.

Aleksei had an idea. "I think we could trade our wetsuits, they're almost new. Let me do the talking."

"Don't worry," Vladimir agreed and the three entered the small shop.

They left the shop a half hour later looking less like Russian seamen—and smelling less like bilge water—but otherwise no less conspicuous. Aleksei wore a pair of faded blue jeans, too short for his long legs, with a thread-fringed hole in the left knee and a bright purple Monterey Bay Aquarium sweatshirt. Vladimir wore a pair of off-white painter's overalls—the only trousers in the store that would fit around him—and a red Disneyland sweatshirt. The tops of Mickey's ears peeked over the front of the overalls. Ivan had on dark blue denim jeans with the legs rolled up and a green plaid shirt that hung around him like sails on a calm day. They had all kept their heavy leather shoes. Remembering their first night under the trees, their turtlenecks, heavy wool coats and watch caps were tucked away in their sea bags.

"You smell much better now," Ivan said to Vladimir as he pretended to sniff his friend.

Vladimir only grunted, admiring his new look in the glass.

The three set off back toward the pathway by the bay.

Tony collapsed into his chair and rummaged in his desk for an aspirin. He found a couple in his pencil tray. The meeting with the Chief hadn't gone particularly well, which was no surprise, and he was beat. He'd forgotten all about Woody and his "invasion" until he saw his partner come into the office.

DeBurke pulled out his cigarettes, then stuffed them back into his jacket pocket. "Wish we could still smoke in here," he said. "Hell, I wish we could smoke anywhere."

"Relax, you'll live longer," Tony said. "Anything from Harbor?"

"Oh, that." DeBurke opened his notebook. "Nothing out of the ordinary. There were no distress calls intercepted, no small craft unaccounted for. They did get a call from the airport around noon though. Seems a private pilot spotted what looked like a small slick and some debris four or five miles out on her approach this morning. She said it was small and might not be anything. I asked the Coast Guard to swing out and see if there's anything to recover."

Tony raised his eyebrows and blinked at his partner.

"I knew you'd give me a hard time if I didn't," DeBurke said.

Tony blew the dust off his aspirin and washed them down with a gulp of cold coffee. He noticed the message light blinking on his phone, picked it up and hit the recall code. He started to write something down, then stopped, hung up and turned to his partner.

"That was Woody," he said. "He saw his Russians again. This time at

Jewell Park." He crumpled the notepaper and threw it in the wastebasket. "Wonder what's really going on?" he muttered.

"He's lost it this time, that's what," DeBurke said.

"But that pilot saw *something* out there."

"There's nothing out there, Tony. Woody's seeing things," DeBurke grunted. "I'd bet my pension on it."

Tony's phone rang. "Scaperelli." He listened for several minutes while DeBurke played with a cigarette, flipping it into the air and trying to catch it between two fingers. Tony hung up, finished his notes and turned to his partner.

"You might find this interesting," Tony said. "That was a Phyllis McBride, runs a thrift shop on Forest. She wanted to know if we'd had any reports of stolen dive equipment."

"So far, not very interesting," said DeBurke, missing another catch.

"There were three men in her shop this afternoon, wanting to trade brand new wetsuits for second hand clothes. Said she could barely understand the one doing all the talking. She thought it sounded like Russian."

"Okay," DeBurke said. "Getting a little interesting. Go on."

"The suits had foreign writing inside and she thought it might have been the name of a fishing boat. The guys smelled a little ripe to her and since they took next to nothing in trade for new wetsuits, the whole thing smelled a little fishy to her. Pardon the pun."

"She get descriptions?" DeBurke asked, no longer playing with his cigarette.

Tony referred to his notes. "That's the best part. She said they left looking like a circus act. I've got it all here."

DeBurke waited for the "let's go talk to her" that he hoped wouldn't come.

Tony looked at his watch. "Let's pack it in for today. I'll check us out. We'll go see her tomorrow."

Relieved, DeBurke stuck the cigarette in his mouth and headed for the door.

The next morning, Tony and DeBurke were having their warmed-from-the-night-before morning coffee when Tony's phone rang.

"Sure . . . send him back." He looked at his partner. "Guess who?"

Woody walked back to where Tony and DeBurke were sitting. "You find 'em yet?"

"Not yet, Woody. Sit down," Tony said, pulling an empty chair over for him. "We have to talk about your Russians."

"So let's talk. How's the investigation going?"

"There is no investigation, technically. I haven't filed a formal report."

Woody looked hurt. "C'mon, Tony. I saw 'em! Twice!"

"You saw something . . . we're just not sure what yet," Tony said.

DeBurke's phone rang and he picked it up. He listened to the caller, then hung up and turned to Tony with a smirk.

"That was the Coast Guard," he said, smiling even broader. "Nothing at all on the water out there. Told ya."

"Coast Guard? What's that about?" Woody asked Tony, turning his back completely on DeBurke.

"A pilot reported seeing what might have been a slick outside the bay. They checked it out, but . . . nothing."

"You asked them to check it out because of what I told you?" Woody asked.

"Actually," Tony said, "DeBurke called it in."

"I'll bet he did," Woody sneered. "Only because if he hadn't, he'd have caught it from you, right?"

"We're just about to check out another possible lead on your guys," Tony said. "Wanna come?"

"What do you think?" Woody said. He was already on his way out of the office.

Tony and DeBurke had just pulled out in Tony's cruiser with Woody in the back seat when the radio squawked. "Go ahead, dispatch," Tony said into the handset.

"Sara called from The Grill, Tony," the woman's voice said from the speaker. "Some divers brought something up at Lovers Point beach that she thought you needed to see right away. I told her you were on a call but she said it might have something to do with what Woody saw the other night, so . . ."

"Ten-four, thanks," Tony said. He dropped the handset on the seat and headed for Lovers Point.

Sara motioned down toward the beach as the three men walked up to the window at The Grill. Tony saw a crowd of divers and others looking down at a dark shape on the sand. As he walked down the steps, Tony felt his stomach tighten. He'd seen some pretty gruesome things pulled out on that little beach. As he neared the knot of people, his nerves settled a little. He could see that the object of their curiosity wasn't a body, but a flattened inflatable, tangled with kelp. Woody had beaten him down the steps and stood with the crowd looking at the deflated boat.

"Who found this?" Tony asked.

"We did, officer," answered a young woman in a wetsuit. "It was caught in the kelp 150 yards out. We looked around, but there was nothing else there."

Tony knelt by the rubber boat and lifted one of the wrenches tied to the side lines. The writing on the wrenches was clearly not English. Tony ran his finger over the raised form of a star at the end of one of the handles.

"Looks Russian to me," Tony said.

DeBurke knelt beside his partner and picked up one of the wrenches. "I'll be damned."

"*Now* you believe me," Woody said, smiling down at the two officers.

"Gotta hand it to ya Woody," DeBurke said, brushing the sand off his hands. Woody only grunted, but the smile on his face grew even bigger.

"Let's get this thing into the car," Tony said. They rolled up the boat, hauled it up the stairs and wedged it into the trunk.

The three drove to the thrift shop and talked with Mrs. McBride, but the proprietor added little to the information she'd given on the phone the day before. Tony and DeBurke walked out of the store and DeBurke lit a cigarette. Tony looked back to see Woody standing in front of the full-length mirror at the back of the shop.

"They only want thirty dollars for 'em," Woody said, holding up one of the wetsuits and checking the length of the arms. "Can you loan me a twenty, Tony?"

"What would you do with a wetsuit, Woody? Put it back on the rack and c'mon. Some of us have work to do."

Woody didn't like the idea, but Tony finally convinced him that there was other police business to attend to and they dropped him in front of his house. "We're working on it, Woody," Tony said. "We put the descriptions out. They'll turn up. We'll call you."

"Well?" Helen said, as Woody closed the door and hung up his cap.

"They're here, all right," Woody said. "They did some shopping at the SPCA thrift store on Forest yesterday."

"Well heck," Helen said, "if they went shopping, how dangerous can they be? I don't know how they got here, but I just have a feeling they're trying to get away from a bad situation."

Woody nodded. "They did look like regular guys when I saw them at the park," he said. "I still think it's a little fishy, but you could be right."

"You know," Helen said, "they may want to stay in America. If they do, they'll need help."

"What are you suggesting?" Woody asked.

"I'm just saying, that if it turns out all they're trying to do is seek asylum, they might need a little help."

"And?" Woody said, raising his eyebrows.

"And . . . we could do it," Helen said, smiling.

"Not likely," Woody puffed.

"Why not? You found 'em," Helen said, tilting her head and smiling at her husband.

Woody folded his arms and whistled softly, *"That'll be the day . . ."*

Tony and DeBurke were almost back to the station when another call scratched through the radio. "Scaperelli," Tony said into the handset.

"Monterey located your be-on-the-lookout's walking toward PG from the aquarium on the rec trail."

"Ten-four, dispatch," Tony replied, looking over at Deburke who gave a quick shrug.

"Off we go," DeBurke said, as Tony gunned the cruiser toward Monterey.

As they approached the aquarium on Ocean View, moving parallel to the bay, they spotted three men walking on the trail below, heading back toward Pacific Grove. The colorfully-dressed trio virtually gleamed in the bright sunlight. Tony made a quick U-turn and moved ahead of the three, pulling to the curb around a curve on Ocean View.

The two officers made their way to the trail just as the three Russians came into view. The short one saw them first and stopped cold. The other two looked back, then spun forward, following his terrified stare. He started to run, but the heavy set one in the Mickey Mouse outfit grabbed his arm. They stood like statues as the two officers slowly walked toward them.

Tony and DeBurke tucked the three into the back seat of the cruiser without incident. As the car moved toward the station, Ivan, sandwiched in the middle, leaned toward Aleksei and said softly, "I hope you're right about not being shot."

Vladimir elbowed Ivan gently from the other side. "No firing squad, I think. They'll probably hang us."

Ivan groaned.

"Vladimir, be quiet!" Aleksei said to the mechanic. "This is no time for bad jokes."

"Some joke," Ivan said.

Aleksei continued, in a more subdued tone, talking only to Ivan. "We knew all along that sooner or later we'd have to go to the authorities. So . . . the authorities came to us first. Not so bad." He hoped that he had been able to keep his own misgivings out of his voice and he noticed that

Ivan had been calmed some by what he'd said. He looked over at Vladimir and, even though he was twenty-some years the mechanic's junior, gave him a stern "you behave" look.

Helen shook Woody awake. "Woody," she said excitedly, "it's Sergeant Tony."

Woody grabbed the phone. "Tony!" he said quickly, blinking sleep from his eyes. "What's . . . did you . . . wha, what?"

"Slow down, Woody," Tony said. "We picked up your Russians for questioning. I shouldn't be doing this, but what the hell, you want to meet 'em?"

"You bet your ass I do!"

"Woody, such language!" Helen said, stifling a laugh.

"I'm on my way," Woody said. "Thanks, Tony." He hung up the phone and grabbed Helen, giving her a big hug and a quick kiss on top of her head.

"Oh, for goodness sakes," she said, with exaggerated impatience.

Aleksei sat dejectedly on the hard wooden chair, contemplating the decision he'd made aboard the *Borscht*. It had been just a few days ago, but an entire world apart from the small interrogation cell he found himself in now. He'd just finished giving a statement to the police with the aid of an interpreter. The woman had thanked him for his cooperation, collected her papers and recorder and left to talk with the others. He was alone in the room and the pale green walls began to close in on him. A sour wad formed in his stomach and the coffee he'd been given after being brought in was only adding to the caustic mix creeping toward his throat.

Tony and DeBurke were standing outside the interrogation room when Woody arrived.

"Well, well," DeBurke said," if it isn't *Detective* Woodall."

Tony laughed.

"Got 'em, huh?" Woody said to Tony, as he joined the two men.

"Yup," Tony said, tossing his paper cup into the trash. "You were right, Woody, they are absolutely Russian."

"I knew it," Woody said, chest swelling.

"But you were wrong about the invasion," DeBurke interjected.

"Oh?" Woody said, turning to acknowledge the officer for the first time.

"That so?"

DeBurke fiddled with an unlit cigarette. "They were on a submarine, you know."

"That right?" Woody said, totally absorbed now by what DeBurke was saying.

DeBurke nodded. "Ran completely out of supplies, diesel, food, water, everything. The rest of the crew abandoned ship onto a supply vessel out there somewhere, but these guys were sleeping one off and missed the boat, so to speak. They got the empty sub in somehow, sunk it outside the bay and rowed ashore. That's when you saw them. They say they want to stay in America . . . say they've had it with the homeland."

Woody grinned. "Well, I'll be."

DeBurke flipped the cigarette into the air and caught it in his mouth. "Need a smoke," he said and left Tony and Woody standing alone in the hall.

"Congratulations, Woody," Tony said. "Good work." Woody was smiling too broadly to form any kind of reply. "Immigration and the Army are on their way, so we don't have much time. You ready?" Tony asked, looking up and down the hall.

"Sure," Woody was able to say finally.

Tony opened the door and they entered a small conference room. Woody saw the tall young man in a Monterey Bay Aquarium sweatshirt sitting in a straight-backed chair behind the square table in the center of the room. The young man looked up alertly, first at Tony, then at Woody. A frown flicked across his face when he saw Woody, but he sat still, folding his hands on the table in front of him.

"This is Aleksei Ivanov," Tony said. "He's sort of the spokesman for the group."

"I saw you at the park," Woody said, looking down at the man. He sat opposite Aleksei and something about the bearing of the young man struck Woody as familiar. The stranger held himself gracefully erect and his alert blue eyes met Woody's evenly. In an odd way, he reminded Woody of himself in an earlier time. "You were in a submarine, they tell me," Woody said, trying to draw the man out of his silence. The two stared at each other for a long minute before Aleksei spoke.

"You are police?" he asked in a clear, strong voice.

"This is Clarence Woodall, Mr. Ivanov," Tony interjected. "He saw you come ashore and he's been helping us catch up with you."

Woody smiled at Tony's words. He couldn't remember a time when his association with the Pacific Grove PD had ever been characterized as "help."

"They also tell me that you three want to stay in this country," Woody continued, still trying to open the stranger's shell. Aleksei turned his eyes to Tony, then back to Woody.

"Da . . . yes," he said softly. "We want only to stay in America. But . . ." He looked around the room, then began to study his hands.

The door opened and a young uniformed officer looked in. "The INS guys are here and a couple of Army types just parked outside," he said to Tony.

Tony tapped Woody on the shoulder. "Time to go."

They stood in the hallway as Aleksei was led away by the young officer. Aleksei looked back at Woody and their eyes met again. Woody couldn't understand why he was beginning to feel so strongly about the fate of this young man and his friends.

Tony looked at his watch. "Hey, look," he said. "It's lunch time. Got any plans?"

Woody watched the tall stranger until he turned the corner at the end of the hall. He looked back at Tony blankly. "What?"

"Want to grab some lunch?" Tony suggested, holding up his arm and tapping his wristwatch with his finger.

"Oh, sure, yeah," Woody said.

"Where?"

"Fine, that'd be fine," Woody mumbled.

"Woody, are you with me here?" Tony said, chuckling.

"Yeah, I'm with you," Woody said, finally focusing on Tony.

"Good," Tony said. "I'm hungry. You up for another one of Sara's cheeseburgers?"

"Sure, let's go," Woody said, pulling his thoughts back into the present.

Tony and Woody sat at the end of one of the gray tables on the patio of The Grill. A few high clouds spread across the sky and the sounds of children playing on the beach below rose on the gentle breeze. The Grill was crowded now with tourists and locals enjoying the day. Tony smiled at Woody, his eyes twinkling.

"What!" Woody said, not used to seeing his friend so unabashedly happy.

"Nothing," Tony said. "You've softened a bit on the subject of Russian invaders since yesterday is all."

"Yeah, maybe so," Woody agreed. "What'll happen to those three?"

"Not sure. My guess is they'll probably just be sent home. Haven't really broken any local laws, if you don't count polluting the bay."

"What would it take for them to be able to stay?" Woody asked after a moment's thought.

"I'm not an expert, but I guess they'd need somebody to help them work through all the immigration hassles. I don't know that part of the law." Tony noticed the peculiar look on Woody's face. "Where are you going with this?"

"It's Helen's idea, really," Woody said. "At first, I thought it was pure foolishness. But now, after talking with one of 'em . . . I don't know. I'm thinking maybe Helen's right, we could, you know . . . help 'em."

Tony shook his head and laughed. "That's quite a turnaround, pal."

"Guess it is," Woody sighed. "But it seems like the right thing. Do you think there's anything we can do?"

"Beats me," Tony said, still shaking his head and laughing. "If you want, I'll check with INS and find out if it's even worth trying."

"That'd be good," Woody said.

"Order up, Tony," Sara called from the window.

As Tony approached the counter, Sara leaned forward on her elbows. "You sure look happier than the last time I saw you," she said.

"I'm feeling pretty good. I've made a couple of decisions and it's good to get the load off my mind."

"What'd ya decide?"

"Number one, how'd you like to have dinner tonight?"

She stood up straight and put her hands on her hips. For a moment, Tony couldn't read her expression. "What time?" she said with a wink.

Tony tried to keep the excitement out of his voice. "Seven?"

"See you at seven," Sara said. "What's number two?"

"I'll tell you tonight," he said and picked up the bags.

"How's Woody?"

"He's doin' good," Tony said. "We caught up with his Russians this morning and now he wants to help 'em stay in the country."

"Wow!" Sara said, then added, "Seven?"

"Seven," Tony answered.

The Grill's little eating area was packed, so Tony suggested they take their lunch up the recreation trail. They ended up sitting on the bench where Woody was sitting when the whole thing started.

"You know, Woody," Tony said after they'd eaten, "you and I have known each other for a long time." He let the statement hang in the air.

"Yeah, we have," Woody replied.

"And we've worked on several things together over the years."

"Yeah . . . we have," Woody said again. He began to wonder where his friend was going with all this sappy reminiscing. "What are you getting at?"

Tony was quiet for a time, then said, "I've been thinking of makin' a change myself. You know I've been kinda working toward Lieutenant for a while now."

"Yeah?"

"Well, it doesn't look like that's in the cards for me, Woody."

"So what?" Woody said. "Everybody likes you in the department. You're the best cop they got and you know it."

"Next month I have 25 years with the department. I think that's enough, don't you?"

"What . . . you're going to *retire*?" Woody said, turning to face his friend.

"Well, yes and no," Tony said.

"What's *that* supposed to mean?" Woody said. "What am I going to do without you in the department? My God! I may have to deal with that idiot, Fowler!" Woody put his head in his hands and bent to rest his arms on his knees. "I guess I could work with DeBurke, but . . . oh, man, Tony . . . are you sure you want to do this?"

Tony patted Woody on the back. "I wouldn't exactly be quitting the business altogether," he said.

"What are you trying to say?" Woody asked, looking sideways at Tony.

"A friend of mine has a small private detective agency in San Jose. Remember Harrison?"

Woody nodded, straightening on the bench. "Yeah, I do . . . short, red hair, good man. Retired from the department a few years ago, right?"

"That's him. Anyway, his business has grown. He's doing work from San Francisco to King City now and he can't handle it alone anymore. He's asked me to come in with him."

Woody didn't know whether to be happy for his old friend, or miserable for himself. The idea of not seeing Sergeant Tony anymore felt like a knife in his stomach. "Well, I guess that's good for you," he said finally.

Tony could hear the disappointment in Woody's voice. "That brings me to the second thing I wanted to talk to you about." Woody turned curiously toward him again. "I'm going to be covering the southern end of the business, from Moss Landing down to Big Sur, but a lot of the work will be right here in our backyard . . . Monterey, PG, Pebble, Carmel . . ."

"Sounds like you'll be pretty busy," Woody said, slipping deeper into his gloom.

"That's what I'm getting at, Woody," Tony said. "I'm going to need an assistant, from time to time. Somebody I can trust. Somebody with good powers of observation. Somebody like you, Woody."

"What, Tony? You want me to work with you . . . officially?"

"From time to time," Tony said, smiling at the look on Woody's face. "You up to it?"

"Ha!" Woody laughed and clapped his hands on his knees. "Well, I'll be . . ." He stood up and walked back and forth in front of the bench rubbing his hands together.

"Is that a 'yes'?" Tony asked. He'd never seen Woody so animated.

"Hell yes, it's a 'yes'!" Woody said. "Partner!"

Ralph jumped as Woody slammed the front door and threw his cap in the general direction of the peg. Helen, curled on the chaise in the small patio behind their kitchen, looked up from her book as Woody almost skipped out of the back door. He knelt beside the chaise and gave his wife a big kiss, knocking her glasses onto her lap.

"What in the world's gotten into you?" she said, patting her hair back and straightening her sweater.

"You'll never guess," Woody said, "so I'll just tell ya." He slid a chair over next to the chaise and sat down. "Tony's quittin' the department. Retiring next month."

Helen couldn't understand the connection between the news she'd just heard and the silly grin on Woody's face. "And that makes you happy?" she asked.

"That's just the half of it. The best part is he's going to work for Harrison as a private eye. He'll be working right around here mostly and he wants me to be his assistant . . . now and then, you know. Isn't that something?"

Ralph moseyed out to the patio to see what the fuss was about and Woody grabbed him up into a warm, but totally unwelcome cuddle. He put the struggling cat down and Ralph blinked at him indignantly before starting to casually groom his hindquarters.

"I think that's wonderful," Helen said. "What about the Russians?"

"Huh? Oh! The Russians, heh, heh, almost forgot about them. I met one, the leader, I think. Aleksei's his name. Looked like a nice, quiet guy. Has smart eyes, you know what I mean?"

Without waiting for Helen's reply, Woody continued. "Tony says he'll check with INS to see if there's anything we can do to help." He sat back in the chair, grinning.

"Well, well. This has been a busy day for you, hasn't it?" Helen said. "Sounds like we're going to have our hands full, what with your being a part-time detective now and the two of us maybe getting your new Russian friends settled. Isn't it funny how things work out?"

"It'll be different," Woody said. He went into the kitchen and opened the refrigerator, bending at the waist to peer inside.

Helen couldn't quite place the tune Woody had started to whistle. She smiled and turned back to her book. Ralph flopped down on the patio and yawned.

About the Author

KEN JONES moved to the Monterey Peninsula in March of 2001, after retiring from the Boeing Company. He and his wife, Southern California natives, felt a growing attraction to the Central Coast for many years, which became too powerful to resist during a visit in the fall of '99. Ken's working career involved a great deal of technical and business writing, but he began writing for pleasure in 1985, focusing mainly on short story fiction. Ken is an active member of the California Writers Club as well as several other area writers groups. He and his wife, Anne, live in Pacific Grove with their deaf, one-eyed cat Lucky.

Resurrected

by Chris Kemp

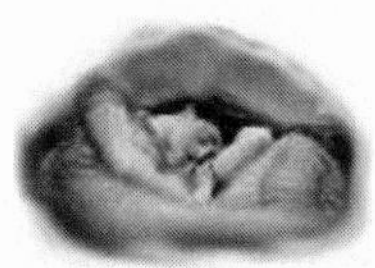

Last Indian summer, in that pristine template of a city, Pacific Grove, I awoke to my destiny. It was like being pushed out of bed into a tub of ice-cold water, but I'm okay with it now.

I think.

A series of sometimes infuriating events led up to this reckoning, beginning a few months earlier in my hometown of Palo Pacifica. That's when my mother, Rosalind, began to suffer from—for lack of a better term—chronic fatigue syndrome.

Her timing proved particularly inconvenient for me. Out of economic necessity I had returned home to live with my family after college graduation, hoping the arrangement to be temporary. But Mom's condition changed all that since it spelled potential calamity for our family.

I'm not overstating the case. You see, Mom practices the preternatural arts as often and as casually as a maid makes beds. It's a unique circumstance that distinctly colors family life, one of the more prominent hues being paranoia. If the good folk of Palo Pacifica ever learned what went on in our house, we'd be tarred and feathered, burned at the stake, or at the very least buried in lawsuits.

Very stressful, not to mention our fear of discovery grows each day. Dad and I may be garden-variety human beings, but my twelve-year-old brother (Joe) and eight-year-old twin sisters (Ann and Elizabeth) have inherited certain "gifts" from their mother. She's managed to keep them in check so far, but like most kids their age, they lack self-control. You have to assume that it's only a matter of time until they attract unwanted attention (at best) or wreak widespread havoc (at worst).

So when Mom began to burn out it was damn serious, not like in most households where long-term exhaustion means Mommy stays in bed past noon, shirks household duties and wanders the halls like a housecoatted zombie. No, in our house, things just . . . went wrong. The garbage disposal oozed an odious, viscous liquid. A neighborhood dog began to mew like a cat. A salesman's shoes spontaneously combusted as he walked (then ran) past our house.

Mom didn't mean to do any of it. She was like a nuclear power plant with a compromised containment structure. Unfortunately, lapses like these could only lead to unwanted attention and eventual persecution.

Unless we did something fast.

In a measure of the gravity of the situation, Dad—who would rather stick his head in an oven than associate with Mom's side of the family—contacted her older brother, the enigmatic Phineas Biggs.

Dad especially keeps his distance from Mom's self-appointed mentor. My Uncle Phineas is a shaggy man with—how shall I put this?—a different set of priorities. His raggedy clothes, questionable hygiene and fiery gaze make him more than a little unnerving. Not to mention his predilection for disappearing months at a time to live on the streets. He's so different from Mom—who goes ballistic if she finds a hair out of place—I sometimes wonder if the two are related.

But there's no arguing that Phineas is a powerful man and since he taught Mom most of the things she knows, for the greater good of the family Dad put his misgivings aside . . .

. . . and left me alone without warning the day Phineas came over to discuss Mom's condition.

I could have killed my father, and not just because my uncle's words and actions are as difficult to decipher as an ancient Lemurian tome. Discussing Mom's welfare was the last thing I wanted to do; after a summer at home my relationship with her had reached an all-time low.

That it had sunk to new depths was no mean feat. After all, I'm normal, she's not, and while a hint of dysfunction flavors most mother-daughter relationships, it had long saturated ours.

But commencing with my return from University, the friction between us intensified. True, I had lived with the shackles of the uncanny and the weight of the weird most of my life, but its full heft didn't seem all that burdensome until I came back. Mom's mastery over her Craft had grown, her arrogance and insufferability proportionally so. The distance between us yawned wider than ever before.

Mostly she was unavailable, busy with the kids or pouring over texts or practicing some fantastic discipline. When we did interact, conversation flowed in one direction: from her to me. Hands on hips, chest out, standing tall in one of the flowing dresses she favored, she would pontificate on a variety of subjects: how I should vote, whom I should date, where to look for a job.

Given that no one had less of a clue about the realities of everyday living, I found such advice laughable and useless. Mom might be able to heal a pulled muscle with her touch, or cast a pesky ghost out of the attic, or whip up a tasty treat to turn a child's nightmares into sweet dreams, but she was all thumbs when it came to dealing with me, her most ordinary daughter. If I told her she didn't understand me, she simply replied, "Ariel, that's the way you see it."

After an entire summer of this, I tried to avoid her whenever possible, a challenge given that she seldom left the house. Destined to be somewhat of a homebody because her powers are charged by a stable home environment, Mom would at least make sure she balanced this predisposition with regular turns of outside activity and exercise. But that was before her condition, and by autumn she had become a constant and palpable presence in the house, upping the tension between us significantly . . .

. . . and now here I was in the den, an unwilling participant in what I supposed would be a plan for Mom's future.

My uncle and I sat in the muted light of the diminishing day. Phineas had gotten my younger siblings out of the way by passing them through to an alternate reality (comparable to a trip to Disneyland for most kids) and had securely ensconced Mom in her bedroom with a containment hex that absorbed her angry cries of protest. He now slurped, with great gusto, a cup of noodles I had fetched him, downing the last of the broth out of the container and ripping loose a belch potent enough to peel the paint from the walls. After that he squatted motionless on the couch, or should I say on the sheet I spread over the couch to shield it from his oily brown overcoat.

For an eternity I twisted and turned on the recliner, its squeaking springs the only sound in the room. Finally he spoke, vocal cords dragged over broken glass.

"Thanks fer goin' on this trip with yer mom."

It was a mortar shot, complete news to me. "Huh?" was the best I could manage.

"Ya dint know? She needs time away t'fix her up. It's all arranged. Little town named Pacific Grove's got jest what she needs. But you gotta go with."

My stomach clenched. It felt like a granite block. I strung some words together. "What . . . do . . . you . . . mean?"

He shifted in his seat and regarded me with a focusless gaze. Looking into it was like spiraling down an 80-foot drop.

"Now don't go worryin' nun, Sweet Pea."

I wanted to protest but didn't, intimidated more than I wanted to admit. With a gargantuan effort, I managed a question.

"Why me? I don't know anything about you . . . special people. Especially ones with shot nerves. I'd be useless."

He looked around the room like he forgot where he was. Then he came back.

"Nah. Jest get her there and don't worry 'bout nothin'. Life's wheel'll be crankin', turnin'. That'll be enough."

Enough? Not even close. The stone in my stomach cracked and trickles of panic leaked out. I gripped the armrests hard and gaped at the dark TV screen, taking in the rich scent of eastern spices permeating the room (a conjure Phineas uses to mask his body's odor—never mind that his manner and appearance remain steadfastly unkempt!)

My uncle shut his eyes and kept them shut. Was he snoring? I became acutely aware of the grandfather clock ticking in the corner. It ticked and ticked, louder and louder, until I couldn't stand it.

"Uncle, this idea is insane! Mother and I don't get along! At all!"

He opened his eyes halfway like he was trying to make out who I was. Then he laughed so hard he started to shake. Before long, the laughing had turned into a coughing fit.

"That's where ya got it all wrong," he said after clearing his throat and wiping his mouth with the back of his hand. "She'll take right to the trip if she knows yer goin'."

I rubbed my temples. He used his tongue to flick away a drop of soup from his yellow-gray mustache. The man could not, or would not, see that my relationship with my mother was dead; a burned-out cinder. Though I'd said only a handful of words, I felt wrung out.

Seconds, minutes or hours passed before he got up and shuffled toward the hallway door, head bent forward. Before he exited, he stopped and put his hand to his brow like he had just remembered something. Then he turned and said, "Oh, yeah. Pacific Grove's got what yew need, too."

Further details failed to surface and no one seemed to care. I didn't put up a long, hard fight due to a number of factors. First, Phineas had given us less than 24 hours to prepare and the rush of events overwhelmed me—like white water having its way with a cast-over rafter.

Second, alternatives didn't exist. Phineas' delusion that I could catalyze Mom's well-being and his infuriating lack of specifics regarding the mandatory sabbatical were worrisome ("you'll jest know when t'come back"), but maintaining the status quo was unthinkable.

Third, Mom didn't kick and scream when informed of the plan, likely due to a lack of available options and her reluctance to cross her older brother—one of the few beings capable of neutralizing her powers for finite periods (which he did in the brief time leading up to our departure).

So never mind that we didn't get along and that Mom had never functioned for an extended period of time without powers and that no instructions were provided.

We were going to Pacific Grove and that was that.

Phineas stuck around the Palo Pacifica Airport until we were in the air, at which time Mom's powers became a moot point since they are bound to the earth. For the short duration of the flight, she brooded in her window seat, looked down at the billowy floor of cloud, ate nothing and said less.

I managed to relax, even dozed for a few moments, but after we landed, in the short time it took to grab our bags and wind our way to the front of the airport, apprehension began to scrape at my spine.

There weren't many people about, and a solitary cab, trunk open, waited at the curb. The driver, a few years older than me in his mid-twenties, stood next to it as if he'd been expecting us. His yellow print Hawaiian shirt, curly blond hair and flaxen goatee complemented his cab's exterior and contrasted with his deep tan. Pretty cute, actually, but I didn't have time for that.

He smiled broadly, wordlessly took our bags and placed them in the trunk before moving around to open the door. As Mom slid into the backseat, she uttered her first words of the trip.

"This cab smells like a toilet!" She frowned, holding her fingers to her nose. "He smokes cigars in here. Ugh!"

Before I could slide out in embarrassment, the driver bounced in behind the wheel, turned and smiled.

"Sorry, ma'am?" he said, cupping his hand to his ear, blue eyes twinkling.

"Isn't there some kind of ordinance that prohibits you from smoking those disgusting cigars on the job! Ariel, I shouldn't have to put up with this!"

But she crossed her arms and made no move to leave.

The driver shut his door. "Ma'am," he replied, "I would never *dream* of smoking cigars." He adjusted the ID photo hanging on his dashboard, which showed him smiling broadly—as broadly as one could with a cigar propped in his mouth. The words "William Wilson" appeared below his face in black block letters.

"Anyplace in particular, ladies?" William Wilson inquired.

"The Centrella, please," I instructed.

As the cab eased its way out of the airport, Mom asked me if it was my idea to let Phineas make the arrangements. "My God," she said, "the man lives in a cardboard box half the time!"

"Like I had a choice." I opened my purse, hand burrowing for a piece of gum. "You wouldn't say that to his face," I added.

"I would."

"You wouldn't."

She sighed. "Ariel! I assure you I would! Why do you think he imprisoned me the day he met with you? He didn't want any part of *my* opinions!"

I caught William Wilson's reflected stare in the rearview mirror and figured it was time to drop the subject. Soon after, Mom grew restless, twisting the ends of her long white-streaked black hair, pulling at the sleeves of her Hensley top. She rubbed her cheek, then down low and out of sight, tried to initiate a minor hex of some sort, tracing an invisible circle in the air with her index finger, then jabbing its center. When nothing happened she balled her hands into fists, struck her thighs lightly and grimaced. I found her frustration satisfying.

Welcome to my world.

Densely packed pines lined each side of the wide road we traveled, just like they did back home. The surroundings felt more familiar than they should have, which intensified the tingling that ran up and down the center of my back. I tried to ignore it.

"Don't worry, you'll like the Centrella," William Wilson reassured us. Had he been talking the entire time? "It's a charming, historical Victorian."

Mom arched an eyebrow. "'Charming' and 'historical' being euphemisms for 'old' and 'weathered'?"

"Don't pay attention to my mom, William," I intervened. "She's been a little . . . stressed lately."

"Billy—call me Billy—and don't worry," he said, "a stay in Pacific Grove does wonders for your nerves."

"Well, excuse me, but I didn't ask . . . *Billy*," Mom said. "And Ariel, I can certainly speak for myself, thank you." Again she crossed her arms, wearing the face of a petulant child.

Billy turned on the radio. A country "singer" cawed about waking up and seeing double. Mom decided to continue the conversation. "You know, Ariel, arrogance doesn't suit you."

"I didn't ask, Mother. Or to put it in your words: 'that's what *you* think.'"

Billy turned up the radio. The cab merged onto a highway. I tried to glimpse snatches of surrounding civilization through treetops and branches while Mom, evidently bored with me, resumed gestures and motions of enchantment behind the seat, each an exercise in futility.

At a sign that read "Pacific Grove/Pebble Beach" we exited the freeway. Which is when the sun vanished. One minute crisp, autumn light bathed us; the next a wet cocoon of fog consumed us, visibility a few yards at best.

Dampness preyed on the car, threatening to creep inside as we wound our way on a curvy stretch of road. Solid white faced us down in every direction. Mom wrapped her shawl tightly around her. Billy didn't seem bothered.

"I'm used to this," he chuckled.

"It's like someone dropped a bale of cotton on us," I replied.

"Think cotton *candy,*" he offered, "and you'll feel better. Anyway, chances are this'll disappear as fast as it came in."

I rubbed my neck and closed my eyes, the lids of which suddenly felt heavy. The onset of drowsiness seemed odd, given my general state of agitation, but I know I must have slept because the next thing I remember is the cab out in the sunshine again. I opened my eyes just in time to see a sign. It read:

Welcome to Pacific Grove, Butterfly Town, U.S.A.

I wondered exactly what a "Butterfly Town" might be, as I took a few moments to get my bearings. I never did, though, because the vista coming into view wouldn't allow it. I, Ariel Smith, have seen many unbelievable things in my time. Some (my mother) have called me jaded. But what lay before me made me stare in disbelief: Pacific Grove looked just like my hometown of Palo Pacifica.

And it didn't.

I nudged Mom, who had fallen asleep, too. "Look at this!" I cried.

Her eyelids fluttered before springing open, at which time she leaned forward, stared ahead and soundlessly formed her mouth into a small "o".

The landscape and geography looked identical to Palo Pacifica, including the body of water that filled the horizon. The streets were configured in the exact same grid and, from what we could see, of identical length and width.

What covered the surface, however, differed greatly. The A&W Root Beer stand at the edge of town was a French bakery here. A fitness center thrived where our Sizzler would be. A set of non-descript commercial buildings took the place of "Fast Food Row". Where I expected to find a court of small cottages lay a half-occupied shopping center.

"This is unbelievable!" uttered Mom.

"Sure is," Billy enthusiastically agreed. "I told you Pacific Grove is one-of-a-kind."

We traveled down a generously proportioned street that sloped lazily toward whatever body of water spread before us. Forest Avenue here, back home we called it Broad Street. A nice enough thoroughfare in Palo Pacifica, here it could only be described as sterile. No kids playing on the sidewalks, no toys on the lawn, no pedestrians visible—like someone had vacuumed the life out of the street.

Mom turned to me. "I can't believe my eyes!"

"And it's only the residential area," Billy chirped.

"Doesn't look like *anyone* resides here," Mom stated.

"Norman Rockwell re-invents Palo Pacifica," I whispered.

By the time we reached the heart of downtown, a drive of a few minutes, curiosity replaced disorientation. We now saw neatly attired, proper-looking people scattered along the sidewalks, a pastel pastiche of faces, many of retirement age and older. The streets and buildings seemed to have been scrubbed clean. The whole thing struck me as a living Fifties TV show—minus the children and teenagers—someone's idealized interpretation of small-town America.

Where Palo Pacifica had neighborhood taverns, an outdoor magazine stand, an auto parts store and a Sears catalog outlet, Pacific Grove boasted antique shops, specialty furniture stores, insurance agents and real estate offices. When Forest Avenue ran into Lighthouse Avenue—our Main Street—the contrast continued. No Woolworth's, no "Ralph's Buy and Trade", no Nickerson's Cafeteria. Just fancy florists, boutiques, more antique stores and corner cafes that looked like they belonged on a movie studio back lot.

We turned left onto Lighthouse. Billy slowed to obey the painful 15-mile per hour speed limit. To my surprise, Mom said, "Pull over, driver."

Finding an open nose-in parking spot adjacent to a furniture store that looked like a museum, Billy pulled in, easing the cab carefully between two other cars. Mom ordered me out. I bristled at the command, but only for a moment.

Too much happening, too fast.

I joined her on the sidewalk. "I don't know what that brother of mine is up to," she said, "but don't you think it would be fascinating to see what passes for you and me in this town?"

Fascinating? I was stunned. Mom hadn't shown this kind of curiosity in months. Too bad it was ill-advised.

"No," I stated. "Seeking out our doubles doesn't sound fascinating or even intelligent. What if it's like one of those science fiction stories where matter meets anti-matter and both cease to exist?"

"Such an imagination!" she exclaimed, straightening her posture. I thought she might begin lecturing me, but what I heard was worse.

"Whatever corresponds to our house on the corner of I Street and Main," she persisted, "can't be more than a half-mile that way." She pointed down Lighthouse opposite of the direction we had been traveling. "Maybe we've been sent here to see 'us'."

"Is that so? And what do you think our doubles will say when they catch a glimpse of us?" I asked. "I can't imagine *that* would be a scene. In case you forgot, you came here to relax, not go on some stupid and dangerous adventure."

"I didn't say we wouldn't be careful," Mom snapped. "For someone who's always complaining about the dulling effects of home life, I should think you'd jump at an opportunity for some intrigue."

I looked around. Familiar faces I couldn't quite place flowed by. Slicked up, sartorial versions of people I knew looked right through me.

"See?" said Mom. "They don't know you from Abdul-Alhazred. We're anonymous."

"For now."

"We'll stay in the car. Until we know it's safe."

"Mom, it's not like you have anything extra at your disposal here to get us out of trouble. You're away from home. Remember?"

"I'm *extremely* aware of it."

"I think I liked you better when you were burned out."

She frowned. I leaned against the front of the cab. I had always pictured Mom without powers as weak, withdrawn, and ready to hole up somewhere. Instead she seemed shot from a cannon and ready to take on the world—well, this world, at least. It might have meant that the trip was already working, in which case I should have been happy. But I only felt jittery—needles and pins under my skin.

Without warning Mom returned to the cab and got in. I followed, entering on the other side. "Driver, change of plans," she said. "Make a U-turn. We want to look around before we go to the hotel. Some of those 'charming' neighborhoods you mentioned suddenly sound quite interesting."

"Yes, ma'am!" Billy exclaimed while backing out. "U-turns are illegal, but . . . "

He swerved around and began to crawl down Lighthouse squeezing the cab between long rows of angled-in parking. This civil engineering nightmare likely prompted the excruciatingly slow speed limit; you never knew who might rocket backwards into you, or when.

As we approached Lighthouse and Ninth, closing in on whatever substituted for our neighborhood, it became evident that development did not thin out here as it did in Palo Pacifica, where commercial structures and homes gave way to an expanse of shallow rolling hills leading up to a dark line of vegetation at their summit. Instead, houses blanketed the area, squeezed next to each other like boxes in a pantry.

Amidst them rose a plain-looking church of pinkish stone. Nothing much to look at, except that it sat squarely on the corner, a position precisely parallel to the three-story Victorian with shuttered windows and peeling paint in Palo Pacifica that we called home.

"Turn left," Mom ordered. To my dismay she added, "and pull over."

Billy smoothly executed the order and the cab rolled down Ninth, coming to rest in front of a low-slung brick house, painted the same pinkish-brown color as the church across the street.

She flung open her door and got out. "Let's look around."

I flung open mine and stood to face her across the cab's roof. "Is this what you call 'being careful'!"

"Then stay in the car," she hissed.

"I will," I said. "You're obsessed!"

Behind us, a door clicked open and a strange yet familiar voice rang out. "Ann, I thought that was you!"

We turned. A smiling man of medium height and indeterminate age peered at us from the doorway of the house: Palo Pacifica's mayor and one of Dad's few cronies, Matt Nelson. Except it wasn't Matt Nelson. This man was a priest, his white collar plainly visible under his rumpled navy blue pullover.

"Well, this is quite a surprise!" he said in a warm, engaging voice. He closed the door behind him and stepped forward, a chilly breeze tossing his longish blond hair. "I never thought I'd see you again. When did you get in from New York?"

Mom went with it. "Why, just now," she said. A unique blend of relief and horror flowed through me.

The priest passed by me to cross in front of the cab, leaving a trace of cheap aftershave in his wake. He cast a brief, puzzled glance my way before walking up to Mom and hugging her. She stiffened for a moment, arms limp at her sides, then her ego beat back her uncertainty: she returned the hug. Though only an act, it had been a long time since I'd seen her greet anyone that warmly—with the exception of my younger siblings.

"You must have come to see the fruits of your labors," the priest stated.

"Of course," she proclaimed.

He made a sweeping gesture with his arm toward the other side of the street. "Well it's all waiting for you down in Immaculate Conception Hall. Let's go."

He put his arm around her. Mom hated being touched by strangers, but not here. She glanced back at me, but I couldn't read her. The priest turned, too.

"I'm sorry," he said as if his car had run over my foot. "I didn't introduce myself. I'm Father Patrick O'Flaherty."

My mind locked tight; cognition out of the realm of possibilities. I simply extended my hand and blurted, "Jane, Ann's friend."

Doubt clouded his face before rapidly dissipating. "Is that so?" he said, a glint of something in the sharp grayness of his eyes. "Well, that's one special friend you've got there. Come on down and see her creation. There's lots of God's love going 'round."

"In a minute," I replied.

He guided Mom across the street to the church. Viewed from the middle of the block, it took on a different aspect. From the front, the church appeared to be at ground level—an illusion caused by the sharp decline of Ninth Street toward the water. In reality, the building had a bottom story accessible from the rear, which I assumed housed the parish hall. A large parking lot spread out from the back of the edifice. A few cars and three small buses—similar to those used by rental car companies—were visible.

Several older women milled around the lot, colorfully dressed in reds and teals, their white hair glistening in the sun. When they saw the priest and his "friend" moving toward them, they became animated, waving and shouting greetings.

"Ann!"

"Sakes alive!"

"You're back! What a grand surprise!"

Too much. I flopped backward through the cab door and onto the seat. I lay supine, throwing both arms across my face, feeling like I had been held underwater for an extended period of time.

The cab stopped idling. The music stopped, too.

"You okay?" Billy asked.

"Yeah. Fine." The breeze carried faint voices from the parking lot.

"Why'd you call yourself her friend?" The driver asked. "Aren't you her daughter?"

I sat up way too fast for someone discouraging attention.

"Pardon me?"

Billy laughed. "I shouldn't be getting all in your business. My bad."

"Sure is," I said rather weakly as a mob of three elderly women converged on Father O'Flaherty and Mom. They looked ready to pull out autograph books and pencils. I clearly heard their squeals of delight.

Father O'Flaherty disengaged himself from the trio who then swept Mom away toward an open door and disappeared inside.

"I've turned off my meter," Billy offered.

"I'm so proud of you."

"Hey, be nice. I'm just saying you can hang out here for awhile until you feel like joining her."

"Where did you get the idea I was going to join her?"

"Sounds like she did something great. Don't you want to check it out?"

"Maybe I just want to stay here and collect my thoughts."

"Whatever."

I lay down again, this time on my side, and drew my knees toward my stomach. Who was this guy, anyway? Cute or not, he had a lot of nerve.

I shut my eyes. Seems I had spent a ton of time and energy at home unsuccessfully avoiding the supernatural, only to find myself in the middle of something as nerve-wracking here. It couldn't be that bad. Phineas set it up. But who knew? Phineas was half deranged. At least!

Thoughts fluttered away for a while, then came back. Billy was droning on when they did:

". . . because, you know, if *my* mom or friend or whatever did something special, I'd be right there."

"Okay, Billy," I sighed. "I get it. I'll go down there, if only to get away from your voice!"

Harsh words, but my sanctimonious driver didn't need to know that I'd concluded, upon waking, that it might be better to see what I was up against. I vaulted out of the cab and started across the street.

"I'll wait," he called after me.

I didn't argue. Though annoying, Billy didn't unnerve me like the rest of Pacific Grove. I almost liked the thought of having him around.

My watch revealed that almost an hour had passed. Had I really dozed off that long? The revelation stirred up earlier forebodings, which grew stronger with each step away from the cab. I wasn't Mom. I wasn't full enough of myself to march into the unknown with nary a second thought. Besides, her double might be 3,000 miles away, but what about mine? The concept of another "me" wasn't fascinating—it creeped me out. And the way that priest kept looking at me . . .

Damn you, Mom!

Still, here I was, first descending the stairs to the parking lot and then in full view of the parish hall, its front wall a mosaic of clear glass panes. Through it, I saw dark figures moving.

I stopped. Dead leaves tumbled by, rustling around my feet, when—not again!—that priest came through the door, marching toward me like a freshly wound mechanical man.

Up close the character lines in his face belied his humanity. "Ann's divorce was a tough one," he said. "I'm frankly shocked to see her here."

"She never talks about it," I said, hoping to keep the exchange to a minimum.

"Well, I guess if *I* fought long and hard to help these poor souls—not to mention getting the city to let us help them—I'd want to come back, too," he said. "Despite the painful memories. That's one tenacious and blessed friend you've got there."

An awkward silence followed. He must have felt it.

"Got to run," he offered breathlessly. "Great meeting you."

My turn for a hug. When he pulled away, he placed his hands firmly on my shoulders and fixed his eyes squarely in mine. "You sure I haven't met you?"

"No. No way." Water. I needed a glass of water.

He smiled absently, then jogged off and up the stairs. Grinding my teeth, I braced myself and resumed walking toward the parish hall. Entering through the door from which the priest had exited, I crossed the threshold, got popped by a small burst of heat, and found myself in a plain-walled shallow anteroom that ran the width of the building. Pictures of Jesus and the saints hung from the walls. Several weathered, disheveled men set up long rows of tables and chairs, helped by one or two guys who looked as if they had driven right off a golf course. A few women, dressed in casual quality, moved throughout, covering table surfaces with orange and brown paper tablecloths, place settings, small pumpkins and other autumnal decorations.

No one noticed me, so I kept moving toward a doorway that led to another room. Someone cooked; you could tell from the smell: dishwater minestrone pulled right from a grammar school memory. I stepped through into a gymnasium-sized space with a low ceiling. Heavy, floor length window curtains were drawn shut, and the lights were dimmed, perpetuating an indoor twilight.

Scattered blankets and sleeping bags covered at least half the floor and a group of about three-dozen obviously disenfranchised men, some shirtless, flocked about them. Some arranged their small piles of belongings. Some sat. Some lay on their sides or flat, looking at the ceiling, knees pointing upward. In the back, a big screen TV faced an audience of empty metal chairs.

The scene contrasted starkly with the picture-perfect quaintness of the streets up above. I had slipped through a crack in the socio-economic strata, into a depository full of Pacific Grove's shadows.

To the left of the television viewing area, a small group of the homeless milled around talking to my mother. She looked right at home. When a lanky man in a soiled flannel shirt hugged her, I expected her to push him away, or deck him. Instead she hugged back.

My legs tingled, a physical reaction that I knew, from experience, foreshadowed disaster. We didn't belong in plain view like this. Why was Mom—a card-carrying xenophobe only 24 hours earlier—ignoring that fact and embracing society's dregs?

What was Phineas doing to me?

A door opened to my left, releasing spirited shouts, the clanking of glass and the sizzle of grilled meat.

The kitchen, hot and busy.

A short, portly woman in a hairnet appeared at my side, leaning against the sprung door to keep it open.

"That Ann's somethin', ain't she?" she said, wiping red sauce off of her hands onto her apron.

I licked my lips. "May I have a glass of water?"

The woman disappeared into the kitchen. She returned with a paper cup.

"What she put together here don't look like much," she continued, "but for these people it's everything. A chance to get back on their feet, to get help findin' work. Not easy to do considerin' in these parts people don't take kindly to pimples on the scenery."

"Uh-huh," I said, gulping the tepid water. I couldn't take my eyes off Mom. She looked as if she were enraptured by a spell of tranquility. In contrast my insides simmered—a stew of agitation and perplexities. Where was this empathy at home? Or was it a ruse to throw off suspicion?

Somebody hit the power button on the TV and the group around Mom shuffled off to view what was, for them, surely a novelty. Mom spotted me and slowly walked over.

"So you finally came down," she stated when she reached me. "You look angry, Ariel. Are you angry about something?"

"You've dispensed more goodwill toward strangers in the last five minutes than I've received in five years," I replied, somewhat surprised that it had come out of my mouth.

"Well, that's self-centered," she shot back. "These people are outcasts in their own city. Think about it. If we ever got found out back home, we'd be outcasts, too."

She paused, furrows forming in the pliable skin of her brow, then added, "And how would you know what I've been doing the past five years? You've been gallivanting around in your so-called 'real world'."

"That's it, put it all back on me."

Her eyes blazed with a familiar fire. "Tell you the truth, I didn't know you gave a damn. You go away to school, never drop us a line. Then you show up back home doing your best to selectively ignore your surroundings, which—last time I checked—included me."

A few of the homeless stared.

"Let's get out of here," I said. "We can talk about this later."

"I'm not going anywhere," she insisted. "Phineas sent us to work something out."

"And if we get discovered?"

"I worry about getting discovered every day, when the stakes are much higher. Besides, the real Ann is out of commission, Ariel."

"Yeah, but what about the real . . . whoever my double is? She might be close."

"You don't know that for sure."

"Mother, I *do* know that the priest looked at me funny."

"Then go to the hotel and keep to yourself if you wish, but I don't feel imminent danger."

"You're probably too busy getting off on the attention," I asserted.

"I'll ignore that comment only because it's nonsense. But I *will* say there's something quite refreshing about attending to people who are so undemanding, so grateful."

"You can call me a lot of things Mom, but 'demanding' isn't one of them."

"My God, Ariel, what's gotten into you? This isn't about you. I was speaking of your brother and sisters."

"How presumptuous of me to think you were focused on me."

She rolled her eyes, opened her mouth and—

"Praise the Lord!" a munchkin voice rang out. "It's a miracle!"

I dropped my empty cup and turned to see a tiny woman with glasses under a gray pageboy haircut leaning on a metal cane. She was flush with the scent of lavender and had to be 80. She gazed at me spellbound, like I was the risen Christ.

Turns out I was the next best thing.

"Glory!" she cried, her shout cutting through the din. She pointed at me. "It's Glory! She's alive!"

Everyone got quiet.

The woman with the hairnet hurtled out of the suddenly quiet kitchen. "Saints be praised!" she exclaimed, getting close and studying me like I was some kind of specimen. "I knew you looked familiar, but . . . you was dead!"

I stood in mute panic, my worst fears realized. A few of the homeless shambled toward me, chanting, "Glory. Glory."

I looked for an escape route, but the crowd hemmed Mom and me in. Mom didn't look concerned.

A murmur spread through the crowd, gaining in volume until it became a roar. I hear Catholics aren't particularly demonstrative in their faith, but this group began to witness with the fervor of charismatic Pentecostals. They dropped to their knees. Laid hands on me. Shouted out. Talked in tongues.

Paralyzed, but not numb, I felt droplets of perspiration gather on my brow. People grabbed and tugged at me, sucking the oxygen out of the immediate area. The swarm's questionable hygiene poisoned what air I could get into my lungs. I lost my balance and toppled over. Four or five people fell on top of me, before everything went black.

I awoke under the covers of a bed tilted roughly 45 degrees upward at the waist—like a hospital bed, only I wasn't in a hospital, though a trace of antiseptic hung in the air.

Eight to ten people, some seated, crowded the room. My surroundings—from what I could see of them—were Spartan and decidedly low-tech: a plain wooden desk, a non-matching chest of drawers, several beat-up hardback chairs.

Most revealing were the large black crucifix next to a smallish, half-open window, a painting of the Virgin Mary in the clouds surrounded by winged cherubs, and the brick walls of the room—the same brick that covered the facade of the low slung building from which Father O'Flaherty had emerged to greet us. It seemed likely that he lived here.

I brushed damp strands of hair back out of my face. Someone sighed in relief.

"Thank God, she's okay," proclaimed a rasping voice.

"If she's returned from the dead, it'll take more than a fainting spell to keep her down," Father O'Flaherty said with surprising flippancy.

Beside him I recognized some of the ladies from the shelter, as well as a shorter Asian priest and a handful of complete strangers. My mother was there, too, along with someone I didn't expect: peering through the window from the outside, from a vantage point to the rear of the assembled, grinned a familiar face topped with blonde curls.

Billy.

When my eyes caught his, he put his index finger to his lips. I fought back a smile, despite my impossible situation.

And impossible it was. There would be no sneaking away now; no low profile. I lay before these people naked, so to speak, about to be held accountable for the actions of a life of which I had no knowledge.

All that, and I was resurrected, too.

The tiny bespectacled woman who first "recognized" me came forward. Her eyes, magnified by her lenses, were wide with childlike wonder. So was her voice: "What's it like on the other side, Glory? Did you see Jesus?"

I rubbed my forehead. Would I be asked to walk on water? Cast out demons? Might some opportunist phone a tip into *Dateline? The National Enquirer?* God, what was I going to tell Glory's relatives and friends!

Father O'Flaherty stepped forward and put a hand on the woman's diminutive shoulder. "Henrietta," he said gently, "this young woman has been through a lot. Let's give her some space. If she wants to talk later, we'll make sure it's her choice. Okay?"

Semi-articulate sounds rolled through the room, some of doubt, some of agreement. When Henrietta stepped back, my mother moved forward to fill the space. She leaned over as if to examine me before turning to address the crowd with the authority of a physician. She crossed her arms in front of her and placed her index finger at her chin. "Yes," she said, "she definitely needs rest."

She leaned over me a second time, even closer, and mouthed wordlessly, "amnesia." Then she stepped away.

At first, I couldn't fathom what she meant. But when Henrietta took issue with the priest, flatly stating, "We have to tell everyone of God's work here," my brain kicked into gear.

"Ohhh," I groaned, placing the heels of my palms to my temples. "Where am I? I can't remember . . ."

The admission was greeted by gasps, blank stares and one or two looks of outright dismay. Mom nodded, ever so slightly.

"Please everyone," Father O'Flaherty implored with an authoritative flair likely crafted from years at the pulpit, "we need to take some time to reflect on this; to ask the Spirit to guide us. Let's not jump to hasty conclusions. This is probably a bizarre coincidence. Keep this to yourselves until we know more. Please."

Silent disappointment drained the room of life. I know the priest must have felt it, but he remained steadfast. "As Catholic Christians we have an obligation to respect this woman's privacy." Traces of steel reinforced his voice. "We don't want our hunger for a miracle to procreate injustice."

One or two protested meekly, but Father O'Flaherty quelled objections with great speed and efficiency—his word ostensibly holding great weight with his people. He ushered everyone out of the room except for Mom.

Some came up to me before they left. One clasped my hand. Another kissed me on the forehead. The Asian priest, smiling broadly under his balding pate, said in gentle accented tones, "No matter what this is, no matter what you are, something about you blossoms hope."

The tranquil words calmed me. Good thing, because after they all left the priest closed the door and stayed. Billy, still at the window and yet to be seen by anyone else, looked like he was watching his favorite TV show.

I expected Father O'Flaherty to say something like "the jig is up," but he didn't.

"You'll have to excuse the congregation," he said apologetically. "They want so badly to believe in the extraordinary. Not like you and me, Ann. We know the Church is all about rolling up your sleeves and doing good works."

Mom smiled benignly. "Thanks for protecting the privacy of my friend."

"I'm really protecting my parish. Getting excited over alleged miracles only leads to disappointments and faith crises," he continued. Looking at me he said, "I'm sure your similarity to poor Glory is an unfortunate circumstance. She was, after all, a homeless addict, without family or friends."

A moment passed, during which he began to look uncomfortable, as if his undershorts were riding up on him. He took a deep breath. "I also have an, um, more practical reason for keeping this 'resurrection' talk under wraps. I am not at all eager to attract scrutiny—police, media, or other—after all the machinations we went through to get our homeless program on its feet. Once people start snooping around, they might find any excuse to shut us down."

Well, what do you know? A paranoid priest. No surprise in these scandal-ridden days.

"Now let's get your friend some medical attention."

"I won't need it!" I almost blurted out, but Mom spoke before I had the chance. "Well, if necessary we'll consult with our doctor back home," she said. "But let's hope it's a temporary state."

"But I feel like the parish is to blame," he said, and I knew he just had to be worried about legal action.

"Don't be silly," Mom replied, "And if you really want to do something for us, let me volunteer at the shelter for awhile."

He exhaled, obviously relieved. "You can stay as long as you like," he smiled. "I can put you and your friend up in the rectory and I'll try to stave off any foolish and redundant questions you might encounter."

"No thanks," Mom replied. "We have our own arrangements."

He thought about it for a minute. "Then come by tomorrow and we'll make it official," he said. "Now I'd better start spin control on this whole, er, unfortunate incident. Take your time leaving."

With that he was off. How odd that a Catholic priest stood in such strong opposition to the possibility of the miraculous. A day or two at our house would straighten him right up.

"Isn't it ironic?" Mom asked.

"About the priest?"

"No." A wry smile crossed her face. "I was just thinking that since the only people who really knew Glory are camping out in that hall over there, you might say they're your family in this world."

"Not funny," I replied. I glanced up to notice Billy had left the window.

"I just assumed," Mom persisted, "that if you're dissatisfied with home life, you might leap at a viable alternative."

I brushed the comment aside. "Don't get too full of yourself just yet, Mom. That priest may be squelching the story, but what about our cab driver?"

"What do you mean?"

Pointing at the window, I said, "Billy was looking through there the whole time. He must have heard everything."

"You're quite sure?"

"Dead sure."

"Then I hope he hasn't left."

She started toward the door. I threw the blankets off of me. "I'm coming with you."

As I slipped my feet into my sandals, I braced myself for an argument that never came. Mom even waited for me.

We walked down a dark hall until we found a door that looked like it led to the outside. We opened it and saw that the cab hadn't moved. Billy sat on its fender, legs dangling, kicking the tires with his heels.

"It's a good thing I turned the meter off," he joked.

Mom went into full-bore, take-no-prisoners mode. "Spare me the witticisms. Why, you're no better than a Peeping Tom."

"Gee," he said with affected babyish wonder, "you guys aren't from around here, are you?"

Mom raised her right arm, crooked it at the elbow, and made a loose fist with her palm outward. Moving her forearm forward slightly, she flicked all fingers simultaneously in the direction of Billy. Nothing happened, of course.

"Cool hand jive," he said and it sounded sincere.

Undaunted, Mom strode aggressively toward him. She looked like she wanted to throttle him, which, of course, she did. He swept his arms into an "X" in front of his face and bent backward slightly, an exaggerated gesture of warding her off. "Take it easy," he said laughing.

The three of us noticed a small crowd milling around in the lot across the street, their collective gaze locked on us.

"We should talk," Billy said. "But not here."

"And just what do you have to say to us?" Mom inquired.

"To steal a line," he replied, "I have an offer you can't refuse."

After a short ride, and some half-hearted protests by Mom, we found ourselves in the flickering darkness of a coffeehouse. It was literally that—a house—and it was nameless, or at least without apparent outside signage.

The pungent aroma of dark beans and cinnamon soaked every nook and cranny. The murmur of other customers filled the air. We sat in one of several small rooms crammed with tables and a hodge-podge of floor cabinets and wall hangings. As we sipped cappuccino—Billy's treat—out of cups that looked like soup bowls, our unsolicited escort held forth.

"I just want to help," he said. "It doesn't matter who you are or what you do."

"That's big of you," Mom replied, and you could have dusted the salt off of her words. "Excuse me if I don't take the offer at face value. Just how do you suppose you can help us?"

Billy looked hurt, or maybe he was tired. I felt sorry for him—a little bit, anyway. He looked my mother in the eye and spoke again: "Look, you want to stay here for awhile, right?"

Mom nodded slowly.

"And your daughter here—your great, fantastic, dare I say beautiful daughter—wants no part of whatever it is you want to do, right?"

The table rocked when I placed my elbow on it. Until that moment I had kept my mouth shut while I tried to figure out how an amnesiac would act, but when I heard that comment I couldn't contain myself.

"Can you be any more insulting, you condescending jerk!"

Billy continued, undaunted. "Hear me out. Doesn't it make sense that I keep you company while your mom does her thing?"

"I do *not* need a keeper!" I barked.

A few customers looked over. "You're a rank excuse for an amnesiac, you know that?" Billy chuckled. "And I'd be your escort, not your keeper, there to carry out your every wish and keep you away from unwanted attention."

Mom took hold of my arm, but kept looking at Billy. "Why should we trust you?"

"Mother," I complained, "You can't be considering—"

"I knew someone would ask that," Billy said. He reached into his back pocket and drew out his wallet, pulling out a card that looked like a driver's license. He tossed it onto the table. It clinked against the base of the sugar bowl.

"Take it," Billy insisted.

Mom fingered it gently like it might singe her. "A cab driver's operating permit," she said. "So?"

"Keep it. Think of it as insurance."

"Not the most reliable of policies," Mom stated.

"No, no, listen. I've got it all planned."

"I bet you do," we said in unison.

"No, please, listen. I know a guy who owns a small, clean motel a few minutes from here. Off the beaten track. It's even got kitchenettes. Go over and check it out with me. Ariel can chill there and keep a low profile, while you stay at the Centrella and do whatever. You can say your friend went back to New York or something."

Mom looked at the permit thoughtfully, the kind of contemplation that a few hours ago would have made me edgy. Now I felt disoriented, like I was a spinning top.

"And how do you expect to make a living without your permit?" Mom asked. "You don't know how long we'll be here."

"I've, uh, got a little something put away. I'll be fine."

Mom now looked so reflective that I half-expected smoke to plume out of her ears. It seemed I should say something—my immediate future was in the balance—but oddly enough, the consideration was more of an intellectual exercise than a true desire.

Then Mom did the last thing I expected: she asked my opinion.

"What do you think, Ariel?"

Mom. Asking, not telling. I felt the tip of something icy began to thaw.

"You can still see your Mom and stuff," Billy interjected.

Somewhere in the fiber of my being, certain impressions, thoughts and feelings fell into place like tumblers in a combination lock.

Staying. For the first time, I didn't flinch at the thought. Mom was mellow. I'd calmed a little. Probably wouldn't stay like that if I left. Not to mention what Phineas might do if I came back early and alone. And there was Billy . . . so irritating, but . . . so intriguing. I added up how long I had been without enjoyable male companionship and cringed at the sum.

"Why do you want to do this?" I asked him.

"You mean besides the chance to hang with a stone fox who doesn't have an attitude problem? I dunno. You two . . . just look like you need to be here."

Mom and I glanced at each other and shrugged our shoulders. "Okay," she said, pocketing the ID.

"Okay," I said, finishing my drink.

"Though if something goes wrong," Mom added, "you better believe I'll find you. Fast."

Billy just laughed. "No problem," he said.

When we got to Billy's friend's motel, Mom inspected every last inch and grilled the manager. It may have been a kindler, gentler Mom, but she could still bulldoze with the best of them.

I didn't mind, though. She was doing it for me.

Cloudbreak: the best way to describe the remainder of my time in Pacific Grove.

Turns out I didn't see Mom all that much. She busied herself with Immaculate Conception's homeless ministry, and when I did see her—say for a midnight coffee at Carrows—we made small, but comfortable, talk about our day.

Billy, a true gentleman and—as it turns out—much, much more, placed himself at my beck and call. He took me to get groceries, escorted me to the beach, even drove me to Big Sur. He helped me pick out hats and sunglasses to disguise my appearance, although that priest must have done a good job keeping his thumb on his congregation. I didn't have a single embarrassing encounter with a "true believer".

Best of all, Billy never crowded my space, never pried. He wore the mystery surrounding me like an old comfortable sweater—as if he were used to taking care of strangers living a lie.

I became comfortable with him, too.

One evening, we climbed high upon a boulder that overlooked the ocean. We must have been two stories high. The dying sunlight painted everything amber. There was no fog in sight.

I sat in front of him on the rock, in-between his legs, wedged in so my back touched his chest. He gently wrapped his arms around me, protecting me from the chill ocean breeze. I closed my eyes.

I considered how unusual it was for me to feel so at ease with a guy my age, and how it was becoming downright bothersome that I couldn't be totally open with him. That, along with my required low profile, had come to feel stifling.

Then, right in the crash of the waves, came a new realization: what must Mom go through every day, having to hide the fact that she manages a supernatural household? Talk about stifling! Not to mention that she plays out the charade juggling a ton of responsibilities she can't pass off to anyone else.

Feeling oddly satiated by the new awareness, I dozed off in Billy's arms.

Several nights later—I can't recall how many exactly—I found myself in Mom's antique-filled room at the inn. Past midnight, we had been to a nice dinner at a restaurant called The Old Bathhouse and were sipping sherry, a rare alcoholic indulgence for us.

I sat cross-legged on a fluffy comforter spread across the bed. A matching framed quilt hung on the wall. Mom sat erect in a torturous-looking wooden chair painted with black enamel.

On a mahogany desk a few candles flickered, emitting sweet vanilla throughout the room. From the arcane symbols carved on them and their conical shape, I recognized them as rest and revival candles.

The conversation began with the light touch we had lately come to master. We talked over the events of that week. I asked her how it had been going at Immaculate Conception.

"Well, dear," she replied, "I have to say it's liberating to walk around in the open and help people without fear of repercussions. I never expected that functioning without extras could be so therapeutic. I work hard, but it's energizing."

When she commented on how much I had seemed to mellow, however, the exchange veered toward deeper territory.

"Have I?" I inquired and thought about it for a minute. "Maybe this place is letting me look at old things in different ways. Like I've been thinking—really thinking—about what you do every day back home."

She said nothing and drank deeply.

"Maybe the scales have been lifted from my eyes," I mused.

Her look softened. She walked over to me and brushed back my hair like I was a little kid. Put her arm around me in a way that, if I recall correctly, was very Mom-like.

"Ariel, I know you think I'm an overbearing bitch. Lord knows I probably could have handled you better in your teens. But power like mine can be so overwhelming that it distorts your perspective, and maybe things that don't seem so extraordinary . . ." her voice trailed off, ". . . get lost at times."

She hugged me tight and held it, crying. I cried, too, and we sat like that for a long time, mother and daughter united, immersed in a comfortable, dreamy silence.

As you might well imagine, the knock on the door jarred us.

Mom got up and peered through the peephole. To my surprise, she slipped the chain off without hesitation, and swung the door open wide.

Billy stood smiling in the hallway. He held two plane tickets up for us to see.

"Congratulations. Your flight back leaves the day after tomorrow. And Mr. Phineas Biggs sends you his best."

Closure—for that period in my life, at least—came about a week after our Pacific Grove sojourn.

By the way, there had been no disheartening crash back to reality. True, family chaos flooded Mom and me the minute we stepped over the threshold of our Victorian (Joe—angry that his sisters had given his hamster wings—had shot sparks out of his fingers at them in retaliation), but it soon became evident that some things had changed for the better.

Mom and I convinced Dad to handle the kids at least one night a week, freeing us to spend quality time together. It did come at a price—I had to agree to babysit those little terrors occasionally—but it's worth it, because it allows Mom to have a little quality time with herself and, when he's lucky, Dad.

Anyway, on our first Friday back in Palo Pacifica, Mom and I walked up the hill to our house. It was dusk. We had just taken a stroll through town, something we had done often that first week. My initial cynicism regarding Pacific Grove had dissipated—it was the perfect place for Palo Pacificans to undergo life-changing transformations—but my time there gave me a new appreciation of Palo Pacifica's lived-in character. Our town now seemed anything but confining.

On the night in question we were talking animatedly about Billy, who was to pick me up later for dinner and a movie. I had come to know more about him, namely that he often helped Phineas with "special projects". Mom said this was a sure indication that Billy had been a paranormal reprobate at one time or another. My uncle had likely rehabilitated him, creating a debt of service. This somehow added to Billy's appeal.

At the foot of the stairs leading up to our new redwood deck—its clean orange and amber planks almost luminous in the twilight—we became aware of someone or something moving around above us.

We shot up the remainder of the climb to find a shabby figure bending over the black cauldron Mom had set out to cool earlier. In horror, we watched as the stranger scratched his filthy pants around the crotch, then dipped his index finger into the pot's ingredients to taste them.

Mom recognized him first. "Phineas! Where's your sense of hygiene!"

She made a few quick motions with both hands—a sterilization conjure—and the cauldron glowed like charcoal for an instant.

Wetly sucking his finger, my uncle scratched his head with his free hand. "Good t'see yew, too," he said after taking the finger out of his mouth.

He walked over to the picnic table where we sometimes ate dinner on warm nights, trench coat rustling as he slid onto one of the benches. We waited. Falling darkness made it difficult to see, but he looked to be engaged in his favorite pastime: gazing at nothing.

Mom moved with purpose, however, like she knew something was coming. She sat on the bench across from him, and motioned me to join her.

"Good trip?" he asked. He sat directly in front of the day's last light so we couldn't see his face even up close.

Mom said nothing. My uncle was asking me.

Was there a correct thing to say? I tried the truth. "Yes. It was. I think Mom and I changed a lot. We understand each other better."

He mulled it over.

"Think so?" The cackling that followed set off the neighborhood dogs.

He stilled himself and got up, turning to the fence that ran the perimeter of the deck. He spoke with his back turned, so I had to strain to hear him.

"Well, there's no denyin' yer momma needed rest, and that's why I sent her. But I don't think she changed much at all, Sweet Pea. Yer the one that changed. Ya had to. How else yew gonna help keep this family out of trouble? T'do that ya gotta see what you're looking at, instead of pretendin' it ain't there."

I didn't know what to say—not because I was stunned, but because it made so much sense. My family needed someone young, energetic and normal to help them fit in, to guarantee their survival. They needed me. And I hadn't been ready to recognize or accept that fact until now.

"Ain't such a bad thing, izzit?" my uncle asked, as if reading my mind.

The answer was undoubtedly complex and dependent on the future. But my uncle didn't wait for my reply. He vanished, his disembodied voice hanging in the air.

"Yew kin thank me later," it echoed. "I'll figger out a way."

Mom moved over, put her arm around me and said, "I won't lie. If you stick around, life might be hard."

"Yeah," I replied, "but at least it's a life. I didn't think I had one until now."

About the Author

CHRIS KEMP is . . . well, a writer. His day job is as a technical writer for Starfish Software, he runs a side business as a marketing communications consultant, and his hobby is authoring what he calls "a subtle breed of supernatural fiction." Teenagers and young adults figure heavily in his story cycles, one of which concerns an unusual family that lives in a fictional town (Palo Pacifica) based on Pacific Grove, California. A story from that series, "Resurrected," is presented here. Another, "Rooted," won Honorable Mention in the L. Ron Hubbard "Writer's of the Future" contest. Chris lives in Pacific Grove with Linda, his lovely wife of over twenty years. He holds a Bachelor of Arts Degree in English from Cal Poly, San Luis Obispo, and is a founding member of FWOMP.

A Flash of Red

by Frances J. Rossi

The pain merged with the rhythmic roar of the sea.

As the cold whiteness settled over Lisa, a gentle voice came to her out of the drifting fog, as if from a distance.

"You are badly hurt."

Leaning on the door, her hand came to rest in warm, wet stickiness, but she was too weak to do more than pull it back. She'd made it up the block from where he'd left her wounded and bleeding, managing to climb the steps to the door of St. Augustine Church without knowing if anyone would be there at this late hour.

"Oh, I get help! Oh dear God!"

As a hand worked its way gently behind her head, Lisa opened her eyes, dimly conscious of the heavy dark hair that hung close to her, filling her nostrils with the scent of damp earth. Another hand slid under her knees, managing to help her lie down. ". . . So the blood go to your head," murmured a man's voice in the slightly staccato tones of someone out of breath or, perhaps, with a slight accent. "Here, I leave you my jacket, so you stay warm." He arranged it awkwardly around her shoulders.

Gratefully she huddled in it, shaking, as the cold fog moved in like an extension of the tide this August night. She closed her eyes, lulled by the muffled sound of foghorns.

A second voice reminded her somehow of Colorado. "The ambulance'll be here in a few minutes. Don't worry." On her forehead she felt the pressure of a hand, blessing.

Sirens punctuated her stupor, and then new voices. "Stop the bleeding!

We need an IV now!"

Were they medics who wrapped her tightly in a blanket and lifted her onto a gurney? The prick in her arm was nothing compared with the stabbing pain of the knife. Then they were moving. Someone held her hand. "Blood pressure 70 over 40," a low voice reported.

At a distance, someone else was saying, ". . . stabbing victim, St. Augustine Church in Pacific Grove. Multiple knife wounds will need transfusion . . ."

When the ambulance door opened, she caught a whiff of pine forest carried on the damp night air. The entryway lights of Community Hospital of the Monterey Peninsula roused her, as they wheeled her into the ER. Shrill voices broke in on the grayness of shock engulfing her.

Troubled dreams swirled her down into a vortex, into which sporadic episodes of surrounding activity worked their way. Finally a persistent beeping roused her. As a young nurse attached a new IV bag, Lisa tuned in to the pulsating waves of pain.

"Squeeze the pump when it starts to hurt, hon," the nurse advised. Stripping the protective wrap from a thermometer, she added, "You startin' to look a little better." A small white name badge on her pocket read, "Vicki".

The aroma of bacon and coffee drifting through the door made Lisa's mouth water around the thermometer.

Noting the food cart outside, Vicki added, "You ain't gonna be eatin' for a day or so yet."

"What day is it?" Lisa mumbled.

"Hon, keep your mouth closed while I'm takin' your temperature," Vicki scolded. "It's Thursday." Pulling out the thermometer, the nurse looked at it, frowned and shook her head. "You been sleepin' a lot, you know."

Lisa tried to shift her weight, only to have the pain crash over her. She eased back carefully, squeezing the morphine pump, as Vicki maneuvered the blood pressure cuff around her upper arm and inflated it.

She woke again to see a trim man in green scrubs looking down at her.

"Still feeling quite a bit of pain, huh?"

She'd squeezed the morphine almost automatically. "I guess I'm getting used to it a little."

"I'm Dr. Thompson." He took her wrist and felt the pulse. "We're dealing with some infection here, Lisa. Not unusual with wounds like yours. The good news is we were able to repair the internal injuries pretty well."

He sat down in the chair by her bed. "Quite frankly, we've got to be thankful you're alive after an attack like that. You're responding well so far, considering."

She tried to formulate an appropriate question. "How long will I be here?"

"That all depends on how quickly you heal, and on the way this infection responds to the antibiotics." As he stroked his trim beard, the large ruby of his class ring caught Lisa's attention, making her oddly uncomfortable. Yet his eyes, like the deep blue outer bay, reassured her.

Her eyes closed involuntarily and she drifted, only dimly aware of his cold stethoscope against her chest. As he left, she opened her eyes to see two men in uniform come in, stopping at the ICU nurses' desk.

"You can't stay long," Vicki, warned them. "She's still pretty weak."

"Are we startin' to feel a little more human?" the stockier of the two said as he reached the bed. "I'm Bill Clark from the Pacific Grove police, and this is Hal Jamison."

Clark was solidly built, reminding Lisa of a football lineman, but he spoke as if he were a quarterback detailing plays during a time-out. "We understand you still aren't feelin' too good, but we've gotta ask you a few questions so we can get this investigation on the road."

Jamison, who had more of a basketball player's build, nodded in agreement. "We hope that's okay with you, Lisa." His blue eyes seemed to probe for answers. "After your ordeal, you're probably not quite ready for this. But whatever you could tell us sure would help."

She nodded. Encouraged, he went on. "Can you tell us what happened?"

Her mind balked at the thought of that night.

Clark, holding a notebook in his thick hand, resumed. "Okay, Lisa, you were found with multiple stab wounds at the side door of St. Augustine's in Pacific Grove on Tuesday night. But the trail of blood indicates you came from down the block, just below Central. Do you remember how you got from there to the church?"

She strained to recall the events her mind was rejecting. A man had come at her from behind, grabbed her by the arm, and roughly pulled her close. The hot, sticky muskiness of his body commingled with the damp sea air, as she tried desperately to push him away. Suddenly he pushed back, pulled a knife and plunged it into her. Pain tore at her shoulder. Then at her chest. More struggle, more tearing pain. The sound of a siren caused him to stiffen, release his grip. Cold damp concrete against her cheek.

"I don't remember exactly. He left me lying on the sidewalk and ran. I got up . . . tried to walk . . . The church was just up the block, and I felt . . . it would be safe. Everything got so foggy. Then, someone came.

Who was he?"

"A homeless fellow that hangs out over there," Jamison answered. "He was still up and saw you. Said he heard some moaning."

"Then I heard another man's voice, and he touched my head."

"That would be Esteban the maintenance man," Jamison confirmed. "He called 911."

Clark turned another page of his notebook. "What do you remember of the person who attacked you? Did you get a look at him, Lisa?"

Pain reverberated through Lisa's back. "I've gotta change position before I can talk any more . . ." As she groped for the bed control, Jamison found it and pressed. The head of the bed adjusted upward, rubbing against her tender skin, but relieving the pressure on her back.

"That any better?" Something about the rich mellowness of his voice made Lisa want to hear more of it.

"I think so."

Clark waved his pencil impatiently. "I know this isn't pleasant, Lisa, but we've got to start hunting for this guy. If you can give us some idea of his appearance now, we'll have the artist come in tomorrow, when you're feeling stronger."

Again, Lisa clutched at memories that dissolved into the mist. "Had dark hair . . . kind of a regular face . . . I couldn't see it very well. All that hair . . ."

"What about his hair?" Clark asked.

"It was dark, coarse, and bushy. Kind of hung down over his face."

Clark frowned and jotted notes, then looked up. "Anything else about his looks?"

"A flash of red—somewhere."

His head jerked up. "What do you mean by that?"

"I don't know."

Jamison urged her, "Could you just tell us what happened? What were you doing down there so late? When did you see him? What did he do?"

Managing to clear her thoughts, she recounted what she remembered of the events, and by the time she had finished, terror engulfed her once more.

"Was he attempting to rape you, Lisa?" Jamison asked, shifting uneasily.

"It seemed that way." The musty damp smell of his coarse, heavy hair crowded into her consciousness. "He was very close, holding me . . ."

Clark scribbled furiously. "And . . .?"

"I tried to get away from him. Then he pulled the knife." Talking about it triggered a renewed throbbing from the wounds. "This is too hard to talk about." Wooziness welled up like a wave from her stomach.

"You must have fended him off somewhat," Clark persisted, "because he missed your vital organs. That's very fortunate."

"I suppose so." The pain deafened her now. "I must have fallen. Then I heard a siren . . . must have been several blocks away. Maybe he thought I was dead, because he ran away."

"And then you got up and started—walking? Why didn't you go to one of the nearby houses to get help?" Clark flipped over a page of his notebook and waited.

"I think they were dark already." She struggled to keep her eyes open. "All I know is, I wanted to get away from there. To . . . the siren. Or Lighthouse Avenue. I got to the church, and it . . . felt safe." As her eyes closed, Lisa began to see Clark and Jamison shrouded in mist on a dark path. Waves were crashing in her ears.

Later that same morning, awakening as the ICU nurse replaced the IV, she caught the sound of a voice at the door.

". . . and we had to call *The Monterey County Herald* to make sure they didn't make the same mistake the TV stations did, making it look like this happened right there at the church." The speaker—a tall, sanguine-looking man wearing a Roman collar—stepped into the room. Lisa noted his trim, neatly groomed dark hair, as he stood near the small nurses' desk to one side of the door, conversing in a low voice with the nurse.

As he came over to her bed, Lisa felt confused. Brought up in a church-going family, she'd stopped attending when she left home. Why would a clergyman be coming to see her now? All she could think of were recollected tales of deathbed conversion.

"Am I going to die?" she asked him.

"I'm here to pray that you won't. I'm Pastor Jim Peterson of St. Augustine's Church." He reached down to pat her shoulder gently. "I just wanted to let you know that our people are praying for you." His brow furrowed as if in concern. "Do you belong to a church?"

"No . . . I was baptized as a baby."

Somehow, that had made a difference. Minutes later, he was marking crosses on her forehead, hands and neck with oil, and pressing her head in his hands. "We anoint the sick with oil, as a sign of God's healing power."

Slightly irritated, she wondered if she'd consented to this. Still, she felt strangely comforted.

Feeling somewhat more lucid Friday morning, Lisa tried to cooperate with the police artist who came in with her briefcase full of charts. With her chocolate brown suit and blond hair efficiently caught up in a bun, th woman asked questions about the attacker's appearance.

Along with the dusky hair and muscular body, Lisa mentioned the flash of red that came back to her mind.

"Yes? Can you go into a little more detail for me?" the woman urged "Jewelry, perhaps? Something he was wearing?"

Lisa felt stupid admitting that she couldn't picture where the red ha come from.

The artist rolled her eyes, and let out a sigh of frustration when Lisa faile to pinpoint the eye-type of the attacker, explaining that this was an important key to identification, and going on in some detail about Mongoloid versus Mediterranean eye types. "Plus there's the less-familiar Gallic eye," sh added.

"But I barely got a look at him," Lisa told her, at which the woma shoved her charts back in the briefcase, complaining, "I can't pull a face ou of nowhere, girl!"

Lisa sensed blame in the woman's words. An overwhelming feeling o anger and despair flooded over her. But a surge of pain blocked it out, an she took refuge in the morphine.

Saturday morning, still in the ICU, Lisa was picking at her breakfas when Clark and Jamison came in.

Clark began in his brusque, awkward manner. "We've been out her talking to your parents."

Her mom and dad had come over from Hollister early Wednesda morning, when they first got the news. They had immediately suspecte her ex-husband, Michael.

"He's stalking you, Lisa!" Mom had said after one of his particularl menacing phone calls, and now Clark was picking up on it, echoing th innuendos of censure she'd heard in her parents' remarks.

They'd never liked Michael, so it was easy, now, to settle on him as a suspect. Or was a vestige of love for him still blinding her to reality?

By the next Monday, Lisa had been moved to a private room near th nurses' station, where she could be closely monitored. The search for th attacker was in full swing. *The Herald* had published statements from th police department, and included a rudimentary artist's sketch.

Late that morning Vicki had helped her walk down the hall to the bac window, overlooking the forest below. Winded, Lisa sat on a bench an gazed out at the pinewoods. Among the salal bushes, glowing white, dove picked its way. Peering to get a better view, she thought the bird might be symbolic, somehow.

Then from behind a bush it blew toward her—a discarded white plastic bag. *Symbolic, sure!* she thought ruefully. *Of my life.*

The next day they took her for further rehabilitation at Hospice House. Her wheelchair safely secured in the back of the van, she watched, intrigued, as they turned off Highway 1 and onto a road leading back into a deep oak forest. A few weeks before, a setting like this would have piqued her curiosity. Now, though, the deep shadows beneath gnarled trees, draped in ivy and hanging with yellowed Spanish moss, made her shrink from whatever mysteries they might conceal.

Once inside the rambling one-story building, Lisa felt relieved. While she had once associated *hospice* with end-of-life care, this place exuded an air of healing and renewal. They passed a lunchroom where patients sat eating with family members. On the right was a bright therapy center with windows looking out on a sunny flowerbed.

Finally in her room and propped up in her bed, Lisa noticed, with discomfort, that the glass-paneled door in the corner led outside to a tiny veranda. When a white-uniformed nurse with a thick black braid brought her lunch tray, Lisa asked her if the door was locked. The girl checked it, smiling indulgently.

"Well, could you just make sure the curtain is pulled, please?"

Family could visit at any time, so Lisa's mother came over for a while every day, sometimes eating lunch with her. A couple of her closer friends from the school in Salinas dropped in one evening. Pastor Peterson stopped by, too. He meant well, Lisa supposed, but he made her uncomfortably aware of having lapsed from her church. As the words of his prayers washed over her, she fixated on the large red enamel cross that hung on a silver chain around his neck. His dark hair, less controlled now than before, had grown out enough to expose silver roots at the hairline. When he had finished praying, they exchanged a few words, and he left, promising to come again.

But Clark and Jamison hadn't appeared in over a week. While Clark's impatient grilling had tired her, Lisa had appreciated Jamison's empathy. She hated the insecurity of not knowing how the case was progressing, but at least therapy had begun to absorb her attention. She focused on her daily healing goals, trying not to think of the tangled forest obscurity outside the windows.

Toward the end of her second week at Hospice House, Lisa was sitting in her chair reading when Jamison entered carrying a briefcase. "Hi," she said, looking past him, expectantly. "You're alone today?"

"I am." He took out a small notebook. "I hope you aren't disappointed."

Was there a trace of irony in his tone?

"We've done some shuffling down at the department," he continued, "so from now on I'll be in charge of your case." He pulled over a chair and sat down, then extracted a pen from his pocket. Unlike the abrupt Clark, Jamison moved to a calmly measured tempo. "I'll have another person working with me, but she can't be here today. Are you comfortable being alone with me? Otherwise we can call in a nurse."

Lisa nodded. "I'm fine."

He leaned down to pull pictures from his briefcase, and his thick hair, the color of maple sugar, brushed against the sheet. "Here we are! Do you recognize any of these people?"

The first picture depicted an Asian-looking man with slightly unkempt hair.

"That's the man who found me at the church—isn't it?"

"You're still not sure?"

"If I heard his voice . . ."

"Does this one look familiar?" He showed her a broad-faced Hispanic-looking man.

"I think I've seen him."

Next, he held up a more familiar face. "That's my ex-husband, Michael." Reluctantly, she examined the photo, which displayed his hair in one of its wilder moments. In his earlobe, like a drop of blood, she noticed the ruby stud he'd worn for years.

Lisa stared at the three pictures, trying to imagine any one of these men attacking her. She hadn't seen the face clearly, so hair was the feature she'd been most aware of.

Jamison gave her time to consider, then asked, "Did any one of these men attack you on the trail?"

She looked up apologetically. "I don't know. I'm not sure I could rule any of them out, but I can't say any of them did it."

"This is not going to be an easy case," Jamison sighed, sliding the pictures back into their envelope. "There's virtually no evidence so far. Quite frankly, we thought at first that it would turn out to be your ex, but he has an alibi of sorts. Not airtight. So far, nobody's corroborated it. But my instincts tell me it may well pan out."

Jamison sat more deeply in his chair, crossing his legs. "We're still checking out the homeless men in the area and known sex offenders. So far, nothing fits. An arrest will depend on your identifying someone, unless someone confesses." He leaned back, clasping his hands behind his head. "So at this point,"—he put emphasis on each word—"everybody's a potential suspect."

A breeze from the hallway swept the curtain aside at the door, revealing a darkening forest, as clouds covered the sun. "And," he added ominously, "someone out there knows you didn't die as he'd intended, and likely fears you'll identify him. That's something to worry about." Forehead furrowed deeply, he rose to leave.

"Will you be back?" Lisa asked, hoping that he might again be forced to come without his female partner.

"Probably. I'm available any time you need me to be here."

"Do you think it's safe here?"

"Absolutely. You're under 24-hour supervision."

Although remaining apprehensive of the surrounding forest, Lisa began to heal rapidly during her stay at Hospice House. After two weeks the doctors agreed that she was ready to move into the apartment her parents had set up for her in Pacific Grove, hoping to keep her address private. Still not able to drive, she was fearful of going out and felt isolated, missing the community of the rehabilitation environment. But she was determined to get back to the freedom of normal life, and rationalized that her attacker didn't know where she was now, whereas he might have been able to locate her at Hospice House.

One day, trying to organize her snapshots in an album, she came across a picture of herself from the end-of-school picnic. Light-brown hair, highlighted gold, framed her sun-gilded face. She turned laughing blue eyes toward the camera, brandishing a large pair of barbecue tongs.

I looked good.

But now, even if her body was healing, she didn't feel like the person who'd ended the school year on a high note back in June. She'd had to give up her teaching job. Friends from school were too busy to spend much time with her. Much of her enjoyment in life had involved the out-of-doors, and now, even though her body was healing—or so they said—she still lacked the strength for walking and beach combing. Depression built its nest and settled in. She tried to catch up on reading, but ended up watching TV a lot. And crying.

One bright and clear Tuesday morning in early October, when daybreak carried just a hint of frost, Lisa felt a fresh burst of energy and garnered the nerve to break out of her seclusion. It was two months since the incident on the trail.

She decided to walk down to Lighthouse Avenue, two blocks up from the Monterey Bay, along which thrived much of Pacific Grove's business community. After a couple of stormy weeks, the morning sun sparkled on the expanse of blue, triggering her usual sense of awe at the sight of *so much* water.

Stopping at Pier 1 Imports to catch her breath, she admired the fall harvest display just inside the door. Cold perspiration made her shiver. She'd never before realized how much of an uphill climb this was.

Just up the next block was Caravali's, where the regular crowd already sat at outdoor tables drinking coffee over the morning papers. As she neared the coffee shop, Lisa glimpsed her reflection in a shop window and paused to assess it. She'd combed her light brown hair forward in bangs, and fluffed it out on the sides to round her thin face, but the breeze now blew it back, and her makeup failed to hide the hollows in her sallow cheeks.

Chunking four quarters into the *New York Times* box on the sidewalk outside, she retrieved a paper, propped it gingerly under her arm, and went in to order *café au lait* and a scone. The sunshine beckoned her to brave the street-side tables, but instead she settled inside at a back corner table. She'd opened the paper and begun to peruse it, when suddenly she was aware of someone standing across the table from her.

Her heart plunged.

It was a thin, weathered man wearing a tattered brown plaid sport jacket, his thick black hair encircled by a worn red bandanna. He held a steaming cup of coffee.

"Mind if I join you?"

She recognized the gentle accented voice immediately. "Are you the one who . . .?" She stopped short, unsure.

"I found you at the church . . . when you were hurt." Uninvited, he pulled out a chair and sat down.

"What do you want?" she asked guardedly.

Looking around furtively, he held a finger to his lips. "You're not safe here. They haven't found him yet."

"I know, but this is a public place." She realized it was a non-sequitur as soon as the words had left her mouth.

"He could follow you if he sees you in town." He picked up a sugar wrapper from the table and, hand shaking, began folding it.

"I guess I should be thanking you for saving my life." Lisa broke off a bit of the scone, but it had lost its appeal.

"Lotta good it did me!" He scowled, pulling the lid from his coffee cup "They think I did it. Sure, I had bloodstains—from when I tried to move you. But, thank God, you did not identify me as the one."

"But it wasn't you," she said tentatively, studying his face as she spoke. *Or was it*? He had the high cheekbones, the narrow eyes she thought she remembered. *Could he have followed her up to the church, planning to finish his work? Only seeming to rescue her?*

"They don't think you could really tell." His eyes narrowed, scrutinizing her.

"What's your name?" she asked.

"Glenn." He took a sip of his coffee.

"Glenn, how *did* you happen to be there that night?"

"See?" he complained irritably. "You don't believe me either." He got up, coffee in hand. "I sleep across the street from where I found you." As abruptly as he'd come, Glenn walked out.

Clutching her cup, she sipped the *café au lait* uneasily. Was he warning her or . . . something else?

Lisa had built her peace like a sand castle poised just beyond the domain of the marauding sea. The encounter with Glenn was the first aggressive wave in a cold tide that threatened to reclaim the beach, demolishing the fragile creation in its path. Reluctantly Lisa made an appointment to see Pastor Peterson.

Arriving at St. Augustine's church, a receptionist directed her to the pastor's office, in a back room of the parish administrative annex. Rising from the leather-upholstered chair behind his desk, he greeted Lisa and pulled up a heavy chair for her.

On the back wall behind his desk, on one of the shelves of a large bookcase, an aquarium bubbled, with lustrous red-violet and blue fish that slid stealthily in among the fronds of sea plants.

"You're looking much better!" he said, his florid face wreathed in smiles.

"I guess you could say so—physically, at least."

Lisa's eyes again gravitated to his hair. The gray roots were dark again now. *Grecian Formula*? She tried to squelch those thoughts.

As he fumbled with paperclips, she went on to tell him about her fear and frustration, and about the troubling encounter with Glenn.

The minister's face clouded over. "Stay away from that guy. I'm trying to get him to stop hanging out here. The police actually suspect him now, you know."

"That's what he said." She ran her finger back and forth across the brocade pattern on the arm of her chair, feeling perplexed.

"Lisa, you may be suffering from post-traumatic stress disorder. Hasn't your doctor suggested something?"

"He's given me a prescription. But that's not even close to the whole answer for me." Like the doctor, this man seemed to be looking for a quick fix. "I thought I had things under control at one point in my life, but now . . ."

She told him about how she'd just gotten over the divorce, when she'd experienced this attack. "I have to rethink everything. I might even . . . need God."

"You always needed God," he corrected her. "It's the Church you thought you could do without."

"I just need to talk to somebody," she said, mentally disputing the church idea.

The pastor leaned forward, his steely eyes framed by smile lines. "Well, I'd be glad to counsel you, if you'd like."

Her stomach tightened at the thought. "Thank you, Pastor, but what I had in mind was more like . . . a support group or something."

"Hmm. Well, we do have something starting up that you'd be interested in." He shuffled some papers on his desk, pulled out a brilliant orange flyer, and handed it to her.

The announcement read:

Been away? Can we get you to try us again? Seeking a deeper faith walk? Join us!
Starting October 15th: our new Seekers' Group.

On Tuesday night October 15, Lisa approached the open doors of the church basement. Pastor Peterson waited outside with several people to welcome those arriving. As she stepped cautiously inside, a woman about her own age with shoulder-length umber hair, wearing a long, sage green corduroy dress, introduced herself as Rosalie. She found Lisa's nametag, and led her to the refreshment table, where an arrangement of burgundy mums and orange lilies presided over a generous spread.

Taking a cup of coffee and a puff pastry, Lisa headed for the large room where about 40 people assembled. The pastor spoke a few words of welcome. Then a short rosy-faced man wearing a blue sweatshirt that read "St. Augustine Church" stood to share his experience with the group. "Since I joined this community, I feel I've come home," he confessed. "I've never been happier."

Would I *be happier if I stayed with them?*

They were invited to greet those on either side of them. When she turned to her right, she found herself face-to-face with a healthy-looking auburn-haired man in his late thirties.

"Jack Kelly," he said, smiling.

"I'm Lisa Calluso," she told him, offering her hand.

Rosalie was asked to pray. Instructing them to breathe deeply, evenly, she said, "Relax. Imagine yourself in a forest."

She described a scene at sundown, where they found themselves out in the cold. There they discovered a little chapel, from whose windows shone a warm light. "What do you hope to find within?" she asked, and paused for a minute before going on.

"God is waiting for you inside in the warmth and light," Rosalie continued. "God is calling you into a place where you can set aside your burdens, your fears."

"God," she prayed, "we come here tonight to see if that place might be here, in this community. Open our minds and hearts to see where you are calling us to find our peace with you. Amen."

Lisa began to relax; but before she had a chance to ponder whether she, indeed, was going to find what she was looking for, a serious-looking woman in a gray pantsuit stood to explain the evening's agenda. She informed them that they were to form small discussion groups based on the number printed on their plastic-encased nametag.

Looking down at hers, Lisa saw the number "4".

Leaning over, Jack checked her number. "You're in my group," he said warmly.

As they moved their chairs into a circle, adding two more for additional members, Jack said, "I think I saw you at church on Sunday. Have you been coming long?"

"Just a couple of times," she answered, self-conscious over her newness to the community.

A dark-haired, light-complexioned man took one of the extra chairs, while a white-haired woman, casually elegant in a black raw silk ensemble, joined them. She introduced herself as Marjorie Snodgrass, the gentleman as Rod Lopes.

Thank heaven the group was small!

"I guess this is it for our group," Jack said. "We'll start by getting to know each other."

He handed each of them a sheet of paper on a clipboard and a pencil. "We'll start by having you write five things you'd like to have the group know about you. Take your time and reflect for a few minutes in silence; then write when you're ready."

As a dulcimer hammered out clean, sweet hymn tunes, Lisa closed her eyes. What five things could she share with these virtual strangers? Her origins—born in the mid-Sixties in Hollister? Probably safe. College at UCSB? That was okay, too.

After graduation? She'd gone to Colorado's San Luis Valley as a Vista worker, and there, fallen in love with Michael, a volunteer from Michigan. They'd married, and Lisa began teaching high school in downtown

Denver. Very soon, his social drinking had developed into full-blown alcoholism. Michael was a mean and violent drunk. All the idealism and hope that had fueled her existence went down the tubes with the marriage.

Surreptitiously she reached for a tissue in her pocket and, trying to remain unobtrusive, dabbed at the tears gushing down her cheeks. She couldn't share this with them. Struggling to regain her composure, she forced herself to return to the "five things." So . . . there was Hollister, UCSB, Pacific Grove . . . and maybe mention of her teaching. What else? Looking up, she saw that everyone else had finished writing.

Jack looked at his watch. "Gotta move on," he said, glancing her way. "Now we'll share what we've written. Marjorie?"

Marjorie, married to a retired newspaperman, told of her interest in landscape painting. Rod, a civil engineer, tearfully described his roots in the Azores, and the way his mom had worked in a cannery to put him through college.

When he finished Jack smiled in her direction. "Now we'll hear Lisa's story."

She froze momentarily. *My story*? "Well, you know, there's not too much to tell." Instinctively abbreviating her answers, she tried not to let the details she shared stand out from the others. When she was finished, she said, "That's it, pretty much. Not very exciting."

Marge reached over and clasped her hand reassuringly. "I'm sure there's more, dear. I know I have all kinds of questions . . ." She paused, glancing at Lisa's still-blotchy face. "Any pets, for instance?"

Lisa relaxed back into the chair. "I've got a dog named Wilson." Words began to flow a little easier. "He's part golden retriever, part mutt . . . and I love him." She reached for her wallet and showed them a picture.

As they admired Wilson, she remembered the day, soon after she'd left Hospice House, when Mom had taken her over to the pound, cautioning that, under the circumstances, she should have a dog—and not a small one. They'd considered a nice-looking Doberman, but then Wilson had made his presence felt, with his begging brown eyes and silly smile, whining wistfully as they started to leave. Now he was her regular companion.

Would these scars be covering her body had Wilson been with her on that August evening's walk?

"So, where is Wilson tonight?" Rod asked.

"I didn't know if he'd be allowed here." She looked questioningly at Jack.

"You'd have to ask Liz about that." He gestured toward the woman in the gray pantsuit.

"How about you, Jack!" Marge broke in. "What's your story?"

Jack cleared his throat. "I'm from Bellingham, Washington. Went to school at Berkeley during the 1980s—back when there were no issues to protest. I work for an investment firm in Monterey. I have a cat named Fang. And, I like . . . the out-of-doors."

"Out-of-doors?" echoed Rod. "You do any fishin'?"

"Not much. I run, ride my bike. Hike some."

"How about family, Jack?" Marge wasn't giving up. "Are your parents still alive?"

"Still in Bellingham," Jack answered.

The comment sounded brusque, but it was probably his natural reserve, Lisa thought, her eyes probing the suggestion of muscles rippling beneath the folds of his shirt. Glancing at his left hand, she saw no ring. She imagined the two of them hiking together at Big Sur.

Most of the groups had dispersed to the refreshment area. Jack passed a clipboard around for names and addresses, and Lisa carefully wrote in her post office box. At the phone number, she paused again, and then wrote in her parents' number in Hollister. Liz called the large group back together, made some announcements and ended with a prayer.

Lisa stopped at the refreshment table, and Jack joined her, coffee in hand. "Did you enjoy the evening?" he asked, as Lisa scooped mixed nuts from the cut glass serving dish.

"Very much. I'm glad I came." It was true. She sensed that this group might turn out to be the community she so desperately needed.

"I enjoyed having you in my group," he began tentatively, smiling in his boyish way, his tanned face almost concealing its freckles. "Ya know, I have to stay for some debriefing after the meeting, but if you don't mind waiting, I wondered if you might like to go somewhere for a cup of coffee or something afterwards. I'd like to know you better."

It was very tempting. "How long before you can leave?"

Someone beckoned to him from the other room, and he looked at his watch. "Man, it's already 8:45! Probably by nine."

Lisa felt drained. "Jack, I'd better get home tonight. Could I—take a rain check?" Sometimes good sense was a tyrant, she thought ruefully.

"How about lunch? You free Thursday?"

"Yes, I think so. Meet you . . .?"

"I could pick you up."

"No, that's alright. I need to do some errands anyway. In front of the post office?"

"Sure," he said, and headed over to Liz and the leaders' group.

As Lisa turned to leave, she almost ran into Rosalie, who'd come up behind her.

"I just wanted to say goodnight," Rosalie began. "How was the evening for you?"

"Good!" Lisa answered.

"Well, our meeting's started, so I've gotta run. But give me a call during the week if you have any questions—okay?" She handed Lisa a half-sheet of paper with a phone number written on it.

Lisa awoke with a start at 2:59 the next morning, chilled by the nightmare that had taken her back to the path that damp, foggy night. There'd been other dreams over the past months, all of them dark, uncertain experiences of attack. She'd be trying to walk up the street and not able to move her feet. And always the fog obscured her view.

But tonight the fog had cleared. This time she saw the attacker's face more clearly, his jaw set, eyes flashing anger and hate. The face was vaguely familiar, with the black bushy hair she remembered most clearly. There was a flash of red. Where? Straining to catch the dream image as it slipped away, she felt she could see Pastor Peterson's face retreating in the dark as Glenn watched.

Wilson stood growling by the door. Fear gripped her as she turned on the lamp.

The police.

No, you can't call the police at this hour unless it's an emergency.

But Wilson heard something! What?

She got up, slowly, carefully, quietly. Trying to think calmly, she recounted the events of the past weeks to herself. No one knew where she lived. She'd been careful about that. Could anyone have followed her home? She'd driven home last evening from the church, but had noticed no one following. Checking, she found the curtains tightly drawn; door, locked. She took the small, silver-gray cordless from its cradle and dialed the number Hal Jamison had given her.

"Pacific Grove Police," a woman's voice answered.

"I'm Lisa Calluso. Officer Jamison told me to call if I suspected any danger."

"An officer will be over right away," she said, "and I'll contact Officer Jamison."

Wilson, over his alarm, came over for petting. "At least you're here," she whispered, scratching his head. Quickly she put on a pot of water for tea, before going to the bathroom to splash water on her face. She'd barely thrown on a robe over her nightgown when the doorbell rang.

The sight of the petite officer with neatly styled short dark hair reassured Lisa.

"I'm Officer Santucci," the policewoman said breathlessly. "I was down at Asilomar when I got the call. Officer Jamison will be along in a few minutes."

"Thanks for coming," Lisa said, beckoning her in. The teakettle whistled impatiently on the stove, and Lisa left Wilson sniffing approvingly at Officer Santucci's trousers.

In the kitchen, hands shaking, Lisa poured the boiling water into her little pot and dropped in a bag. The doorbell rang, and she heard Santucci open it.

"C'mon in, Hal!"

Lisa left the kitchen to welcome him.

"Sorry I'm late," Jamison apologized. I guess you've already met my partner, Beatrice Santucci."

"We've met." Officer Santucci's mouth betrayed a droll smile. "But I guess this makes it official." Directing herself to Lisa, she said matter-of-factly, "So, ya heard a noise?"

Lisa told them about her abrupt awakening. "I thought I'd heard something, but I'm not sure." *They must think I'm an alarmist.*

"How 'bout the dog? Did he hear it, too? C'mere, big boy!" Reaching over to the ever-ready Wilson, she scratched between his ears.

"When I got up he was by the door, growling."

"So, it wasn't your imagination." Bea took out a little pad and scratched some notes.

"I'm going out for a look-see," Jamison said. "Bea, you stay here with Lisa. I'll let you know if I find something."

He left, and Lisa offered Bea a cup of tea.

"Something hot'd taste pretty good right now. That fog is damp and nasty."

They walked into the kitchen. After pouring tea into a mug with a picture of a butterfly on it, Lisa set it on the table, and got a squeeze bottle of honey from the cupboard.

Bea sat down. Stirring in some honey, she said, "Lisa, I was there the night of the attack. So if ya feel like talkin' to me about it, go ahead. It must feel awful knowing somebody's out there tryin' to get ya."

Before Lisa knew it, the story began to pour out if her. As it did, she found herself in tears more than once. As Bea took her hands and held them in solidarity, Lisa noticed the wide gold band on her ring finger. So, maybe she and Jamison were partners in more ways than one. Lisa felt a twinge of regret, but told herself how nice it must be for them to work together like that.

She'd finished describing her dream just as Jamison came back in. "Bea, come and take a look at this, will ya?" he asked. "I think somebody's been out in front." Lisa watched as Jamison led his partner out to the small flowerbed just outside the living room window. Through the window, in the dark, she could only see the spot of light made by his flashlight.

When they came back in, Jamison informed Lisa that he was going to make a plaster cast of some footprints they'd found in the soil. "It won't tell us much," he said, "but it might figure in. Odd part about it is the shoes, far as I can tell, show the person was facing toward the street. You'd expect him to have been trying to see inside."

Lisa pulled her yellow chenille robe more tightly around her.

"Well, her lights weren't on," Bea pointed out.

"No matter. He'd still try to see in." Jamison sat down to make some notes. "Ya got any of that tea left, ladies?"

Sipping it thirstily, he said, "Bea, how about if you stay here with Lisa, so she can get some sleep? I'll be patrolling the area. You can call me if anything turns up." Lisa poured him a cup.

"Sure, no problem."

It was after four when Lisa went back to bed, comfortable with the thought that Bea was in the other room watching.

Around eight, she pulled her robe around her and tottered out to the kitchen. Bea, yawning over an old *Sunset* magazine, looked up, "How'd ya sleep?"

"Like a baby. I think telling you about it helped."

"Jamison's on his way over with coffee. I hope you don't mind."

"I don't think so!"

Lisa had just dashed cold water on her face when Jamison arrived. He spread large cups of coffee and warm raisin-nut twists from Pavel's on the table. Prying the plastic lid off his coffee cup, he took a sip.

"Discover anything new last night?" Lisa asked hopefully.

Setting the cup down, he drew a slow breath and let it out. "The main thing we found out last night is that homeless guy, Glenn, is hanging around your neighborhood. I saw him. I have a suspicion the prints in your yard are his."

He pulled off a piece of pastry and ate it. When he spoke again, his voice was grave. "We'll bring him in, of course, but he wasn't close enough that we can get him for stalking. We'll have to let him go. Just a heads up, Lisa."

The thought of Glenn lurking around outside kept Lisa inside the rest of the day, looking forward anxiously to tomorrow's lunch with Jack. If anything, her anticipation had intensified after the discovery about Hal and Bea. They would protect her, she reasoned, but she imagined Jack becoming a confidant, and maybe more. Meanwhile, staying in the house depressed her more than ever, as she mulled over her stalemated life. It would be like this until they caught the guy, she thought bitterly.

From her porch on Thursday morning Lisa looked down over the bay, which mimicked the blue innocence of a baby's eyes. The horizon formed a crisp line against a cerulean sky. Full of anticipation, she pulled on a peach-colored sweatshirt, and left to meet Jack.

Wearing an olive-toned sweater over khakis, he waited by the newspaper boxes in front of the post office, where he leaned to squint at headlines. Looking up as she approached, he waved. "Hi! I was afraid you might not make it."

"Am I that late?" Her watch indicated a couple minutes after twelve. "I had trouble parking." They weren't on a hugging basis yet, but she couldn't resist touching him affectionately on the arm.

"Uh, I took the liberty—I hope you don't mind . . ." He held up two bulging brown paper bag lunches. "I thought we might eat this down by the water, if that's okay with you."

"Oh, yes." *It would be fun, wouldn't it?* She'd avoided the waterfront since the attack, but with someone like Jack, now might be the ideal time to venture back to the part of the Peninsula she loved most—the shore, with its limpid tide pools and rocky promontories to climb on, its crashing surf and gentle waves lapping lazily onto the sand.

They headed down to Ocean Drive, dodging across the street to the path.

"Watch it, Lisa!" He grabbed her arm, pulling her back, as a cyclist whizzed past on the paved portion of the path.

Pain swept over her, dizzying her momentarily. "Whew! Guess I'll have to pay better attention." The wounds, although mostly healed now, were still tender deep down. For some reason, she wanted to cry.

At Lovers Point Beach, he paused. "What do you say we go down a little farther, to one of the more interesting beaches?"

"Sounds good. Maybe one with fewer people."

Walking along the trail for a ways, they came to a short stretch of beach, where smooth, round, stones nestled at the base of the rocky bank, giving way to sand at the water's edge. They agreed that it looked good, and climbed down a trail worn between the rocks. On either end were rocky outcroppings, one of them stretching out some distance into the water. Waves crashed hungrily against it. Closer to shore, too, the waves were larger than usual.

"Let's sit over here, where there's a little shelter." Jack led the way to a protected niche at the base of the cliff, where they could sit partly out of the wind, but still look down the coast toward Monterey.

It felt good to sit down on the warm sand next to Jack, good enough that Lisa could partially ignore the throbbing of her back wounds when she leaned against the rough rock. In silence, she studied his classic profile:

strong chin, straight nose, hair the color of sweet potatoes. Suddenly she wanted very much to tell him everything that had happened.

When the time was right.

"Well, *bon appetit*!" Jack reached into his bag, pulling out a sandwich ensconced in a plastic baggie. "Tuna. From a little lunch counter at the liquor store on Grand. Best kept secret in Pacific Grove!"

Dubious, Lisa sampled hers. "This isn't bad!"

"So, what do you think of St. Augustine's?" he asked.

"I'm liking it more than I expected to—the people, especially. And Pastor Peterson . . . seems very spiritual, but also . . ." She groped for the right words.

"Approachable? He's not perfect, but hey! I find him refreshingly human."

Lisa continued munching on her sandwich, enjoying the warm haven. A seagull was perched on a nearby rock, watching them. Out of the corner of her eye, she detected Jack's eyes on her as well.

"Tell me more about your work, Jack," she suggested, hoping to find a more personal topic.

He expanded on the investment company for a bit, then stopped to take another bite of his sandwich. Pulling out a napkin, he wiped his mouth and directed the conversation her way.

"So, did you say where you work, Lisa? I don't seem to remember."

"Well, I'm not really working right now. I've been, uh, recovering . . ." So it was out. She'd planned to tell him, but suddenly she felt qualms.

"Recovering?" He set his sandwich down on top of the empty baggie, all his attention on her. "From what?"

"An . . . accident. I . . . I can't really talk about it yet." Her hand shook as she lifted a cold, moist bottle of mineral water from her bag.

His eyes, still questioning, softened slightly. "Whew! And you actually had to stop work? Well, I understand. That could be hard to talk about, all right. But sometimes a person needs to talk, Lisa, and I'll listen if you need that. Okay? When you're ready."

She twisted off the top of her bottle. The ogling gull lowered his head, as if to be inconspicuous, and flew to a closer perch, on a ledge above them on the cliff.

Although the wind still whipped waves against the rocks, the sunlight in their secluded spot was making Lisa perspire. Automatically, she pushed up her sweatshirt sleeves. Jack stopped, sandwich poised in mid-air, eyes fixed on her scarred arms. Cheeks burning, she quickly slid the sleeves back down.

From above, so swiftly that neither of them saw it coming, the seagull swooped down, grasped Jack's sandwich from his hand in its yellow bill, and flew down the beach to a safe refuge. Jack's mouth dropped open in shock, causing Lisa to laugh. After a moment, Jack joined her.

"Where did you say you live, Lisa? Pacific Grove, right?"

"Yes, up on . . ."

About 30 feet out from shore, in a kelp bed, she saw the unmistakable head of an otter.

"Look!" Struggling to her feet, she brushed the sand from her clothes and headed down toward the rocks.

Jack followed. At the water's edge she stepped out gingerly onto a rock and then over to a larger one leading out to a craggy promontory. He was close behind, when she stopped to peer down into one of the tidal pools. The water sucked nervously in and out through the narrow spaces in the rocks, working its way into this tiny world, where anemones concealed by sand waited for tiny prey on each new wave and hermit crabs camouflaged as snails prowled every nook and cranny.

Drunk on newly found daring, Lisa climbed over the rocks, hoping to get a better look at the otter. Behind her, Jack shouted against the wind, "Careful, Lisa! You know about the rogue waves on this coast." Coming up beside her, he added, "A couple of newlyweds were climbing out on rocks like this, and a freak wave came and swept them out to sea."

"I'm watching," she assured him, scanning the white-capped water for the elusive head.

Momentarily she lost her balance, and Jack slid his hand up her back and onto her left shoulder, taking her right arm gently with his other hand to steady her. She felt herself relaxing back against him, and he tightened his hold reassuringly. Below them, foam-edged waves surged against their rock, splashing up in triumphal challenge.

Suddenly, from behind, voices pierced the sounds of birds and surf. They turned to see a couple of teenage boys scrambling down the steep path leading to the beach.

Jack loosed his hold, and, stepping back, said, "Lisa, I need to get back to work."

"Oh, okay. This wind *is* getting nippy."

On the walk back, Jack talked about the people at the church, the possibilities of a recession, and the car he hoped to get, now that the new models were all out. Lisa half-listened, still savoring the thought of their moment together on the rocks.

At the post office Lisa stopped. "Well, Jack, I've really enjoyed this." She meant that. "I feel . . . as if I'd known you for a long time."

"Funny how that happens sometimes," he agreed, smiling down at her.

Except for the Sunday morning service at St. Augustine's, it was a dreary weekend. Lisa had seen Rosalie up in the choir, and Jack was busy. Pastor Peterson had made a point of hugging her as she left church. It struck her as unctuous.

Probably just my bad mood.

On Tuesday morning, determined to forget her despondency, Lisa put on her new walking shoes and set out with Wilson for Bookworks, a healthy walk through the back streets where she could admire the fading fall bloom in the carefully groomed front yards she passed. Marigold burst magnificently in gold from between the white pickets of a fence; red chrysanthemum shared a bed with a blue sage. A few late roses staged a fall showing, and—up against a blue Victorian cottage—pyracantha, true to its name, boasted of fiery orange berries.

Wilson still resisted the leash, trying to investigate the lawns for his own purposes, and she had to keep reining him in. "It's obedience school for you, fella!" she warned, as he sniffed interminably at a fence corner.

Once she reached the bookstore she felt fairly safe. In among the shelves she felt secluded. Browsing through the new novels and biographies kept her mind off her life's uncertainty. She picked out a couple of Elizabeth Peters mysteries. Then, after winding Wilson's leash around a barstool, she sat down for a cappuccino.

She'd started for home when, turning to urge Wilson on, she saw the now-familiar figure of Glenn half a block behind her. Hat pulled down on his forward-bent head, hands plunged resolutely in pockets, he trudged toward her. He didn't seem to notice her, so she continued her course, yanking Wilson back from the Infiniti tire he was investigating. Despite her breathlessness—this was the farthest she'd walked since the attack—she hastened her pace. Home was still a number of blocks away.

Trying to avoid the sight of Glenn, she looked into the wind, toward the water beyond. A bank of clouds was forming across the horizon, while icy strokes of white brushed the blue of the sky. Resolute hydrangea paled and shivered in flowerbeds under the filtered light.

Again Wilson stalled, intensely interested in a clump of grass protruding through the fence. As she pulled on the leash, Glenn caught up with her.

"I can walk with you for a while," he stated, pausing until she got Wilson under control.

"This dog!" she exclaimed, agitated by Glenn's presence.

"But he's a good watchdog. You need him with you."

Preferring not to discuss her safety further with Glenn, Lisa changed the subject, asking him where he was from.

"San Francisco," he began, speaking with his characteristic disjointed formality. "My parents have a laundry there—hard-working people. I went to school there, and I did pretty well in math and science. My dad wanted me to become a scientist."

He chuckled humorlessly. "Too much pressure on me. If I don't get A's, I get whipped. I can't go out at night with other kids. Got to study. So, I rebel. Somebody gives me a drug that makes you very happy. Then I don't need to go out. I just take it and have a good time wherever I am. But I took too many of those drugs, and they wrecked my mind. My parents found out and threw me out. So here I am. I wasted a good life."

Lisa nodded. "But you were there when I needed you, Glenn."

Or maybe . . .

He seemed to miss her comment. "And I help Esteban at the church quite a lot."

When they reached Grove Market, Glenn scanned the parking lot. "There's my friend Sam, sitting over by the shoe repair."

He motioned toward the tall, fair, balding man sitting on the ground, leaning against the small shop opposite them. "Sam *knows* about you."

The way he said it made Lisa's back tingle unpleasantly. She stared at Sam, who sang to himself, waving the handle of the broom he held in his hand.

"Well, I'll leave you here," Glenn said, and with that headed across the lot, dodging parked cars.

Grateful for the reprieve, Lisa guided Wilson over to the market, hoping not to see Glenn again when she came out. Sure enough, when she emerged with her small bag of groceries, Sam was sweeping and Glenn had disappeared.

Her hand shook as she pushed the key into the lock of her apartment door, Wilson panting by her side. The walk—or was it the encounter with Glenn?—had taken more out of her than she wanted to admit.

She put away the milk, took a plastic container of leftover soup and poured it in a bowl to microwave. While it was cooking, she poured some kibbles in Wilson's dish. By the time she sat down with her minestrone, she was almost too tired to eat. She ate as much as she could, then threw the rest down the garbage disposal. After that, she went in to sit in her recliner by the window and closed her eyes. Despite her fatigue, she couldn't relax. What had Glenn meant by that remark, "Sam *knows* about you"?

She'd just begun to doze when, strident, the phone jangled into her consciousness. Lisa groped for the receiver. "Hello?"

I should be monitoring these calls.

She recognized Jack's rich mellow voice. "We're calling the people in our groups to see how everybody is doing."

"That's nice of you . . . I'm doing very well," she said. She wouldn't mention how tired she was.

"I hope you enjoyed our picnic last week."

"Very much!" she said, aware of her face flushing. "I'm glad we could get to know each other better."

"About the group—uh, did you have any questions?—about the Church, I mean. If there's anything I could help you with, I'd be glad to make some time."

"I can't think of any ques . . . tions."

How did he get my phone number?

Old slow-on-the-draw Lisa, she chided herself. "I'm surprised you've got my number, Jack. I thought I hadn't written it on the list." She paused. "I hope that hasn't inconvenienced you."

"Not at all," Jack replied affably. "I got it from the church office. The secretary called your mom for it."

And of course, Mom was *glad* to help. Lisa's misgivings melted away. In fact, she felt flattered by his persistence. Maybe he wasn't just getting to know her out of a sense of Christian duty.

"Thanks for your concern, Jack."

"Will we see you tonight?" he asked.

"Yes, barring unforeseen circumstances." Despite being so tired, she wanted to be there tonight, to see him again.

"Good! Looking forward to it. God bless!"

She'd no sooner hung up the phone than the doorbell rang. Slightly alarmed, she released the foot lift on her recliner, struggled to her feet and went cautiously to the door. Through the peephole, she saw Bea Santucci looking out toward the bay.

"Ah, you're here!" Bea exclaimed as Lisa opened the door. "I hope this isn't intrusive, but I called and left a message this morning, and you hadn't answered. So I thought I'd come by and see how things were going."

"I took a walk this morning," Lisa said. "And I was so tired when I got back that I forgot to listen to my messages. C'mon in." She hated to have the neighbors see a police officer on her porch. People might start to talk.

"Don't mind if I do." Bea sat down at the kitchen table. "So, have ya noticed anybody else hangin' around here?"

"Not exactly." Lisa leaned against the cushioned chair back.

"Whaddaya mean, 'Not exactly'?" Bea leaned forward.

"Well, Glenn seems to be following me. He showed up again this morning."

"Where?" She asked sharply.

"Down by Bookworks. He walked part way home with me."

"And you *let* him?"

"What was I going to do? He wasn't threatening me, really." Lisa leaned forward against the table. "He showed me his homeless friend Sam, though. He says Sam 'knows' about me. It kind of gave me the creeps."

"No kidding!" Bea frowned. "Look, we know he's hangin' around. Hal's pretty sure that footprint was his."

"I haven't heard anything since that night. Maybe it was just a fluke . . ." She wanted this looming threat to dissipate, like fog burning off in the noonday sun.

"No! It isn't a *fluke*! You've got to stop being so passive about this." Bea clenched the fist that rested on the table. "You're like a clam, hiding in your shell!"

Lisa managed a wry smile. "Maybe more of a hermit crab." A cold wave of discouragement washed over her. "I don't know what else to do, Bea. All I can do is wait for . . ."

"Forget about the hermit crab, Lisa!" A smile flickered across Bea's face, softening the impact of her words. "Ya gonna be a real crab from now on, okay? You've seen real crabs in action, haven't ya? They hide down in a little crevice in the rock and watch for their prey t'come crawlin' along and then, *Pop!* with those pinchers. They get that sucker!"

"What're you saying?"

"I'm sayin' it's time we stopped waiting!"

Lisa gulped. This felt like standing in the surf when a wave began to retreat, dragging the sand out from under your feet. "Stop waiting and . . .?"

"Lisa, sorry, but I'm just frustrated. I've been checking out the men on our list. We've got suspects, but no real evidence. Ya know, if he'd raped you, this might actually be easier for us to solve. At least then we would've had DNA. But, as it is, we've got samples from Glenn, your ex, and some other known sex offenders in the area, but nothing to match them to." She got up momentarily to fill a glass with tap water.

"No hairs even?"

"There was kind of an odd hair-like fiber that tested out as synthetic. Must've been from some article of clothing." She sipped the water and made a face. "The point is, I don't see how we're getting anywhere. And yet you seem to think Glenn knows something. And this other guy—Sam—too." She sat back abruptly. "Lisa, you need to wake up! Either Glenn is plotting something in some incredibly sinister way, teasing you with it, or at least he knows something. And either way, you're in danger."

Resting her head on her hands, Lisa wanted to go to sleep. "So it wasn't just my imagination."

"Why aren't you angry about this?" Bea demanded, her voice growing shrill. "*I'm* angry, and it didn't even happen to me."

Lisa sat up straight, aware of pumping adrenaline. "I'm scared, but not angry."

"Some guy stabs you and leaves you for dead, for no good reason, and you're not angry? You can't work, you're in hiding, you're being stalked, and you're not angry? What? You deserved this?" She was wagging her hand.

Shakily, Lisa answered, "I'm in a seekers' group at the church now, and my faith is growing, and I think that's why—"

Bea cut her off. "Nope. God's not calling you to be a wimp!" Her wide brown eyes blazed. "God's friends hafta take charge."

Lisa stared at her. "What do you have in mind? What do I have to do?"

"Nothing out of the ordinary. I'd say, walk home from one of your church meetings at a prearranged time. We'll take care of the rest. Do you trust me?" She paused, waiting for Lisa's response.

Lisa hesitated. "Wouldn't that be dangerous?" *If I'm going to start taking charge, couldn't it be in small increments? This is more like plunging off the high dive.*

"No, I wouldn't consider this if I thought . . . no, it's just t'give us an excuse t'bring Glenn in. I really don't think he's our man, but he *knows* something."

Lisa imagined herself out alone, coming home from the church. Before the attack, she'd loved walking alone at night, the rhythmic rush of the surf, the barking of the seals floating on the cool sea breeze. But the old freedom was gone. He'd taken that from her. She'd been reduced to cowering, waiting for others to rescue her. "Let's *get* him!" she said, anger making her more resolute.

"Ah hah!" Bea exclaimed. "Do I hear some spirit?" She leaned over the table. "When could you plan to go out? The sooner we do this, the better, because I've got a hunch you're in more danger than we realize."

"Actually, the seekers' group meets tonight," Lisa said, "but I'm not sure I'll go. After this morning, I'm exhausted."

"Well, you've gotta call me as soon as you know if you're going, so I can have a watch in place. I'll try to line up some people, but we won't go out unless you call."

"If tonight doesn't work out, we could always do next week," Lisa said hopefully, thinking a week might give her time to work up to this. "Do I need to do anything special?"

Wilson panted hopefully at Bea's side. "I'd bring the dog." She scratched between his ears. "Ya got any mace?"

Lisa said she did.

"Good. Well, get some rest, and let me know what you decide."

After she'd gone, Lisa went back to the recliner. A little rest *would* help her decide on this evening, she thought. Taking a *National Geographic*, she started reading an article on Afghanistan. She didn't notice when the magazine fell from her hand.

Wilson's nuzzling awakened her. Opening her eyes to darkness, Lisa felt disoriented. The wind whistled in the pine tree next door. Peering groggily through the still-open blinds, she saw lights on in the house across the street. From somewhere she heard a horn honking. She turned on the lamp and blinked at her watch. Six o'clock. The Seekers' meeting started at seven. She could still make it if she hurried. Getting up, she went to wash her face. A little refreshing of her make-up, a cup of noodles, a snack for Wilson, and they could be off.

She threw a box of breath mints in her pocket. They rattled down next to the mace. Wilson's leash—where had she left it? Oh, right. It'd fallen behind the table. She fastened it, and put on her pea coat, grabbing a knit hat for the walk home. As she locked the door, she felt good about being involved in the plan to corral Glenn.

Her head cleared by the brisk pace set by Wilson, Lisa arrived at the church fellowship hall at ten minutes before seven. Liz, her face drawn under the severity of her gray perm, was waiting at the door and pulled her aside.

"Lisa, Jack will have a leaders' meeting tonight, so you'll be in a different group," she said in a tight voice. "He wasn't very happy about it, though. Sorry, I hope it'll be okay with you."

Lisa looked around for Jack. "Whatever works." This was frustrating. She'd planned to tell him about the plan to catch Glenn, but maybe later she could say something.

"Whose group am I in, then?"

"You'll be in Rosalie's group tonight." Looking over toward the refreshment table, the thin, angular woman went on, "You met her last time, didn't you?"

"I did. That'll be fine. Also, do you mind if my dog stays? I like to keep him with me when I go out at night."

Liz knitted her brows slightly. "I suppose that would be fine."

Lisa started across the room to where Jack had been setting up chairs for the large group, but seeing him engaged in conversation with Pastor Peterson, she held off. Maybe she'd see him at the break.

A bell called them to sit down. After the opening announcements, Rosalie gathered her group together. Lisa struggled to keep her mind on the topic for discussion—"Living in God's Love"—but her thoughts gravitated to the solo walk awaiting her. Worry gnawed at her; however the walk down here had gone without incident.

She could do this!

Her eyes scanned the room. Jack had disappeared.

"Lisa?"

She surfaced blankly. "Sorry, I was distracted. What was the question?"

Rosalie's blue eyes sparkled invitingly. "How have you experienced God's love this week?"

"Hmmm." Lisa pondered the question, imagining God's love as light against the dark shadow of fear that had been holding her life in thrall over the past three months. "Actually, I've met one person in particular who had that effect on me," she answered, recalling the galvanizing effect of Bea's words that afternoon. "I think maybe she's helped me to get through my fear. I guess that's where I felt God's love."

Several group members nodded.

"Interesting that you used the word 'through' instead of, say, 'get over'," Rosalie commented. "Why was that?"

Lisa combed her tangled thoughts. "Because, I have no control over the fear, but I can stop letting it control me." The answer had surfaced from deep within her.

"That's beautiful, Lisa!" Deftly, Rosalie wove the discussion into a meaningful pattern. The evening progressed as it had the week before.

During the final prayer circle, she saw Jack standing across from her. He caught her eye and smiled. If she could just talk with him briefly before leaving, she thought, she'd feel surer of herself.

Could she really go through with this plan?

After a rousing song, Rosalie squeezed Lisa's hand. "You have my number, don't you? Any questions, problems . . . just give me a call, okay? Do you have a way home?"

"I'm walking. It's only a few blocks."

Rosalie hesitated, hanging onto her hand. "Lisa, I don't think that's a good idea. This is a wonderful town, but things do happen—I mean, they can happen anywhere. Beauty, peace, love—it seems to attract a dark side. Let me give you a ride."

Lisa hesitated. It would be so easy to put off this little operation until next week—until she was more ready. *But what am I? Some kind of wimp?*

"I really appreciate your concern, Rosalie, but I've got Wilson, and I just feel like walking tonight, okay? I process things best when I'm walking."

That's the authentic me, she prodded herself. *I've got my self back. And I'll have help if I need it.*

Rosalie continued to frown doubtfully.

"Look, could you maybe call me after a half-hour—when you get home?" Writing her address and phone number on the back of one of the handouts, she gave it to Rosalie. "One other thing," Lisa said hesitantly. "Do you know where Jack is? I wanted to see him for a second."

Rosalie glanced around. "He should be here any minute. I think he's down in the office making copies."

Wilson was pulling toward the door. "Just tell him I said 'hi'," Lisa said quickly. "I've got to get going now."

She pulled on her hat and made her way out.

Dark clouds crowded in heavy overhead, and a chafing wind blew in off the bay, where lighted squid boats tossed on the mounting waves. Pulling up the collar of her pea coat, Lisa headed up the hill, leash in one hand and her combination mace/billy club in the other. She managed to wave at several participants leaving in cars and even smiled once or twice.

At the corner, she glanced both ways, half-expecting to see a police car with Bea and Jamison in it. Wait! What had they agreed on before Bea left that afternoon? Bea had said, "If you decide to go, gimme a call." Did she really say that? It seemed like Bea'd said she was going to set everything up. But Lisa'd said she was tired, that she needed to decide.

Oh shit! She hadn't called!

Feeling naked to the elements and God knows what else, Lisa stood vacillating on the corner.

I could call her on the cell phone.

She groped in her bag for the little Nokia. Maybe it was too late to set up the sting, but at least Bea'd know she was out here.

Her hand explored every corner of the bag. Nothing!

She felt beads of sweat forming under her cap despite the chill wind. Desperately, she began a more controlled search through the bag, item by item. No phone.

She could go back to the hall and look for a phone, but the thought of walking into the middle of the staff meeting put her off. This would mean delaying the entrapment until next week, but a week wasn't long at all. Was it?

The concrete below her feet seemed to pull at her like quicksand, rendering her immobile.

I've gotta decide!

I've got my mace and my dog now, she told herself, so she stepped off the curb and launched nervously into her taking-charge pace, starting up the narrow block in the direction of home. The gusting wind sent shadows of looming pines in a chaotic dance upon the sidewalk ahead, and the first heavy drops of rain were beginning to fall. She hurried on, glancing back to catch sight of anything unusual. Wilson seemed not to notice, pulling ahead, anxious to get home.

At the corner up ahead she saw a dark figure silhouetted against a porch light. It moved quickly back out of sight. *Maybe just a passerby.* Wilson growled. Anxiously Lisa scanned the homes on either side. A corner house still had lights on. Mentally, she rehearsed the way she'd run to the porch and pound on the door if there was real trouble.

When she reached the corner she scanned the cross street in both directions. No sign of the shadowed figure, but shrubbery and trees provided ample room for concealment. All she could hear were the howling wind and pelting rain. Wilson held back, whimpering slightly, then tried to plunge across the street, yanking her ahead with him. They continued forward into the next block. Here the houses stood farther back from the street, partially hidden by thick shrubbery.

Wilson slowed to a stop, determined to fully investigate his surroundings. Lisa pulled at the leash, but his mass was too great to budge. Like a cold tide, apprehension mounted within her. On her right a high, ivy-draped wall hemmed her in for the length of the block, and parked cars provided obstruction along the curb side. She was just a block from home, but it seemed a very long one.

A low growl from Wilson alerted her to a figure that slid out from behind a car just to her rear. It approached so swiftly that she barely had time to ready the mace. She squeezed prematurely, missing her target. The figure lunged against her, knife raised in one hand. A black ski mask covered its face. Losing her balance, she managed a second squirt of mace. As she fell backward, she let go of Wilson to catch her fall, and dropped the mace. It rolled away from her.

The masked attacker swore, hesitating momentarily. No question the voice was male. Wilson jumped up on him, sending him staggering backward. He regained his balance and went for the dog. Lisa screamed, managed to retrieve the mace, and struggled to her feet. The knife plunged towards Wilson. She managed another spray of the mace, this time closer to his face. Wilson yelped in pain, his sharp cries joining Lisa's screams. Lights went on in the house across the street. The masked man turned again to Lisa, knife raised. She began to run up the block. He caught up almost immediately, grabbed her arm roughly, dragged her back, and thrust her against the wall, his steamy breath striking her face.

She leaned forward and managed to catch the mask in her teeth. He pushed her back, but she held on long enough to pull the mask partway off before the rough stone bit into her back. She caught a glimpse of a strong jaw leading to his earlobe, where a glint suggested an earring. A whiff of a faintly reminiscent sagey musk scent wafted out on the warm air from his body.

Across the street, a door opened. He moved squarely in front of her, as if to shield her from view. All Lisa could see was the knit ski mask, beaded with raindrops. From behind, Wilson's howling subsided slightly. The heavy body of her attacker pressed against her in one final crush before he lunged outward. Again he lifted the knife.

An arm slid deftly around his neck and pulled him backward. As he struggled, another set of arms appeared from Lisa's left to grab the still uplifted hand with the knife. Lisa tried to regain her balance. Blinking into the rain, she looked hard to make out the two dark forms that struggled with her assailant.

One wrestled the knife free, while the other hung onto the attacker's neck, pulled him back and down onto the sidewalk on top of him.

"Sam, help me hold him down!"

Surprised, Lisa recognized Glenn's voice. She leapt over and grasped the assailant's upper arm, trying to pull him back. Fighting to escape Glenn's grasp, he caught Lisa with one hand, loosening her hold, and twisted so that she lost balance again. Sam went for his feet, and tried to pull him off Glenn. The masked man kicked violently, sending Sam to his knees, and pounded Glenn's head, beneath him, with one fist.

"Hey, I can't hold on much longer!" shouted Glenn, still hanging onto the flailing attacker. "Grab his hand, somebody."

Sam grabbed the fist that was pounding Glenn, and hung on.

A set of headlights swung around the corner below, started up the hill, then stopped abruptly. As Lisa struggled to her feet, she saw Hal running over from the squad car. Bea stood by the car, talking into the police radio. "We've got an assault on the corner of Sumac and Wesley. Need a couple officers pronto! And send an ambulance!" Several blocks away a siren sounded.

Looking back at the struggling Glenn, Lisa saw him clinging to a familiar head. The mask lay crumpled some distance away. She gasped. "Jack?"

Bea came over to stand by Lisa. Hal forced Glenn to relinquish his hold on Jack, who sat up, rubbing his neck.

"Talk about suspicion!" Jack roared, straining in the direction of the police. "Look what they've done to me! I come after her to see that she makes it home safely, and these bums jump me! They would've gotten to her, too, if I hadn't made it here when I did. That one even had a knife!" He waved his hand in Sam's direction.

Sam hung back close to the rockery, shaking his head. "Not good!" Lisa heard him say. "It's bad! Bad!"

"You're saying you were attacked?" Jamison asked. Lisa watched, bewildered, as the officer, chestnut hair beaded with raindrops, took Glenn firmly by the arm.

A siren screamed around the corner and the car squealed to a halt by a clutch of curious neighbors across the street. Two more officers jumped out and rushed over.

"Here, Soares, secure this man!" Jamison shouted to them. "And Blake, get that one!"

Sam had quietly started off up the street, and broke into a run at the sound of Hal's command. Blake took off after him.

Bea turned to Lisa and asked brusquely, "Are ya hurt?"

Lisa pressed her hands gingerly against her back. "It hurts where he pushed me against the rocks, but I guess that's all."

"You should probably go sit down." Sounding exasperated, Bea did not wait for Lisa's response, but went over to join the policeman named Soares.

Lisa studied the scene. Glenn stood by Soares, hanging his head and mumbling incoherently. Jack stood talking to Hal, with animated gestures.

More headlights, but no siren or flashing lights this time. A white Camry pulled to the curb, and Pastor Peterson got out, opening a black umbrella. From the driver's side, Rosalie came over to Lisa, fear written on her white face.

"I had a bad feeling when you left," she began breathlessly. "Something happened at the meeting—and then I heard the sirens. We were just breaking up."

She stopped to catch her breath. "I called your place," she went on, "but you weren't home, so I asked Pastor Peterson to come up with me."

She scrutinized Lisa in silence for a few seconds. "Are you okay?"

Lisa nodded, unable to speak, and gratefully accepted the hug Rosalie proffered. They watched as the clergyman splashed over to the two officers and Jack and Glenn.

"What's going on here?" asked Pastor Peterson.

"Well, it appears we've caught Glenn here attacking Jack Kelly, who says he'd come out to see Lisa Calluso safely home." Hal's deep blue eyes probed the clergyman's steel gray ones. "Do you know either of these men, Pastor?"

"Sure do! Jack's very active at the church." He set one hand on Jack's shoulder. "Good work, Jack!"

"And this man, Glenn . . . you know him too?" Glenn was now in handcuffs.

"Very much so. He's hung around the church over the past few years, helping Esteban. I had just issued an order that he not be allowed to loiter around St. Augustine's any longer. Frankly, I was afraid something like this, or worse, would happen—if it hasn't already." The pastor's voice darkened as he spoke.

Rosalie had come over to Pastor Peterson's side and nodded in agreement.

"So . . ." Hal's voice trailed off uncertainly. "Lisa, how about your side of this?"

Lisa stood frozen in disbelief. Had Jack been concerned enough to follow her home, as he said? Had she, confused by the wind and rain, and by her own fear, misinterpreted what had happened? Was his the arm that pulled the masked attacker from her? Or had he himself attacked her, as it had at first appeared? It would make things easier if she could agree with Jamison and Pastor Peterson. But if it wasn't Glenn . . . if it was really Jack . . .

A haunting memory hovered just beyond her consciousness.

"Lisa's feeling a little disoriented at this moment, I suspect," Pastor Peterson said, speaking her own feelings. "But I'm sure she's relieved to know that from now on she may not have to worry. I feel certain that you've got your man, officer." He shifted the umbrella to his other hand to include Rosalie in its shelter.

"Excuse me, Pastor, but I'll have to disagree," interjected Bea sharply. "We can't jump to any such conclusions—particularly since we've not heard from this witness yet." With an uncompromising look at Lisa, she added, "Take a few minutes to think about this, Lisa. I want you to come over to the car and sit down for a few minutes."

Lisa followed her, needing to sort through this welter of contradictory thoughts. She got into the back seat, where Wilson was already established on a dry blanket. He'd licked his wound clean, and had curled up to sleep. Bea sat in front, facing her, one arm over the seat back. "First off, I hafta be honest. I'm really pissed that you didn't call before trying this. You coulda got yourself killed, you know!" Bea's brown eyes burned with intensity.

"I know," Lisa said shamefacedly. "I'm really sorry. I fell asleep after you left, and woke up with just barely enough time to get to the meeting. I—it's no excuse, I know—forgot my cell phone. I just thought we'd set everything up, and then when I realized we hadn't, I figured we'd wait until next week."

"Yes, but didn't you think about the danger? We knew Glenn was hanging around!" She sighed loudly and took off her hat.

"I *did* have my mace, and Wilson."

I sound pathetic. Feeling bad about having let Bea down, Lisa continued, "But you came anyway! How'd you know?"

"Just a hunch. We were gonna cruise past your house and see if anybody seemed to be lurking around." Bea looked over at Glenn, who studied the ground, shaggy dark hair hanging wet over his eyes. "So, go on . . ."

"I was almost home, when this guy in a black ski mask jumped out from behind a car. He was coming at me with a knife." She went on describing the struggle, and Bea took notes.

"Now, tell me," Bea said, raising her pen, "What happened to the guy in the mask? Because I'm confused. When we got here, it looked like Glenn had attacked Jack, and neither one was wearing a mask. Who came at *you* with the knife?"

The flashing ambulance interrupted her, pulling to a stop in the middle of the street. Bea jumped up, beckoned over the paramedics, and turned to Lisa. "Will you be okay for a few more minutes?"

"I can wait." While Bea led the ambulance personnel over to the group on the sidewalk, Lisa stared at Jack, who displayed his usual confidence, despite the struggle. He still had that easy boyish grin, as he spoke with the pastor and the police. She'd wanted to run her fingers through that hair, now dotted with glistening raindrops. *Why would Jack want to hurt her?* It was easier to doubt the evidence of her senses than to let go of her cherished image of Jack. Perhaps her mind had played a trick on her.

Bea came back over. "So, who came at you with the knife, Lisa?"

"I'm not sure." Her stomach clenched.

Bea raised her neatly plucked eyebrows. "Take your time. We need this to be right!" She set down her notebook and turned to look out. "Uh oh! Blake's comin' back *without* the blond dude." She went over to the officer, who panted steamy breaths into the damp air as he trudged up the hill.

Lisa stroked Wilson's head, then went to join Bea and Blake.

"Damn him! He got away, the son-of-a . . ." He rubbed his knee, where he'd torn his pants. "He went over a wall and down through the creek bed. I tripped on the way down." He looked sheepish.

"We'll put out a watch for him." Bea headed back to the car.

Hesitantly, Lisa moved over to stand by Glenn. Peering at his hair and face, she groped for the elusive memory that kept retreating like a sea anemone pulling down in its cloak of sand. He turned to her and said reproachfully, "Not a good idea, walking home alone like that. If—"

A husky blond paramedic with pink lipstick interrupted them. "I'll take a look at you now," she said. Glenn had scraped his knees and elbows in the struggle, and the woman swabbed them with Betadine and bandaged them. Then she turned to Lisa and began checking her arms and legs. "Impressive scars ya got there!" she observed. "Oh! *You're* the one . . ."

As the medic checked her over, Lisa's eyes drifted down the street. No lights on the bay tonight. Down at the end of the block, someone came around the corner and started up the hill. She watched the approach of the tall, thin individual, who walked determinedly, but as if with trepidation.

She slid her arm out of the coat sleeve, so the woman could take her blood pressure. As the figure neared, she recognized Sam carrying a bulging plastic grocery bag.

Seeing him, Blake broke away from the pony-tailed paramedic cleaning up his knee. "Sorry!" He ran towards Sam, who continued on unflinching, and seized him by the arm. "Tryin' t'make yourself look better by comin' back, huh? Ya can't fool me, bud!"

As he roughly pulled the dripping man over to the car, Bea hurried over. "What ya got there, fellah?"

He clutched the bag. "Need t'talk t'my friend."

Lisa pulled her coat around her and followed Glenn over to Sam.

Sam thrust the bag at Glenn, holding it open. "Show 'em, Glenn." In the view of all gathered Glenn reached inside the bag with his cuffed hands, pulled out a dark, matted furry mass and held it up.

"What *is* that? It looks like a dead animal! Why. . .?" Lisa watched as, hampered by the handcuffs, Glenn attempted to pull the shaggy thing apart.

Bea took it from him. "Son of a bitch!" the female officer said. "A wig!" She held it gingerly, turning it over. "Somethin's caked on it—mud?" She pulled out a small flashlight and looked closely. "Could this be coagulated blood?"

As Blake snapped handcuffs on Sam's wrists, Hal pulled out his notebook with calm authority and lifted his pen. Silence fell on the group. "Well, Glenn," he said, "let's hear why *you* think this thing has any bearing on what we're doing here."

Glenn spoke in even tones. "Sam found it in a trash barrel over at Nob Hill grocery. Thought he might use it sometime."

Sam stood frowning, thin blond hair flattened in wet ribbons against his freckled balding head.

"Do you have any idea where it could've come from, Sam?" Hal queried.

Glenn nodded at Sam. "Tell 'em, bro'."

Sam shook his head slowly, and then turned back towards Jack, who stood between Rosalie and Pastor Peterson. "That guy." He lifted his cuffed hands to point. "He dropped it in there late one night. Maybe thought nobody was around. I was gettin' ready t'sleep, over in the corner."

"How do you know it was him?" Jamison asked doubtfully.

"I seen him over at the church plentya times. I was curious." Sam looked beseechingly at Glenn.

Bea turned to Glenn. "Did you see any of this?"

"Nah. He told me about it when he showed me the wig. I knew about what happened to this woman. I found her, you know." He straightened up and shook the hair from his eyes. "I just started to think about it. I kept my eyes open."

"What a crock! What a fuckin' crock o' shit!" Jack shouted, turning to face Hal. "This creep doesn't know me! He's clutching at straws, because he's on the spot." His tawny eyes flashed. "The two of them 're in league on this. How can they deny it any longer?"

Lisa stood close to Jack, shivering. She studied his strong jaw and the blaze of hair that seemed to give off sparks under the pulsating red lights. *The eyes.* Suddenly she was there, leaving the rec trail again. Under the mass of dark hair, those were the eyes whose hate had pierced her. She remembered how, as he'd struggled with her, the dark hair had shifted oddly, uncovering the *red* that hadn't made sense at the time.

Anger swelled up like a great tide inside her. "No, Jack! It wasn't Glenn or Sam. It was you! I remember clearly now." Wilson, having come over, crouched and sounded a low growl at Jack's feet—as if to confirm this turn of events.

Lisa wasn't finished. "But what burns me the most, Jack, is the lie you've lived with us! You led me on! You tried to incriminate these innocent men! You deceived the community! You . . ."

Bea caught the arm Jack raised threateningly. "Gil?"

Soares snapped a set of handcuffs on him.

Shaken, but oddly elated, Lisa turned back to Rosalie and found her wiping tears from her cheeks. "I can't believe this," she choked.

Stonefaced beside her, the clergyman put a hand around Rosalie's shoulder. "This all remains to be seen," he said stiffly. "I guess we'd better get back, Rosalie. I've got an early service in the morning."

Bea stood close to Officer Soares, leaned against him for a second, and, reached up to kiss his cheek. Seeing Lisa's surprised expression, she said, "We met back in fifth grade at St. Angela's School." Then she was back to the business at hand—getting the three men into Soares and Blake's cars, which took off for the police station, leaving Jamison with Lisa.

"I've reached a vet, Lisa," he said, "so we can take this dog over for a checking over. A wound like that shouldn't be left untreated, no matter how well-licked it is." He turned to look into the car, where Wilson lay curled up on a blanket on the back seat.

"Thanks." She didn't move. The rain had stopped falling, and the still air carried the fragrance of damp earth and fallen leaves.

"You must feel like a load's been lifted." He drew a deep breath, apparently enjoying the same sense of relief as she did.

"I guess so," she said numbly. "But it'll take a while to get used to it."

He leaned against the open car door. "You've got a lot to process."

Lisa nodded. "I can't believe I almost let Glenn and Sam take the blame."

"Don't be too hard on yourself," Jamison said gently. "You've been through a lot. And you're still not out of the woods. There'll be the rest of the investigation, given this evidence, and the trial still to come. But things are starting to look hopeful."

"Officer Jamison, one other thing . . ." She knew they had to go, but she couldn't relax with this enigma still so heavy on her mind.

"Sure, what is it?—and, by the way, you can call me Hal."

"Hal." She savored the way the word felt in her mouth—solid, stable—before asking the question that refused to be dislodged from her mind. "I just have to know. Why Jack? I don't understand."

"Who knows? I suspect we're going to find a man with a deep hatred for women. And maybe . . . well, I'll just say there have been some unsolved killings along the coast here in recent years. This could turn out to be our first real break in an ongoing investigation that had almost gone cold."

"Hmmm." Suddenly aware of how exhausted she felt, Lisa got into the car. As Hal shut the door and went around to the driver's side, she pondered this revelation. Once he was seated and starting the car, she said, "Do you mean that if he'd succeeded in killing me the first time, you might still have no clue as to who was responsible for these deaths?" *If I've been instrumental somehow in solving these cases, my ordeal might not have been a total waste.*

Hal hesitated. "It's too early to say, but yes, it could turn out that way."

Only dimly aware of their route through the dark streets toward the 24-hour vet clinic, Lisa settled back against the seat, conscious of a peace she hadn't known in many months. "Hal," she began after a time of silence, "it's thanks to you and Bea that this is over. I can't get over the fact that I'm finally free!"

He smiled back at her, his chestnut hair curling from the moisture. "Free enough to have dinner with me when this is all over?"

"That's something to look forward to," Lisa said, suddenly choked by emotion. "I'd like that very much." She ran her fingers through the dog's soft fur.

About the Author

FRANCES J. ROSSI believes her insatiable need to write stems from her 16th Century French literary ancestor, Etienne Pasquier, known for his encyclopedic historical work, Recherché de la France. *In keeping with that tradition, she has written several articles for publication on the history of the Church. As a fiction writer, at age eight she made her debut in the neighborhood with a novella about an alley cat, but "A Flash of Red" will be her first published story. Frances has worked as Director of Religious Education in Catholic parishes in Western Colorado, as well as on the Monterey Peninsula. She lives with her father, Robert Paquette, in Pebble Beach, and is the mother of three grown children.*

A Place to Heal

by Shaheen Schmidt

The scream of a fire truck in the street below penetrated the closed window, its piercing siren invading the whole office. Steven turned his chair from the window and pressed the phone tightly to his ear while cupping his right hand around the mouthpiece.

"What? Hold on, I can't hear you!" he yelled into the phone, rubbing the furrow between his eyebrows, trying to concentrate. The high-pitched sound started to fade away as the emergency vehicle passed down the street.

"Okay, I can hear again. Some fire crew probably going to save another burning hellhole in downtown L.A. I swear to God, if I hear those damn sirens one more time this week, I'll move the company out of this building." He twisted a pen rapidly between his fingers.

He hung up and looked at his watch. It read 2:15 p.m. "Shit, I'm starving. Where's that damn menu?" He pulled open his desk drawer and searched through a mess of papers and loose business cards, when his eyes caught the corner of an orange greeting card peeking from underneath.

Slowly he pulled it out. The familiar, hand-painted, watercolor flowers on the cover brought a smile to his face. *Happy birthday Steven, hope you are living the time of your life. You probably are because I don't see you any more. Stop by any time. Miss you. Love, Faye.*

Steven felt a heaviness in his chest as he quickly buried the card underneath the papers again. He pushed the button on the intercom. "Julie, I need some lunch. Order me a Philly cheese-steak. It'll be my breakfast and lunch."

A Place to Heal

"There you go again, Mr. Price," a smooth, girlish voice expressed disapproval from a little plastic box on his desk. "You worked right through your lunch hour."

Steven exhaled and turned back to his computer. This day, like any hectic day at Price Investment Company, was taking its toll on him. His mind was filled with a spool of tangled numbers and the buzz of different voices, his life crammed so full there wasn't room for more. Some called it a rat race, but Steven felt proud of owning such a competitive company at the age of 40. It was the family business, left to him after the early death of his father, and it was his chance to have it all, to live his dad's dream.

He liked the attention it brought him, too. At social holiday and business gatherings, Steven always managed to turn heads. The flirtatious attitude of women toward him reminded him of the power his young blood held over the older businessmen.

He used every moment to move ideas into actions, to get ahead and make money, to survive the cruel dog-eat-dog world where life seemed forced to happen. He no longer had any interest in such nonsense as self-discovery, stopping to smell the roses, or slowing down. That kind of thing was fine for his undergrad days back at Yale, but no longer.

A scavenger of time, Steven felt as though each moment was just out of reach. He kept speeding up, turning his switches higher to keep himself going as he hunted and ran after the next minute. "This is a fast life, man," he advised his younger friends and coworkers. "You gotta act quick and jump on opportunities or you get eaten by the pack." He believed it, too.

With his energetic demeanor and his sturdy build, Steven seemed healthy on the outside. As long as he was able to carry on with his normal routine—go to the office to work, find a restaurant to eat at, get home for brief rest periods, and occasionally visit with coworkers—he found life tolerable.

But he often ignored inner physical signals. He took an occasional pill to relieve his aching head. To sleep at night, he took another. And in the mornings, there were eye drops for his irritated red eyes.

He smoked at least a pack of cigarettes a day (his idea of pleasure) to calm his nerves, and to give his body something it craved, something it needed.

He felt just fine.

Steven intensely inhaled a breath of warm smoke into his lungs, sucking the life out of another skinny cigarette. He grabbed his coat, turned the computer off, and left the office. It was Friday night. He looked forward to meeting his office manager, Norm, for a quick dinner and a cocktail. It was an arrangement Norm had suggested three weeks ago which just now was taking place.

Traffic on the 10 was unbearable. Steven held onto the steering wheel so tightly his hands started cramping. "God damn these fucking slow drivers! Shit!" He clenched his teeth and with a tight jaw pulled out another cigarette. "Yeah, yeah, yeah. Get a move on!" The veins on his forehead stood out as he drew in the smoke and let it billow out through his nose and mouth as he cursed.

By the time he arrived at the restaurant, his watch showed that he was 35 minutes late. Norm, a heavy-set man in his late 40s, was used to that by now. He sat at a table sipping on a drink, watching two blonde babes across the room.

"Sorry, Norm. Got stuck in that God-awful traffic again." Steven's fidgety body took a while to calm down as he finished describing the mess on the freeway. Soon, both men were fired up in a heated conversation about politics, investments and the latest in technology. Words came out of Steven's mouth like bullets from a gun. He chewed on each new sentence with barely a pause for breath in between. His heart beat faster and drops of sweat beaded on his forehead. Before he knew it, the waiter had put their dinner bill on the table. The empty plate in front of him and the knot of undigested food in his stomach were the only indications that he had actually eaten his filet mignon.

"So what'ya doing for Thanksgiving?" Norm asked, moving a toothpick around in a corner of his mouth. "You know, you're always welcome at our home."

"I know, I know . . ." Steven looked away. Images of Faye opening a picnic basket and pulling out two wrapped homemade turkey sandwiches brought a smile to his face. *God I loved how spontaneous she was.*

"Norm have you ever been up the coast, by way of Big Sur I mean?" Steven leaned forward as he asked, engaging the man more as a friend than an associate, an exchange that didn't slip past Norm.

Norm's eyebrows rose. "Oh jeez, it's been a while." He twirled his tongue on his teeth under the upper lip. "Why? You going there?" Norm was not accustomed to such a sincere look on his boss's face.

"Nah. Don't have time for that." Steven began to tap his foot under the table and put a hand in his pocket, feeling for the cigarette pack. Norm waited to hear more, but Steven changed the subject.

After the meal, they stepped outside for some air and another cigarette. An early fall breeze caressed Steven's face. He pulled up his collar and reached inside his pocket again. He felt a strange pain in his left arm. *I must've been working too much at the computer today.* After a smoke, they decided to stop at a pub on the next block for a drink and some more chatting. Steven felt suddenly tired but agreed to go along anyway.

At the pub, they picked a corner table. A noisy crowd filled the dark, hazy room. The sound of occasional laughter and music swirled with the smells of alcohol and cologne in the air. Steven ordered an Irish coffee. He sipped his hot drink, watching the movement in the room as Norm talked on. The smoky air twisted and danced into a cloud, like an octopus with long tentacles wrapping around everyone's neck. The sounds were like a jackhammer pounding on Steven's head. He felt the sudden onset of extreme fatigue. The whole room started spinning. At first he ignored it, but when it was followed by strong nausea he felt uneasy and got up to look for the bathroom.

Norm looked confused as Steven left without a word and disappeared among the multitude of bodies. In the bathroom, he felt like he was going to throw up. A sudden pressure in his chest made it hard to breathe, as if an elephant were sitting on him. He broke out in a cold sweat, shaking like a tiny branch caught in a windy storm. His knees felt weak and wobbly as he walked back to the table. Sharp noises scratched his ears. The room started to shrink and become tighter. The glass with his Irish coffee was still full. Norm kept asking him what was wrong, but all Steven wanted was to leave this spooky cave.

So they did.

As they stepped out the door, he felt another sharp pain in his arm and the tightness in his chest doubled him over. "I . . . c-can't . . . breathe . . . I think . . ." the words faded out as he grabbed Norm's arm to avoid crashing onto the concrete.

"Whoa! Hold on buddy!" Norm helped him sit down by the sidewalk. "You look pale!"

Images of people staring at him and Norm talking fast into his cell phone swirled around Steven's head as he was sucked into darkness.

Steven's heavy eyelids slowly opened to a haze of white, quite a contrast to the darkness he last remembered. Behind this filmy layer, he noticed movements and felt the subtle vibrations of sound. He was too tired to see what else surrounded him, and he didn't care. He felt stiff, sore, and all he wanted was to close his eyes and float away again.

He stood in the middle of a playground. Miles of dry, yellow lawns surrounded him. His head felt light and his body heavy. Little holes all over the ground gave it a spongy look. Gray clouds were stuck in the air and everything had a dull, dim light to it. He felt strange, out of place.

Faraway a young woman stood silently facing him, her gray dress blending with the background. He could hear her weep. "F-F-a-a-ye . . ." he called. He wanted to reach her but his feet wouldn't move. He felt like an empty shell looking at faded, hopeless surroundings.

The next time Steven became conscious, he felt someone very close. A woman in a white uniform stared at him with a smile. "Mr. Price?" she asked, softly. "Can you hear me?" She leaned forward to feel his pulse. Steven turned his head toward her, staring into the sterile white room. An IV line hung down on his left side with several tubes attached, poking into his arm. "I'm your nurse, Jasmine," she said, looking at her watch.

"W-wha . . . happen . . ."

"You had a heart attack. You're lucky your friend knew CPR. We have things under control for now." She nodded reassuringly.

The door behind her opened and a man in a white jacket walked in. Steven guessed that he must be the doctor in charge before he faded back into unconsciousness.

The next day, Norm came to visit. He wore a big smile. "Hey buddy, you scared me," he said, reaching out with his hand to touch Steven's arm. "Too much booze and babes, huh?" He sat carefully next to the bed. "Well, at least booze," he jibed.

"They say it was a cardiac arrest . . . I don't have time for this kinda shit," Steven replied wearily.

"C'mon, take it easy now. You need rest. A few days of rejuvenation and medication and you'll be as good as new."

Norm tried to sound reassuring, but he didn't fully believe it himself. He patted Steven's shoulder. "Some of the guys from the company are here, if you're up to seeing anyone. They were really worried."

"Yeah, let 'em in. I'm not contagious. I've got to tell 'em about some of the accounts, since I've missed a day." He pushed the button on the railing of his bed that lifted the upper part of his body until he was sitting up straight. As far as he was concerned, he was ready to go back to work.

Two weeks later, Steven was released from the hospital with a long list of prescribed life changes: a special diet, fewer fatty foods, no salts, no cigarettes, an increase in exercise. There seemed an endless list of do's and don'ts for living a happier, longer life—at least what remained of this life.

Who has time for all this?

Everything was fine once he got busy again. But then, one morning, after a week back in the grind, Steven suddenly saw the world in a different color. An anxious and foggy feeling reached down inside and glued itself to his heart like sticky, black algae. It hung there for the rest of the day. "It's something with that medication, I guess," he reassured himself, putting drops into his red eyes.

Time passed and more of Steven's world evaporated into a heavy, dark cloud. He saw tension all around him and felt fear in the air so real that it touched his skin. He couldn't concentrate at work and became even less patient with others. He could find no reason for this sudden change in his attitude.

Gradually, he started to distance himself from friends and employees, avoiding social affairs. He became suspicious of the motives of everyone who got close to him. In order to protect himself from invisible enemies, he took more control of office operations and became aggressive and rude. People everywhere seemed to be doing their jobs all wrong: the cashier at the grocery store, the waiter at his favorite restaurant, the mailman, and others. Each of them got a piece of Mr. Steven Price's critical mind. Pretty soon the only company he kept willingly was that of his dear, old bottled friend, Johnny Walker.

Norm observed the shifts and mood swings in his friend whom he had known for the past five years. One day he suggested that Steven seek professional help from a therapist.

"Nah. I'm not crazy," Steven said. "Besides, all those shrinks have major personality problems themselves. That's why they chose the profession. They're all searching for an answer to their own dysfunction, created by their dysfunctional families growing up in a dysfunctional society. I don't want those crazies putting a bunch of psychological crap in *my* head."

So he tried to put the pieces together by himself. *I can handle anything.* Somehow, the words did not seem loud enough in his mind. *I'm a strong, confident man who runs this prosperous company and deals with its problems.* The words came from somewhere out of reach, in space, instead of his heart. It was as if he were reading aloud from a blank paper. His thoughts bounced off the empty hole inside his head. He had doubts whether the Steven who had been in charge all his life had ever existed at all. Despair slowly crept into that empty hole. He lost interest in his work. He was living in a shadowed out-of-control world.

Three months later, after he had closed an account that had taken him weeks to settle, Steven made his regular stop at the local pub to relax and have his real medicine. One shot of whisky started to warm him up. As he sighed deeply and prepared to get the bartender's attention for another, a familiar voice called from behind.

"Steven? Hi buddy. Long time no see."

It was Norm, whom Steven had just left at the office. His old friend walked toward him with a beer in his hand.

"Hey Norm, what's up? You following me or something?"

"Maybe. You never know when you'll need someone to drag you to the hospital again," he laughed. "I kinda think of it as job security."

Steven stared at Norm without smiling, then waved at the bartender. "This is what takes the now-and-then blues away," he said lifting his glass and smiling. "I'm feeling pretty good right now, thanks for asking."

"Actually, you look like shit. Your business and your health are going down the drain. And remember, the next time your heart stops, there might not be anyone around." Norm looked straight into his friend's eyes, a bold and clear statement.

With the second shot of whisky, Steven started to loosen up. He began talking about the ugly world around him. This time Norm listened and let Steven pour out words that seemed to have been bottled up inside of him for years. "I just think . . . well, I feel like I'm behind all the time. I see everyone else has accomplished something and they're going on with their lives . . . family . . . all busy with that kinda stuff. My work *is* my family. It's all I have now. But I'm tired of dealing with it."

He rested his elbows on the counter and leaned forward. As a woman passed by them, the mild scent of her rose perfume cut through the bitter odor of whisky. Steven's eyes followed her as he stared at her long, golden hair.

Faye smelled like that. He inhaled deeply to catch more of the familiar scent. His mind wandered back in time . . .

She'd smiled at him and the dimple on her right cheek had caught his eye. Her long, straight, golden-brown hair felt silky to his touch. He could bury his face in her arms, inhaling the scent of her forever. But it seemed like she wanted more and more of him each time they met . . .

The noise from the TV in the corner of the bar took over. The tube showed a crowd at a football game. Fast movements of face after face, body after body, covered the screen. Suddenly Steven felt an impulse. "Hey Norm, maybe we can get away for a weekend."

Norm took his eyes off the TV and stared at Steven. "What? Where do you wanna go?"

"I used to go up the coast, by Big Sur," Steven said. "It's pretty up there, but not much to do." He sat up straight. "It's okay for a weekend but any longer than that, it gets boring."

Norm seemed interested. "You mentioned that before. Where did you stay?"

"Oh, with a lady friend. But there are plenty of places to stay. Anyway, just an idea."

Maybe it's not such good idea after all. Leave it alone.

"Hey, not a bad idea, Steven. I'll drive and we'll go for a couple days, relax, clear our heads and come back renewed." Norm nodded gently as the idea settled in. "I'm sure the wife won't mind. We'll call it a business retreat and deduct it."

Steven realized he was out of his element. He started to regret having suggested the whole thing. "Well, I'll let you know." He looked down at his third shot of whiskey, still untouched.

It was time to leave.

That night, after Steven made it home, he actually had a buzz of energy. Not from the alcohol, but from talking to Norm and being listened to. However, his dreams that night were frightening. A dark shadow chased after him as he ran breathlessly through narrow alleyways that ended nowhere.

In the morning, when he grabbed the eye drops, he saw his tired face in the mirror.

Look at me. I'm getting old.

A strange fluttering sound came from his living room. Something was hitting against the glass window. He walked out of the bathroom wrapped in a towel, the eyedropper still in his hand. A small bird had flown inside his home through one of the three windows he'd left open last night. A few colorful little feathers floated in the air. The helpless, tired bird kept hitting the clear glass, losing more feathers. Steven walked to one of the windows, opened it wide and waved his arms to direct the bird toward it.

"You're trying too hard . . . here . . . c'mon," he said, working his way closer to the little creature. This time the bird flew over to a high lamp and crashed into it, falling to the floor.

"You stupid bird, the window's open. Can't you see it? Can't you feel where the breeze is coming from?" With one fast move he was able to grab it. Holding it, he felt the pulse of its little life. The tiny head peeked out from between two of his fingers and squeaked loudly. He walked back to the open window and held out his arms.

"See, all you had to do was open your eyes." He spread his hands and the bird zipped out of sight in less than a second. "Stupid animal," he mumbled under his breath, then closed the window and turned around. His gaze stopped at the feathers on the floor.

The room around him suddenly seemed confined and tight. His throat felt like it was closing. He had to sit down.

Faye's voice echoed in his head. *Steven, sometimes I think you'll never come back.* A yearning boiled up in his heart and found its way to his eyes. Tears poured out like pus from a painful infection that had been festering for a long while. *She was all I had and I let her slip away, day by day.* He could hear himself crying but couldn't stop it. "I didn't deserve your love! I'm no good for anyone!" he shouted and dropped onto the couch, feeling drained. *It's been five years since I've seen her. I was afraid to disappoint her. I don't know what the hell I want!*

The next morning, as he grabbed a cigarette and looked for his lighter, a spark of light cut through his mind, sharp and clear. *Why not go to a shrink? Getting some Valium never hurt anyone. Plus it would be like taking a shot of whisky with someone there to listen to you.* He picked up the phone and called information.

"Dr. Katarina Broman on Wilshire Boulevard, please." He wrote down the number of the psychiatrist Norm had once recommended to him.

Steven's first visit was two weeks later. He got out of bed early enough to nervously smoke several cigarettes before he left for the ten o'clock appointment. He hoped for a chance to do some talking, and convince Dr. Broman how right he was about the scary and unfair world out there.

When he met the 60-year-old psychiatrist, he found her a non-threatening presence. Her salt-and-pepper shoulder-length hair neatly framed her face, and her soft cheeks showed only a scant amount of makeup. She gently offered him the comfortable couch to sit on.

"So what's going on? What's on your mind, Steven?" She smiled as her blue-gray eyes stared into his.

"Well, I've had some trouble sleeping lately." He shifted his weight on the leather couch. She waited for him to continue. "I don't know. I've been working a lot and I guess I'm just drained." He started rubbing his left eyebrow while his right ankle moved up and down, almost tapping the floor.

"What kind of work do you do?" She said, keeping her steady gaze on him.

"I own my own brokerage company. I'm a busy man. I've got to be," he said, scratching the back of his head.

"That's a very good start. Let's talk about why you have to be so busy." She smiled again, leaning forward to listen as he told his story.

Surprisingly, after it was all over, he found that he had been able to tolerate the one-hour visit. He even booked another appointment without asking for Valium. It seemed he felt an interest in the process of delving into his own confusing life.

After a few therapy sessions, Steven learned to talk less and feel more, something he had never done before. He realized that confronting his own emotions could be quite frightening.

He was facing down his demons.

Steven began to understand that the visits to Dr. Broman were the best thing he'd ever done for himself. It was not an easy ride but all the same, a promising journey, slowly made. He learned how stressful his lifestyle was and how he hadn't recognized it, in part, because of the painful guilt he hid beneath. There were times when he got frustrated or bored with the process, then fell back into his old routines and lost faith. But then pieces of himself would come back together.

That was when he decided to take trips up the coast by himself, without Norm. He wanted to get away from the city. Before long he noticed that when he returned to L.A.—up to a few weeks after each trip—his tension and his desire for smoking seemed to fade. He cut back to a pack of cigarettes a week.

He soon decided not to rush the drive and started taking winding Highway 1 all the way to Big Sur. He'd stop at Nepenthe, a restaurant high up on a cliff.

We used to eat here.

Absorbing the breathtaking view from up on the rocks, he would stare at the blue ocean and reminisce about his time with Faye. The Pacific, stretching out for miles, boldly showed off its power and beauty as if daring someone to stop it. *I feel like I'm home or something. Wonder where Faye is now? She always enjoyed staring at the water longer than I did.* The tranquil coast called him back again and again.

Every time he returned to the Monterey Peninsula, he would drive by Faye's old house in Carmel. Once he tried to call her at the studio where she had taught ballet and jazz dance. But she had moved, and the new management wouldn't give him any information. Still, he kept hoping to see her.

One Saturday afternoon, months later, he grabbed his beach chair and took a walk by the Monterey Beach Hotel, smoking a cigarette. It was a clear, August day. The green hills of the Monterey Peninsula stretched out and cut into the water, creating a backdrop behind which the sun could set. Golden clouds were moving in, and orange and pink colors were gradually spreading out over the sky. He hoped to do a bit of work while he sat in front of the waves. He took out his Palm Pilot, which he carried like a child's security blanket.

After fifteen minutes of browsing the Web and checking on a few stocks, he lifted his head to watch a barking dog chase the waves. Nearby, an older couple was pointing at the ocean.

And there they were. Three dark fins sticking out of the water, sailing slowly toward the left.

SHARKS! A primal voice called out in his head, and suddenly a spark of concern for the surfers and beachgoers washed over him. With wide eyes he stood up and looked for potential victims. *The ocean is full of sharks, ready to attack!*

That's when he heard the smiling couple say to a kid nearby. "Look! Dolphins!"

Their large, curved backs rose out of the water and slowly sank back in.

Dolphins? He gently put away his Palm Pilot and sat down to watch. They came close again, so close to the shore that he could scarcely believe it. He picked up his things and walked toward the water, following them with his gaze. *Son-of-a-bitch! I've never seen dolphins in real life!*

He walked faster in their direction. "Amazing! Look at that!" he said to no one in particular. He smiled at the older couple as he passed them. Time slowed and he became mesmerized by the show opening before him. The dolphins swam gracefully for several minutes while a playful sea otter joined them. More orange clouds appeared and the sandy beach changed as a pink overcast blanket floated in. Overhead, a V-shaped flock of geese flew toward the open ocean, disappearing above the fog. He felt like a child again. *What an amazing sequence! It's like a movie, where they've put all these creatures next to each other in one scene! I'm thinking more . . . well, more like Faye. I wish I had a camera.* He frowned, looking at his Palm Pilot and slowly walked back to his chair. *How many more of these beautiful sunsets am I going to miss if I'm always watching a screen or reading a paper?*

He put his right hand on his chest. For the first time in his life, the sensation of his heartbeat reassured him. He felt alive. He knew how precious life was. *God, do I want to see more of life!* He grabbed the folding chair and headed toward the hotel with a sure, steady pace.

Steven had completely relocated up north, leaving Norm in charge of the office. He settled in the charming little town of Pacific Grove, where old Victorian houses with small cozy gardens lined the streets. He ran his business long-distance, following the path of healing his heart and soul.

As he walked through his new hometown, he felt surrounded by the peaceful lives that existed there. But soon he found this new, slow pace made him restless. He noticed that drivers went fifteen miles an hour, taking their time to check out the scenery, not worrying about anyone behind them. There was no nightlife to speak of and, except for restaurants, most shops closed at five o'clock. Hardly anyone walked the streets after dark.

Steven created more and more time and space for himself. He began to make a deliberate attempt to socialize and seek out entertainment. He drove south to Big Sur one night to watch Native Americans drum and dance under the full moon at the River Inn. They shook colorfully long feathers bound around their waists and became one with the drumbeat. He saw Faye's face on every dancer's painted body.

Other times he drove to San Francisco or L.A. to visit or see a play for a weekend. But it always felt good to come back to his quiet home on the Peninsula, to rejuvenate. He invited friends up from L.A. to visit for holidays, so he didn't feel like a monk, living in a faraway temple on top of a mountain. They were eager to accept his hospitality.

He sometimes took his visitors to the Esalen Institute down the coast, to sit in the mineral baths and share the beauty of the blue water from the cliffs above. Steven's city friends got a kick out of all the New Age folks who hung out at the baths.

As months went by, he met many interesting people who guided and supported his healing process. They were healers, writers and artists who got their energy from the land and spent their time creating masterpieces. The further he explored inside himself, the more innocence and goodness he found. The colors around him became more vibrant and the sound of nature grew louder. The sweet smell of the ocean awakened in him a sense of belonging.

But it wasn't long before another hazy cloud settled upon his life. Norm's phone calls began to alert Steven to the fact that the business wasn't doing well. It got worse. They had lost a lot of money in the stock market and several clients were jumping ship. "You've worked hard for this company and now it needs you again," Norm said. "We have to come to some decisions. You need to think about us guys who are trying to hold it all together for you."

"Well, I know that I've been away for awhile," Steven replied, "but I don't know what to say. Give me some time to think about it."

The old familiar knot formed in his stomach. *Could I give up this new life and go back to the one I'd been ready to leave behind? Can I sacrifice everything my father and I had worked so long and hard for?*

The next day Steven decided he needed to go to a place where life was happening on its own, without the demands of others. He went on a hike at Big Sur. Complete solitude always welcomed him there. Nature's invisible currents charged up his batteries and sharpened his mind and senses.

Still, the thought of his faltering business nagged at him, distracting his thoughts. He considered the plight of his employees who depended on him for their livelihood. He needed the insight and support of a kind friend. *Where's Faye? I could use some of her good old sound advice on this one.*

One Tuesday afternoon he walked out of the movie theater on Lighthouse

Avenue, still disturbed by work and already forgetting the movie he had just watched. As his eyes got used to the bright light outside, he heard a familiar voice. A young boy ran in front of Steven and a woman's soft voice called after him. "Wait for me, honey." The woman sped up, trying to grab the boy.

Steven's eyes widened. "Faye! Faye Courtney?" he asked hesitantly. She turned around while holding onto the young boy's arm. It took her a few seconds to respond.

"Steven? Oh my God, is it you?" A big smile appeared on her face.

"Yeah it's me. I can't believe it!" He turned to the little boy. "Is he yours?" His heart pounded so hard he could hear it.

"This is my son, Robin. I can't believe it, either. It's been more than five years! Wow!" She let go of her son's arm and leaned the boy against her legs while resting her hands on his shoulders to keep him from bolting away.

"Well, I live here now," Steven explained. "Thanks to your inspiration, I mean . . . it's a long story. You're married now?" His face felt hot.

"Yeah, I mean, I was. Three years ago. I'm on my own now. We don't live here, though. Robin's grandparents do." She started laughing nervously. "There've been a lot of changes!" Robin started to get restless and tried to slip away again.

"I sure hope I can see you sometime. We have a lot to catch up on." He couldn't believe he was saying this. *Will she give me a chance?*

"I don't know, Steven. I've moved on and am in a different stage of life now. I don't want to rush into anything." She looked away.

His shoulders dropped, disappointment flooding his thoughts. "I've been waiting to hear from you for a long time," he said in a low voice.

She looked back at him. "We're going to be here for three more days. If I find some extra time, I might call you." She caressed the top of Robin's head.

"Oh, sure . . . sure." Steven smiled, hiding his excitement.

"What's your number?" she asked.

He recited it slowly and clearly.

He gave her one of his business cards and noticed his hand shook mildly. "I live two blocks from here." He watched her fingers move to take it from him.

"Okay, I've got to go now." She turned abruptly away. "Hey, wait a minute you little one!" She held onto the boy as she put the card into her purse.

"I can't tell you how wonderful it is to see you again. I'd love to talk to you." He stopped. *Don't want to scare her now, go slow.*

He watched them walk across the street toward her car.

I may not see her again.

He didn't leave his house the next day, hoping to hear the phone ring. He trembled inside and his stomach felt queasy. *How should I say it to her? Will she give me a chance to explain?*

But she didn't call.

Steven invited Norm up to discuss the future of the firm. He took Norm on a long hike at Point Lobos State Park, south of Carmel. "You look like shit, man," Steven told his old friend. "You should consider moving up here and letting your brain breathe for a while."

He laughed, then followed up quickly, "Just kidding. Someone has to manage the firm, I guess."

"That's exactly what I want to discuss with you," Norm said. "You basically abandoned us down there. What the hell do you expect us to do?" Norm cut loose on his boss and let out all his pent up frustrations.

"I've been doing a lot of thinking about that," Steven assured his friend, placing his hand on Norm's shoulder. "I've decided to dissolve the business. You can all take clients on your own. I'll keep my personal accounts, and we'll divide up the rest, based on who's done the most work with the clients. Meet with the rest of the guys and see what they think. If they want to keep the office open, we can set something up like a monthly rental or cost share or something. I just don't have it in me to hold it together anymore."

And that was it. Steven had taken the last step toward freeing his spirit.

It was a lazy afternoon near the end of December, when the phone jolted Steven out of a daydream.

"Hello, Steven, this is Faye," the calm voice said through the receiver.

"Hi. I'm glad you called." *Breathe, breathe.* He had long since accepted that she would never call him and now he was talking to her!

"I thought we could meet at Wildberries in Pacific Grove. Do you know where it is?" Her words came out sharp and clear. Steven could hear her take in a quick breath, waiting.

"Oh yeah. It's a few blocks from my house, I can walk to it."

"I'm sorry I couldn't get back to you last time I was in town. But things just came up. You know how it is." She paused for a moment. He didn't say anything. "I'll meet you there around two. I can't stay long. Robin's grandparents are babysitting and I don't want to stay away too long."

"That's fine. I won't keep you long." When he hung up, he felt excited and afraid. He was back in school being jerked around by a fantasy. He had to get real and accept that whatever might evolve with Faye would have to be altogether new and nothing at all like it had been in the past. Otherwise, he knew he didn't have a chance.

The small Victorian that had been turned into a cozy coffee house had a warm feeling about it. *This is a good sign,* Steven thought as he entered. It didn't take him long to spot Faye. She sat at a table in the back room. Her long, golden-brown hair was pulled halfway up on top of her head, and her light lavender velvet top shone at the folds of the material in the front. *She looks as soft and beautiful as a rose petal.* With each breath he took, he remembered more of her from the past.

She looked up and smiled.

Steven smiled back and sat down. "This is a great place," he said. "It smells like someone's grandmother's house."

"We should go get our tea in the front," Faye advised.

"I'll get it. You keep this spot. Is your favorite still jasmine?" He got up slowly.

"Actually my taste has changed a bit. Peppermint with a half spoon of honey in it." She rested her chin in her hand while looking into his eyes. He broke away to get the tea.

Minutes later he came back with two steaming cups.

"You haven't changed at all, Faye. You're exactly the way I remember you." He looked down at his cup.

"You've got some gray hair since I last saw you but you look good."

They awkwardly made small talk for half an hour.

"Faye, I went through some rough times. I finally decided to change some things in my life and, thanks to your inspiration, here I am. Can you believe I moved up here?" Steven felt more at ease speaking the truth.

"No I can't. Obviously, when we were together, I didn't make enough of an impression on you to keep you here." She sat up straight.

"Faye, I had to go and figure it out on my own. I didn't know what I was feeling when we were together." He leaned forward.

"Are you saying you led me on all that time, giving me false hope and taking my heart while you didn't know what you were talking about?" Her eyebrows rose.

"Believe me, you wouldn't've wanted to deal with me under the circumstances I was going through. I'm trying to say, I knew what a precious person I had in my life but didn't know how to keep and take care of her. I was afraid of hurting you by keeping you hanging in there for too long." He leaned back and sighed. "I paid a heavy price for leaving you. The guilt and unworthiness I felt didn't leave much room for other things."

"I kept writing to you, sent cards, but you never answered." She looked at her cup.

"I never felt finished with our breakup, Faye. Something about it always plagued me."

"It's been five years. I got involved with someone else and got pregnant with Robin. We got married two years later. It was never right from the beginning. He turned out to be a manic/depressive and committed suicide a few months after our marriage. Well, here we go. I guess I've been through a lot, too." Her eyes filled with tears.

"I'm really sorry." He stared at her. "Can I hold your hands, please?" He leaned forward.

"No, I'm okay." She pulled her hands away and held the cup instead. "He's my whole world, my little Robin." A tear dropped from her cheek.

"He's lucky to have you as his mother." He imagined Robin hugging her.

They slowly sipped their tea. "There are no accidents," he suddenly said.

"What?" She looked up.

"There're no accidents in this world. There was a reason we met last summer like that." He smiled.

"Maybe we can resolve our unfinished business and everyone can go their own way, clean and fresh." She grinned sarcastically.

"This is the place. A place to heal. You always told me that. That's why I came." He looked into her eyes.

Her frozen smile melted and she laughed. "Robin loves short walks in the forests."

"Any chance I could show him some really cool spots on one of your trips down here?"

"Oh, now *you're* the tour guide?" she said, folding her arms across her chest.

"I know of places you haven't seen yet! Any chance I could take you and Robin for a picnic?" He raised his eyebrows.

"Maybe. I don't know. I'll let you know." She looked at her watch. "We're leaving tomorrow. I might call you, but I won't promise anything. I've got to take care of *Faye* as well, you know." She grabbed her purse.

"I totally understand. Take as much time as you want. You know my number if you ever need anything. Please . . ." He handed her another business card with his mailing address and phone number on it.

She pushed it back. "I still have the other one."

They walked out of the cafe. She turned around and took another look at him. "Steven?"

"Yes?"

"I do know there are no accidents," she said, and walked away.

One Year Later

While walking his favorite trail, Steven took off his hiking boots and socks and stepped into the cool, refreshing water. He felt an instant awakening spread throughout his body. He saw a blue jay feather lying beside a rock. He bent over and picked it up, twisting the quill between his fingers so he could see all the different shades of blue.

Steven took a deep breath and contemplated his surroundings. A constant whir of insects filled the air. The Big Sur River rolled over rocks, its sounds adding to the symphony of birds chattering. Small lizards hid in the bushes and rattled the branches with little movements, capturing Robin's attention. Faye sat a few steps further down river watching both of them. Tiny sparkles of bright green and purple flew before their eyes as Robin reached out to touch a dragonfly. Life was happening right there, in that moment, like everywhere else in the world. But now, for some reason, Steven could feel the pulse of nature in his body more strongly than ever before, tingling and filling him up. It had taken him quite a long time to develop an appreciation for these surroundings. His mostly silver hair shone under the sun's rays. His hazel eyes peered into the green hills, watching a hawk flying, way out there. He had a good reason to live and be in this part of California, a reason worth remembering and acknowledging. He knew if he had to do it all over again, he wouldn't change a thing.

As he stepped out of the river, he remembered the past as if it were a movie. He walked toward Faye and sat down. He thanked God for that part of himself that had forced him to choose life in this sacred part of the world. He thanked God for the opportunity to be alive, to witness it with Faye. She leaned her head on his shoulder and he took a deep breath.

About the Author

As the saying goes, "Beauty is only skin deep." But as a beautician, SHAHEEN SCHMIDT doesn't just do people's hair. She is an expert at dealing with the proverbial "bad hair day." Her talent for knowing about interesting local activities and events, aimed at improving one's mind, body and spirit, has proven invaluable to Shaheen's friends and clients. Living nearly twenty years on the Monterey Peninsula, she has experienced much of what the area has to offer for a lifestyle makeover. Shaheen has an insatiable interest in the arts, and is an accomplished painter, photographer, videographer and dancer. Now, as a founding member of FWOMP, *she makes her writing debut with "A Place to Heal".*

If the Tubs Could Talk

by Pat Hanson

Did I tell you that a favorite pastime of mine on long road trips is to find off-road pit stops? Squatting in a gully next to a cornfield, or an almond orchard, or an artichoke field, or even rows of desert palm is much better than inhaling the reeking odors of a dank cement room behind a gas station.

Today I'm on one of my favorite off-road treats, turning off Highway 101, glad at last to lighten my foot on the pedal and leave cars moving at warp speed behind. The view of the fertile valley expands in the rearview mirror as I climb from the exit toward my "secret retreat".

I involuntarily slow my pace as vineyards, rows marked by rose bushes, give way to a grove of looming cypress pines. Weaving through columns of blooming cactus, off to the right I find the perfect dirt road to pee in today. What a calendar I could make of "California Pit Stops I Have Known."

I smile, looking up from my teetering crouch and say, "thank you!" wishing as I let go that I could as easily relieve myself of things I no longer need to make me feel worthwhile. Somebody else's project to report eloquently on. Another client's program to evaluate. Whether my business account will have enough in it to pay my quarterly taxes next month. If only stress could be eliminated as easily as pee.

I wobble and I hear my knees pop as I pull my panties up, my skirt down and stand, glad the wind didn't wet my sandals. A flash of "what if my mother saw me?" hits. Taking three hours on a weekday between business meetings for yourself? Not her generation. But then there's something to that work ethic I've inherited. I'm grateful for the salary, but I probably need a twelve-step program for work addiction. Let me recover from keeping busy with someone else's details to escape the void I'd feel if I slowed down. Busy-ness is an anchor, it holds down my creativity, it doesn't get me anywhere; it's an illusion. It doesn't protect me from anything. Depressed, lethargic, and bored are states I've managed to avoid quite well over the years, thank you very much. Give me manic any time. Still? Me? Well . . . I'm getting better and better at it, the older I get. Each trip I make to this hot springs helps.

Cypress Hot Springs* is one of the Central Coast's best-kept secrets: 24 oak hot tubs with names like *Serenity* and *Tranquility,* each totally private and protected by its own redwood fence, nestled in folds of California-gold hills dotted with scrub oak, sycamore and grape vines.

At the desk a twenty-something college student in khakis and Cypress-branded Polo tee shirt smiles and takes my twelve dollars. The springs, open 22 hours a day, offer soothing mineral waters for respite from whatever one wishes to escape, just as they have for thousands of years.

"Would you like an upper tub or a lower one?"

"Oh upper," I say relishing the climb. "Is *Rendezvous* or *Lookout* available?"

"You're in luck, *Lookout* is, but *Rendezvous* has been reserved."

"Great," I say as I select lavender-scented bubbles for another dollar and choose a bottle of Sobe "Serenity" Elixir, which the clerk pours in a non-breakable container.

"You know the drill then. Up the second flight of stairs and turn right at *Twilight. Lookout* is just past *Déjà Vu.*"

A fortyish college-professor type is just ahead of me as I slowly ascend the three-story staircase entwined in flowering jasmine and ivy. I can't see his face, but imagine rows of worshipful students looking up at his penetrating blue eyes, deeply tanned skin, and closely trimmed beard as he lectures. I focus on how the muscles in his lightly hairy calves twitch with each step as I chat with him about the wonders of this place, so close to home.

"Go figure, best kept secret, don't tell too many people," he mutters between conscious breaths as I turn right for *Lookout* and he goes left to *Rendezvous.* I lift the steaming cover from my tub, turn on the jets and pour in the lavender bubbles to soften the bitter sulfur smell. I go outside *Lookout's* gate to turn the red valve that sends more hot water up. Careful to avoid the poison oak, I reach under the deck and retrieve a few crinkling condom and candy wrappers that have slipped through the slats from God-knows-when. A shuffling makes me look up toward *Rendezvous.* My professorial staircase-mate is standing naked, pacing at the doorway to his deck.

"Mmmmm, nice legs," I think, remembering that I might have called across to him in my single days a few decades ago. A light pounding on the steps interrupts further fantasy. A lithe blonde twenty-something, back-pack over a bright pink tank-top, strides the steps two at a time and turns into his tub. For a second I'm blinded by a beam of reflected sunlight from the silver ring at her navel. I smile, shrug and return to my own steaming waters.

I remember to pull off my own ring as I undress, wondering exactly what minerals Mother Earth releases from her womb for our pleasure that can also turn silver black and if the blonde's ring was as easily removed. I sink ever so slowly into the 106-degree water, and stifle a cry of shock from the heat. I push aside thoughts of the workshop I'll lead tomorrow, the impending deadline for the report that remains precariously perched on my desk at home. Arms above my head almost in prayer formation, I slip in. I shudder. I close my eyes, remind myself to let go. Another thought of the professor and his blonde of the semester floats up and I wish it away. I sink into the oak tub/womb, floating in fetal position, my muscles Spanish moss melting from my bones. As I notice the tingly bubbles gently massaging every pore of my body, I find myself wondering what these tubs would say if they could talk.

My, what they must've have witnessed over the years! These waters have cradled literally thousands of bodies in their depths! I can't get the words of the Eric Burdon song out of my head: "tall ones, skinny ones, fat ones, short ones." Playmate material at eighteen; everyday American spread circa 40. Sagging breasts and siliconed; hairy chests and shaved ones. Muscles and flab. Hearts and bones.

Marital assignations. First dates. Relationships straining from parenting young ones, renewed by leaving a babysitter at home. Closeted gays meeting in private. Single businessmen strategizing after a golf game. College students rewarding themselves for finishing exams, smells of sensimilla mixing with the sulfur. Wine in paper cups lubricating conversation and god-knows-what else. Bones formerly broken, now arthritic; backs twisted from years of improper posture or days of driving, their tension melted and massaged by the spa's muffled jets. Or lone travelers like myself just taking an hour to let go, to listen to the silence.

As I soak, I wonder if, during the middle of the night, *Tubby* might ring up *Hideaway* and compare notes. Or would all the tubs have a conference call and put in their two cents?

"Okay," *Nirvana* would gurgle. "What was your most special treat today?"

"Well, I had that television newscaster and her cameraman again," *Tubby* would babble. "The energy those two have! Get this. I caught each of them looking at their watches while they were making love, so they'd get back to the studio by five. That's responsibility, eh?"

"So what! Good for them," *Shangri-La* would spout up. "At least they 'do it.' I haven't felt anybody make love in weeks. Maybe my thermostat is too hot. Water ain't the best lubricant you know."

"My favorite today was Gramma and Pops," *Twilight* might bubble. "Didn't you think it was cute, how they were kissing and holding hands? 'Round' is the only word to describe those two. Seventy-odd years of meat and potatoes wrapped round their middles, their pale skins mottled. They even gave each other a massage. He didn't even flinch when she touched his scar from gallbladder surgery. And I loved it when Pops suckled the dark nipples of her one full breast, then actually kissed her chest where the missing one should've been. I could tell that mastectomy had to have been at least twenty years ago. No silicone replacement therapy for them. If their grandchildren only knew how touching and totally accepting of each other they are. Who says they're ain't life after 60!"

"Aaah, how sweet," *Hideaway* would slosh. "Quite a contrast to what I saw today! Two dark unshaven men took me from eleven o'clock 'til three in the morning! It wasn't the gang numbers on the back of one's neck, or the talons of the dragon tattooed around the other guy's shoulder that got me. Nope, not even the lines of coke they snorted. Or even the shots of Jack Daniel's they drank. It was the guns! They were so angry, so tweaked! I was afraid one of them would shoot a squirrel he got pissed at for dropping acorns on the deck. It took everything I had to soothe the savage inside those two. They just didn't belong here. But when they turned on my jets full force, for a few minutes I helped them forget what it was they were running from."

"We sensed something dangerous going on," *Harmony* would pipe in.

"Do you think they were drug dealers?" *Enchantment* would splash." Darkness rarely shows its face here, but we all knew you'd be all right."

Gemini changed their flow with: "Well, did any of you catch Mrs. Whitney and Mrs. Rockford today? They treated themselves to lunch after tennis this week, and had a whole bottle of wine. They almost tripped coming up the stairs they were giggling so much. Eleanor actually convinced Esther to forgo the bathing suits! They took a tub naked! Thirty years of keeping their boring husbands happy; their only solace is their weekly tennis game and soak. But listen to this. After a while Esther held Eleanor's hands as she wept about her daughter's divorce. And you know what? For a brief second I thought they wanted to kiss."

"Nah, you're kidding," *Lookout* would answer.

"Nope," *Gemini'd* reply. "If I'm not mistaken, I felt the vibration from a lust that dare not speak its name."

"Speaking of lust," *Rendezvous* would burble in, "did you see Professor Clapham and his latest young thing this time? I wanted to spew over the edge of my tub. If I hear about 'the validity of subjective measures of competency-based education' one more time, I'm going to boil over. I wonder if she realizes that he dyes not only that reddish quasi crew cut of his, but his chest hair, too!"

"Ah come on, doesn't he get that we all age?"

"Exactly. What do you think the nineteen-year-olds are about for him? But this one really spars with him. He's actually beginning to be smitten by her. She'll go places with that thesis of hers; that is, if she lets go of the fantasy that he'd leave his wife and settle down with someone nineteen. Is she dreaming?"

"Ssssh, come on now," *Lookout* would foam. "We're all absorbing a bit too many human traits here. We're about healing, not judgment, remember? I had that writer again today. She always picks *Rendezvous* or me because she can see more through the trees at this height. She's taken another contract with the county; important work, good money. But I had to remind her that's not what she's really supposed to be doing, what she's here for. As I surrounded her, my minerals whispered not to be afraid of her own creativity, to let that voice be heard. I actually sensed a shift in her. Very little, but some movement in the direction of quiet, calm."

"Wow, quiet," *Atlantic* would continue. "Wish *I'd* had some peace today. All my customers were gabby. Sometimes I want to put a gag in their mouths. My minerals are still being replenished from four o'clock's insomnia, five o'clock's marital troubles, and seven o'clock's arthritis."

"Now, now, you know how long it takes sometimes," *Erewhon* burbled in. "Cut your writer a little slack, *Lookout*. At least your customers do something meaningful. I got mostly high school girls in bathing suits, worried they don't look more like someone named Britney Spears, all trying to attract the same guy, who wouldn't know what to do with one of them if he caught her. And, yikes! The language young girls use these days! When did the "f" word become something young ladies let slip from their mouths?"

"I totally agree," *Shangri-la* might burst up to *Starlight*. "And when did this body piercing thing start? That guy I had at nine o'clock had enough jewelry on to short-circuit a computer! Must have been his first time, because he forgot to take it off. I was worried I'd turn into a battery from the chemical reaction!"

"It's different now than it used to be," *Tranquility* slurped. "Most of them move so fast. We're here to slow everything down, remind them that time is precious, help them remember what it was like when the Native Americans first discovered us. I can still smell the sage, hear the chanting. I miss the ceremonies they used us for."

"Holy water!" *Paradise* complained, "I'm just about steamed out. Just look at what we've absorbed! No wonder they drain us every morning between five and seven o'clock. Look. Anthony's on the first level releasing the valves. I'm ready to be sucked dry and be re-mineralized for two hours. We'll all be one again soon. Let's chant before our stress filled waters go back down into Mother Earth."

If the Tubs Could Talk

"OOOOOMMMMMMM."
"Oooooommmmm."

The chime outside the gate to my deck rings. Stunned, I open my eyes. Fifty of my 60 minutes are already up! My arms feel heavy, my head light, as I sit on my towel and rub cream slowly into my callused heels, between my toes, up my legs. I realize these conversations weren't imaginary. They are the voices in my own head. And yes, they do stop when I turn the jets off, lie back and float, resting enough so that all I can hear is my own breathing, the beat of my own heart. I feel ever so grateful, so blessed for having taken one more step to *Learn to be Still* like the Eagles song.

I slip back into reality and pull on my clothes, forgoing the bra—too constricting. No, I thought, if the tubs could talk, they wouldn't. As I slip back to reality and dress, I get that these tubs wouldn't gossip, they wouldn't care. They wouldn't be concerned with conditions, judgment, evaluation.

If they could talk, it's not secrets these tubs would tell!

They wouldn't care if you were alone or wonder why you weren't a couple, or even whether you loved the one you were with.

They'd just tell you to slip in, slide under, float . . . just BE.

"Look up through the trees," they'd beckon.

"Notice nature."

"Let the squirrels and birds sing you to sleep."

Serenity wouldn't whisper of jealousies or *Tranquility* spurt inconsequential comparisons between body parts. *Erewhon* would never ripple in judgment, victimizing someone for causing the disease that brought them here seeking relief.

Infidelities wouldn't interest *Harmony,* nor would *Nirvana* brag about the orgasms enjoyed in its embrace. *Starlight* certainly wouldn't care about someone's weight, or how much water they displaced.

I finally get it. These waters are about acceptance. Their supply from geothermal depths is endless, infinite. If the tubs could talk, *really* talk, they would wonder what the hurry is all about. They'd ask where people have been to so tightly knot their muscles; what forces wind them up so much inside that it twists humans' god-given architecture. Waters which spring from the center of the planet and rise from molten rock, to fill man-made chalices in which we play, or pray, would only ask us to hope. They'd wish us to leave renewed. Reminded. Remembering our source. Cypress Springs only envelop. If they did speak it would be in a whisper:

"Surrender."

"Float."

"Forget."

"Fly."
"Wrap yourself in love."
"Be with me now."

I descend the staircase, one step at a time, notice that the professor has left before me, and hear his student arranging with the timekeeper to stay another hour—alone. I smile and head out to the parking lot. I put my gym bag and wet towel smelling of sulphur in the trunk. I gasp when I look at my watch, which I'd left in the car on purpose. I have a meeting at six o'clock in Salinas and less than an hour to make it. I quickly set the CD player to the Rolling Stones, roll the windows down and head for the freeway. On 101, my foot firmly on the pedal, I scan for police cars as I zip into the left lane, and then pull back over as a dark maroon SUV in the rear view mirror tailgates and dwarfs my Honda Civic. I am doing 77 as he passes me. Not three minutes later, I see the SUV stopped by a cop. I wipe my brow, relieved it's not me and smell a hint of sulphur on my skin from the tubs. I ease over into the right lane, switch the CD to Enya, and remind myself that there's always enough time.

*** Author's Note:**
Cypress Hot Springs is a fictional representation of two very real hot springs on California's Central coast:

Sycamore Hot Springs
1215 Avila Beach Drive
San Luis Obispo
www.sycamoresprings.com

-and-

Monterey county's Paraiso Hot Springs
Soledad, California
831-678-2882.

About the Author

PAT HANSON has a doctorate in Community Health, a nine-page resume, is a veteran health and sexuality educator, Chair of the Santa Cruz/Monterey Local 7 of the National Writers' Union, and owns her own consulting business, HEALTH MATTERS. Her hobbies (when she allows them) include film, Tai Chi, new thought spirituality, sunbathing and tub-soaking.

Dot's Dad Visits Dinosaur Town

by Mike Tyrrel

My nickname is Dot, so when Dad called me Elizabeth I knew I was in BIG trouble.

He wanted to know why I didn't want to eat dinner, but I didn't say anything right away. Instead, I just stared out the dining room window, looking at the setting sun bathe far away Fremont Peak in pretty swirls. It looked like pink and purple cotton candy, not the yucky gray fog I knew I'd see if I turned my head toward Monterey Bay.

I also knew if I wasn't careful how I answered Dad, tonight might be yucky, too—at least yuckier than it had to be.

Mom had put homemade pasta with my favorite salmon and Alfredo sauce on the table—it's even good on corn flakes. But tonight I was going to eat somewhere else, somewhere far away from my home in the foothills outside Salinas, farther than Pacific Grove or Monterey, and much nicer than Carmel.

Tonight I planned to eat in Dinosaur Town.

I turned to Dad, next to me at the table, hoping for the best.

"I'm not very hungry," I told him gently. "I only want a small helping."

He looked at me sternly. "Elizabeth, did you eat candy or cookies before supper?"

Uh-oh! That was the *second* time he used my full name. I had to answer very carefully so I wouldn't get grounded. No way was I going to miss out on Dinosaur Town.

"I didn't eat anything, Dad," I said, even though I'd gladly have had two helpings any other time. Mom's sauce is that great!

He wagged his finger at me. "You're eight years old, young lady. Your body is growing and needs *all* the good food we serve you."

"I know, Dad. 'Nature's building blocks will build me up.'" It's a favorite saying of his, one he always repeats when I don't want to eat something that smells like it belongs in the curbside trash. "But tonight is special. I'm going to Dinosaur Town. I'll eat there. The steaks, potatoes, and even cauliflower taste like candy, and according to King T-Rex the food is very nutritious." I sighed when he squinted at me. With that look, I knew he didn't believe anything I'd just said.

"Dinosaur Town, Dinosaur Town, Dinosaur Town! Every time you don't want to do something it's Dinosaur Town!" After he'd said it, he turned to Mom. "What should we do with her? Where does she come up with this Dinosaur Town, King T-Rex, flying dragons, and candy-flavored food? Is there a TV show that I'm missing out on? Maybe you could tape it for me so I can understand."

Mom smiled. Holding my hand she said, "Well, she's your daughter. I'm sure she hears how often you say you could improve your company, or be a better President of the United States, or drive better than all the other maniacs on the road. Her fantasies are just as real as yours. Why not go along?"

I couldn't tell if Mom was on my side or just talking to Dad. Besides, Dinosaur Town is real!

"Okay! Okay!" he said throwing his arms in the air. "Dot, I give up. I won't run for president this year, but you do need to eat half the food on your plate."

"All right, Dad." What a relief to be "Dot" again! I parted my pasta right down the middle of my plate, so there wouldn't be an argument that I didn't eat half.

Then Dad looked at Mom and started to smile, the kind of smile I knew would lead to trouble. "So, instead of going to Yosemite for our summer vacation," he said, "why don't we go to Dinosaur Town? What's the temperature there in July?"

I couldn't believe my ears. "Wow! That's a great idea! Tonight I'll ask King T-Rex if we can stay in his castle. Then we won't have to camp out in Yosemite with all those mosquitoes."

Dad reached behind his chair and grabbed the vacation maps that were lying on the dining room cabinet. He looked through them as I finished eating half my pasta, hoping my stomach wouldn't announce it was still hungry. "So Dot, tell me again," he said when he was finished. "How do you drive to Dinosaur Town? I can't seem to find it on any of these Triple-A maps."

"Dad, you can't drive to Dinosaur Town! Fifi the fire-breathing dragon picks me up at midnight. It takes her ten minutes to fly there. Then she makes sure all the kids are back home before sunup."

"Is Fifi a safe flier?" Dad snickered. "I hope you don't take your sister with you! She could fall off!" As he made that ridiculous statement, he wiggled his eyebrows at Mom.

I swallowed my last bite of pasta before I answered. "Fifi is very safe. Her scales are sticky and kind of hold onto our pants so we don't fall off. I don't bring Katy along because I don't want to baby-sit her while I'm in Dinosaur Town."

"I no baby!" Katy said, jamming her fork into her plate.

Dad shook his head and looked real hard at the pasta sliding off his fork. "Interesting." The word came slowly out of his mouth. "Do you think I could go with you tonight? Does T-Rex allow adults to visit Dinosaur Town?"

"Great idea!" I shouted. "I have an extra ticket! But there's one rule when we get there: you have to listen to me, otherwise you could get into trouble. Okay?"

Dad muttered "humph" a few times. Then shook his head up and down which I guess meant he agreed. "Okay," he finally said. "I'll go with you. You can be in charge while we're in Dinosaur Town tonight."

"Yippee!" I yelled. I pushed my chair back from the table and ran up the stairs to my bedroom. "I have to find where I put that extra ticket!" I shouted.

Mom cleared the table and rinsed the dishes while Dad placed them into the dishwasher. "So you're really going to Dinosaur Town?" I heard her say. "Mike, don't hurt her feelings, okay?" There was a pause and then she said, "What are you going to wear?"

They both laughed after that, but I was too busy to continue listening. Dad needed that ticket or he couldn't go. I looked in my chest of drawers. I searched my treasure box. Then I dug through my other secret hiding places. I started to worry that the washing machine might have eaten it (that happens a lot to me). Then I remembered: I'd hidden it inside my pillowcase.

I pulled out the ticket and looked at it. It has a cool hologram of T-Rex's castle that rotates and sparkles in the dark. When you hold the ticket up outside at night, Fifi sees the sparkles and stops at your house.

I placed it in my pants pocket and began to organize my clothes on the corner of my dresser. When I was finished, I turned off the bedroom light and went downstairs to play with Katy. Katy would go to Dinosaur Town as soon as she was older. Since I'm the queen, she'd be a princess, according to T-Rex.

"All right, time for bed!" Dad yelled. He always has to yell to get our attention at bedtime. "Everyone upstairs!"

"Katy, come on, up to bed." I said. "Tonight's special. Dad and I are going to Dinosaur Town. So we *really* have to get ready. No goofing around tonight." Using my big sister voice I added, *"Now get going! Hut-hut!"*

Katy said, "No fair. Me go, Dino Town, too."

"Not until you're six. It's too dangerous."

Katy insisted. "Me no 'fraid! Me hold Dada's hand."

"I only have one ticket," I was sorry to tell her. "It's for Dad. But you can go without a ticket when you're six. I'll take you on your birthday."

That calmed her down. Being her big sister, she always trusts me. I tell her what TV shows to watch, what food tastes good, and I'm never wrong!

We brushed our teeth, washed our faces, and got ready for bed. Soon after we shouted downstairs that we were ready for our prayers and a story. Dad always reads a story out of our kids' Bible, then prays with us. Afterwards he exercises by lifting us over his head about twenty times before giving us our final goodnight kiss. As he bent over to kiss me, I reminded him that we were leaving at midnight, so he'd better set his alarm clock.

He patted my head. "Okay Dot. But if I'm not up, go ahead 'n' wake me."

He turned off the light and to complete our nightly routine he said, "Good night, sleep tight. Don't let the bed bugs bite."

"Good night, girls," Mom said while standing in the doorway, to which we pretended to be asleep. It's better that way because if Mom thinks we're awake she might check how well we've washed our faces. Dad doesn't.

As they walked away, I heard Mom ask Dad, "What're you going to do when Dot wakes you at midnight?"

"If she does, which I doubt, I'll play along," Dad replied. "We'll have some cookies and milk downstairs, then I'll put her back to bed. She'll probably say Fifi was scared."

"Don't underestimate her," Mom said, but then I couldn't hear any more after that because they closed their door.

Dads sure are funny. This would be his greatest adventure, and he wasn't excited. Didn't even believe it! Not everyone gets into Dinosaur Town, you know.

I placed the alarm clock under my pillow so it wouldn't bother Katy and soon fell asleep. The next thing I knew the clock beeped in my ear. I turned it off, hopped out of bed, and quickly dressed. Then I knocked on my parents' bedroom door (we're supposed to do that to be polite).

Dad's snoring was the only reply, so I entered the room and gently shook his arm.

"Dad! Dad! Wake up! It's almost midnight. Come on Dad, remember Dinosaur Town?"

He opened his eyes. "What time is it?" he asked. "Oh, gee, Dot, it's midnight. Is everything okay?"

I held his clothes in my outstretched hands. "Here's your pants and shirt, Dad. Let's get going! Fifi will be here any minute!"

Normally Dad's the one trying to get us ready to leave and now here I was trying to get him going! "Come on, Dad, let's go!" I pleaded. "Hurry up! Tie your shoes outside! We're going to miss Fifi!"

That got him up and moving. He dressed fast, then followed me down the stairs and out the door. We hurriedly walked to the edge of the driveway to wait for Fifi. By now he was fully awake. He rocked back and forth on his toes as he looked at the sky, while I started to wave the ticket so she would be sure to see it.

"So, how does Fifi know we're waiting?" he asked. "Really, Dot, I'm getting cold! How about having some cookies and milk and waiting for her in the house?"

How do you tell your dad to be patient, when he's always telling you that patience is a virtue? "Dad, one more minute. Hear that whistle? It's her circling. She has to be certain that no cars are coming."

Dad looked up to try to spot her, but he looked in the wrong direction. "Alright," he said. "I'll wait another minute, then it's back inside the house."

I knew he really didn't believe in her, but boy was he was about to be surprised! When she landed, he leapt backwards onto the lawn. I'd never seen him jump so high. If his shoes hadn't of been tied, he'd have left them on the sidewalk!

No words came out of his mouth, only gibberish, like my Pig Latin code. The whole time he kept pointing at Fifi. I couldn't blame him. Fifi's frightening when you don't expect her. She's about as large as a hippopotamus. Her head's at the end of a long thick neck and she has a mouth like a crocodile. White smoke puffs from her nostrils and her eyes send out red flashlight beams (the light from them helps me mount her at night). Greenish-red splotches cover her skin all the way to her pointed tipped tail, which she now tapped on the ground to let us know that it was time to go.

I climbed on top of her. "Come on, Dad," I said. "Show her your ticket and get on."

Dad just stood there shaking his head. I think the loud rumbling from her ribs bothered him the most. I had to climb back down, grab his hand and pull him forward. "It's okay, Dad, she's purring," I explained. "She never bites, trust me, don't be afraid. Now we gotta get going before a car comes."

I led him to a place just in front of her wings. He looked at me like he was about to get on a really scary roller coaster, but then he finally climbed up and sat down gently. I climbed up and sat behind him.

Fifi turned, nodded her head, and winked. Then she shook her neck and rippled her scales which grabbed our legs tight. She flapped her ears, a signal for us to get ready, then her leg muscles tensed and she leapt into the air.

Before long we were flying through the clouds. Dad gripped her neck tightly, shaking like a leaf. Too bad he was scared because he missed out on seeing me reaching high and swatting the clouds as we flew through them.

Fifi followed the Salinas River eastward. The moon reflected off the water and I could see green fields off to the sides of the river. Everything was nice and quiet because the farm tractors were turned off, and the smell of sweet strawberries was everywhere. Just a few semi-trucks traveled down Highway 101. Dad missed out on seeing all of this, too, because his eyes were squinted shut. Tears rolled down his cheeks.

Right after that we flew over Soledad Prison, its orange lights blazing bright but casting no shadows (don't get scared, Fifi knows not to stop there), then she turned north toward Pinnacles National Monument. We could feel the cool mist from the sprinklers watering the vineyards.

For cars, the road to Pinnacles is long and twisty, and it's much better to fly in. But even so, you've gotta love roller coasters to appreciate the last few moves Fifi makes when we close in on Dinosaur Town. First, she pivots on her left wing and goes into a steep dive. Then she normally does a tight corkscrew by twisting her head and using her ears as flaps.

But she didn't do it this time because she sensed Dad was terrified. Instead, she tucked in her wings and legs, stretched her long neck straight out, and gently entered one of Pinnacle's caves (by the way, I've searched all the caves on our many family picnics there, but I've never yet found an entrance to Dinosaur Town).

As we entered the damp, dripping cave, Fifi made a high pitched puppy-like whining sound through her nose, like she always does, to scare away bats. After a couple of quick turns she headed down a deep hole, then with one more swoop we came out into bright, sunny, Dinosaur Town, which was part of a big valley bordered by the mountain range we had just flown through.

Fifi spread her wings wide, lifted up her chest, and extended her feet for a gentle landing in the large field below us. She picked a spot right next to the Rex River (which is named after the king, of course).

After we landed, I hopped off first and tapped Dad's leg. "We're here, Dad. It's okay to come down."

He opened his eyes and rubbed them in disbelief before carefully climbing off. His legs shook as we walked in front of Fifi. I patted her head and gave her an apple I took from home. I always do that. She loves Granny Smiths.

Dad moved his head rapidly like my budgies do. Boy did he ask a lot of questions. "Where did the sun come from? Where are we? Is it safe here? Can I call Mom? Can she pick us up? Can we go now? Please?"

I knew he was scared so I spoke slowly, trying to calm him. "Dad, it's okay. You're safe with me." I paused thinking it would be a short night if we went home. And if we went home, he would never let me come here, ever! "Dad, I've been here a hundred times. Come over here. Remember, I'm the queen. The dinosaurs have to listen to me."

Dad moved and stood behind me, nervously clutching my arm. "Dot," he asked, "does she really breathe fire?"

I wrapped my arms around Fifi's neck and gave her a big hug. "When it's cold out she breathes fire, so the air is warmed. Would you like to see her do it?"

He waved both of his arms as if there were a swarm of bees around his head. "Oh, no, no, no," he insisted. "I was just curious. Please, please, don't ask her."

I gave Fifi one more pat and she leapt back into the sky on her way to pick up a few more kids. "Let's go find some wheels," I said, trying to sound like Dad.

We walked to where the cars were parked. The cars are here for guests, since dinosaurs don't need them. Dad mistakenly entered the first car he saw, a blue one, and I had to tell him to get out. The blue cars are slow because they're for new visitors. We had to find a red one, because reds are the fastest. Only kids that have been here about a hundred times get to drive them.

I went to the information stand to get a copy of today's planned events when I heard Dad shout my name. "Over here, Dot! I found one—it's a Mustang." He waved his arm so I could see him.

After making a few reservations, I walked over. He sat in the driver's seat and tried to lower it. Since kids drive the cars in Dinosaur Town, I told him to move over. He argued with me. He told me he'd been driving for fifteen years and had never had a ticket or accident, so he should drive, not an eight-year-old!

Listen to him, I thought. *We've only been here a few minutes, he's no longer scared, and already he's being a pain!*

"Dad, you've never been here before," I explained. "You don't know the rules. They're way different than back home. There's one basic rule in Dinosaur Town: listen to the kid! Back home you promised you'd listen to me. So you'd better, otherwise you might be sent to the timeout room."

Reluctantly he slid over to the passenger side. I started up the car, and as we drove away he pouted, his lower lip curling down. He held his arms tight across his chest. "Humph," he growled, "this isn't going to be much fun."

Waiting for him to get over his mood, I looked around at the road we traveled on. It started out lined with mulberries on one side and raspberries on the other, then changed to orange and white berries, then to blue and pink ones. It's beautiful and the best part is anytime you want you can stop and grab a handful. It's totally safe, because there are no bees, flies, or bugs in Dinosaur Town. They're not allowed.

We traveled a few miles and I thought Dad had calmed down until I went through a red light. We were moving into the left lane because a blue car was in front of me. You can go through red lights in Dinosaur Town, and it's safer for faster cars to travel in the left lane, but Dad didn't know.

"Stop!" he shrieked. "The light is red!"

He tightly gripped the door handle as we breezed through the intersection. He turned to me. "Why are you driving on the wrong side of the road and going through red lights?" he shouted. "Are you trying to kill us?"

"Well, in Dinosaur Town," I explained, "green means stop and red means go. But to tell you a little secret Dad, it doesn't really matter. There's no cross-traffic. So calm down!"

He didn't really listen and I could tell he was panicking. "Dot," he kept repeating, "this is a two-lane road and we're on the wrong side!"

I pulled the car over and stopped.

"Dad, this isn't Highway 68!" I said, waving my hands. "Do you see any cars coming our way? Take a good look, 'cause the answer is no. Since everyone lands in the same place, everyone has to drive in the same direction to get to the other side of Dinosaur Town. Don't worry, King T-Rex has thought of everything. Please. Just relax and enjoy the ride."

"Okay," he said, and sank lower into his seat with his chin resting on his knees.

I pulled out and started to pass another car. It was Tommy Two Shoes. We call him that because he's always losing one of his shoes. He honked at us. His dad was with him, too.

Tommy's dad yelled to my Dad, "Hey, you'd better listen to your kid. I just got out of the timeout room, and IT'S BORING!"

Dad waved back. "Thanks for the advice!" he shouted. Then he turned to me. "Say, Dot, I just noticed that there aren't too many adults here. Why is that?"

I glanced at him like he should know the answer. How many fathers play Chutes and Ladders? Or hide and seek on a rainy day? Or organize scavenger hunts in the mall instead of going shopping? My dad does all those and acts like he enjoys it. "It's because most parents don't play with or talk to their kids," I answered. "You see, I've got the best dad in the whole world."

"Oh, no," he replied. "God gave *me* the best kids in the whole world."

"Oh, no. *You're* the best dad in the whole world."

It's a routine we go through almost daily, but it's true: he *is* the best dad in the whole world, which explains why he came with me to Dinosaur Town.

After we had been driving for half an hour, we decided to stretch our legs. We passed several souvenir places looking for a place to stop, but it wasn't until I spotted Deino Gems, my favorite gem store, that we pulled over so Dad could buy something to take home.

He walked up to the counter and tried to pay with his credit card. The buck-toothed Raptor (all dinosaurs have bad teeth, an orthodontist could make a killing in Dinosaur Town) hissed from behind the cash register, "No pla-s-s-s-tic." Then he politely explained that he only took paper money. Coins are impossible for dinosaurs to pick off the floor with their claws, so they're not allowed, either.

He hopped out of the car and ran inside before I had a chance to warn him, and it took me a while to get into the store because a few kids wanted my autograph (I am the queen, after all). By the time I entered, Dad was standing with his mouth open in the middle of all the rubies, opals, sapphires, emeralds, and diamonds. He held a big ruby high in the air. "Look Dot!" he said excitedly. "This is only ten dollars! Your mother'll love it! I'm sure going to save a lot of money by getting it here."

"Dad, you should've waited for me before you went in," I told him. Then I broke the bad news. "You see, one ruby costs ten dollars. But ten rubies cost one dollar."

Dad gave me that puzzled look of his: eyes squinted, with lips curled back to show his teeth. "What're you talking about?"

"One diamond, one ruby, or one emerald costs ten dollars. Or you can buy ten of them for one dollar. Two bucks gets you a lot, too many to count or carry. I don't know who set it up that way, but that's just the way it is in Dinosaur Town. Now, give him a dollar and pick out ten more."

I guess Dad goofed because he was afraid to ask the clerk what the sign hanging on the wall meant:

10 for 1 — 1 for 10

I could understand his fear, though. Sometimes the Raptors purr or gurgle while they scrape their claws across the slate counter, which can be frightening to a first-time visitor. But it's Dinosaur Town, so of course they're harmless!

When we got back outside Dad grumbled that someone should've explained the sign to him. I didn't understand what the big deal was. After all, he wanted to buy one ruby for ten dollars. He should have been happy that he had eleven rubies for eleven dollars.

As we were about to get into the car, he asked, "Dot, what's that white key around your neck?"

"This one?" I said holding the key out in my left hand. "This white key opens the white door which allows you inside a movie. Everyone can buy one. Since I'm the queen, I get mine for free."

"You mean the key allows you to walk into a movie theater?" Dad asked, thinking he'd corrected me. He likes to help me like that. Well, he was about to be corrected!

"No, the key gets you *into* the movie that you want to be in. Pop a movie into the machine, turn the key, fast forward to your spot, push the yellow button, then you're in the movie."

"Are you saying I can be in any movie I want to be in?"

"Yeah, any movie," I replied. "But T-Rex doesn't allow any of the violent action movies you enjoy watching because once you're in the movie, you could get hurt. That's why us kids watch a movie over and over until we have it memorized. We stay out of trouble that way. See Dad, it wouldn't be a good idea to get into the Bambi movie just before the fire scene. You could get burned up! Oh by the way, do you know I can outrun Thumper?"

"So you're really *in* the movie?" he asked like he was all out of breath. He didn't even hear about me beating Thumper!

"Yeah Dad. In fact, if Mom happened to be watching the movie you entered, she would see you in the movie. She would rub her eyes, not believing what she saw. But she's sleeping now, so it's okay."

"What movies have you been in?"

"I did *Bambi* and some John Wayne movies. *Roger Rabbit* is one of my favorites. He's really goofy in real life, Dad."

Then I made an offer knowing the answer. "Would you like to borrow my key, Dad?"

He closed his eyes. "Let me think." Then he smiled. "There's a bunch of movies I'd like to be in," he said.

"Just remember, Dad, be careful. I don't want to have to tell Mom something bad happened to you. We'll do a movie after dinner, it's less crowded."

So we got into the car and continued our drive. He kept his elbow on the doorsill, and I could tell by the way he pointed his big ruby toward the hills that he was daydreaming. He held it up to the sun, viewing the star in it. It was hard to tell if it was bigger than a mini-Halloween candy bar, but it was close. Speaking of candy bars, Dad was amazed that they don't exist in Dinosaur Town. But with the food tasting like candy, who needs them?

Since he had been pointing his ruby towards the hills, he noticed the cows grazing and asked what they were.

"Well Dad," I answered, "they look like cows. Occasionally they moo like cows. They have that dumb cow-look on their face. So they must be cows!"

Then he asked another really dumb question. "What are they for?"

I looked at him and frowned. "Dad, these dinosaurs are meat-eaters. They raise the cows for food."

"Cool!" He sat up quickly and turned to me. "Can we watch them eat?"

"Gosh Dad! What a thing to think! First off, Dinosaur Town is not a zoo! Second, dinosaurs don't cook their meat. Watching them eat live food would be very rude!"

I couldn't believe him. I mean, my dad never takes a restaurant window seat because he doesn't want people watching him eat!

"I guess you're right," he admitted, then changed the subject, something he'd done a lot since we'd gotten to Dinosaur Town. You'd think he'd be able to focus on one thing!

"Hey, Dot, look at that field by the fence! There's sparkling lights coming from it! Can you pull over?"

I stopped the car, and just like before, he hopped out before I could caution him (I gotta have T-Rex install door locks on the passenger side!) He found himself surrounded by wild flowers with emeralds, diamonds, or sapphires in their centers, jewels smaller than those back at Deino Gems. As I came up to him, he had a bouquet in his left hand and was about to pick more.

That embarrassed me. "Dad, stop picking them! The flowers are here for everyone. If everyone picked them, nobody would be able to enjoy this field." I shook my head as I took the emeralds and marigolds he'd picked, and started to bury them.

"Dot, what're you doing? Now that they're picked, can't we just take them home?"

I looked up from the ground wondering where he was when they explained that seeds make flowers. "If you wanna take some home, I can stop at the next gem store. But these gems are seeds. Tomorrow these emeralds and the gold from these flowers will start to grow. So it's okay you picked 'em but, no, you can't take them home."

He reached into his pocket, held out his ten-dollar ruby and said, "You mean if I plant this at home, it'll grow into a flower and that flower's seeds will be rubies?"

"Yes, that's what I said. I've tried many times, though, and it hasn't worked. Maybe you can do better."

Together we planted the seeds from the flowers he had ripped up. Afterwards we lay on our backs in the field as a gentle breeze swayed the flowers back and forth, playing gentle musical themes, one for each type of flower. Together we listened and enjoyed the shimmering lights—like a kaleidoscope—that came from the wild flowers as the sun reflected off of them.

Dad told me that when he was younger (I didn't know he was!) he used to lie in a field of daisies as they rippled in the wind. He liked that a lot, but agreed that this field was tops, better than the white daisies of his youth.

After a few minutes we got up, holding hands as we skipped together back to the car. It wasn't long before we were passing blue cars again. Then Dad suddenly yanked on my arm. "There's Arnold!" he said over and over again. "There's Arnold!"

I'd talked to Arnold and his daughter before, so I just waved. "Yeah, Dad, I see him. Just calm down and say 'hi' to him. I'll slow down so you can talk."

"Hey, hi!" Dad said awkwardly. "Uh, how are you doing? I'm Mike."

Arnold took the cigar out of his mouth (the dinosaurs sell a safe one, so it's okay). "Mike, I'm pleased to meet you," he said. "Hi, Dot, this your Dad?"

"Yes," I replied smiling.

"This your first time, Mike? Well, I think you should know I enjoy this place better than any of my movies."

Soon Dad and him were talking about Arnold's past movies, and he invited Dad to join them in his newest flick. I quickly interrupted and politely declined. I said we had other plans, but maybe next time we could join them. Besides, it was hard trying to drive the exact same speed as another red car for too long. So I drove away as Dad waved goodbye.

"Ain't he something, Dot? And he knows you! Wow!"

"Yeah, Arnold's a nice guy. He brings his own movies and takes his daughter into them."

"So he does come back after all," Dad said laughing. I didn't get the joke.

"You know, Dot," Dad continued. "This all looks pretty familiar. The hills over there remind me of what it's like when we drive on River Road towards Marina. And I can envision the Salinas strawberry fields on my left. Of course the river is on our right just like back home."

I coughed even though I really didn't have to. "Well, remember the county map that was missing a few years back? I gave it to T-Rex so he could build this road to town." I paused for a second before asking, "So you like my design, huh?"

He didn't say anything, but just smiled. One of the biggest I'd ever seen.

Finally, we came to the end of the road, where it emptied out into a big gravel parking lot. At this point, if you try to drive further in any direction, the car's engine conks out.

The parking lot overlooks a large lake with a wharf jutting out into it. A number of good restaurants surround the lot, but my favorite, Raptor Café, sits atop a bluff overlooking the lake. It only took us a few minutes to get up there, and at the entrance, I asked them to place a table outdoors by the water fountain, so we could have dinner next to it. Since I'm the queen, they did it, no questions asked. With the nice view we could see sea serpents in the distance pulling kids on inner tubes.

While we waited, Madonna walked up to us with her daughter. She said hello and gave me an envelope. Dad waited until she left, then asked what was in it. "Great," I was thinking, "just great!"

He was about to learn my biggest secret.

"Sometimes an entertainer gives me front row tickets to their show and I sell them at school so I can donate the money to help poor kids," I explained. I opened the envelope. "She gave us four tickets for next week's San Jose concert. Interested in going?"

"No. But does Pink Floyd ever come here?"

"I don't know, I'll ask T-Rex. We better order, Dad."

We began to open the menus, as a pair of Pterodactyls flew over our head. Dad hunched down and immediately covered his head with the menu.

"Dad!" I said, embarrassed again, "you look ridiculous! This is Dinosaur Town! Pterodactyls don't splatter on anyone. Now take the menu off your head!"

Peeking from underneath he pointed upwards. "Dot, what's hanging from their feet? Food?"

I looked up. "Those are kids, Dad! Kids can safely hang glide in Dinosaur Town. Interested in trying?"

He finally put the menu down. "No, but maybe next time. Being in a movie sounds more interesting. I'm still trying to decide which one to go into."

The menu had only pictures, no writing. That makes it easy for kids to choose what to eat. All you have to do is point at what looks good and the dinosaurs do the rest. I ordered steak, potatoes, broccoli, and cauliflower. Dad shook his head in disbelief, since I never eat that stuff at home, but it tastes a lot better here. He ordered the exact same thing.

The food came in a few minutes, because no one has to wait in Dinosaur Town. Dad quickly took his first bite.

"This is excellent," he said. "Is there a cookbook that we can take back home? That way Mom can make the food taste great!"

"No, it's a secret. She wouldn't be able to. Just enjoy it."

And he did. Gobbled it up in no time flat.

After dinner he carried me on his shoulders and I told him to walk down a cobblestone path that led away from the restaurant and the lake. It led through a small village of bamboo huts that were home to a group of local dinosaurs, mostly ones that worked at the restaurants and entertained the kids.

As we walked, passing dinosaurs bowed down to me. Dinosaurs looking out their windows shouted my name and waved. I could tell Dad enjoyed seeing this, because he grinned and waved back to them.

Finally, we came to the end of the path, where there was a big stone building with a row of white doors. This was the movie place. A black rock with a yellow stone hung on each door. This was the "out" button.

We walked up to the ticket booth. The attendant was a teenaged Iguanodon in a white jacket. Dad immediately asked him for a Pink Floyd movie. Luckily someone had already checked it out (they're too loud for me). Dad then asked if they had *Let It Be*. They did.

The clerk gave the tape to me. I looked at the label. It had "S" for "safe" printed on it. Approvingly I gave it to him. He shouted, "Yes!" and jumped up and down holding the tape near his chest. I don't know why he got so excited. But hey, he's my dad and I'm glad he was.

We walked up to a white door. I took the out button off the door and placed it around his neck. Then I inserted the white key and the door sprung open. "When you want out of the movie firmly press this yellow button," I explained. "Whatever you do, don't lose it! You'll be stuck in the movie."

He nodded. I told him I was going to go water skiing on the lake and that I'd meet him at the door in an hour-and-a-half. If he wasn't there I'd push the door's emergency button to end the movie.

When I came back later, he was outside jumping around and playing his air guitar.

"Did you like it?" I knew the answer but I asked it anyway.

"Fantastic! Tremendous! Outta sight! Terrifical! Never in a million years could I imagine doing that! Thanks, Dot!"

"Glad you liked it, Dad, but now it's time to go to the parade. And we have to hurry. Or we'll be late!"

Everyday there's a parade in Dinosaur Town. And since I'm the queen, whenever I'm in town I have to review it.

The parade site is on the other side of the restaurants, far away from the movies, so we had to run like Raptors to get there on time. Dad kept up with me, but we still arrived late. Parades don't wait for anyone, even me!

In the grandstand's first row, next to King T-Rex, two empty seats waited for us. When we entered the private box, the king moved so we could sit on either side of him.

For a T-Rex he's not much taller than a climbing tree, though I could see he was twice as tall as Dad. And his red tuxedo looked great against his green skin. A gold replica of his castle dangled from a gold chain underneath his bow tie. No meat dangled from his sharp teeth. At least right now.

When Dad and I sat down, the king turned to me. "You're a little late,

Dot," he said in his deep booming voice. It echoed. "Any problems I should be aware of?"

T-Rex is a good king. He's always improving things around town. When I told him my idea for planting wildflowers in the fields, he made sure they were planted the next day. "No," I replied. "We're late because Dad went into the movie *Let It Be*. I think it's about some bug band."

"Did you enjoy the movie, sir?" King T-Rex asked.

"I played tambourine!" Dad exclaimed, so overwhelmed with excitement that he forgot to shake the king's hand. "And I sang all the songs with them! Can you imagine, Paul even asked me how I knew all the words to the songs. Wow! I can't believe I sang with the Beatles! Thanks, King T-Rex. This is the best day of my life."

King T-Rex smiled at Dad, with a look that showed he didn't really understand what Dad was saying but wanted to be polite. Then the king turned to me with a twinkle in his big eyes and said, "Fifi's eggs have hatched. She's coming this way to show us her little fire-breathers."

I looked up from the grandstand to see Fifi pushing a red wagon full of her babies toward us. We were in the front row so she could wheel them right up to us. She scooped up two, walked over, and showed them to us. They looked so cute with their wings flapping, and their heads darting around as they looked for pieces of food. Before I could warn Dad (again!), he took one of Fifi's babies from her without asking. She became angry and was about to blow fire on him. But T-Rex put his claw up just in time to keep Dad from becoming a toasted marshmallow. You just don't take a newborn baby away from its mom! Dad should've known better!

It didn't take long for him to learn another lesson: baby dragons have no control over their fire. When this one burped, a ball of flame shot out and burned the palm of his hand. Everyone looked real worried until Dad burst into laughter. Then everyone laughed, including Fifi.

Dad handed the little dragon back to Fifi. "It was foolish of me to take your baby without asking," he apologized. "I'm sorry. Thank you for letting me hold it."

We turned our attention back to the parade. The Pterodactyls had long kite streamers tied to their feet. They swooped and did acrobatics so complicated you would've thought they'd get their streamers tangled. But they didn't. They're that good. Better than the Blue Angels, even.

The Raptors—they always try to make money—sold cotton candy. It's okay to eat since, even though it tastes sweet, it's made of shredded carrots, beets, and turnips. (They won't tell me how they do it, but then Raptors are pretty sneaky, anyways). The Sabertooth Tigers leapt back and forth on top of Woolly Mammoths. A couple of lucky kids rode on top of them. I remember the first time I did it.

Plateosauruses did somersaults, laying on their backs and juggling Coelophyises on their hind feet. The Ankylosauruses painted their knobby tails to look just like their faces and bounced balls on their tails.

Dad had as much fun as anyone. It was good to see him laugh at the jugglers and clowns. He clapped a long time when they were finished, being careful not to touch the burned part of his hand.

After the parade, T-Rex invited us to his castle to put some medicine on the burn. As we entered his home, Dad asked him if his castle had a dungeon.

Before answering, T-Rex looked at me. "You didn't tell your Dad?" he asked.

"No," I replied embarrassed, "he doesn't know."

"Then I'll tell him the story."

He invited us to sit down on a big comfy sofa made out of an animal fur I've never seen back home. There are certain things you don't want to know, this was one of them. Other skins covered a wall made of stone blocks. Some furs were real soft, others as coarse as sand. T-Rex promised me a coat of the softest fur once I stop growing.

"Dot did something very brave," the king began. "Captain Hook and his pirates captured me and placed me in my own dungeon. Try as I might, I could not escape. Dot came up with a plan that cleverly distracted the pirates. Then she slipped past them and helped me out of the dungeon. For that act of bravery, she'll always be the Queen of Dinosaur Town."

Dad told T-Rex he couldn't get over how brave and resourceful his little girl was, and after the story he kept looking at me like he was seeing me for the first time. We talked for a little while after that, and then T-Rex stood up and said it was time for us to go. "I don't let Fifi fly during the daylight hours in your land," he explained. "She might cause a problem if she's seen."

So T-Rex walked with us to where Fifi waited. I guess she must have left her babies with the sitter. We climbed on, waved goodbye and the next thing we knew, we were up in the air. While flying, Fifi gave Dad a special treat by blowing fire. Often people on the ground mistake the flame for a shooting star.

Fifi took the long way home. We exited on the Big Sur coast and twice flew under the Bixby Bridge. The second time she did a barrel roll while Dad held his hands high in the air, yelling at the top of his voice. I was so proud of him!

We followed the Carmel River east, then crossed the Santa Lucia Mountains to our home. In no time at all, we landed. Dad jumped off first and walked up to Fifi to pat her head. Then he hugged her neck and thanked her. Two steps and she leapt into the air without a sound. We continued to wave till we could no longer see her.

After that, Dad went to the tool shed and pulled out a small shovel. He dug two rows on the terrace and planted his ten rubies. With a sprinkler can, he watered the seeds real good. I hope they grow for him.

After such a long day, I was tired. Dad carried me up to my bed. Katy was snoring, just as I soon would be. Dad hugged me. "Thank you for taking me to Dinosaur Town," he said. "It's the best place to visit."

He kissed me. I closed my eyes and fell asleep.

The next morning I awoke to chirping magpies. Down in the kitchen, Dad whistled and I smelled his traditional Saturday banana-pecan pancakes. I got out of bed and met Mom at the top of the staircase.

"Did you have a good sleep?" she asked. I nodded my sleepy head and went downstairs with her.

While we were eating breakfast, Mom noticed Dad's burn and asked him how he had scorched the palm of his hand. He started laughing before he answered. "It doesn't hurt that much," he told her. "It's only a baby burn." I laughed with him. Mom didn't understand, which made us laugh even longer.

The rest of the day was great. Dad treated me like an adult, not like a kid. He even canceled his golf game to be with me. Amazing! He never cancels golf, even when it rains!

We talked about many things, and went outside to lie on our backs, describing which clouds looked like animals. We were tired, so we took an afternoon nap right there on the freshly cut grass. It almost smelled as good as Dinosaur Town!

Later, Dad watered his rubies three more times while holding the ten dollar one in his hand. For some reason, precious gems in Dinosaur Town look like ordinary rocks here. Still, he carried that ruby all day. That night he placed it in a special spot on his dresser.

For supper Mom prepared fried chicken and other food I liked. As she served my portion, I made the announcement that I was going to Dinosaur Town that night and I didn't want to eat a lot of food.

Mom looked at Dad and said, "Well?"

He lowered his head and winked. "Dot, here's what I'm thinking," he began. "You'll have more time to play in Dinosaur Town if you eat at home rather than eating there."

"That's a good idea," I had to admit. Mom smiled and nodded in agreement. Not only is my Dad the best Dad in the whole world, he's pretty smart too! In fact, he suggested that I write this story down so you, too, could go to Dinosaur Town. As for tickets, just ask around. And don't forget to bring Granny Smith apples.

By the way, if you see me in Dinosaur Town, you don't have to bow. Just say, "Hi, Dot."

Oh, I almost forgot. Does anyone need Britney Spears tickets?

About the Author

MIKE TYRREL is the grateful husband of a fine wife and the proud father of two daughters who have turned their home into a resting place of homeless lizards, snakes, birds and other creatures. Because the Tyrrel household doesn't have a television, Mike tells them adventure stories nightly, one of which is included in Monterey Shorts. *Mike has worked with computers throughout his 30-year career. He designed and currently oversees the software in a factory that builds an automobile that typically wins the annual award for best American-made compact automobile/truck. It did exactly that in 1999, 2000, and 2002.*

ORDER ADDITIONAL COPIES OF MONTEREY SHORTS

____
NAME

____
ADDRESS

____

____
CITY STATE ZIP

____
PHONE E-MAIL

QUANTITY	PRICE	SUBTOTAL
______	**$12.95**	$ ______
	TAX *:	______
	SHIPPING**:	______
	ORDER TOTAL:	$ ______

MAIL ORDER FORM AND CHECK OR MONEY ORDER TO:

FWOMP
22597 Black Mountain Rd.
Salinas, CA 93908

* Tax: California residents only.
** Shipping and handling: $4.00. Add $.50 for each additional book.

Copyright Acknowledgements